'If God Will
Spare My Life...'

'If God Will Spare My Life...'

Mike Lewis

Victorina Press
www.victorinapress.com

Typesetting and layout by Jorge Vasquez
Cover design by ©Fiona Zechmeister
Calligraphy by Hubert Unger

British Library Cataloguing in Publication Data
A catalogue record for this book is available from the
British Library.

ISBN: 978-1-8380360-4-1

Typeset in 11pt Garamond
Printed and bound in Great Britain by 4edge ltd.

For Sue, Joe, Catrin, Davy, Erin and Tommy.

'How often have I lain beneath rain on a strange roof, thinking of home.'

William Faulkner, *As I Lay Dying*

"My life's a vain pursuit of meaningless smiles Why can't God touch me with a sign?"

Scott Walker, *The Seventh Seal*

CHAPTER 1

Little Bighorn,
Montana Territory,
Sunday June 25, 1876

The gypsy's curse had done for him, he knew; but how cruel a fate to not even possess the means to dispatch yourself into the eternal blackness and so bring down the curtain on this ghastly tableau of horror ...

Haverfordwest
Pembrokeshire
April 28, 1904

Arthur Nicholas glanced up from his desk as the sound of parting voices signalled Reginald Eaton had opened his office door. Having paused in the doorway to shake his master's hand, two visitors duly emerged, the elder catching Arthur's inquisitive eye.

Living in the port of Fishguard, in the south-west corner of Wales, the young apprentice solicitor immediately recognised the man as Gwynne Austin Roberts, well-known and highly-respected manager of the town's Lloyds Bank in West Street. The face of his tall, angular companion also looked familiar, although, try as he might, Arthur could not quite place it. The second visitor bore the weathered complexion of a man of the Pembrokeshire soil and when they shook hands moments later, Arthur noted he bore the callouses of one too.

'Well now, young Arthur, I'd clean forgotten that this was where you worked,' said Roberts, a pleasant, avuncular man in his mid-forties, extending his hand. 'This young fellow, Henry,' he said, turning to the other man, 'is Mr Arthur Nicholas, the son of a very dear long-time friend of mine, Charles Nicholas, the late blacksmith from Dinas Cross. Arthur, please allow me to introduce you to Mr Henry Rees, of Carne Farm, Goodwick.' The pair shook hands and nodded at one another.

Turning to Rees, Roberts stroked his chin thoughtfully and said: 'Come to think of it, it's a damn shame Charles is no longer around to assist us in our somewhat daunting quest. He knew cousin William well. Shoed his horses on many an occasion and, I daresay, probably had a hand in some of Will's little japes as well!' Rees smiled knowingly and nodded. The trio made small talk for a few moments, before the two men turned to depart for the town's railway station. 'Please be mindful to remember me to your mother,' Roberts told Arthur, returning a bowler hat to his greying head as the two visitors took their leave.

Arthur was 21 years old and had been working in the Haverfordwest office of Eaton, Evans and Williams for five years. Lately, he'd been finding the work, or at least that which Mr Eaton passed his way, particularly humdrum and had even started to question whether the life of a solicitor was truly for him. Working in a stuffy office in which a smoky coal fire needed constant tending left Arthur with a splitting headache most days. And even after five years he still possessed the uncomfortable feeling that he did not truly fit in.

His father had worked as a blacksmith all his life and Arthur was becoming more and more convinced he too would be better suited to a manual occupation. And preferably one in the open air to boot. Yet his parents had been so thrilled when he landed a job which they felt would be a significant step up the social ladder that he felt compelled to make the most of it.

The day a letter arrived informing him he was being offered a position saw his mam proudly conveying the news to every soul in Dinas Cross. She had even told old Evan Williams, the one-time saddler, though he was as deaf as a post and in a somewhat confused frame of mind. The look in the poor man's drowned eyes as she relayed her news suggested he was having a devil of job trying to remember who he himself was, let alone some young chap called Arthur Nicholas.

Two minutes later Arthur was summoned by the head solicitor into what office staff termed 'the inner sanctum'. 'Take a seat, will you, lad?' said Eaton briskly, clearly in a business-like mood. 'I gather you were a bit on the late side this morning. Least said about that the better, I suppose, but I have every confidence,' he continued, as Arthur slid awkwardly into a chair on the opposite side of Eaton's desk, 'that this little oversight will not be repeated.'

'Terribly sorry, sir, I'm afraid the train was delayed by ...' Arthur's blurted response was cut short by a deft wave of Eaton's hand.

'Spare me the details, dear boy, least said, soonest mended. I have an important assignment I'd like you to tackle and a somewhat unusual one at that. And the fact that you hail from that charming village of Dinas Cross suggests to me that you are eminently qualified for the task.' Arthur was both puzzled and curious at this intriguing disclosure.

'Assignment, sir? Of what precise nature, exactly?' he enquired.

Sliding a file of papers across the desk towards him, Eaton explained, in his usual clipped manner, that his two visitors were the executors for the will of one John Clement

James, a cousin of Roberts, who had died in Swansea of consumption, that hideous wasting disease, aged 52, in May of the previous year. Arthur had vaguely known the gentleman farmer who had owned the large farm of Llanwnwr, out on the rugged peninsula of Strumble Head, which protruded like a giant's muscled bicep into Cardigan Bay. A couple of years before, James had officiated the first football match ever held between Goodwick Welsh and Fishguard Rovers, for whom Arthur played as a defender.

Despite being billed as a 'friendly', and the County Echo newspaper's pre-match entreaties for 'brotherly love to prevail', the match had turned into something of a bloodbath and Arthur still bore the scars on his legs to prove it. There had been precious little brotherly love displayed on the pitch that day, he recalled ruefully. In fact, Mr James's whistle had sounded so frequently that it had been a wonder the somewhat breathless, ruddy-faced little fellow had not run out of puff. Eaton went on to explain that, as John Clement James had died a bachelor, it was imperative to establish whether there were any living heirs to the farm before it was sold at auction. 'Four of John Clement James's five brothers are known to be deceased,' he went on. 'However, there are question marks over the fate of the fifth ...'

'How come, sir?' Arthur wanted to know.

Eaton lit a cigar and, rising from his chair, slowly began to pace around the office. 'As things stand, William Batine James, possibly the sole surviving brother of the late John Clement James, is poised to inherit one of the finest farms in the north of Pembrokeshire,' he explained. 'T'is a property I wouldn't mind getting my hands on myself, if truth be told. Trouble is, no-one from these parts has seen hide nor hair of the aforementioned William Batine James for well over thirty years. Through letters John Clement James left behind,' he said, indicating the file in front of Arthur, 'we know his brother travelled to Canada in the March of 1871 and from there to the United States a couple of years hence. The last missive John Clement James received from his brother came from a town called Opelika, in Alabama, down in the Deep South of the country.'

'Do we know what occupation William James pursued out there, sir?' asked Arthur.

Eaton flopped down opposite him with a weary sigh and shook his snowy head. 'Unfortunately not,' came the reply. 'Infuriatingly, from our point of view, the letters he left behind tell us precious little about Mr James' activities, let alone his current whereabouts if, that is, the gentleman is still in the land of the living.

'William James would only be in his mid-fifties by now, however, so it is perfectly feasible he is out there somewhere. The question is where exactly and how the deuce do we set about finding him?'

'Is there any evidence that James is in fact deceased?' queried Arthur. 'The mere fact he has not been heard of in over thirty years suggests to my mind that he might well be.'

Eaton drew long and hard on his cigar before tilting his head back and releasing a stream of blue smoke into the veritable fog already suspended over his desk. 'Well, John Clement told his will executors that he'd received notification of his brother's death many, many years ago. He said one of the letters he dispatched to America was returned with the word 'deceased' written thereon. Suffice to say, the letter imparting that information could not be found among his private papers, so as things stand we simply cannot verify William Batine James's reported demise.

'Of course...' Eaton looked at Arthur and smiled, 'if one were of a cynical nature one could argue it would have been in John Clement's interests to put it about that his elder brother was no more. John Clement stood to inherit Llanwnwr, after all, and it could be argued that the last thing he'd have wanted prior to being handed the keys to that fine property was brother William turning up from North America unannounced and somewhat queering his pitch, shall we say?'

Eaton took another drag on his cigar. 'John Clement, a long-time sufferer of poor health, spent his final years living out there on Strumble,' he went on, as Arthur swallowed hard in an attempt to stave off a coughing fit. 'Prior to that I gather he lived and worked in Swansea for a time. On his death he left a considerable amount of money to the Welsh Terrier Club, of Swansea, but no apparent heirs to Llanwnwr, which his family have owned for well over a century.

'Terrier club? A somewhat unusual beneficiary, I'm sure you'll agree, sir,' observed Arthur.

'The gentleman evidently loved his dogs.' Eaton nodded his head and rolled his eyes. 'I have it on good authority,' he continued, in a bored tone of voice, 'that the late Mr James was never happier than when holding court on the merits and intricacies of the breed to anyone unfortunate enough to be within earshot; hence his decision to donate to the Welsh Terrier Club a generous sum of money. Each to his own, I suppose ...'

Eaton sat back in his chair and frowned. 'Brother William remains a true mystery man, however. We don't even have so much as a photograph of the fellow to go on. Apparently left for Canada in considerable haste by all accounts, which makes me wonder whether he may have committed some form of foul play. The James family were respectable God-fearing farmers who were well-known in Fishguard and Dinas, yet I'm told seemed to suffer some form of collective amnesia whenever the name of William Batine James popped up. They didn't speak ill of the fellow, you understand; just didn't speak of him at all,' Eaton again shook his head perplexed. 'What particular skeleton did this chap have in his cupboard, I wonder?' he said, examining his well-manicured nails. 'Gwynne Austin Roberts, who was very young when James departed for Canada, suspects he was, as he put it, the black sheep of the family who farmed Pencnwc on the Cardigan side of Dinas Cross, by the way.'

Having grown up in the village, Arthur was well familiar with Pencnwc, a large farm perched above the Gideon chapel in the shadow of Dinas Mountain. As a small boy he and his friends had habitually collected conkers in its nearby woods whilst running the gauntlet of the reclusive and belligerent elderly farmer who lived alone there. His angry shouts as they scampered back towards the village across his fields, pockets bulging with conkers, had been an entertaining part of such youthful adventures. The fact Arthur had no recollection of the James family was unsurprising as he would duly establish they had vacated the farm a good twenty years before he was born.

Eaton removed his cigar and stabbed a nicotine-stained forefinger at Arthur. 'So this is where you come in, young man. I want you to make enquiries into the possible whereabouts of William Batine James, or at the very least seek to establish whether he still walks the Earth.

'Unless we can learn his ultimate fate, or at least be seen to have moved Heaven and Earth in order to try and establish the full facts, the future of Llanwnwr will technically remain unresolved, which is obviously the last thing his brother's will executors want.

'You're a smart fellow, Arthur, with a good head on your shoulders, who to some degree reminds me of my younger self,' Eaton beamed at his young charge, 'I have no doubt that you will excel at a little Sherlock Holmes-type of detection and, should you be successful,' he paused, squinting slyly at the apprentice, 'why, I might even be minded to rustle up a little pay rise, plus ...' he continued, raising his voice a couple of octaves, 'I could also be prepared to overlook the fact that you rolled up for work well over an hour late this morning looking like a man who'd slept in a hedge!' Eaton returned the cigar to his mouth with a curt nod of his head.

7

'Yes sir, thank you sir, you can rely on me sir,' stammered Arthur. 'Please rest assured that I will leave no stone unturned. I'm more than happy to accept the challenge and shall begin my quest for William Batine James forthwith. And I can assure you, Mr Eaton, that you will not find me wanting!'

***

'They say you drink to forget, yet all the drink did was make me remember all the bad things I'd done; and all the bad things that were done to me.

'Look, having arrived at my destination a tad sooner than expected I'm happy to give full chapter and verse. And I won't take offence if deemed guilty of spinning a web of falsehoods 'cos, if truth be told, I can scarce make head nor tail of it all myself ...'

Powder River Depot, Montana Territory, June 8 1876
(17 days out from the Battle of the Little Bighorn)

'Huna blentyn ar fy mynwes Clyd a chynnes ydyw hon; Breichiau mam sy'n dynn amdanat, Cariad mam sy dan fy mron; Ni chaiff dim amharu'th gyntyn, Ni wna...'

'Letter for Sgt William B James!'

When I hark back to those distant days of childhood, I remember the toy sailor, wooden rocking horse, tatty tin soldiers with flaking paint, the Noah's Ark, chipped painting of Lord Palmerston and vast, blue-patterned bedspread. But what I can't recall for the life of me is the name of that sweet Welsh lullaby Mother would sing softly whilst tucking us all in.

Whatever it was called was cut short by that crude shout exploding like a cannon inside my head. Caused me to tear my heavy eyelids open and sit bolt upright in my blanket with a start, right hand fumbling for the Colt. The piercing cry seemed so loud and so near that I'd have sworn someone was sat plumb in the middle of that foul-smelling US Army tent with us. I stayed motionless for a jiffy, blinking foolishly at the cream canvas like an owl shaken awake on its roost, slowly taking stock of all around me.

All I could hear over Ogden's snores was the buzz of those infernal mozzies that made camp life such a misery, the chomping of the horses and the picket's call of 'All is well!' from way over yonder. As I came to my senses, I lay back with a weary sigh as it dawned on me where I was. The letter I yearned for so badly existed only in my dreams...

They say the howl of a coyote is the most lonesome sound out on the prairie; a lament that penetrates right into the heart of a fellow's soul. Lying in our three-man pup tent next to the gurgling Powder I wasn't about to argue. The critter was perhaps a good few miles distant, yet his mournful refrain steadfastly kept me from returning to slumber. That and Ogden's snoring which seemed to have gotten worse in the three weeks since we'd ridden out of Fort Abraham Lincoln past lines of weeping soldier wives as Custer's band played 'The Girl I Left Behind Me'. T'is queer how a fellow can feel so alone when he has 1,200 men of war and hundreds of horses and mules all seeking to rest their weary heads around him.

All the boys could sense a battle looming even if it went largely unspoken. We enlisted men were never told when or where we were going; those officers would just say they'd tell us once we'd gotten there. Yet being soldiers we could feel something was coming in our bones. The same kind of feeling you get afore a prairie storm blows up. Fellows who talk much go real quiet and those who don't normally say boo to a goose just won't hold their tongues.

We knew those will o' the wisp Indians couldn't run and hide forever and although we'd reckoned on finding them in the Badlands a week or so back, there was now barely a fellow among us who didn't anticipate a pretty hot fight and that old Chief Sitting Bull would think he was caught in the middle of a hornets' nest once the fighting Seventh caught up with him.

The one fellow in camp who thought different was surgeon DeWolf. He was treating Hohmeyer, our prickly first sergeant, for a boil on the backside when he said he thought we wouldn't see an Injun all summer, though Fred told us later he reckoned old DeWolf didn't truly believe that. Hohmeyer felt DeWolf was trying to convince himself the hostiles had skedaddled for that was what he kept telling his better half in letters back home to save her getting spooked. DeWolf, who really pined for the old lady, had said it so often he'd pretty much come to believe it himself.

Hohmeyer, a German-born, dark-haired and ornery son of a gun on his third enlistment, begged to differ. Scratching his scraggly whiskers thoughtfully as we huddled around a firepit one night, he said those US Government bigwigs wouldn't have spent so much expense on sending an expedition this big out into the back of beyond to locate those troublesome hostiles unless they were pretty damn sure we were going to find them. And with a fellow like General Custer at our helm it wasn't so much a matter of if, but when. 'Once Custer gets his orders, he's like a starvin' mutt with a Goddamn bone,' said Hohmeyer, in his heavy German accent. 'He'll see 'em through even if it means ridin' through Hell and back and takin' us dumb asses with him. Them Injuns' gonna find out real soon that there ain't no prairies, forests or mountains in the whole of Montana Territory big enough for 'em to hide from Ol' Iron Butt.'

We had a decent camp on the Powder. Fish, game and berries were plentiful. T'was no wonder those Indians had chosen this area for their favourite hunting grounds. Once Reveille was sounded at five that first morning, we had the finest breakfast since leaving Lincoln; bacon, beans, biscuits and hardtack with butter, washed down by an ocean of coffee, scalding hot and black as soot. Our huge column coiled like a giant serpent down the river which became one huge laundry tub as scores of men stripped to their waists, splashing, scrubbing and wringing their outer as well as inner garments.

The boys, some of whom had plainly done little scrubbing afore, washed trousers, shirts, drawers and socks, some bloodied and soiled following the long march, as best they could in the muddy waters. Their faces were a picture once they realised that those garments had been rendered even grubbier despite their very best efforts. If those laundresses back at Lincoln had caught sight of the hangdog looks of us unhappy washer men, they'd have split their sides.

And dwindling supplies didn't buck up our spirits. Hohmeyer got wind that the steamer, The Far West, packed to the gunnels with vital supplies, had reached the mouth of the Powder, only for General Terry to commandeer her to try and get a message through to Gibbon. Seemed like we were having no more luck in finding the Montana column than we were in locating the hostiles.

Leaving Lincoln on May 17, we'd reckoned on catching up with Sitting Bull and his band by early June. Now here we were, a damn sight further West than we could ever possibly have imagined, and we still hadn't caught so much as a glimpse of one God-forsaken red man. Maybe DeWolf was going to be proved right after all. Fellows were going crazy for the want of tobacco, some offering five or even ten

11

dollars for a plug or bag of the stuff. Some of the boys with scarce a dollar to their names were so desperate they ended up smoking grass, coffee grounds and even those dried-up buffalo chips we used to make firepits.

Once we'd arrived on the Powder the order had come down from above that campfires were strictly forbidden as, with the surrounding country pretty much crawling with redskins, it was felt the smoke would reveal our location.

A lot of the boys spent the best part of the day writing out their last will and testimonies, though I didn't see no point myself. The family back home in Yr Hen Wlad (The Old Country) had no inkling I was a bluecoat in the Seventh, so if some Indian were to come along and lift my scalp how'd they even know where to collect my measly few dollars?

The thought of my scant funds barely covering one of brother John's fine dinners in one of Swansea's swanky hotels had me smiling ruefully to myself in the near darkness. By then I hadn't heard a squeak from anyone back home for well over a year. John's last letter had come when we were chasing redneck moonshiners and the Ku Klux Klan down in the Deep South. Mother's last short note a couple of months hence. Seemed to me like my own kith and kin had clean washed their hands of poor William Batine James and I'd be lying if I said it didn't trouble me.

This got me thinking of the package I'd left for dispatch the day we'd rode out of Lincoln. Given the change in my personal circumstances the time had seemed ripe to pen a letter home to Elizabeth for the first time in the five years that had passed since we'd last clapped eyes on each other. Truth be told, I just couldn't get what'd happened 'twixt me and that woman out of my mind. Try as I might I just not could unburden the guilt I felt; t'was like a hideous gnawing toothache that tormented me the longer I was out West. How I yearned to tell her of my great sorrow at our unhappy parting and the terrible reasons, concealed for so many years, I now knew lay behind it. While I appreciated that kind of heartfelt stuff was the sort of thing to say to Elizabeth's face, not in some letter scribbled in haste in a leaking army pup tent with a fellow sergeant snoring, farting and belching besides me, I also knew our paths were destined never to cross again. Yet what had happened way back then was one of the reasons that kept me chasing sleep night after night after night ...Ogden, on t'other hand, always seemed to snooze like an infant, but then not even the roar of a passing freight train had disturbed the fellow's shut-eye when we'd unwittingly pitched our tent a mere stone's throw from the railroad at Yankton a couple of years previous.

After one particularly hard march, Johnny Og had even felled asleep with a great lump of salt pork wedged in his sauce box. Eagan, our fellow bunkie, always lay dead to the world at night as well. But then Ogden and Eagan weren't beset by the type of troubles that plain drove me off my chump in the dark. I was still all at sea over what had happened in the final days ... no ... make that the final hours, afore we'd rode out of Lincoln. The way my poor head was hurting I reckoned it'd take days or even weeks to get a handle on everything. Although Elizabeth belonged to my past, I fair itched for a chance to put her right on a few things I'd never previously been able to tell her. Suppose you could say I wanted to wipe the slate clean afore it was too late. I reckoned that by now she might've married some master mariner from Newport, or some rich farmer from Dinas, who'd doubtless provide her with countless children and ensure she enjoyed wealth, happiness and comfort for the rest of her days. A woman like her would ne'er want for potential suitors, of that I had no doubt.

And what of John, the only brother I had left on this good Earth? I found myself again pondering how his letters had been so irregular and then just dried up. John was ne'er big on writing, true, but had he taken affront at my request to send money to my bank a while back? Back then I was gambling like a blessed fool, I confess, but now I was on a sergeant's wage of eighteen dollars a month with no need to go cap in hand to John or anyone else for that matter. I ne'ertheless brooded on his silence. As his elder bro, I felt I'd always looked out for him in those now far-off days in Dinas Cross. Together we'd come through the horrors of Peniel School, which had trailed me like a black crow down all these years, and the grievous loss of Father and five of our dear siblings. We two boys may not have had much in common but we were the closest in age. Now it seemed we were a damn sight more than one vast ocean apart. Aye, I really needed to square matters with John as well. I just couldn't countenance the fact that, as far as he was concerned, I was out of sight, out of mind.

T'is queer how the mind wanders on nights when sleep doesn't come; leastways mine always did. I lay there taking in the usual camp sounds: the snorting and munching of the horses, the braying of the mules, bawling of cattle, barking and whining of Custer's dogs and the faint, lazy sound of Meyer's mouth organ picking its way through 'Shenandoah' in the still prairie air. There were times on the long, wearisome march West when I'd felt like hurling the blessed thing into the muddy brown waters of the Yellowstone; the mouth organ, that is, not Meyer. Yet now, in the dead of night out in the midst of this vast rolling ocean of grass where ev'ry shadow seemed a potential hostile, each ravine concealing some unknown menace, those gentle refrains were strangely comforting.

As usual my mind turned all melancholy and I began to think again of death and the day John Tuttle met his Maker. Back in the August of '73, we'd had a big fight with the Sioux down near the mouth of the Bighorn. It was the first action I ever saw and poor Tuttle's the first close-up death I ever witnessed; in battle, anyhow. There must have been a thousand or more of the red devils yipping and whooping as they locked horns with around 450 of us bluecoats from across the river. Suppose you could call it something of a running fight. Those painted fiends would come at us in numbers shrieking like banshees from Hell with those shrill, piercing eagle bone whistles they always used in battle and we'd be forced to high tail it. Then a few volleys from our Sharps unleashing a deadly torrent of lead would see us gain the upper hand and drive them back across the Yellowstone. Back and forth it went for hours in murderous heat. The red tide would come in, the blue tide would push it back, and so on and so forth.

Anyway, Custer positioned twenty of the Seventh's best marksmen, myself included, behind trees along the banks of the river to fire on the enemy at a range of around 400 yards. Tuttle was Custer's striker, or soldier-servant, and the crackshot of E Company, the Gray Horse Troop, with a reputation known throughout the regiment. He'd lie deathly still like a snake about to strike for what seemed an eternity. Then he'd let fly and split the skull of an Indian a quarter of a mile distant as if it was a watermelon. Some of our company's greenhorns reckoned the fellow could even slow his heartbeat. That may have been tall talk, but what I do know is that when it came to company shooting practice, old Tuttle had no equals, myself included, and I was considered a pretty good shot. He was a fellow profuse of whisker but short on words; I know that Custer valued him highly and like some of the other boys he'd fought for the Union against Johnny Reb a few years previous.

I was crouched just a few yards away from Tuttle when our carbines opened up with a roar. Afore those Injuns on the far bank knew what was up: 'Crack! Crack! Crack!' He'd sent three of their braves straight to the happy hunting grounds, one after t'other. We were getting ready to mount up and charge when the Sioux caught Tuttle in a crossfire and put a bullet clean through his skull. I heard him grunt, saw him shudder and slump back against the tree where he'd concealed himself. He pushed his right leg hard against the stump like a man would try and shake himself free of the cramp and then moved no more; not ever. Around the campfire that night some of the greenhorns were really curious and wanted to know if Tuttle, one of four bluecoats lost that day, had said anything afore departing this life? Don't know what those fools expected. A few fond last utterances for me to convey back to his sweetheart home in Michigan, maybe? A plea to take good care of Dandy Dave, the horse he'd grown so fond of? Truth is the poor beggar was stone dead in an instant; the bullet that slew him entering one side of the head and exiting t'other. 'It was really clean and really quick,' I told them over beans and bacon in a tone of voice that begged no more discussion.

What I didn't tell them was how my heart leapt in my breast with joy that it was Tuttle who took that bullet, not me. Up to that point it'd been about the nearest I'd ever come to the Grim Reaper and, while I'd never have admitted it to those new recruits, I suppose I was still pretty shook up by just how close I'd been when death stalked that riverbank. After we'd sent those Sioux packing by charging across the river, Miller the blacksmith spied blood on me and enquired whether I'd been hit. Turned out I still had some of Tuttle's lifeblood smeared all over my face, but none of his brains, thank God. A bluecoat for just 18 months, I'd now had my first taste of Injun warfare and it would not be my last.

Now, I'd never really been afeared of death myself; death, I always reckoned, ought be afeared of me! Yet I couldn't stop thinking what a grievous blow the end of my time on Earth would deal dear Mother back in Pembrokeshire. Having been widowed and left alone to raise nine children, the wretched woman had lost five of her offspring in two years. When, if ever, would fortune smile on us Jameses again? For that reason, after considerable thought, I decided to conceal my enlistment with the Seventh once I'd signed up for five years at Chicago in the bitter February of 1872. I signed my letters home 'F A Lynchon' so no one back in Pembrokeshire would cotton on to the fact that I was now a soldier of fortune employed by Uncle Sam. Or a soldier of non-fortune in my case.

As there was damn-all West of Lincoln other than grass, buffalo, rattlesnakes, coyotes and redskins, I reckoned there was little danger of letters from home going astray and failing to reach their far-flung destination. Unless some unfortunate mail-rider fell victim to an Indian ambush and ended up resembling a porcupine with his bag and its cargo decorating the inside of some teepee, that is. Seemed to me that Mother had endured enough grief without having to worry about her eldest nearest and dearest being ritually disembowelled by some bloodthirsty savage in the wilds of Dakota Territory. Indeed, while I was many, many leagues from western Wales, the Indian wars were being reported in all the newspapers back home, even thrilling readers of the Cemes and Dewisland Guardian over their breakfasts back in Pembrokeshire, for Heaven's sake. So while I saw no real shame in signing up for Uncle Sam, a fellow must do what he can in order to survive, after all, I felt it made sound reasoning to keep my own counsel. As the saying goes, what the mind doesn't know the heart doesn't grieve over, or something like that.

Did I believe in the Hereafter? I saw no reason to. Had I witnessed signs that Father and my brothers and sisters dwelt in Heaven above? Nope, afeared not. Seeing was believing in my book and I'd ne'er seen their ghosts nor heard them sighing in the wind. I oft dreamt about my dear departed siblings, though. Remembering the good times at Pencnwc afore we lost Father. A respected deacon at Ramah Chapel in Dinas Cross, religion was a big part of his life and a big

17

part of our childhood. The older I got, the more things I saw and the better I understood people: the good, the bad and the sheer downright plain evil, the less important my faith seemed 'til in time I more or less clean forgot all about it, if I'm honest. Ne'er went to chapel on leaving home at 15.

Thought about going a couple of times during my time in London; but an honest day's toil, earning a wage, chasing women and going for a gargle down the East End with my chums just seemed better ways for a lusty young fellow to pass his time. In time, I would come to regret that. Yet those bygone days at Brynhenllan, the preachings, the hymn-singing, the essay-writing and memories of what us Welsh folk called the hiraeth, the spirit that bound us together, had stuck with me like flies to a dung heap no matter how far I roamed. T'was queer, but even in the US Army, where oaths and profanities abounded, I still found myself unable to suppress a silent shudder whenever I on occasion blasphemed. Usually when bawling out some raw new recruits who didn't know their arse from their elbow, much less ride a horse or fire a gun. In my early days with the regiment the boys were always saying they found it queer I never, if ever, cursed. Ogden once enquired whether I'd been a man of the cloth in my past life which, in view of some of the things I'd gotten up to, gave me real fits.

I was 27 by now, but looking a fair bit older, it has to be said. I sometimes felt those arse-battering rides over the plains and long hours in the saddle had ground my backbone down to nothing more than a fine dust and aged me at twice the usual rate. Aches and pain were constant companions of us all 'cos soldiering made you old afore your time. T'was a life for young fellows and, in truth, I was by now pretty much sick to the back teeth of it, even if it was reckoned by others that I was a soldier of excellent character. I'd been made a corporal in '75 and then, on my 27th birthday in March, a sergeant. But five years' service would be more than enough and I'd no desire to make the army my life like fellows such as Ogden, whose spare and wiry frame made him an ideal cavalryman. That son of a gun already had the bow legs of one! He'd first joined up at 16, left after a few years on account of some young fresh down in South Carolina, and then re-enlisted in '72 after she'd switched her affections to a shoemaker and, I suppose you could say, given old Ogden the boot. Ne'er was a fellow so glad and so eager to don that US Cavalry uniform, as blue as a bluebottle's hide.

Ogden's folks back home in Massachusetts thought he was the bee's knees and when E Troop were down in the Deep South he'd proudly tote his carte de visite around where e'er we went. He'd hand out copies to those giggling young Southern fillies we came across in every saloon and restaurant with their high hair and fluttering eyelashes like he was some bigwig actor or politician or something. On the back he'd wrote: 'With compliments – Sgt John S Ogden, Seventh Cavalry.' The Southern belles always seemed really impressed and I suppose their laughter and feminine charms made a pleasant change from the evil stares we got from those sullen rednecks with their great big beards, wolfish eyes and whisky breath. Fellows who'd slit your throat just as soon as look at you.

Those diehard Rebs had lost the war and just couldn't get over it. While that was ne'er any business to do with the likes of me, or Ogden come to that, those hostile glares our uniforms drew plain wore a fellow down after a while. Sometimes it seemed to me that being a soldier of the US Army was a couple of steps lower than a junkyard dog. At least that's how some folks made you feel, never mind those officers who treated their horses a damn sight better than they would a lowly buck private. Small wonder John's lack of letters from home cut me to the quick.

Ogden saw it different. 'You gotta fine blue uniform, James, you gotta horse,' he'd say in answer to my gripes. 'You get fed three times a day an' a warm barracks to rest yo' head in winter. Most folks kinda look up to you when you ride inna town an' they knows you belong to Custer's Seventh.' A languid, curly-haired fellow, Ogden's rural farm boy drawl may have drawn the mockery of our fellow sergeants, yet it cloaked a fierce and driving ambition. He'd set his heart on becoming an officer one day and few of us doubted he would make it. His horse Sky Dancer was the fleetest mount in the company, one of the fastest in the regiment and his proud rider was ne'er slow in letting anyone know it.

Only a few years older than I, Ogden seemed a great deal more world-weary and it was pretty hard to strike up a conversation with him that didn't involve either soldiering or his blessed horse, come to that. Despite this dogged single-mindedness, his kinfolk back home were ne'er far from his thoughts and I knew he'd dispatch some greenbacks their way from time to time as they were finding it tough to make ends meet after their crops failed two summers on the trot.

Aye, Sgt Johnny Ogden had a good heart, to be sure, yet in some ways he was no different to those dapper, mealy-mouthed officers who'd sweet-talked me into signing up at that recruitment depot back in Chicago. 'The US Army needs young men of your calibre, James. We feel you have all the necessary attributes to become a successful soldier.'

What they didn't tell you about were those long, hard marches in temperatures so low the snot freezes inside your nostrils, the tinned meat stamp-dated back to Civil War days with green mould growing over it, the maggot-ridden hardtack, infestations of bed lice and rampant plagues of yellow fever and cholera that put many a young soldier in the ground afore they'd even fired a shot in anger.

I must have returned to the very edge of sleep when that accursed coyote howled again from somewhere up in the hills, jolting me wide awake and momentarily interrupting even Ogden's snores. Reveille would be sounded within the hour so there was precious little hope of sleep now.

For some queer reason I remembered the date and realised it was nigh on thirteen years to the day since the galloping consumption claimed the life of Father back on our farm in Dinas. When sleep eluded me, as it did oftener now, I'd lie in my camp bed ruminating on the fates that had brought me, a rural farm boy from little Dinas Cross in western Wales, all the way out onto the Great Plains as a soldier in the US Seventh Cavalry.

No doubt each and every one of us reach a crossroads in life which sets us on our ways, for better or for worse. For me, that point came when poor Father breathed his last. No-one was to know it, but life for all of us would ne'er be the same again ...

Haverfordwest
April 29, 1904
Case re: John Clement James Deceased

Under the Will of one Thomas Griffiths who died in the year 1808, certain real estates in the Parishes of Llanunda and Fishguard in the county of Pembroke, in and previously to the year 1891, stood limited to the use of Mary Mortimer during her life; with remainder to the use of Thomas James during his life; with remainder to the use of the first son of Thomas James and the heirs of such first son lawfully issuing with remainders over. Mary Mortimer died on May 12, 1891. Thomas James died on January 31, 1865, having had issue John James, his first son and other children. John James was married on March 2, 1839, and had issue (with other children) five sons viz: 1st Thomas

James born May 7, 1845 drowned around 1870 2nd James James born Jan 9, 1847, died 1871 3rd William Batine James born March 3, 1849 – ?4th John Clement James born November 24, 1850 and 5th Francis Batine James. John James died on June 17, 1863. Thomas James, eldest son of John James, was drowned at sea upwards of 30 year ago. He had married but left no issue. James James (2nd son of John James) died a bachelor on February 22, 1871. William Batine James (3rd son of John James) went to America in 1871 and is believed to have died a bachelor within a few years afterwards. Upon the death of Mary Mortimer in 1891, John Clement James, the fourth son of John James, entered into possession of the real estate of Thomas Griffiths, and continued in uninterrupted possession thereof until his death.

On December 23, 1891, he executed a disentailing deed limiting the real estate of Thomas Griffiths to himself in fee simple.

John Clement James stated in his lifetime that letters addressed to his brother William Batine James by himself and their mother had many years previously to Mary Mortimer's death been returned from America, accompanied by a letter from the landlady of William Batine James, announcing his death, but no such letter could be found. Letters from William Batine James to John Clement James (the last dated November 1875) have since the death of John Clement James been found amongst his papers.

John Clement James died on May 17, 1903, having by his Will dated October 21, 1902 devised and bequeathed the whole of his real and personal property unto Henry Rees and Gwynne Austin Roberts, upon trust to sell, call in, and convert the same into money and out of the proceeds to pay his funeral and testamentary expenses, debts, and legacies, and to pay the residue to the said Gwynne Austen Roberts for his own use; and he appointed the said Henry Rees and Gwynne Austin Roberts, Executors of his said will which they have since proved. The legacies amount to £3,100. The personal estate has been got in and has proved insufficient by about £1500 for payment of debts and funeral and testamentary expenses. The trustees are anxious to sell the real estate (about £6000 in value) by public auction, but feel themselves in a difficulty consequent on their being unable to furnish any evidence of the death, without issue, of William Batine James. The position would appear to be this:

If, as is believed to be the case, he died unmarried in the lifetime of Mrs Mortimer, John Clement James's title would have been good. If he had survived Mrs Mortimer, the claim of himself or any issue he may have had would be barred under Section 1 of the Real Property Limitation Act 1874. If, however, he had married and subsequently died in Mrs Mortimer's lifetime leaving issue, the claim of such issue may not be barred, as the 3rd Section of the Act would apply. The trustees feel that there would be little or no chance of effecting a sale with a special condition obliging the purchasers to presume the death of William Batine James without issue, and that if they effected a sale without such a condition, the purchasers might successfully refuse to complete.

Counsel is requested to carefully consider the trustees' position and to advise them as to the course they should take under the circumstances. Dispatch is requested.

London
May 2, 1904
Notes of barrister James G Wood:

It would be very hazardous and prejudicial to sell under the present circumstances.

The letters of W B James will probably afford information as to his last residence and enquiries should be made there to ascertain the fact of his death and that nothing was known of his having married.

As the result of such enquiries, it may be possible to frame a condition which would not prejudice the sale.

CHAPTER 2

Lying there in my blankets on the banks of the Powder, craving slumber whilst knowing full well that Reveille would sound all too soon, I tried one last sleep-inducing trick which'd served me so well as a child back at Pencnwc afore the night terrors closed in with their talons. I'd run my mind through all the surnames of children in my class: Abrahams, Allen, Buckley, Davies, Ebenezer, Jones, Nicholas, Pepper, Phillips, Prosser, Samuels and so on; each one bringing blessed sleep ever nearer. Now, listening to the camp sounds of horses, mules and pickets along with the splash of fishes jumping in the Powder, I'd tick off the names of my comrades in E Troop: De Rudio, Reily, Smith, Sturgis, Abbots, Ackison, Baker, Barth, Berwald, Boyle, Brogan, Bromwell, Brown, Bruns, Chapman ... and so on right through the alphabet, Woodruff being the last ... And I still couldn't get myself back off to the Land of Nod ...

When I cast my thoughts back to that horribly damp, cold and miserable winter of 1862/63, t'is the coughing and retching I remember most. Father was seized in the grip of the disease which would kill him the following June and while he was an upright and God-fearing mainstay of Ramah Chapel, I well recall my elder brother Tom's eyes moistening when he told us, his dear siblings, that no amount of prayers would save Father now. There were nine of us still living on the farm that winter; elder sisters Mary and Elizabeth having already flown the coop. Mary had been betrothed to James Lloyd, an egg and butter merchant from Prendergast, near Haverfordwest, the October previous, whilst Elizabeth was working as a servant down in a farm near Bwlchmawr. Pencnwc, the family farm perched snugly on the lower slopes of Dinas Mountain above the great granite edifice of Dinas Head, was the only home we knew. Father and Mother had settled there on land Grandfather Batine owned a few years afore I was born.

I entered this world on March 3, 1849, the sixth of their brood. Mary, Elizabeth and Ann were my older sisters, followed by Tom and James. John Clement came after me followed by young Frank and Ellen. Mother would have another little one every two years, regular as the rising of the dawn. Ann, dark, severe and pretty, was the third-born who, looking back, was somewhat in the shadow of her two elder sisters. Mary and Elizabeth were gay and carefree types, who from their teens enjoyed lively social lives and drew a whole host of young male admirers along the farm track to Pencnwc. Ann was a home bird who read much, prayed oft and based her life around the chapel. As the eldest girl now still at home, much fell on her slender shoulders and we younger children, James, John, Frank, Ellen and myself, came to rely upon her much. With Mother keeping an eye on all household tasks, as well as helping Father around the farmyard and out in the fields, Ann more or less became mother hen to us all from the age of about 11.

It was a role she took seriously and one she performed well. Not for nothing did little Ellen call her 'Mam Fach'. (Little Mother). T'was truly like having a second mother. Alas, poor Ann wouldn't live to bear children of her own. Tom was the eldest boy, a fine strapping fellow of 17 with a thick mass of black curly hair who already looked older than his years. Tom was the type who grabbed life by the scruff of the neck; every day seemed an adventure to him. He had a temper as quick as his fists and made just as many enemies as he did friends. I recall seeing him set upon a group of gypsy boys for picking on little girlish-like Evan Williams outside the Freemasons Arms in Dinas one bitter winter's night. By the time he was done two of the gypsies lay insensible and bleeding and the other two had taken to their heels. Tom's sole wound was a split lip which didn't stop him sinking a quart of ale prior to making his way home.

By 17, he was already away at sea much, having decided that a mariner's life would be the making of him. The sea was a calling and Tom's intention was to eventually join the ranks of master mariners in Dinas and Newport. None of us had the slightest doubt that he would achieve what he set out to do in life; gungho spirit was infused in his veins. He was possessed with a sense of derring-do and whatever fate threw in his direction ne'er seemed to rattle him. I envied Tom much and wished to be like him.

Next came James, at 15 a smaller and wirier version of Tom, but minus his elder brother's reckless temperament and wild ways. Tom and I would josh with James that he was Mother's favourite; I say we joshed, and pulled one another's legs, but all three of us knew it to be true. Eternally good-natured, strong and steadfast and always willing to help, James was the family's bedrock, the glue who bound us all together. Having left school the previous year, he was, due to Father's worsening condition, now having to take on a greater burden of work in the fields, yet did so readily and always with ne'er a complaint. James had oft talked about following his elder brother to sea so it came as no surprise to any of us when he did the very same next year.

After me, there was John Clement, light-haired and brown-eyed, who although similar to myself in appearance always lacked my robust health and nature and, fortunately for him, my occasional bouts of melancholy. Small of stature and reticent by nature, John grew into a quiet, studious boy who was always happier with an open book afore the fireside than making fishing trips down to Pwllgwaelod or Cwmyreglwys, building driftwood campfires or shooting rabbits down in the cwm, which was probably just as well 'cos he was like a cow handling a musket. On a couple of occasions he fell victim to a couple of the village bullies, but word got back to Tom who went down and exacted swift retribution. John ne'er had any more problems after that, though as far as health was concerned he was a long-time sufferer and no amount of fresh air and exercise ever seemed to put him right. Of all us children, he was the one Mother troubled herself about the most.

Frank, my youngest brother, had more in common with Tom; small wonder that he held in high esteem his big brother who always looked out for him. Dark-haired and stocky, Frank would in a few years develop into a fine physical specimen, mainly through those long, hard hours he spent grafting down the slate quarry at Porthgain. However, after barely two years there the siren call of the sea grew too strong and he too became a mariner like his elder brothers.

And last, but by no means least, came Ellen. The only redhead in the family, she had Grandmother James's side to blame for that. Hence she was oft referred to as 'Ellen Coch' (Red Ellen). An excellent scholar, she took much joshing from us boys, mainly on account of the striking colour of her hair, but woe betide any of the Dinas Cross ruffians if they were e'er unkind to her! Once, on hearing a boy called Owens had called her names on the way back from school, Tom and I tracked down the miscreant and tossed him into the village duckpond. The following day we learnt we'd been mistaken and it was his older brother that had been the culprit! And to think I'd held the wretched fellow's head underwater for some considerable time at that! Unsurprisingly, Father had given us both the strap when we'd gotten home that night. But t'is true what they say: blood is thicker than water. Some families like us can scrap like cat and dog, but when someone else starts throwing their weight around with us, well, that's quite a different kettle of fish. You crossed one James, you crossed us all. T'is queer how families are like that.

And what of me? The one who somehow made his way out to the Great Plains of North America, land of the buffalo, bear, mountain lion and wolf and the red man? According to my US Army recruitment papers I was five feet nine with light hair, a light complexion and hazel eyes. I'd have described them as more of a brown shade myself, but I won't quibble. I didn't look like your typical dark and swarthy Welshman, it has to be said. Yet, take it from me, I was the finest singer of us all!

With hindsight, I can now surmise that I was very much trailing in Tom's wake. The two of us scrapped constantly, with Tom, being the elder by four years, always gaining the upper hand. In spite of this, I had more in common with Tom than James and Frank and certainly John. We were both sturdy, lusty young fellows who thrived on the outdoor life and, at the end of the day, were always up for a fight or a frolic. It was not until I was somewhat older that I became aware of my reputation as something of a rogue or troublemaker, though I never, ever, saw myself like that. I felt I was always sticking up for the kind of people who couldn't fight back. A sort of defender of the underdogs, you might say. Someone who stood up for the downtrodden. Very few others were of the same mind, alas, and I confess I tasted the sting of Father's strap a damn sight more than my brothers.

My problem then, and indeed would remain as I became a young man, was that if I witnessed a perceived injustice, regardless of the circumstances, I always felt compelled to speak out. James, Frank and John would know when to hold their tongues. I was also possessed of a fierce and fiery temper which did not seem to afflict the others, 'cept Tom. 'Hot as pepper', Mother would say. But then if I wasn't rubbing at angles 't'would be going against the grain of myself! T'was queer as I could oft take no end of riling without so much as turning a hair. Then something would happen, a sharp remark, an ill-timed jest or gesture or perhaps even a look, that'd cause me to lose my rag completely. Afore you'd know it I'd be in there hurling punches like some whirling dervish. Never knew when to stop, or when I was licked, either.

There were one or two happenstances in my young life that try as I might I just can't shake. When some of Father's coins went missing and were found in our bedchamber, I was wrongly deemed to have been responsible. Despite my fervent denials of any wrongdoing I duly received the strap, like.

Unbeknownst to my brothers, the tears I shed that day were not at the pain I was dealt, but rather at the burning injustice I had suffered. The true culprit had lain low whilst I took the blame. I regret to say that Tom's relentless mocking of my tear-streaked face and barbed suggestion that I was somehow less of a man plain sent me off my chump. Tearing myself free from Father's restraints, I dramatically announced my intention of running up to the top of Dinas Mountain, launching myself off its highest crag and dashing myself to pieces on the rocks below. He must have thought I meant it as he shouted for Tom and James to follow my headlong flight. Must have made it halfway up the mountain afore they collared me and dragged me kicking, biting and screaming all the way back to the farm. T'was a pity the pair failed to buckle me sooner as they might've stopped me busting both my hands on the trunk of a large elm tree. Curiously, I did not receive my anticipated scolding, merely being sent to bed without supper. No-one mentioned ought about my conduct as the doctor was sent for next morning or, indeed, e'er again, which was just as well for I'd truly meant to end it all that day.

My constant companion way back then, and one who always remained true and steadfast, was Spot, our big-hearted and soppy young Welsh sheepdog. He'd be by my side as I spent hours shooting rabbits down in the woods or marching faithfully at my heel along the rugged and windswept coast

30

path. The two of us were inseparable. When I was away Spot would sit patiently awaiting my return at the end of our lane. On seeing his master he'd be overcome with joy, bounding up to me, head hanging low, whining with excitement, tail wagging furiously all the while. Father and Tom, who were both not averse to dealing poor Spot the occasional slap or kick when he incurred their displeasure whilst herding the cattle, reckoned I fair ruined that dog. 'A dog is a working animal and should be treated as such,' quoth Father. Suffice to say, I trenchantly ignored such views. Why anyone could think they'd get the best out of an animal through free use of the rod and stick was beyond me; yet similar punishment was habitually meted out on young scholars down at the village school.

Ne'er was I more grateful to be assailed by Spot's warm presence and comforting doggy smell than on one queer and terrible afternoon down on the thickly-wooded banks of the River Gwaun, near Fishguard. Beset by a severe fit of melancholy I'd sat down on a large boulder, peered down at the shotgun in my hands and calmly debated putting the barrel to my head. The sound of the nearby waterfall would mask the report, I reasoned. No one would be any the wiser. Why not replace the blackness in my heart with a blackness that would stretch for all eternity? If, as had been implied, I cast a stain on my family then surely I would be bestowing upon them a favour by eradicating such a stain forthwith? Few would weep for me. And while my end would no doubt prompt much shock and discussion among the congregation at Brynhenllan – why would such a happy-go-lucky young fellow take such a course? they'd enquire - by the following week, my mortal remains would have been consigned to the chapel cemetery; my short, wretched and miserable existence all but forgotten.

So I'd positioned the shotgun under my chin and was tensing my finger on the trigger when suddenly out of nowhere came the crash of breaking branches as Spot charged madly up from the direction of the river. Providence had arrived fortuitously in the form of a shivering and soaked bedraggled sheepdog!

Afore I could act, he set about frantically licking my face and shaking himself dry, showering me with spray from top to tail to leave me resembling the proverbial drowned rat. I just didn't have the heart to pull the trigger after that. The thought of a bereft Spot returning home alone to Pencnwc was heart-breaking. Besides, t'was such a beautiful location there on the Gwaun so why sully such a scene by scattering my brains all along its buttercupped banks?

We lost Spot when I was 13. Didn't take sick and die, you understand, simply lit off after a rabbit one day and ne'er came back. T'was a most queer happenstance I could ne'er quite shake. Having spent days and weeks fruitlessly scouring the surrounding fields and woods whilst all the time plaintively calling his name, I grieved long and hard for my dear friend. James surmised Spot had gotten stuck down a rabbit hole from whence he'd been unable to extricate himself. Already feeling as miserable as sin, I heartily wished my brother had kept such an opinion to himself. The thought of my poor dog condemned to suffer a cruel and lingering death trapped helplessly deep underground was all too terrible to contemplate. It took me months to get over Spot's loss. We had other dogs on the farm, of course, but none could ever match up to him. In truth, none of them even came close.

Being able to read and write from a young age opened up a vast world of exploration and adventure for me. How well I recall eagerly devouring newspaper accounts of the first overland crossing of Australia when I was about 12. I found the heroism, endeavour and ultimate tragedy experienced by that band of hardy souls all-consuming.

What stayed with me was how the last doomed survivors of the British expedition had for months battled extreme hardship to struggle to the depot which should have been their salvation, only to find that the relief party had departed mere hours afore. Had those wretched fellows not dallied to give one of their number a Christian burial, they'd have made the rendezvous and so lived.

To my young and enquiring mind this tragedy highlighted the fine line that existed betwixt success and failure, of life and death, and, most importantly, how the lives of us all are governed by the fates; and fate had failed those poor devils cruelly just as they'd struggled into sight of the finish line. Where had God been then? I wondered. Perhaps looking t'other way?

Around the same time, I read one of Father's books called The Whale which similarly fired my imagination. It told of a master mariner's obsessive quest to kill a great white leviathan which took him to the very ends of the earth. For some reason, I especially identified with its narrator, who called himself Ishmael, and wished that I'd been named so. For a time I even insisted that my siblings addressed me such! 'Call me Ishmael ...' I'd say. Tom and James, who did not share my love for books, both reckoned I was a tad queer in the head.

So that was the James family of Pencnwc in that winter of 1862/63; a period that would affect us all in myriad ways. T'was as if Father was the foundation stone of our little world and, once that cornerstone was removed, all four walls came tumbling down upon our heads. T'was as if we'd been struck by an earthquake.

Night after night I'd awaken to that dreadful rattle of impending death while my brothers slumbered peacefully on either side of me. As my eyes grew used to the inky blackness, I'd peer towards the flickering candlelight coming from my parents' chamber across the hall and listen to our father wheezing and gasping as his life force slowly and inexorably drained away. Occasionally, I imagine Mother would give him a draught of water; anything to help clear those tortured lungs or ease that fevered throat and thus provide a small and passing degree of comfort. But more often than not this would only provoke a fresh bout of spluttering so fierce I feared that at any instant he might choke and expire and t'was as much as I could do to stop myself from leaping from my bed, running to him and burying my head into that once-broad chest as I had done when I was very little. Yet for as long as I could remember it had been a set rule that we children should never set foot in our parents' bedchamber and one that even now I could not quite bring myself to challenge.

Up 'til then, life had been good. Owning one of the largest farms in the parish, Father had the means to take on a couple of agricultural labourers and, as more of us children showed up, Mother employed a domestic servant. My earliest memory is of being held in her arms, watching Father and Tom drive our herd of coal-black Pembroke cattle up the lane to our farmhouse. Those cows were damn fine milkers and for years hence I'd fall asleep to the sounds of their lowing on the slopes of Dinas Mountain, like.

Another early recollection is of the old Welsh tradition of the Mari Lwyd coming round one Yuletide. I was terrified by the appearance of this sinister spectral figure in our yard: in truth a horse's skeletal head perched on some fellow's shoulders, not that I fully understood that at the time. Such was my four year-old's terror that I fled to our chamber upstairs, steadfastly ignoring the entreaties of Mother to remain with our visitors and participate in the ensuing singing and feasting. That was the only occasion I can recall the Mari Lwyd ever calling on us, although other neighbouring farms received visitations in the years following. What irony, given my future path, that the sight of a horse's head should have induced such terror in a fellow destined to become a US cavalryman!

On January 13, we would celebrate Hen Galan, the

old New Year as marked by the Julian calendar, prior to the coming of the Gregorian. For us children, the tradition of Calennig, the practice of visiting nearby homes and farms bearing twigs from evergreen plants and cups or jugs of water, carried far greater weight than Yuletide.

Having sung a selection of traditional Welsh rhymes to welcome the New Year, we'd use the twigs to splash water at our neighbours; a practice that Tom in particular seemed to relish, and in return would be given calennig, gifts of small copper coins. Father and his cronies would enjoy a rare chance to go shooting while Mother, Mary and Elizabeth would busy themselves preparing a sumptuous repast of goose and figgy pudding in the farmhouse kitchen. Away from the farm, the chapel held sway. We'd attend three times on Sundays; seemed to spend as much time there as we did at Pencnwc.

We spoke Welsh at home and I must have been around six when I first heard the English tongue down at Brynhenllan. Mother and Father pressed our use of the language for they believed it would help us get on in life. All the well-to-do people spoke English, they said.

It did seem queer to me that the mother tongue in which we conversed back home was not just frowned upon at school, but outlawed. Indeed, as I was to find out soon enough, any child caught using Yr Hen Iaith (The Old Language) would not be merely harangued or chastised, but was likely to end up slapped and beaten.

And while Father occasionally had just cause to curb us boys, the punishments he administered were a mere trifle compared to what we were forced to endure at Peniel School. Father's younger brother, our uncle William, was very big on the Welsh; in truth, save the occasional profanity, I don't think I ever heard that fellow utter one word of English in all the years I knew him. Uncle William differed much from Father. The two of them could not have been more unalike. William was an out-and-out scallywag who had no truck with religion of any kind. He gambled and drank much, consorted with painted women and was once or twice pulled up before 'the Beak' at Felindre Farchog on account of some drunken escapade or another. In his younger days, he'd partaken in the Rebecca Riots, when men dressed up as women and smashed up a load of tollgates in protest at paying road charges, I think. He'd have us children in fits by saying the bit he'd relished the most was dressing up as a woman! Never had his collar felt for the part he played in the kerfuffle, which saw the tollgate smashed down in Clynderwen, as far as I know.

That Rebecca's Riots tale of his became as much a part of our Yuletide gatherings as renderings of Good King Wenceslas and Once in Royal David's City. Then, after a few ales, sure as eggs are eggs, he'd start rowing with Father over what Uncle William regarded was his indifferent attitude to Welsh. Now Father was a proud Welshman who wasn't against the Welsh language by no means, but his trenchant support for the English tongue would see them quarrel endlessly. Uncle William would wind up taking offence or getting on his high horse, as Father'd say, and insist on riding all the way back to Grandfather James' farm of Caerlem out on Strumble Head oft through drifts of deepening snow. 'They took our land, and they made it their land,' he once said to me of the English, only in Welsh, of course. When I was about 14, I overhead Mother tell a fellow chapel-goer one of her biggest fears was that I would turn out like Uncle William! I suppose those fears of hers pretty much came to pass ...

I was 13 years old during Father's last winter and, in the coming months would have to grow up fast. As Father neared his end, myself, Tom and James took on more and more chores around the farm. We were young, fit, increasingly able and eager as young pups to share the increasing burden that poor Mother now toiled under. Like the hearty farmer's daughter from Strumble Head she was, Mother remained stoic and steadfast, only those black-rimmed, hollow eyes betraying the sleepless nights she spent caring for a dearly beloved husband on his death bed.

At the same time, the poor woman was undertaking the duties of the head of the household of a farm of many hectares as well as administering to the needs of my younger brothers and sister. Yet, for the most part, Mother stoutly maintained a bold front that seldom slipped.

But once, while undertaking a search for hens' eggs in the barn, I heard her weeping softly in the woodshed: the sorrow and shock on hearing those wracking sobs, low moans and anguished sighing: 'O Arglwydd Duw ...' (Oh Lord God ...) haunt me still. Father had been a robust man of the soil all his life, as had his father at Caerlem and his father before him. As a Methodist minister, he preached temperance, shunned alcohol and constantly warned us young fellows on the perils of the drink. The Cross Inn, Miss Morgans' little tavern a mere stone's throw down the road from our farm, was never graced with his presence, although once Father was no more Tom would partake of many an ale there and regale an impressionable James with tales of life at sea.

From a very young age, Father had toiled six days a week from dawn 'til dusk. For much of his life he was as fit as a butcher's dog. The James menfolk had widely attained their full span of three score years and ten. Grandfather James lived 'til over ninety; Grandfather Batine to a great age also. But soon after the age of fifty, Father was struck down by the galloping consumption which was such a scourge in the locality. His decline was swift and cruel. The day he was unable to mount his loyal Shire horse Soldier without steps was the day I knew his days were short.

The wedding of my eldest sister, Mary, is a rare pleasant memory from that sorrowful time. Defying his increasingly frailty, Father downed his medicines, arose shakily from his sickbed, donned his Sunday best and proudly walked his beloved first daughter down the aisle at Dinas Parish Church as she was betrothed to James Lloyd. T'was one of the first weddings at the new church since St Brynach's had to be abandoned due to the invasion of the sea at Cwmyreglwys. Despite his stooped and aged countenance, Father was a happy man that morning, e'en prepared to make light of the fact his new son-in-law spoke not one single word of Welsh. I well recall him jesting that the union of the happy couple would mean that we Jameses would not want for eggs or butter again for the rest of our days.

As winter marched on, we resigned ourselves to the approach of Father's death. By the coming of spring he was fast sinking. By now he had discontinued the hymn-singing that had sustained his spirits, and he groaned much. Kindly Dr Phillips was providing a draught to calm him at night when he pronounced that Father was in a dying state. Yet Father rallied again and again. Just when it seemed he would succumb to the eternal sleep, mother said he'd somehow move from his bed to the easy chair for a short while afore going back again.

The day we lost him remains etched on my mind. It was the first time I could remember being allowed into the chamber he'd shared with Mother for so long. Dr Phillips, who'd arrived early that morning, stated that father would expire afore 12 noon, but he was still alive, though like as if dead, three hours hence.

Suddenly, and unexpectedly, he became quite agitated and began calling for his late sister who'd expired a full thirty years previously. 'Mary, Mary fach, dewch yma,' (Little Mary, come here), he implored piteously, then just a little later: 'Ble ydych chi? Dyma fi, cariad (Where are you? Here I am, love). T'was truly heart-rending to witness. He was calling out so loud that James, out working in the fields as was his custom, later said you could hear him half a league distant. The good doctor administered an anodyne draught soon afterwards whereupon Father mercifully slept for about an hour. When

I next saw him his mouth was quite open and his eyes closed. I excused myself and left the room immediately as it was too hard for me to stand about and in about 15 minutes he took his last breath.

The funeral at Brynhenllan, where as deacon he'd consigned so many others to eternal life, was very large. My abiding memory is of his obnoxious fellow deacon, William Sparks, that supposed champion of temperance, attending the proceedings in such a drunken state that he tumbled into the open grave. In retrospect, my lack of zeal for religion perhaps stemmed from there. I imagine Father's lifelong religious faith had sustained him to an extent, in the same way it'd provided some succour to Mother. But in the years to come her attendance at chapel grew more infrequent and later, especially when in drink, she would sometimes even question the very existence of God and take task heatedly with those who demurred.

Death was already no stranger to me. In the November of 1859, the Pembrokeshire coast had been besieged by a storm of unrelenting fury which carved a swathe through the fishing boats of the county with a resulting frightful loss of life. That storm had no equals. We later discovered that among those vessels lost was the Queen's own Royal Charter. Over 400 wretched souls went down with her somewhere off north Wales. The wind howled around Pencnwc like a thousand demons that night, prompting my terrified ten-year-old self to bury his head in the blankets of our bed and fervently pray for the onset of the dawn. I am man enough to admit I even shed some tears during those dark hours. How my elder brothers would have mocked me had they awoken! But for several hours I truly believed the strength of the wind would uproot Pencnwc's rock-like foundations and blow us all down the hill into the sea. At one point, I even called out to Mother, but I doubt she could hear me amid that screaming tempest which wreaked so much death and destruction as chronicled within the pages of The Dewisland and Cemes Guardian the next week.

The next morning, Mr Mayler of Cwmyreglwys rode up our farm track to say a catastrophe had befallen St Brynach's Church which had been destroyed by mountainous waves. 'For God's sake, Mr James, make haste,' he bellowed. 'The dead sleep in peace no more; the sea is awash with corpses!' On arriving at the scene one glance indicated he had not been guilty of exaggeration. The seaward-facing wall of the church had been swept clean away, as had part of the graveyard. A sight of unimaginable horror lay before us as we gazed at the sight of mortal remains lying amid the shallows or scattered here and there along the foreshore. Everywhere one looked one could spy either a grinning skull or glistening ribcage.

'The church has been dealt a mortal blow; St Brynach's is no more,' declared Father grimly. And he was right; despite the very best efforts of the congregation, within two years the church had to be abandoned and a replacement constructed at Brynhenllan in the heart of the village. A week after the great storm, Tom and I were fishing down at Cwmyreglwys when a macabre sight met our startled young eyes. The naked body of a drowned man, mouth agape and arms stretched out above his head, almost in the manner of worship, drifted slowly past our rocky outcrop. As we gazed horrified at his sightless stare, Tom, who was himself destined to perish at sea a dozen years hence, pronounced him a victim of what the newspapers was now calling The Royal Charter Storm.

The mariner, if that's indeed what he was, was buried in an unmarked grave in the new cemetery at Brynhenllan the following day. During his address at the wretched fellow's graveside, I well recall Father telling his congregation that the nameless unfortunate was known only to God. A wave of sadness swept over me as I contemplated the possibility of my own loved ones perhaps ne'er knowing of my own demise and final resting place. Will there be anyone to weep for me at my own graveside? I wondered, with all the maudlin self-pity young hearts so readily engage in.

Death stalked us all in those days. What I could not have known was that the same accursed disease that carried off Father would also claim poor little Ellen at the age of 14 a mere six years hence. Working in Llanelly as a commercial traveller in 1869, I was spared the anguish of witnessing my youngest sister's decline which was mercifully swift once the wasting disease ensnared her in its grip. Poor Mother became almost paralysed by grief, so Ellen's nursemaid in her final weeks and days was the noble Ann who did all she could to ease her little sister's pain and discomfort.

Less than three weeks after Ellen had passed, our distraught mother fell into a swoon on finding Ann herself prostrate and insensible on the kitchen floor, as cold as the flagstones upon which she lay. Dr Rees subsequently pronounced her deceased from a ruptured blood vessel although our elder sisters swore blind she'd died from a broken heart. And how could we have foreseen that within two years both Ann and Ellen would have been joined in death by their three stout-hearted brothers, Tom, James and Frank?

So by the time I set off for Canada in the March of 1871 five of my precious siblings had departed this life so young. Thank God Father was spared the misery of witnessing his dear family torn asunder. Alas, it was Mother who had to bear alone the anguish of burying five of her nine children as well as selling off the lands of Pencnwc for monies to support her diminished brood. Although death was a constant companion in Dinas on both land and sea, I brooded over the fact that we Jameses of Pencnwc seemed particularly ill-starred. When the black dog descended upon me, as it did oftener, I'd invariably reflect on the day we became the unwitting subjects of a gypsy's curse.

In the autumn prior to Father's sad decline, he, Tom

and James had cause to drive an encampment of Romany gypsies from one of our lower fields. A number of pigs had gone missing from neighbouring farms and, rightly or wrongly, blame was apportioned squarely at the door of the travelling folk although our own family held no real quarrel with them. Some time later, Tom had encountered, in his own words, 'this self-same parcel of rogues' whilst riding along the mountain road across the Prescelis on his way to Haverfordwest. While the gypsy menfolk appeared not to recognise him and issued cheery greetings, one old crone had unleashed a stream of blasphemous remarks in his direction, prior to laying a curse on the entire James clan. Whilst Tom was unabashed, and later related the tale with considerable mirth, this unsettling encounter would prey upon my mind from time to time during the difficult years that followed, not least when we suffered the dire misfortune of losing three of my brothers within little more than a week. At the time, Tom had airily dismissed my concerns. He told me I thought overmuch. But I know that James, who stepped out with a gypsy girl around this period, shared my dark forebodings.

While grateful for the Sunday School chapel lessons that enabled me to read and write, I could not deny that I was no great believer, despite oft regarding those who did believe with no little envy. God, should he indeed exist, had dealt my kinfolk a pretty poor card, it seemed to me. I resolved that, come the Day of Judgment, I'd freely express my litany of grievances to Him in person. He would have some considerable explaining to do, I decided. However, it does pain me to admit that having attained the age of 27, I find myself completely incapable of reciting the Lord's Prayer, Yr Arglwydd Duw, in Yr Hen Iaith, for painful reasons that have only now become apparent. Such an admission would grieve Father, a man who served as chapel deacon for over twenty years, deeply.

And so, within a couple of months of Father breathing

his last, our days at Pencnwc were over. We left the farm with heavy hearts as the place we children had known as a once happy, noisy and cheerful home below Dinas Mountain now stood silent and empty. Mother moved us into Tyllwyd, a fine new house perched high on a spur above Cwmyreglwys, where we lived as tenants thanks to the proceeds of the land sales. She took young John Clement, Frank, Ellen, Ann and myself with her; Mary had just commenced married life down in Prendergast and would shortly become a mother, while Elizabeth was by now working as a servant on a farm near Cwmyreglwys. We four youngest were still attending Peniel School in the centre of Dinas at this time. Each weekday morning, and again on Sundays, we'd depart Tyllwyd washed and brushed in our best outfits and troop wearily like a veritable line of ducks up the rise from Cwmyreglwys towards the village, little Ellen invariably singing Welsh hymns in her beautiful clear voice. I cannot speak for the others, but my belly would be sick with dread at the prospect of what the coming hours would bring. I hated that school with a vengeance or rather, if truth be told, Thomas, the grotesque, one-eyed schoolteacher, whose great and unreasonable rages we all feared. His black eyepatch mirrored his soul; as dark as the ace of spades. Ellen's outwardly gay countenance can only have masked the forebodings she bore within.

Thomas was not from those parts, I believe he was once a mariner who originally hailed from south Wales. I well recall Tom, the recipient of the teacher's lashings on numerous occasions, recounting with wicked glee how this cold-hearted fish came to be washed up in Fishguard like some beached porpoise, as the sailor of a ship which foundered in Fishguard Bay. 'Had it been down to me I'd have thrown him straight back in the briny,' declared Tom. Father once told us that the Calvinistic Methodists of Fishguard held a collection to send Thomas back from whence he came. Sadly for us, he only got as far as Dinas Cross where he promptly decamped and, within time, resurfaced as a preacher at Tabor Chapel. From then on, he became a towering figure in the community. A pillar of respectability, one might say. He set up prayer meetings and fellowship meetings, a Sunday School and Bible class swiftly followed. Quick-tempered, almost demonic, his eyepatch making him appear ever more sinister, he'd brandish his arms wildly from the pulpit while berating his hapless congregation over what he perceived to be their countless wrong-doings. Unsurprisingly he caused much rancour and division, many of his flock wisely departing for other chapels and our own dear Father had precious little time for him. They say Thomas's somewhat timid wife made good progress in curbing his temper, but as one of his unfortunate young scholars I saw scant evidence that this was the case.

I was nine years old when he took charge of Peniel School, whose children numbered around seventy. Thomas set up a kind of school council whereby a jury of children would judge a wrongdoer; the purpose was to deflect criticism from the miscreant's parents who were members of his congregation, and he used the stick as a means of enforcing discipline. Suffice to say, he used it greatly. His favoured method was to order some unfortunate to climb aboard the back of a classmate to enable him to wield the full force of strap or stick. I myself was punished oft, usually for speaking in Welsh out in the playground or for neglecting to do my homework.

What proved the day of reckoning came on a cold January morning in 1863 when Thomas flogged John Clement for having the temerity to keep coughing in class. Unlike his elder brothers, poor John had ne'er been blessed with a robust constitution and the sight of his anguished, tear-streaked face, quivering lower lip and rapid gasps for breath unleashed a fierce and terrible anger from deep within me. Just like the great storm that had laid waste to St Brynach's, it rose up unexpectedly, with consequences that were far-reaching.

Rising from my chair I heard myself exclaim: 'Peidwch!' (Stop!) as the red-faced, panting headteacher prepared to strike my younger brother for the umpteenth time. Thomas turned slowly and glared at me; the look of sheer disbelief and shock on his face would have been comical in any other circumstance. In that instant both he and I knew that a line had been crossed and that things could ne'er return to how they were. My blood was up and I readily hoped he would rush at me brandishing the cane above his head, thus giving me just cause to stand my ground, plant my feet, strike back with both fists and so administer the instant and fitting retribution that had been so long in coming. Yet striding across the classroom towards him I sensed something else within this man who had ruled our lives for so long; t'was the smell of fear.

Standing five feet eight inches tall and weighing a wiry yet muscular ten stone, I may not have been quite the oldest scholar at Peniel, but I was by now unquestionably the tallest. Moreover, even by that point, I had developed a reputation in the village for, how can we say, being somewhat handy with my fists judging by the occasional dust-ups I'd had with the gypsy boys. Only that very week I'd rendered a full-grown fellow I'd seen whipping a horse insensible with one blow.

Snatching the cane from the teacher's trembling hand, I gazed fiercely into his eyes and promptly snapped it hard across the nearest desk, causing the poor lad sitting there to jump as if having suffered a dose of buckshot. The sharp crack it made was magnified a thousand times in the now-silent classroom. 'As God is my witness thou will ne'er strike any one of us ever again,' I rasped in a voice that brooked no argument. As I spat out those words I swear all the colour drained from the schoolmaster's spiteful face. No meek scholar had e'er addressed him such. As a sailor he may have had occasional recourse to use his fists against fellow shipmates, but in this clearly enraged farmer's son from Dinas Cross he had quite evidently met his match.

Pulling the afeared John away from him, I turned to take hold of Ellen's hand while motioning with my head for Frank to follow. We four Jameses flounced out of that school through rows of gaping classmates with our heads held high, a band of soldiers on some great march, myself heading the procession like some cock of the walk. I'm told that those who were there that day talk of it still. My own schooldays ended forthwith and from that instant Mother insisted on sending my younger siblings to the chapel school at Brynhenllan, although in a show of solidarity with her children she always made a point of never sitting in on one of Thomas's sermons, bless her.

Tom and James, having for a time entertained thoughts of taking the Queen's Shilling, left home to become mariners. Over the next few years they would sail the seven seas while I worked for a number of years as a carpenter in Narberth, a rough and ready and poorly-paid trade that at least provided board and lodge and a bunk to rest my weary head above the workshop, a decent situation for a boy of barely fifteen who had just left home.

Having been raised with horses, the job of a coachman appealed and while still at Pencnwc I'd frequently enjoyed discourse with those ruddy-faced, weathered, top-hatted individuals who drove the Haverfordwest omnibus from Newport into Dinas each morn. After they'd shed their load of mail at Mr Harries's post office next door to the Cross Inn they'd invariably adjourn inside for a glass of Porters or two. When these hale and hearty fellows emerged, faces aglow, an hour or so later they'd inevitably find me patting, feeding or simply admiring the coach horses while ruminating on the lure of an occupation that boasted the attraction of travel.

Those early days in Narberth were bewildering times, I confess, as I sought to make headway in life in an unfamiliar town at a time when so many constants as well as constraints had vanished around me. The work I was engaged in was quite humdrum and not of my choosing; I missed life on the farm as well as the company of my brothers sorely. But at the same time I took solace in the fact I was now, at the age of 15, a working fellow with ne'er a soul to trouble about but myself.

Moreover, my pay, although meagre, was ne'ertheless my own and I was able to do with it as I saw fit, oft seeking gay and colourful company in the taverns and ale houses of the town and indulging in both the drink and vices that had hitherto been denied me home in Dinas. These carefree days were a welcome diversion from the sorrow that had been. I was a strong, good-looking boy with an eye for the fairer sex and stepped out for a time with a servant girl whose parents hailed from Fishguard. Emily and I became quite fond of one another, leading me in time to entertain thoughts of marriage. Yet for all Emily's comely appearance and engaging ways, a persistent, louder voice sounding within me could not be silenced. It told me that my wandering days were not yet over; indeed, they had scarce begun. I may have left my home village behind, yet a far wider world lay beyond dear old Pembrokeshire. I well remember James saying that a mariner's mind would be elsewhere days or even weeks afore he departed on a long voyage. 'T'is hard to explain, Will,' said he, 'but when a fellow's within sight of sailing it's as though he's already gone, and the distance 'twixt him and those he's leaving behind widens by the instant.'

The same was true of me during my days in Narberth. Like a sailor preparing for some great voyage I sensed my time ashore would be short and, in a queer way, the journey ahead would not be of my own choosing. In short, I felt guided by a stronger and higher force, not that I would have imparted as much to my elder brothers.

James Lloyd, my rather grand brother-in-law, was busy

laying plans to set up as a market trader in London and the giddy prospect of travel both enticed and enthralled me. One night, Emily, whose grandmother told fortunes, insisted on reading my palm. 'Alas, Will, your future lies not with me,' she said softly. 'I see you travelling far and wide across a fathomless ocean to a distant land where you will take up the gun and cutlass.' Though she'd not have known, the idea of me becoming a soldier was no mere folly. Mother's great-uncle, Thomas Batine, was a Major-General in the Indian army who served in the artillery for 47 years across much of the north of India. Here he was involved in a considerable number of engagements, including the Nepal War of 1814-15 and the Third Mahrata War of 1817-18 in what became the state of Maharashtra.

After more action in Uttar Pradesh in 1819, he was brevetted Lieut-Colonel. He died at Lahore in 1851 from 'severe bilious fever'. An obituary said of him that: 'He was an officer much esteemed and in private life greatly regarded.' Nor was he the only soldier in the family. Grandfather Batine joined the Pembroke Cavalry soon after the French invasion of Fishguard in 1797 and an uncle, Francis Batine, who young Frank was named after, served in wars of colonial conquest in India. He was an Ensign in the 31st Foot in Bengal in 1833; transferred to the 9th Foot in 1835 (then in Mauritius); and was then promoted Lieutenant in the 9th Regiment of Foot. He was later brevetted captain and returned home sick from Simla in July 1838. He retired from the army in April 1839, and went to live with our grandparents at Llanwnwr. Although he died two years afore I was born, I was well familiar with some of his soldiering tales as related to us boys by Mother.

One of my earliest memories was of hearing Father discussing The Charge of The Light Brigade with Grandfather James. The war in Crimea was in all the newspapers and the story of that heroic dash into the Valley of Death both thrilled and excited me, my interest piqued even more on learning that one of the Bowens from Llwyngwair, near Newport, had taken part in some capacity and survived.

The charge was immortalised by Tennyson's famous poem which stirred the hearts of all us young boys. I'd learnt it off by heart at the age of six and Father would oft summon me to recite it during family occasions, wearing a soldier's hat and clutching a wooden sword. Standing afore an audience of expectant adult faces in my Sunday best held no terrors for me and reciting it undoubtedly stood me in good stead for all the hymn-singing, poetry readings and eisteddfods which lay ahead. Those words of the Poet Laureate became fixed in my young head. John and I endlessly recreated the charge with our toy horses and I spent many a night dreaming of thundering into the Valley of Death.

> 'Half a league, half a league,
> Half a league onward,
> All in the valley of Death
> Rode the six hundred.
> 'Forward, the Light Brigade!
> Charge for the guns!' he said.
> Into the valley of Death
> Rode the six hundred'.

Aye, Tennyson's account enthralled all us young fellows. Ne'er once did we stop to contemplate the pain, terror and horror of what unfolded, the reckless folly that had led up to it or the enduring misery of the loved ones those slain horsemen had left behind.

So though responding at the time to dear Emily's fortune-telling with great mirth, inwardly I felt there might be something to it. And, as I lay pondering in my pup tent ten years on, a war-weary soldier in the US Seventh Cavalry readying himself for an anticipated great battle, how uncannily prophetic that sweet girl's words seemed. Taking stock of my position, I calculated I had but mere weeks to serve afore laying down my gun and cutlass and commencing a return to civilian life; a life I now would share with my one true love awaiting me countless leagues distant; the girl I left behind me…

CHAPTER 3

Haverfordwest
May 8, 1904

Arthur Nicholas sat patiently in Eaton's office as the head solicitor finished dictating a letter to Miss Gray, the typist. Eaton had earlier explained that as Messrs Roberts and Rees wished to spare no expense on the investigation into the whereabouts of William Batine James, he had accordingly suggested they enlist the services of London-based solicitors Messrs Peacock & Goddard. They, in turn, from their Grays Inn headquarters where they habitually utilised a range of contacts from across the globe, would instruct a firm of US solicitors to launch the search on their Haverfordwest colleagues' behalf. Eaton duly informed Arthur some days later that Peacock and Goddard had recruited the services of the New York firm of Messrs Owen & Sturgis, of Wall Street, who would embark on the quest for the missing William Batine James with immediate effect.

Arthur could not help feeling very excited at this speedy turn of events. Having already spent considerable time poring over the five letters from America contained in John Clement James's bundle of private papers, he was starting to feel something of a sleuth. Suddenly the life of an apprentice solicitor did not seem quite so humdrum. Yes, America was a mighty big place, which realistically meant the chances of a successful resolution were minimal, yet the James case certainly beat the usual assortment of petty land disputes and trivial poaching matters that Eaton habitually dropped on his small desk. The fact his office colleagues had expressed pessimism over Arthur's chances of success also provided ample incentive to prove them wrong. The previous week Eaton had made Arthur feel uncustomarily important by seeking his opinion on the best means of instigating the hunt for a man who had in all probability been dead for thirty years. 'Well, sir,' Arthur had told him, 'I would respectfully suggest we follow the barrister's advice to concentrate the search on the places from where we know James posted those last couple of letters; Greensboro and Opelika down in Alabama.'

'And how exactly do you propose we go about doing that?' frowned Eaton, cupping his chin in his hand and giving Arthur the distinct impression the wily old fox was testing his initiative. Despite his nerves, and Arthur had always been hampered by a lack of self-confidence, the young solicitor cleared his throat and carried on. 'My initial enquiries indicate Greensboro and Opelika are small farming towns with very modest populations,' he said. 'Bearing that in mind, I suggest we get our New York colleagues to place advertisements in the local newspapers in Alabama appealing for any information on the whereabouts of William Batine James.'

Eaton nodded thoughtfully. 'Bit of a long shot, I suppose, but then we don't have too many options open to us, do we?' he grunted. 'Are you suggesting that if the advertisements state that the aforementioned Mr James is entitled to the keys of a significant property here in west Wales, it might just flush him out of the woodwork?'

'No sir, definitely not,' answered Arthur. 'On the contrary, I suggest we mustn't be too specific. An advertisement of that nature will inevitably attract the usual n'er-do-wells, cranks and madmen all seeking a piece of the pie. No, I would strongly advise we keep it vague and hope that, by hook or by crook, the advert is seen by James himself or, failing that, someone of his immediate acquaintance.'

Eaton nodded again. 'Assuming William Batine James still lives, of course,' he said, stroking his beard. 'I'm sure you will agree, Arthur, that there is significant irony in the fact that much time, effort and money will undoubtedly be expediated in trying to locate a man who, in the balance of all probability, has been lying six feet under for God knows how many years.'

'You could well be right, sir, but we obviously have to try,' replied Arthur. 'And I don't know why, but I now possess an intuitive feeling that William Batine James may indeed still live. Admittedly, all I have to back up that hunch at present is a feeling in my gut, you might say.'

'Ha! I always did like an optimist,' replied Eaton approvingly. 'Very well, Arthur, we will proceed in the manner you suggest, although now you have read the William James letters you will know only too well that they afford us precious little to go on.' Arthur wholeheartedly agreed with his master's assessment. How could the contents of no fewer than five letters amount to so little? he pondered.

Rising to his feet and ushering Arthur towards the door, Eaton then added as an afterthought: 'I trust that you will, of course, provide me with weekly updates on any progress that you may make?' 'Of course, sir,' answered Arthur whose confidence at solving the riddle he had been posed with was not nearly as fulsome as he hoped it appeared.

A bright and studious young man, Arthur could easily grasp why Eaton's pessimism was so well-founded. The letters William Batine James had sent home from Canada and the United States were dreadfully light on detail. In fact, almost deliberately so, it appeared to him.

In the first, date-marked Toronto, its writer had alluded to getting 'a situation in one of the best shops in the city', but what occupation he was pursuing there remained a complete and utter mystery. In one of the later letters, WBJ alluded to some illness which had precluded him from attending business for some time. Once again, there was nothing to indicate what business that might have been. Arthur nevertheless found himself studying the letters again and again. They fast became something of an obsession. He even took them back to the little terraced home of his widowed landlady, Mrs Canning, in Fishguard Lower Town's Bridge Street to read by candlelight in bed at night.

From Toronto, the next letters jumped to 'F A Lynchon, Dakota Territory', a couple of years later, and then the final two were dispatched from Alabama down in the Deep South. By now a certain suspicion had formed in Arthur's mind. 'This chap just did not want to be found,' he said to himself, sipping a cup of hot chocolate whilst sitting up in bed late one night. 'It is almost as if he is taking great pains to cover the few tracks he leaves behind; and he is covering them well.' Could something indeed have happened back in Dinas Cross, Arthur wondered, to make the writer flee the shores of his native land in unseemly haste?

Arthur found himself unable to resist divulging details of his assignment to Louisa Perkins, the young Goodwick seamstress he was courting. At first, she had displayed polite interest, but the last time Arthur had raised the subject while they enjoyed a drink at Fishguard's Royal Oak he'd noticed her barely stifle a yawn.

A couple of weeks on, Louisa would complain she felt this William Batine James character was competing with her for Arthur's affections; the trouble was, Arthur sensed she was only half-joking. His curiosity as to the fate of this man he sought was well and truly whetted, however, and in order to find out more about the type of person he was seeking, any clues as to what his business had been in Canada and North America and, perhaps, possible reasons for his sudden disappearance, Arthur decided his home village of Dinas Cross would be the best place to start. And what better person to speak to first than his own mam?

'Do I remember a William James from my childhood?' Mari Nicholas had replied when Arthur turned up at his old childhood home a couple of days later. 'Dewch, Arthur bach, I must have known a good half-dozen fellows of that name!' Sitting comfortably in her easy chair in front of the parlour fire, Mari, a cheery, middle-aged widow with grey hair, twinkling eyes and rosy cheeks, was clearly more than eager to cast her mind back to her teenage years. 'His full name was William Batine James, mam, and he was born at Pencnwc Farm in March 1849, just one year ahead of your good self,' said Arthur. Mari smiled warmly and nodded. 'Well, duw, duw! William James, of Pencnwc! Otherwise known to all as 'Will o' the Wisp'. Of course I remember Will, and most of his family too. Strong chapel, although I suppose we all were back in those days.

'Will's father was a deacon at Brynhenllan and I numbered among his congregation for a couple of years. Ruled Ramah Chapel with a rod of iron, he did. My, how us children were afeared of him! Mr James died quite young, as did most of Will's brothers and sisters. Tragedy was a constant bedfellow of that poor family. You'll find most, if not all of them buried down at Ramah Cemetery. So, pray tell me the reason you seek Will? Should you be successful please be mindful to pass on to him my best regards.'

Arthur patiently explained that William Batine James would undoubtedly prove considerably more elusive than his mother seemed to appreciate. 'He went out to Canada in 1871, and then on to America a few years later,' he told her. 'The reason we are so keen to find him is that following the death of his younger brother, John Clement James last year he stands to inherit the family farm of Llanwnwr.'

'I see,' Mari nodded slowly. 'I was aware of the sad recent passing of Mr James and sincerely hope your search yields results. Llanwnwr is a most splendid farm and should Will indeed be found I have no doubt whatsoever that he would make a grand success of the place.

'I'll tell you a story about Will James,' she smiled, clasping her hands across her midriff, 'in truth, I can tell you a few! I well remember the day he and his brother Thomas raced their horses at breakneck speed from the Cross Inn right through the village to the parish pump on the green here at Bwlchmawr and back again.'

'A horse race through the village?' repeated Arthur. 'Who was the victor?' 'Why, Will, of course,' replied Mari. 'By a neck unless I'm not mistaken. He was a very fine horseman who could ride like the wind from a very tender age. Poor Thomas cut up a bit rough afterwards, though. Swore blind he'd been diddled as Will had turned his mount around a few yards short of the pump! That caused much mirth back down at the Cross. But those who'd observed the spectacle sided with Will so Thomas ended up paying him some shillings. The two of them had struck a wager following a few bevvies, I seem to recall.

'And t'wasn't the only race they had through the village, mind. There were a whole host of complaints and the matter of young riders galloping through Dinas was brought up in the council. The constable was ordered to keep an eye out for Thomas and Will when they were out riding. He never caught them though. Not that I can remember.' 'Where was the Cross Inn, mam?' frowned Arthur, the name of the pub being unfamiliar. 'Next to the old post office up from the Gideon chapel, not far from Pencnwc,' she answered. 'Real spit and sawdust type of place which called 'stop tap' for the last time many years ago. Probably round about the time of which we speak, in truth.' Arthur pressed Mari on what Will was like as a person. And what occupation did she think he could be following now?

'He was a good-looking boy, with brown eyes, light-coloured hair and a ready smile,' she remembered. 'One of the teachers at chapel said that disarming smile of Will's would take him a long way, I recall. He was a bit of a rascal to be honest and, indeed to goodness, he could certainly put it about with those fists of his. Most people liked him though. Beneath all that front and cocksure bluster beat a kind heart. I suppose you could say that Will James was the type of fellow who'd make a great friend, but a frightful enemy.' Mari halted in her recollections for a moment and scratched her head absently as she continued to hark back to a time when she was young. 'The other thing about Will was that he was the first, and so far only fellow I've ever known to ride a horse backwards,' she told Arthur, smacking herself on the knee.

'Backwards?' her son repeated incredulously. 'You mean he got a horse to trot backwards?'

'No, twpsyn!' (silly) replied Mari scornfully, 'I mean he rode the horse whilst sitting about-face in the saddle; looking down past the horse's backside and holding the reins behind him!'

'Really?' answered Arthur, in astonishment. 'Would I be right in venturing that this was down at the Haverfordwest County Show, by any chance?'

Mari shook with laughter. 'Mynyfani! (Hell!) Indeed it was not!' she exclaimed. 'It was right along the bloody main street of Dinas, mun! He did that for a wager too!'

Although somewhat taken aback at this revelation, Arthur found himself laughing along with his mother. This William James was evidently something of a character, he thought. 'I imagine the local constable wouldn't have been at all happy at such antics on the main street,' he said.

'Indeed to goodness, Constable Jones wasn't,' agreed Mari. 'When he heard all about it he came looking for Will. I sincerely hope, bach, that you have a damn sight more luck in finding him than that policeman ever did!'

'So he never collared him?' Arthur wanted to know.

'Dewch, of course not! Will had disappeared back to Narberth or wherever it was he was working at that time,' said

Mari. 'And he once showed the Haverfordwest constabulary a clean pair of heels, too!'

'In what way?' queried Arthur.

'From what I can recall there was some big kerfuffle down in this tavern by the Cleddau one Christmas,' said Mari. 'The constables were summoned and collared a number of fellows including Thomas, but Will broke free, leapt out of a window, jumped on his mount and galloped off through deep snow. The constables followed his tracks on horseback and thought they'd cornered Will down by the river, and do you know what that wily bugger gone and done?' Arthur shook his head.

'Rode his bloody horse across the frozen Cleddau and got clean away again!' Mari chuckled delightedly. Arthur looked at her astounded. 'Good God,' he said at length, 'I've never previously heard of such a feat.'

'Indeed to goodness, it was the talk of Dinas for weeks,' replied Mari. 'That was why he was known as Will o' the Wisp, see? He could never, ever, be caught; always melted away like some ghost in the night. And vanishing down to Narberth or wherever,' she concluded with a wide smile, 'well, that was Will James to a 'T' for you.'

Arthur frowned again. 'What exactly do you mean by that, mam?' he asked. Mari paused for a few moments, as she again collected her thoughts. 'Well, bach, Will James was always, and I mean always, getting into scrapes and yet … and yet …'

'And yet what, mam?' asked Arthur, by now becoming slightly irritated at his mother's tendency to spin out a yarn. 'And yet, by damn, you could always count on him somehow finding a way to get out of them!'

7 Wall Street
New York
June 10, 1904

Dear Sirs

Your favour of May 20th with enclosures relative to obtaining information of one William B James, has our attention. We have instituted inquiries with the expectation of ultimately finding some trace of Mr James, although it will probably take considerable time to reach any satisfactory result, if such can be obtained.

With regard to the expense, we are entirely satisfied to leave that matter with you, depending upon the outcome.

We will advise you as we obtain any information of value.

Messrs Peacock & Goddard
Grays Inn

Mouth of the Tongue River, Montana Territory, June 19 1876

(six days out from the Battle of the Little Bighorn)

We'd endured hard riding afore, but this was something else. The ten-day scout undertaken by Major Reno from the Powder River depot pushed the endurance of men, horses and mules to the limit.

T'was a truly devilish slog. Horses and mules played out, men exhausted from pushing and pulling the Gatling gun through gullies and ravines; this torturous day seemed to have no end. As we finally plodded towards camp, just a few miles distant from Terry and the rest of the Seventh, I half-dozed off in the saddle and found myself again thinking of Liz Penfeidr ...

Elizabeth Morgans was a scholar of eleven years with pigtails and wearing a straw hat a couple of sizes too big when I first clapped eyes on her during a recital at Tabor Chapel in Dinas. There she was, sandwiched in the pew 'twixt her brothers with the bored expression on her freckled face suggesting she'd rather be somewhere else.

Glancing sidelong at her from time to time I noted how she kept fidgeting and looking around, showing no interest whatsoever in the sermon taking place. When our eyes finally met we tried to stare one another out. We remained locked on each other's faces, gazing solemnly across the pews for what seemed an eternity.

Finally, I crossed my eyes at about the same time as she poked out her tongue. I looked away again, but when I stealthily turned my head back found that she was now saucily returning my cross-eyed stare. So straightaway I stuck my tongue out at her. She gave a slight start, blinked a couple of times in surprise, then slowly, very slowly, broke into a broad grin. That was my first encounter with Liz Penfeidr.

She was from a monied family who lived at Penfeidr, a large farm on the road to the Gwaun Valley. We Dinas children always said that those who dwelt in Cwm Gwaun differed from the rest of us. To go up the Cwm t'was not merely like venturing into another country; t'was like returning to another century. Spoke a different type of Welsh and clung on to so many old customs from yesteryear.

Over the next few years, I'd see Elizabeth at various chapel events or Sunday School excursions. We might pull the odd face at each other, though ne'er speaking. By the time she was 14 she'd turned into a young woman of terrible beauty; a girl whose mere appearance on Newport's Long Street would halt discourse among us boys.

She became an object of fascination; not simply for her startling looks, but also for how she held herself. 'Liz Penfeidr', as we came to call her, though ne'er to her face, was tall, brown-eyed and pale-skinned with hair the colour of a raven. Staunchly Welsh, she was not averse to berating those whose mastery of Yr Hen Iaith (The Old Language) failed, in her opinion, to match her own. And she was occasionally inclined to reply not at all should any stranger have the temerity to address her in English.

She oft bore the knitted brow of the fierce Gwaun Valley princess. Untouchable, I thought a little wistfully. Away from home she tended to wear her hair loose, allowing those jet-black locks to tumble well down her back.

When I got to know Elizabeth later, I'd josh her by stating that her parents had evidently bought her as a babe-in-arms off some passing family of gypsies, a suggestion that never failed to goad her into dealing me a sharp slap or cuff.

She also disliked being called Bessie, the name of one of her aunts, which duly spurred me to address her as such whenever possible. Once, while horsing around outside Tabor one cold winter's afternoon, she punched me so hard on the nozzle it bled profusely. When Mother later enquired how I'd sustained the injury, Tom replied: 'The daft beggar forgot to duck, mam.'

Another time, when a group of us had gathered outside the chapel, I told all and sundry it was my understanding that Elizabeth's father had found her abandoned as an infant in a cave up on the Prescelis. Everyone fell about holding their sides apart from her. She simply arched an eyebrow and indicated with a slow nod of her dark curls that her vengeance would not be long in coming.

Not long afterwards, I emerged naked from a swim down at Pwllgwaelod to find someone had made off with my clothes. Acutely mindful there were chapel elders about, I'd had to dash straight back into the chilly waters again in order to preserve my modesty. Sitting shivering in the shallows while James vainly scoured the beach for my garments, I suddenly spied a tall and slim young woman waving gaily from a clifftop. She appeared to be brandishing a bundle of clothes. I knew in that instant who was responsible for my embarrassing plight...

Elizabeth was the Morgans' youngest daughter and I once overheard one of the chapel elders say they were having trouble containing her headstrong ways. 'That girl is as wild and untamed as those ponies up on the Prescelis!' he exclaimed. The fact that Liz Penfeidr was already attracting disapproval from such quarters, coupled with the fact she did not appear to care one jot, enticed me towards her even more.

We first got talking during a Sunday School picnic down at Pwllgwaelod, that did not involve bathing, I'm glad to say. I was taken aback when Elizabeth proceeded to lecture me and Tom, with no little knowledge, on the best way to catch fish from the rocks. Her elder brother, a mariner, had taught her not only how to fish but also how to make a fair rod and line. I was more of a crabber myself and would oft be found prowling the rocky outcrops of local beaches in search of those big brown crustaceans that dwelt in their crevices.

While my brothers tended to use small grappling hooks to prise them out, I opted to use my bare hands even if the sharp rocks caused much bleeding. I'd subsequently regale the impressionable village girls with tales of crabbing along the foreshore at dawn, proudly displaying my supposed scars of battle as evidence of my great pluck. Elizabeth was not so easily fooled. 'Get along with you!' she cried, 'crab claws be blowed! If those supposed wounds weren't caused by barnacle-blistered rocks then I'm Florence Nightingale!' And to my chagrin she proceeded to refer to me as Barnacle Bill for pretty much the rest of that summer.

Much as I loved my sisters, they differed greatly from

Elizabeth. Even at 14 she was well at ease in the company of boys and took great delight in taking the mickey out of them. For me it was not mere looks and poise that stood her apart; she was different in every conceivable way. Although always very womanly, Elizabeth did have this unusually direct way with her. Women in Dinas Cross many years her senior weren't like that. Unlike so many of the local young womenfolk, who'd rather study their own feet than look a fellow direct in the eye, she'd return your gaze in such a manner that'd make poor John Clement blush furiously. 'Why, I can assure you, Master James,' she'd coo mischievously, 'that it is not my intention to eat you.'

Although they were almost the same age, she seemed a full-grown woman; shy and stuttering John Clement, who had a frightful crush on her, a mere boy. Once, when a group of us were out working in the fields above Pencnwc, Elizabeth had sharp words in Welsh with my sister Ann about something or other. Ne'er did find out what exactly, but Ann made it clear to me and Tom more than once that she had no time for that Morgans girl. 'Just because her family have wealth, she feels she can lord it over the likes of us,' she said. When I mischievously relayed this back to Elizabeth she for once reacted pretty much how I'd anticipated. 'Don't you just hate women, Will?', she sighed, gazing out upon Newport Bay whilst fanning herself under that big oak tree at the back of Penfeidr.

'I fervently wish the world was peopled by men and children alone. If I'd had my way I'd have been a boy; it would have made my life so much easier. Count yourself fortunate, Will, that you will never have to contend with all the unkindness that a woman will go out of her way to impart on others of her kind.'

All the time Elizabeth was speaking she had this resigned but slightly bemused look on her face. The cool summer breeze kept straggling her dark locks across her face which she kept having to flick back. Far from being angered or discomfited by Ann's haughty reaction, she evidently took considerable amusement from it. She once told Ann bluntly she was too accepting of her lot and that there was far more to life than going to chapel and carrying out menial duties around Tyllwyd day in, day out. Ann, who once archly opined she felt Elizabeth 'wasn't quite all there', went to great pains to try and avoid her completely after that.

Another time, when Elizabeth was stepping out with Tom, the talk at the dinner table turned to the approaching 1868 General Election and how fellows from all walks of life were now getting the vote. Over boiled mutton, mashed potatoes, peas and gravy, Elizabeth shocked the assemble by stating she considered it unjust that women were denied the vote. One day, she opined, citizens of Great Britain would look back aghast on this lamentable state of affairs. Such views were completely foreign to Mother. The way she shifted uneasily in her chair whilst glancing nervously across the table at Tom had me choking with suppressed mirth into my napkin.

One could always count on Elizabeth to set the proverbial cat among the pigeons. 'You know me,' she shrugged afterwards. 'I speak as I find.' Maybe, as Ann maintained, she was over-indulged by her parents and minded not who she upset or angered. But she was a young woman who knew her own mind and, when seeing something she found disagreeable, just could not hold her tongue. One reason I found myself drawn to her was because I could ne'er be quite sure what Elizabeth would do or say next. Moreover, she evidently considered herself the equal of men; and went out of her way to let a fellow know it.

She may not have smiled overmuch, but those eyes of hers were always full of jest. She also had a habit of coming out with a statement quite profound and unexpected. 'Just like I trap rabbits up on Carningli Mountain, beware that one day I won't trap you, Will James!' I well recall her saying. Another time she told me the one question in this life that mattered above all else was what happened once we'd died. 'Your soul and mine will fly arm-in-arm to the top of Carningli, the Mountain of Angels,' she said. 'There we will dwell for evermore, surveying all that surrounds. And should you arrive afore me, Will, be sure to await me there.'

'Indeed I most surely will,' I'd replied, though by no means convinced by thoughts of an afterlife. 'I'll be watching all the ships roll in and then I'll watch them rolling out again.' Once, whilst gazing up at the mist-shrouded peak from Newport Sands she confided she'd long harboured the desire to run down its wild slopes 'as naked as the day I was born'. I could only gape at her in astonishment. Elizabeth oft regaled me with tales of the fairies she maintained dwelt atop the mountain and professed to have spied them on dawn-time strolls on more than one occasion. 'This is our time, Will, our time and we have to grasp it,' she once exclaimed as we strolled together around the graveyard surrounding Newport Church poring over tombstones one summer's afternoon. 'It may seem that these are our days without end, yet afore we know it they will have slipped through our fingers like grains of sand. All of us, Will, are just passing through and we must never lose sight of that fact.'

Elizabeth likened life to a lighted match struck in the darkness. Whilst we'd been born in the flash of light, all too fleetingly, she'd say, the match would be extinguished, darkness would descend again and then reign for all eternity. T'was why we had to seize each day as if it was our last, she'd tell me. Despite this, she fervently believed in some form of afterlife. Aye, Elizabeth Morgans was a young woman who did not bow to any convention nor yield to any rules. Such women were unheard of in Newport and Dinas which is why she put the fear into a lot of us boys. Not I though. I told her on more than one occasion she'd met her match in me.

Over the course of time my feelings towards her gradually changed until they amounted to more than mere friendship. Her friend Annie Lewis once told me about a Sunday School outing that Elizabeth had been forced to miss due to a bad head cold. As it happened, I also could not attend due to farm work and when Annie mentioned my absence to Elizabeth she'd replied she hadn't missed much as 'Will Pencnwc is the only boy who holds my interest in any case.'

We started corresponding while I continued to work in Narberth. She wrote as she spoke; her letters were funny, forthright and wise. The initial trickle gradually became a torrent so almost afore I knew what was happening we seemed to be writing to one another each day. Interminably dull hours sawing and hammering away in that carpenter's shed were brightened only when the coach brought yet another letter from Newport; the address on the envelope scrawled in Liz Penfeidr's distinctive hand. I was becoming besotted with this girl and found myself craving those handwritten jewels like a drunkard craves his ale or a desert misses the rain. My trips back home to Dinas, supposedly to catch up with Mother, John and my sisters, but in reality to see Elizabeth, grew e'er more frequent. Once, while calling around at Penfeidr on the pretence of delivering a catch of mackerel, I was taken aback to find her padding around the farmhouse bare-footed, her long hair flowing loosely behind her.

Mr and Mrs Morgans were away attending Barley Saturday in Cardigan that day; when the cat's away the mouse will play, I thought. While I harboured a strong, almost overwhelming desire to scoop Elizabeth up into my arms, she acted really proper, made us both lemonade and we sat out in the garden in the summer sunshine talking earnestly about life and in which direction we hoped it might take us.

Like me, Elizabeth hankered to travel. Her great ambition was to live and work in London as her aunt Bessie had done as a young girl. 'Newport is too humdrum for me,' she once said. 'Prying eyes on every corner. Too many ears seeking to eavesdrop. Busybodies looking to meddle. I wish to live anonymously in some vast city where I can lose myself.' That more or less tallied with what I desired. As a young boy visiting our grandparents at Llanwnwr I'd spend hours lying on my own in their fields among the dragonflies and honey bees idly watching the sailships and steamers weave their lazy way around Strumble Head and out into Cardigan Bay to the Irish Sea beyond.

While I harboured no ambitions of becoming a mariner, the idea of crossing the Atlantic to America was fixed in my mind from that early age. As a child visiting Grandfather and Grandmother Batine, I became obsessed with a large oil painting which hung over their mantelpiece depicting Pegasus, the white, winged horse, riding through the clouds above a dark, storm-lashed ocean. Would that Pegasus suddenly appear on those windswept Strumble Head clifftops to bear me away to some distant land or city, I'd think. Lying in my blankets in the loft at Narberth at night, I'd find myself imagining Elizabeth and I forging a new life together in the great metropolis of London where my elder sister Mary and her husband James now resided.

So the news that Elizabeth had started seeing my eldest brother came as a cruel and jarring shock. Tom was four years older than I and already with a reputation as a ladies' man. Ann, rather viciously I thought, suggested Elizabeth was driven less by matters of the heart and more by the fact Tom was fast rising up the ranks of the Merchant Navy. 'She likes to see herself as the wife of a master mariner,' she said. 'Mark my words, that one will stop at nothing 'til she gets what she desires and woe betide any man who falls for her suspect charms.'

Tom and Elizabeth did a lot of their courting up on Carningli, or so John Clement told me. After learning that disclosure it was an awfully long time afore I could stomach setting foot on that upland again. Elizabeth's father was a tax inspector and something of a dour old cove. I suppose Ann was right: he evidently thought of himself and his family as above the likes of humble farmers such as us Jameses. He was none too happy to learn his youngest daughter was traipsing around the fleshpots of Newport in the company of some uncouth young mariner and, on spying Elizabeth with Tom outside The Golden Lion one stormy winter's night, sternly forbade her from ever seeing him again. His warning failed to have the desired effect, though. When Tom came home, Elizabeth and I had a sort of unspoken agreement that we would keep our friendship in the shadows, so to speak. The pretense and subterfuge were bad enough, but the anguish I felt on sharing her with my brother gave me unremitting agony to the point I sometimes felt I would go mad.

I had no wish to fall foul of Tom, though I felt sure he was tomcatting around during his trips away from home, but Elizabeth and I both knew full well our situation was perilous, Newport being the sort of place where everyone made a point of knowing each other's business, like. The seeds of our own romance, which had been conducted within my own head for some considerable time previous, were sown when I'd quite literally bumped into Elizabeth coming out of the bakery in Newport after I'd paused to water my horse at the Llwyngwair Arms on the road back from Cardigan.

As we exchanged pleasantries that morning, I sensed she seemed somewhat distant; as if something was burdening her mind. Perhaps, I conjectured, I might have offended her in some way? When I delicately observed that she appeared, perhaps, somewhat fatigued, she snapped: 'Thank you for that, Will James! As if my day wasn't bad enough already, now you come along and have the sauce to suggest I look like a cowpat!' Although she was a spirited girl, oft given to blaspheming on occasions, her sharp response left me taken aback. Such a queer riposte to a wholly innocent remark. So much so that, try as I might, I couldn't help but burst out laughing.

This only served to infuriate her further. And when angry or upset Elizabeth had an enchanting way of sticking out her lower lip. I could not help but notice that Miss Morgans' lip was extremely pronounced as she turned smartly on her heel and flounced up High Street in the manner of a woman who had detected some great stink. Still puzzling over the episode on the long ride back towards Narberth the next day it dawned on me that the reason for Elizabeth's queer conduct might have been 'cos she possibly quite liked me. Could it be that she considered me as more than just a friend?

Casting my mind back to some of our recent conversations, more through hope than expectation, I persuaded myself that she did indeed appear to enjoy my company. When together, the two of us laughed much, oft at the same untoward subjects. 'For a farm boy from Dinas Cross, you're quite the conversationalist,' she once said. 'When you and I are together we talk much, but I can't pretend to properly know you, Will James, you hide your true feelings behind a veil.'

Elizabeth told me on more than one occasion that she sometimes felt that I was her one true love and that she would explain her feelings to Tom in due course. Other times she'd say she couldn't see herself finishing with him. 'You bad James boys will be the death of me yet,' I well recall her saying. 'How can this poor girl decide 'twixt the pair of you?' Once, she said she was afeared of how Tom would react in the event of them parting, provoking my reckless young fellow's response that, if need be, I could deal with him with my fists if necessary. I meant it too, even though Tom was by now a full-grown man. I felt sure my superior fighting prowess would prevail if it came to fisticuffs, although I hoped and prayed such an encounter would never happen.

Tom had been a good brother to me and what a form of repayment if I was to make off with his sweetheart!

Maybe old man Morgans' constant disapproval might have had some bearing in the end, because Tom's romance with Elizabeth always appeared doomed to me. The pair seemed to finish on countless occasions; what proved to be the final parting of the ways coming when poor Ellen was in the final stages of the sickness that killed her. Then Ann joined her in death not three weeks hence, a dual loss that drove poor Mother near-mad with sorrow. With Tom away at sea as usual, Elizabeth became my closest confidante during that unhappy time. She was compassionate, understanding and kind.

One crisp winter's morning while walking together in the field above Tyllwyd not long after we'd buried my sisters at Brynhenllan, she told me she and Tom had parted for good. Her breath, as she spoke, was frosted in the still air, yet at that instant I could feel no cold at all. So on finally hearing the news from Tom's own lips that his romance with Elizabeth had ended, I had to effect an air of surprise. How was my poor ignorant brother to know that I had by now formed quite an attachment to Elizabeth and she with me? How could something so awry become something so right?

By this time I was 20 and on the verge of leaving Llanelly where I'd been working as a commercial traveller in order to seek work in London. With Tom increasingly away, Elizabeth and I had continued seeing more and more of each other in secret. It was a dangerous game, I confess, as Tom had numerous friends in Newport and Dinas; lusty fellows to a man. I will readily admit, however, that my feelings of guilt at our illicit meetings were more than outweighed by feelings of longing and lust towards sweet Elizabeth.

Whenever I was home from Llanelly and an opportunity presented itself, she and I would arrange to go blackberry-picking on the slopes of Dinas Mountain or picknicking up on Dinas Head. At least that's what we would say we were up to. Once or twice we'd ride over to the Salutation Inn at Felindre Farchog or the Trewern Arms in Nevern where we'd be relatively safe from prying eyes. Many's the time we held hands and talked for hours in the shadow of The Bleeding Tree at St Brynach's Church in Nevern. Time seemed to stand still on those occasions and that ancient old yew came to know so well this pair of young sweethearts who sat there engrossed in the shadows of its great boughs. We also spent much of our time tramping the coast path between Dinas and Newport in all weathers, lost in endless conversations 'about anything and everything' as she put it.

As children, we'd been warned to stay away from the cliffs, but that delightful track meandering as it did among flotillas of gaily-coloured wild flowers while affording spectacular views of Newport Head was a far more agreeable alternative than walking the coast road and getting a clod of earth thrown in your face by some unthinking rider or being soaked to the skin by the passing Fishguard omnibus thundering through a puddle. The clifftop route also afforded us both much privacy, with less chance of being glimpsed by some interfering fool who'd take great delight in reporting back to Elizabeth's folks at Penfeidr.

On fine summer nights the two of us would huddle together before a driftwood fire at Aberhiggian Beach or Aberfforest, sometimes imagining that we were the last two persons left in this old world. Elizabeth would oft bring a pan on these excursions and we'd cook fish that I caught afore finally wandering back to Newport well past midnight with just the light of the stars to guide our way. Such encounters made me truly believe that I would be at Elizabeth's side for the rest of my days and she beside me.

Once we were caught out at Aberfforest by a sudden storm that hurtled in from the Irish Sea with breathtaking ferocity. Gathering up our drenched belongings, the two of

71

us seized each other's hands and hurried along the path back to Newport, having to shout at each other above the howl of the wind. The tempest rose to an almighty crescendo and the waves were booming far below us as we finally rounded the headland to see the blessed lights of Newport twinkling ahead. There was something almost unearthly about that sudden onset of wind, rain, and thunder. As we scurried through the deserted streets of the town like two sodden and bedraggled mice, I expect lost Ellen and Ann ran at our heels. We finally arrived, shrieking with laughter and on the very brink of hysteria, on the Gwaun Valley road back towards Penfeidr, as wild and woolly a pair as some of those mountain sheep we oft came across on the higher slopes of Carningli.

As we parted, a soaked and giggling Elizabeth blew me a kiss before making her way to the trusty oak tree outside her bedchamber whose branches she'd expertly use as a ladder, unhindered by her wet blouse and billowing skirt, all the way up to the window she'd invariably leave open whilst we were out on one of our night-time jaunts. Her climbing ability was the match of any boy. Nimble and sure-footed, she was nevertheless feminine and heart-stoppingly beautiful, yet also adventurous and something of a rascal to boot. Afore too long, I'd fallen hard for her.

Jesting with her once, and how it gladdened my heart turning the tables on Liz Penfeidr once in a while, I professed to knowing how to palm-read, having been taught, I held forth, by an old gypsy woman. Studying Elizabeth's pale hand intently, I solemnly forecast that she'd one day marry a handsome farmer's son from Dinas Cross who would provide her with many children. When I glanced up into those saucer-like brown eyes she was looking at me transfixedly with an intensity I found un-nerving. For an instant I thought I'd over-stepped the mark, but as I returned her gaze her face broke into a wide grin. 'Well now,' she said at length, gently withdrawing her hand from mine. 'I hope this handsome farmer's son will be able to keep Miss Morgans in the manner to which she has become accustomed.' Imagine Ann's scorn had she heard that!

'You do love me, don't you, Will?' she continued in a small voice. And the way she addressed it as a query rather than a statement made me desire her all the more. That was the secret of Elizabeth's great allure, I decided. While outwardly assured almost to the point of nonchalance, she'd occasionally reveal a surprising vulnerability I found irresistible. Few fellows would have understood that. Me being me, I chose to answer Elizabeth's query with a non-committal shrug. 'You have undoubted qualities, indeed,' I replied, with an effort. 'But whether you have the necessary attributes to be a farmer's wife it is really far too early to say.' She continued to scrutinise me searchingly with that faint, enigmatic smile playing on her lips; she knew full well that I was joshing, of course. Later she'd say that it was my ability to make her laugh which had drawn her to me.

I may not have been no great scholar, but I was no fool; the signs of mutual attraction couldn't have been plainer. Back in Newport three days later I made a point of loitering outside the chapel where Elizabeth taught at Sunday School. T'was a fine afternoon and when she appeared I suggested we go for a stroll on Newport Sands, the beach where we'd so often played as children. There, watching the breakers roll in across Newport Bay, among dunes the colour of milk about to turn, I asked her to be my bride. Then it was as if I'd unleashed this great flood and all my pent-up feelings of the past two years, no, make that the past twenty years, poured forth. Ne'er in my life had I experienced the sheer rush of emotions I felt on those sands. Came as much of a shock to me as it was to her.

Sobbing uncontrollably, I told her of the moment I'd first seen her at chapel and how it remained entrenched on my mind; the time when I first realised I had strong feelings towards her, feelings that became all-consuming; the unending pain in my heart whenever I saw her with Tom and the dire feelings of guilt catching stolen moments with my brother's girl that I'd been forced to endure. Once I started I just could not stop and the tears continued to flow in a raging torrent until eventually I broke down and wept on her shoulder as she held me as tight as a mother clutches her new-born infant. 'What took you so long, Will James?' she replied softly, stroking my hair. 'There have been times when I thought you held about as much emotion within your heart as Needle Rock. There were so many occasions when I felt that you too were as still and passive; and now you have crumbled.

'But, dear Will, pray tell me what in Heaven's name lies behind all this? Watching you so overwrought and anxious causes my heart to bleed. T'is not the Will James I know, or thought I knew.' As to what ailed me, at that point I neither knew nor cared; I carried on blubbing for what seemed like an eternity. When I finally raised my head there were tears running down Elizabeth's cheeks also. And ne'er had I known her to shed a tear afore. I believe that at that charged moment I could have lain there with her among those dunes forever and a day. 'Oh, Will, cariad Will …' (dear Will) she said, wiping my tears away. 'What on Earth is it that torments you so?'

I well recall the letter in which Elizabeth spelt out her feelings for me; feelings she'd evidently nursed for some considerable time. Her words still echo down the years; indeed, how could I e'er forget them? I will carry them in my heart to my dying day. 'How?' was the single word she'd used to start the letter, followed underneath by 'Why?' Her ensuing sentences, tumbling out one after another like a waterfall, suggested she had been left surprised, indeed completely bewildered, by the turn of events and the unexpected well of desire she harboured for me, Tom's younger brother.

'Please tell me, Will, how in God's name has this state of affairs come to pass?' she implored. 'I have been thinking about you so much my poor head hurts. Please help me, I beg, as I can no longer think of anything else. The feelings I have for you I can contain no longer. In days past I pledged, promised and convinced myself that dear Tom was the only man for me. Indeed, I swore blind on my own mother's life that no other man would ever turn my head again. All the time I was seeing him, building our dreams and hopes for the future and laying down plans to become a faithful mariner's wife I vowed to myself that I would never so much as even look at another man!...

'And then you came along...'

On reading that last sentence I felt a rush of blood to the head and momentarily feared I was about to swoon. I'd never afore realised that such passion, conviction and, yes, honesty could be conveyed in the written word. How could an ordinary fellow such as myself be the recipient of such longing? Without even knowing it I had evidently awakened the most extraordinary feelings within the most beautiful woman I'd ever clapped eyes upon. Elizabeth's intensity weighed heavily on me; indeed, it almost frightened me. This was a love affair like no other and, for me, the raw and powerful beauty of those heartfelt words bore a profound, yet simple truth. Elizabeth Morgans, of Penfeidr, loved me! Yes, me! And only me!

Mike Lewis

CHAPTER 4

As the summer of 1904 progressed, young Arthur Nicholas was beginning to appreciate the magnitude of his task. Gazing at a map of the United States one afternoon, he found himself suddenly gripped by a terrible sense of futility. Assuming William Batine James does indeed still live, finding him will be like trying to find the proverbial needle in a haystack, he thought. And what if that needle is constantly on the move and may not even wish to be found? Arthur's constant readings of the James letters had unearthed one small clue. In one of the missives 'WBJ', as Arthur had taken to referring to him, had advised his brother John to approach a number of businesspeople in Llanelly, stating that they were 'the best customers in town'.

Thumbing through the Llanelly trade directory for 1869, Arthur had established that those people referred to in the letter were drapers. This suggested to him WBJ was at the time working in the supply industry. Knowing that John Clement had himself worked as a commercial traveller in Swansea for several years, Arthur now deduced it probable that WBJ had pursued the same line of work; and was endeavouring to pass on a few tips to his younger sibling as he followed the same path. Staring idly at the map of America spread over his desk in front of him, Arthur wondered aloud whether WBJ had pursued the same occupation in the United States. This, he reasoned, would at least explain why the letters sent back to John came from four different locations.

Alternatively, given WBJ's reputation as an expert horseman, could he perhaps have been working as a rodeo rider at a fun fair or even a circus? Gnawing his pencil deep in thought, Arthur reflected on how his quest had come to occupy so much of his time; he was not yet to know it, but before too long the chase would even come to invade his dreams.

Like most young men, Arthur had been raised on enthralling tales of the Wild West and had a number of books on cowboys and Indians at home. As heavy rain rattled the windows of the Haverfordwest office, Arthur imagined himself at the head of a posse, doggedly on the trail of the mysterious William Batine James; a trail with myriad twists and turns. 'Folks may well have called you 'Will O' the Wisp', but I will catch up with you one of these days,' he muttered, staring fixedly at the map. Arthur liked to envisage the pair of them eventually meeting up over a beer at the Freemasons. They would clearly have much to discuss. And the very first question he would ask WBJ was what had prompted his sudden departure for Canada?

> **7 Wall Street**
> **New York**
> **Aug 18th, 1904**
> **Messrs Peacock & Goddard**
> **Grays Inn, London**
>
> Dear Sirs
>
> Replying to your inquiry of the 28th all relative to James, deceased, we would say that our progress has been very slow. We have simply, after long intervals, been referred from one party to another, without obtaining any information. We will, however, continue our inquiries in hope of learning something.
>
> Very truly yours
> Owen & Sturgess

By now Elizabeth was occupying my thoughts night and day. It became difficult to recall what life had been like without this all-consuming passion that burned so fiercely in my breast. That girl was in my thoughts from the moment I awoke 'til the moment I retired to bed at night. I read newspapers as oft I could as well as the occasional book. Just seeing the name Elizabeth brought a pang to my poor heart. Even coming across the name of Newport in print had the same charged effect. I simply craved Elizabeth's presence more and more. While we were apart, how I longed to hold her close. Everywhere I went I seemed to see young lovers, yet far from attracting my envy they merely served as a reminder of how fortunate I was. I knew beyond all doubt they could not possibly possess a mad passion as strong as mine and that Elizabeth and myself had embarked on the love affair of the ages.

But what of Tom? How would my brother react when he learnt that Elizabeth's affections now lay elsewhere? And rather more closer to home than he could ever have possibly contemplated? Up to now, my love for Elizabeth had been smouldering like an underground peat fire, concealed from sight, yet growing in heat all the while. Now it had fully ignited and was out in the open and raging like one of those vast summer gorse fires in the hills above Dinas. And there wasn't enough water in the whole of the Atlantic Ocean capable of dousing it.

The truth was I had been so blind to all else that I had ne'er given a thought to my elder brother. While I consoled myself that the romance between Tom and Elizabeth had been flickering at around the time mine was being stoked, I knew in my heart of hearts that both Elizabeth and myself were guilty of a betrayal. Whatever way I dwelt upon it, however many excuses I put forward in my fevered head, there could be no doubt about that. Had I been in Tom's boots, I thought darkly, I'd have been so enraged I might have committed murder. How I dreaded imparting the news to him. And, dear God, how I feared his reaction. By now Tom's lengthier absences away at sea and my employment first as a carpenter down in Narberth and later as a commercial traveller in Llanelly meant we were fast becoming strangers.

For a while I thought that contacting him in Cardiff via letter might be best, but ended up dismissing the idea as too cowardly. No, although the paths we were following were now markedly different, I liked to think I still knew Tom as well as anyone. Accordingly, I resolved to meet him for a heartfelt discussion over a quart of ale in one of Newport's many taverns when he was next back in Pembrokeshire. Then, and only then, would I spill out my true feelings for Elizabeth; the feelings I had struggled with all my might to contain for so long.

I'd been glad to turn my back on carpentry. Although I was regarded as deft with my hands with a sound eye for detail, I cannot pretend my heart was ever truly in it. The job had been a reason for leaving home and all its attendant sorrows and learning to stand on my own two feet. The fact I was now courting Elizabeth made those long solitary rides across the bleak Prescelis and back seem ever more wearisome and monotonous. While the situation of commercial traveller spelt more time further afield, it meant better renumeration and possibly, I thought, the first step towards setting myself up in business.

The occupation involved riding on horseback around Llanelly and its surrounds, oft e'en as far afield as Cardiff, distributing goods to trade customers who were either retailers or manufacturers. While I seemed to possess the gift of the gab which enabled me to sell goods and samples or trade catalogues and, I'm not proud to admit, talk my way into the bed of the occasional female customer, the job's real attraction was the pay.

Moreover, I quickly learnt I could earn extra by passing

on intelligence about the affairs of customers, the activities of competitors and the general state of rival businesses. I found I was more suited to life as a knight of the road. I enjoyed my own company, found I was good at haggling in order to persuade customers to purchase products they did not really want, plus I travelled most of the distances on horseback and at a pretty fair lick too. I was also robust enough to carry the great weight of my samples and liked the fact you could get pretty much out of the job as what you put in. Moreover, unlike my previous occupation at Narberth, I was the master of all I surveyed.

The dalliances I had on the road were generally with older married women whose husbands were either away on business or who had long since deserted or been prohibited from the matrimonial bed. These ladies would invariably be happy with our little arrangements and never demanded any more of me; nor I of them.

While I could ne'er resist the lure of pleasures of the flesh; what young fellow could when they were served up so freely? I reasoned that I would soon be betrothed and from then on true only to Elizabeth until the day I took the long walk.

The meeting with Tom was difficult indeed, but I felt better after we talked and sincerely hoped he did too. We spent the evening drinking in The Golden Lion and, at first, Tom seemed quite morose. He said that much as he'd loved Elizabeth, he'd always felt sure they were destined to part.

Later, as the ale continued to flow, his spirits seemed to rise and he said that if he had to lose her to any man he was glad it was to his younger brother. He felt we'd make a good couple. But by the time we stepped out into the rain-drenched streets his mood had blackened once more. 'Elizabeth is a woman I've never understood,' he reflected, as we both leapt back in the doorway to dodge a wave of muddy water thrown up by a passing pony and trap. 'There was always something about the girl that made her seem quite distant and apart. Trust me, Will, she is not quite what she seems.' I did not know what to make of those words, as Elizabeth seemed as much of an enigma to me as she'd appeared to my elder brother. Perhaps that was another major part of her allure.

Despite the great distance betwixt Llanelly and Newport, she and I kept seeing each other whenever possible; taking turns to visit one another by train and coach. Though my employment kept me away from home, we oft talked of our plans to marry in secret, all the while knowing Elizabeth's parents would want no part of it. Once, she told me wryly, they were encouraging her to tie the knot with a retired sea captain from Bwlchmawr, 28 years her senior. He was a wealthy widower who lived in a large comfortable home on the outskirts of the village.

The thought of that happenstance, of Elizabeth dropping me like a hot coal in order to become the wife of another, brought on one of my occasional rages. In truth, the notion drove me insane with jealous fury. Elizabeth appeared unmoved and then I realised with a jolt that she was laughing. 'You are easier to stir than a bowl of oatmeal, Will James,' she said wickedly, back-handing me playfully in the midriff. 'How dare you judge me so harshly when you know wild horses would not drag me to the altar to marry a man for whom I possessed no feelings?' This wealthy widower was merely the product of her vivid imagination. To say I felt foolish would be an understatement.

In the spring of 1870, I moved up to London, intent on finding a situation that would go a long way to supporting Elizabeth and myself as man and wife. Having very few shillings to my name, I was fortunate to get lodgings at the West End home of my sister Mary, her husband James and their two infants, who rented the top two floors of a large house in Marylebone. James had established a stall at nearby Portman Market where he would sell butter, eggs and hay and would, from time to time, employ me as a porter. It was back-breaking, poorly-paid work but after a couple of months I found better renumeration by joining the ranks of the hundreds of labourers swarming like soldier ants across the foundations of what in time would become the massive Holborn Viaduct. The toil was long and arduous but being both young and strong I managed well enough, all the time believing that I was, in effect, laying foundations upon which Elizabeth and myself would build our new life in London following our betrothal.

Walking back to Marylebone one hot summer's evening in my dust-caked overalls with money in my pocket and eagerly anticipating a few hard-earned ales in the tavern that evening, I remember thinking how fortune had finally smiled on me now I had attained the age of 21. I was a young man with a delightful sweetheart, the type of woman any man would covet. Moreover, I had my health and a strong work ethic installed in me by my parents, which I was confident would help secure a prosperous future for us both.

Yet the long periods I spent away from Elizabeth were difficult, that I cannot deny. Despite my steadfast efforts to remain faithful, I did lapse on numerous occasions, some of those comely young girls who worked at Portman Market proving an irresistible attraction for a fancy-free west Wales farmer's son such as myself. On one wild drunken night myself and a fellow labourer enjoyed sport with three young sisters who helped their mother run a lodging house in the Spitalfields; and after the two of us had given free rein to our rampant lust we'd shared their mother as well! Whatever can have possessed me at such times? Perhaps these dalliances were the result of the great misery and anguish I had undergone over the previous months. A means of proving that I at least remained a living, breathing being of flesh and blood; albeit one possessed with the usual human frailties. Leastways, that's what I'd always tell myself.

The deaths of my sisters were a bitter reminder of how little time we had on this Earth. 'You're a long time dead,' was one of Tom's favourite expressions and he truly believed in following Elizabeth's advice of living each day as if t'was his last. He himself would not live to see his 26th birthday and I oft think he was somehow aware that his time on Earth would be brief, which was why he approached life in the wild and buccaneering manner he did.

Each time I succumbed to temptation in London I'd reproach myself and remember that I'd be betrothed afore the year was out when I would pledge myself solely to darling Elizabeth, for richer or poorer, for the remainder of our days. Following such lapses, like a lot of Welsh Methodists, I tended to mire myself in guilt, drown my sorrows in alcohol, repeat my sins of the flesh and then wind up flagellating myself all over again. It was a constant merry-go-round which, try as I might, I could never seem to alight. Had Elizabeth become aware of my indiscretions she'd have taken a knife to me. That girl's great temper was almost akin to mine.

I got into one serious spot of bother with a servant girl from Covent Garden, a true Welsh wildcat with whom I occasionally consorted. Black as the night she was. When she began talking of marriage outside a tavern one night and I demurred, she got uppity and took to brandishing a broken bottle.

I was forced to drag her to the ground and disarm her while she shouted and swore amid the cheers and applause of watching patrons. She was a fluent Welsh speaker who resorted to crude Anglo-Saxon whenever we fell out, which was oft. The two of us made up in passionate fashion in an East End common lodging house that night, but I ensured that our tempestuous union came to an end soon afterwards. Why were so many Welsh women of unsound mind?, I wondered. That particular ugly fracas made me earnestly question the wisdom of asking for Elizabeth's hand in marriage!

Throughout the summer of 1870, I saved money for our impending nuptials, Elizabeth having by now said she would join me for a new life in the wicked city where she planned on seeking a situation as an English teacher. She appeared as thrilled and as excited at the prospect as I was. Meanwhile, remnants of our old life back home were fast disappearing. Mother had by now left Dinas, having married a retired blacksmith named Daniel Francis who'd outlived his two previous wives. She went to live with him at his large farm over at Scleddau on the other side of Fishguard. After the deaths of Ellen and Ann, I don't think she could wait to depart Tyllwyd swift enough. For her, it was a new start, which we all welcomed, and Mr Francis appeared a worthy husband and stepfather. Mother told Captain Vincent, a long-time family friend and preacher, that what with her beloved daughters dying following the loss of her first husband she felt she'd never smile again.

For my part, I felt Mr Francis, while being something of a dry old stick, was nevertheless, as a devout teetotaller, good for Mother. For a long time, John and I had noted with mounting alarm her increasing fondness for the bottle. And this was someone who had ne'er so much as allowed a single drop of alcohol to pass her lips 'til attaining the age of forty. For a time, it appeared that both Mother and I would embark on a new and happy chapter of our lives together.

Early that December, I received a letter from John that troubled me. After he'd gone through the usual chit-chat about what was not happening in Dinas Cross and said how he too was now considering a situation as a commercial traveller, John mentioned happening across Elizabeth in the company of Tom in Newport the previous afternoon.

I was surprised, if not unduly alarmed, but nevertheless lay awake that night dwelling upon John's words for some considerable time. Although Tom and Elizabeth's parting was still raw, both still lived in Newport. It was a small village so would it not be inevitable for their paths to cross from time to time? I finally convinced myself that neither wished to allow their change in personal circumstances to affect a friendship dating back to their childhoods. Yet I was somewhat unsettled, I confess. My love for Elizabeth was very young and I was already quite possessive. She attracted many an admiring glance from menfolk of all ages when we were out together and, far from being flattered, I brooded upon it greatly.

I was so insecure in those days that I viewed every fellow as a potential rival for Elizabeth's affections, which she at first found highly amusing, but as time went by less so. When I next saw Elizabeth and asked if she'd seen Tom on his last visit, she readily admitted they'd had a short conversation in Market Street. She acted so matter-of-factly that I dismissed all thoughts of suspicion from my mind, resenting myself for having raised them in the first place.

And then, just afore Christmas, it happened. Returning home to my lodgings in Marylebone covered as usual in white Holborn dust from head to toe, I found a letter in Elizabeth's familiar neat handwriting awaiting me. Glad as ever to hear from her, I tore the envelope open and eagerly withdrew its contents.

'Dear Will, this is the hardest letter I have ever had to write, Thomas has asked me for my hand in marriage and, after careful consideration, I have decided to accept his proposal. I hope and pray that you will respect my decision and that the two of us can still remain true friends.'

Yours sincerely

Elizabeth

Estate Duty Office
Somerset House London W. C.
September 28 1904
John Clement James, deceased

Sir,

Before I can definitely reply to your letter of the 14th instant, I will thank you to inform me in what manner the title to deceased's Real Estate valued at £5850, is defective and how deceased's elder brother became the heir thereto. Is it to be understood that deceased's own title to the entire Real Estate is doubtful? If so, I will thank you to explain how he derived his title whether by purchase or otherwise. If derived under the will of a former testator please give name and date of probate, if under a deed please forward same or a copy. The Estate Duty being a direct charge on the Real Estate should in any case be paid. Legacy Duty should also be at once paid on any portion of the legacies amounting to £3,400 which has been satisfied. A reply at your earliest convenience is requested, as considerably more than a year has elapsed since the death of the deceased. I am, Sir, your obedient Servant,

T Latter Chief Clerk
Gwynne A. Roberts Esq

Mike Lewis

CHAPTER 5

On the Yellowstone,
June 20 1876
(five days out of Little Bighorn)

Even now, from the distance of five years, it is painful to describe the effect of those few words contained within Elizabeth's letter. In short, it was the worst thing to have e'er happened to me. I felt like my heart had not so much been broken, but wrenched from my chest and crushed asunder. In an instant my whole world was shattered into a million tiny fragments. I stood there in my squalid little room, with its cracked vase, thin bedspread and grimy window, foolishly reading and re-reading her missive as if in hope that I'd somehow misinterpreted those few terrible lines, which only served to increase my deepening anguish all the more. Finally, scarce knowing what I was doing, I raced down the stairs, tore open the front door and ran headlong along the street to The Valiant Soldier where the market traders caroused. I found myself a table in the corner and downed several Porters in swift succession 'til the room finally began to spin.

I ended up heaving in the gutter outside for what seemed like hours and was eventually seen home by a kindly policeman who advised my disapproving sister to give me a dose of liver salts and keep a strict eye on me. It was only when I'd sobered up somewhat in the early hours of the morning that the tears began to flow and once they began continued unabated. Small wonder I've barely been able to shed a tear since; I used them all up on that dreadful night in west London.

In that instant, as the fog in my head began to clear, I resolved that my future lay in some foreign land. Going home to confront both Tom and Elizabeth was unthinkable. At that instant I could not even countenance breathing the same air as them, let alone walking those same streets. For weeks I carried a dire sense of loss and could dwell on nothing but their twin betrayal, ne'er thinking that it was I who had first betrayed Tom, to say nothing of the manner I'd betrayed Elizabeth through my own secret dalliances. I was shorn of all sensible thought and reason and consumed with angry and bitter thoughts towards them both. The one thing that kept me sane during those harrowing weeks was the thought that I would soon be setting sail for America from Liverpool so I could consign the wreckage of my unhappy love affair to history. For me that departure could not now come soon enough.

I found myself drinking and rutting like a madman. Woe betide any unfortunate man or woman who crossed my path. An ale or two at night following my long and arduous labouring shifts at Holborn had become customary, but now the drink well and truly seized me in its unrelenting grip. Ev'ry night I'd arrive back at my lodgings, overalls coated in a fine dust resembling flour that gave me the appearance of a baker's roundsman. A quick wash if I felt like it and I'd repair to The Soldier where I'd pour as much ale as I could down my throat. Then perhaps have a scrap on the cobbles with some impertinent market porter who'd made a snide remark against us Welshies, and then I'd drink and drink again.

T'was down at The Grenadier in Belgravia where I met my Waterloo. I'd been drinking at the pub opposite the regimental stables where the Duke of Wellington had once caroused when I quarrelled with a soldier who'd taken strong exception to the disparaging remarks I'd passed on the manner of his riding. The row grew more and more heated until he finally swung a tankard at my head. I felled him with my first blow, only for reinforcements to rally to his aid. The fight spilled out the door, down the steps and out onto the cobbles where he fought back hard 'til I managed to drop him again, eyes going up into his head.

But as I continued to get the better of him he was joined by more and more of his Grenadier chums until, back pinned against a wall, I was single-handedly fighting the entire damn regiment, or so it appeared. I ended up being dealt a proper thrashing and on regaining my senses in a nearby sentry box some time later found myself black and blue, tongue swollen, lips and mouth caked with dried blood, cigar burns all over my arms and a dislodged tooth wedged in the back of my throat. In view of my earlier drunken misconduct, I had to accept it was no more than I deserved.

How could Elizabeth have rejected me so suddenly and so cruelly with no prior warning whatsoever? How long had she and Tom been enjoying clandestine meetings? Had they even stopped seeing each other in the first place? Indeed, did their supposed parting ever happen at all? The more I ran things over in my mind, the wilder I grew. Oh, what bitter irony! I'd subjected myself to months of self-loathing for seeing my brother's girl behind his back only to find out that all the time he'd been seeing her behind mine! What was it Tom had told me about Elizabeth? That she was not who she seemed? I truly felt that I'd come to know that girl better than her own family which made what had happened all the more difficult to comprehend. Part of me yearned to go home to seek an explanation from her own lips. The greater part told me to leave well alone as I just could not countenance how such an unhappy meeting would end.

I'll hold my hands up and admit I'd always possessed a demon within me which surfaced unexpectedly. Once, while drinking with Elizabeth in the Castle Inn in Newport I'd lashed out at some dog of a merchant seaman I'd overheard utter some uncouth remark about her. I'd only dealt him a swift back-hander, for God's sake, yet the soft beggar had collapsed to the floor clutching his snozzle and squealing like a sow. I hadn't even drained my last drop of ale when I was ordered to leave the premises which Elizabeth had already angrily vacated. That girl always had a bit of a tongue on her and, as I'd anticipated, flayed me verbally all the way home. She said I was an obnoxious fool when in drink, that even my own dear Mother was ashamed of my roisterous antics and that she herself felt frightened by my occasional outbursts of temper.

She also made me feel extremely foolish by stating categorically that the seaman I'd slapped had been referring to a woman he'd once stepped out with, not her. Although not fully accepting of what she said, by that point, sobering up fast in the cool night air, I couldn't have felt any lower had I crawled under a snake's belly with a top hat on my head.

On and on she'd raged. There was that time when I'd picked her up and thrown her fully-clothed into the sea at Pwllgwaelod after partaking of a few ales at the Sailors Safety. I, and my friends, Ieuan, Dan and Geraint, considered seeing her flounder in the waves good sport, and I'm sure I recall Elizabeth laughing as well.

But now she told me for the first time that she'd imbibed a great deal of sea water on that occasion and at one point feared she was going to drown. On another occasion she'd apparently taken offence at something I said about her in jest in the presence of her disapproving parents at Penfeidr. Admittedly, on that occasion I'd arrived at the farm slightly the worse for drink but, God in Heaven, I'd had a long and monotonous journey back from London and surely a fellow deserves to slake his thirst after countless hours sat with a cramped arse surrounded by assorted bores in a crowded and draughty train carriage?

So now I began to look at things in a new light. Maybe

what I'd taken to be one of the great love affairs of the 19th century had in truth been a mere dalliance after all. But, no! That could not be! What the two of us had was true indeed. What on Earth could have happened to have brought that love to such an abrupt and unhappy end? Was I really not the sort of fellow I thought myself to be? And so I wept and drank and raged and cursed some more ...

And how I hated Tom! I had plucked up courage to do the decent thing and have an honourable discourse with him that night at The Golden Lion and all the while he was still seeing Elizabeth behind my back. What a complete and utter fool I'd been!

My feelings towards Tom in particular convinced me it would be exceedingly unwise to go home. I had no way of knowing how I would react on seeing him or them, come to that, but I was pretty sure what would happen if I did. No, while I maliciously hoped his next long sea voyage would be Tom's last, I had no desire to set foot in Newport ever again.

One night, after downing veritable buckets of ale down the tavern, I had a dream so vivid I awoke drenched in sweat. I'd seen a ship floundering on its side amid heavy seas, its desperate crew crying out for salvation as they fought vainly for their lives. One of them, I felt sure, was Tom. Had I somehow put a curse on my own brother?

By now, it was February, full of cruel northerly winds, satanic skies and thick snowdrifts. Even dirty old London would have appeared quite magical in its wintry coat had I still been of sound mind. But I was no longer. I was a fellow dangerously beyond control and one Hell-bent on self-destruction. Tom and Elizabeth and their betrayal invaded not just my waking thoughts but also those rare nights when I snatched fragments of sleep out of sheer exhaustion. Looking back, my decision to sail to America was an attempt to escape. What I did not take into account is that the one thing a fellow can never escape is himself. . .

I did go back to Dinas one last time, having received a letter from Mother begging me to visit. I avoided Newport like the plague, of course, and confined myself to my 'milltir sgwar' (My square mile; my own locality). It was a painful return home and one I'd forever regret. Poor James was dying of consumption, that hideous wasting disease, at Mother's new home down in Scleddau and seeing my once strapping and vigorous brother reduced to a veritable husk on his deathbed was truly pitiful. He and I talked little. What was there to say? His fever was rampant and for the most part I suspect he held no recognisance of me.

From time to time, though, James would experience moments of great clarity. Just when it seemed he slept and I'd be making stealthily for the door, he'd suddenly enquire when we could next go fishing in the little wooden skiff we'd kept moored down at Cwmyreglwys. Then he said how much he craved a flagon of Mrs Davies's ale down at the Freemasons. After he started mumbling about some woman called 'Blodwen fach' and apologising to her for his 'ungentlemanly conduct' he finally drifted off into a restless sleep. I was never to see dear James again.

I sought blessed oblivion in a tankard that night. I began drinking at The Gate Inn at Scleddau and then in the Royal Oak and the Haverfordwest and Fishguard Arms near Fishguard Square afore stumbling down to the Ship in Lower Town, getting into a heated altercation with a coachman who almost ran me down along the way.

I then hitched a ride aboard drunken Silas Hughes' roan mare which carried us both up the road to Dinas where we continued carousing in so many taverns I lost count. At the Freemasons, I met up with Margaret Trenewydd, an old acquaintance who'd recently lost her husband. The woman was every bit as drunk and as wild as I was. She offered me free board and lodge for the night provided, she'd laughed, I'd perform my 'usual tricks' with her. I'd taken exception to that and we'd started to quarrel, whereupon she slapped me hard across the face.

I cannot recall too much after that, but dimly remember rowing with my sister Elizabeth prior to finding myself sprawled outside The Ship Aground on the road to Pwllgwaelod some time later. It seemed an apt place to founder as I'd well and truly hit the rocks.

I got up and staggered down to the Sailors Safety where I drank some more. Later I found myself lurching along the coast path intent on reaching Newport a few miles distant. In spite of all that had transpired, I wanted to glean from Elizabeth and Tom some explanation as to why they'd heaped such misery upon me. That clifftop walk was sheer and utter madness. Stumbling along, out of my mind with the drink, pausing occasionally to piss, then to heave my guts, I trod a slim tightrope betwixt life and eternity. With the sea crashing way down below on my left, my every move could have been my last. I can't remember how far I tottered but eventually I must have passed out insensible as I came to lying at the side of a field, a host of curious Pembrokes gazing down at me.

My head throbbed violently, my knuckles were skinned and raw like I'd been fighting and my mouth tasted like the floor of a parrot's cage. Looking back, the vast sea of alcohol in my bloodstream had probably saved me from freezing to death. I was still feeling poorly when my train pulled into Liverpool the next day. It'd been a lengthy journey frequently broken by delays caused by snow drifts blocking the lines. I took a shabby room in a cheap hotel near the docks and set about seeking to book my passage to the New World.

Lean and hungry-looking women haunted the hotel and prowled its environs. Inevitably, I took one to my bed, only to start shouting at the poor frightened girl afore thrusting her out the door after finding myself unaccountably unable to act on my fleeting desire. A monster prowled the great sea port of Liverpool; and that monster was me.

On my second morning, I was surprised to find a letter from John awaiting me in reception. I stared at the envelope askance. I must have told him my destination though I had no recollection of doing so. My tortured mind was still all over the place to the extent I feared I was breaking down in brain. If the arrival of his letter was unexpected, its contents pushed me ever nearer the precipice of insanity. . .

Like I've said previously, John was ne'er a great letter writer, even if the handwriting style he had sown in Peniel was excellent. On this occasion only a few words were necessary to convey the harrowing news of the latest tragedies to befall our wretched family. Dearest James, my second brother, had succumbed to consumption, the very same disease which had carried off Father seven years previous, on 22 February at the home of Daniel Francis in Scleddau. He'd only been ill for a few weeks and repaired to bed there in order for Mother to nurse him when the extent of his increasingly grave condition became apparent.

For Mother, this cruel tragedy must have evoked stark memories of that terrible autumn of 1869 when poor little Ellen succumbed in agony, mere weeks before the awfulness of Ann's sudden passing. Yet there was e'er more worse news to come from John's pen. The very same week that James had expired came a letter stating that Tom's ship, The Avon, of Bristol, had gone missing in the Channel. She'd been bound for China with a cargo of coal and nothing had been heard of her for almost a week. Imagine my complete and utter horror when I went on to read our little brother Frank had also been among her crew.

Frank was 18 and the only boat I could ever recall him boarding with Tom in the past was our leaky little skiff down at Cwmyreglwys. How in God's name had my youngest brother come to be aboard The Avon on her voyage to oblivion? While the mere thought of Tom evoked evil thoughts, I knew in my heart that in the vessel's last desperate moments he'd have selflessly fought tooth and nail to try and save our youngest brother. According to John, the news had plunged Newport, Dinas and Fishguard into mourning. Most of The Avon's crew hailed from the area, indeed I'd personally known the ship's master, Peter Owens, of Goodwick, and the bosun, Caleb Francis, of Scleddau, a relation of my stepfather. We were plainly not the only family left bereft and desperate for news of any survivors; yet none was e'er forthcoming.

The loss of The Avon was a real local disaster in that little patch of north Pembrokeshire whose inhabitants were long accustomed to ships going down, lives being lost and families torn asunder. Yet it was John's third paragraph that left me as winded as if a horse had kicked me full in the ribs. Elizabeth and Tom had been betrothed in Cardiff mere days afore The Avon set sail. She did not have her parents' blessing but eloped to that greaet port to marry the fellow she loved, prior to him setting out on the long voyage East. Frank had been the only member of our family to attend the ceremony. John said the Morgans were evidently against the union as they'd not been present for the marriage ceremony at Cardiff Registry Office. Elizabeth, he went on, had added a year to her age in order to avoid having a parental signature on the wedding certificate.

That letter from my last surviving brother laid waste to my soul. Both elder brothers and young Frank gone within a matter of days and the girl I'd planned to marry left a widow having just become a mariner's wife. The gypsy's curse had returned with a vengeance and would ultimately claim each and every one of us, of that I was now certain.

By now I had more or less turned my back on God; had I not done so I would have questioned how one family could be the recipients of so much dire misfortune? We were honest, working people, in Heaven's name, hardly n'er do wells. What miscreant deeds had we committed in the eyes of the Lord to deserve such harsh and unjust punishment?

After a few ales, my mind turned ever blacker. Had my vicious thoughts towards Tom and Elizabeth indeed brought about their great tragedy? Had I somehow cursed their new-found happiness and future life together and summoned up some demon from the depths of Hell which dragged poor Tom, Frank and their fellow shipmates down to the bottom of the Channel in its fearful claws? I'd yearned to punish Tom for what he'd done, yet poor young and innocent Frank had paid with his life as well! Indeed, was I myself that demon from Hell?

I staggered back towards my hotel, blind drunk and blaspheming. That I could even find my way was astounding given my inebriated state and the fact I was weeping so much I could barely see the muddied, rain-lashed streets afore me. Slumped on my hard and narrow bed, teeth chattering from the cold, I gazed forlornly at the single passage ticket to Quebec on the chest of drawers. Canada, not America, was now my destination, not that it seemed to matter greatly. It then dawned on me that the imminent voyage would present ample opportunity to hurl my wretched body overboard so I'd join Tom and Frank and their unfortunate crewmates down in Davy Jones's Locker. Unless, of course, I hadn't already elected to fling myself into the Mersey afore we'd e'en left port.

I discounted the idea on the grounds it'd be a grievous waste of the twelve pounds my trans-Atlantic ticket had cost. Also, it seemed so unjust to wantonly extinguish my own life so soon after my three brothers had lost theirs through no fault of their own. I somehow got through the next three days although have little recollection of them and, on 7 March 1871, found myself ascending the gangplank along with my fellow passengers of The SS Idaho, bound for Quebec. My mood remained beetle-black, and looking down into the dark swirling waters the thought occurred again that death would be a merciful release. What finally decided me against ending my own life was the thought of poor Mother grieving her latest losses back in Scleddau. Having suffered a fresh onset of tragedy in little over a year, would not my own added demise also hasten her own?

I felt terrible at not going back when James was laid to rest alongside Father and my sisters at Ramah. But although barely 22 years of age, it seemed to me as if I'd already spent half my life standing head bowed at gravesides. Besides, what if Elizabeth was there? And what would be her own state of mind considering she'd been widowed mere days after she and Tom were betrothed in Cardiff Registry Office? As I stood on deck listening to the sounding of foghorns as we quietly slipped our moorings and headed out into the Mersey bound for the open sea, I decided that my lot was surely bound to get better. Could scarce get no worse.

What I could not dismiss from my mind was our family's unstinting ill-luck. I knew in my bones that with no God to watch over me, the gypsy's curse would stalk me to the ends of the earth. It would in due course ultimately claim me, sure as night followed day. Shivering uncontrollably in the morning air I wondered when and how that moment would arrive.

7 Wall Street
New York
Nov 28th, 1904
Messrs Peacock & Goddard
London, Eng

Dear Sirs

We beg to acknowledge receipt of your favor of Nov 12 inst relative to William B James, supposed to be deceased. We cannot say that any progress has been made in the matter. We were last referred to the keeper of the cemetery at Opelika, Alabama, and communicated with him requesting that he examine his records for the name of the party required of. This was some months ago but we have no reply. We will address him again on the subject, although we are not confident of any satisfactory result from this source.

Yours truly
Owen & Sturgess

CHAPTER 6

101 Church Street
Toronto
April 9, 1871

Dear Brother

With pleasure I am sending you these few lines to inform you that I arrived safe after a rough and long passage of 17 days but thank God I am safe and I got a good situation in one of the best shops in the City.

I hope I shall have my health; there is some good shops here, better than London. I have no strong news to inform you this time only that I am in good health hoping you and Mother are the same.

I hope I shall hear from you per return with all news. Please give my best regards to Morgans and my Sister in law and to all my Friends in London and at home. I shall send you a long letter next time.

Please send the enclosed note to Mother, 3rd class stamp will do for Toronto. I have no more at present. Please excuse short letter and all blunders.

I must wish you Good my Dear Brother.

I am

Your Dear Brother

W B James

My address

W B James, 101 Church Street, Toronto, Ontario, Canada

Toronto had not been my intended destination, but it is where this piece of Welsh flotsam washed up having grabbed a ride aboard a boat down the St Lawrence seaway from Quebec. Other than keep moving West, I had no plan whatsoever. May just as well have put a blindfold over my eyes and stuck a pin on the map. By now I'd grown accustomed to being surrounded by strangers' faces though once in a while I'd swear I'd spied a glimpse of someone from back home.

I'd decided to plump for Toronto as my destination following a chance conversation with a fellow passenger aboard The Idaho. A distinguished-looking retired gentleman of middle years, he waxed lyrical about the town where he had been born prior to seeking his fortune in England. 'There are jobs a-plenty, cheap boardings and wild women galore!' he told me over glasses of whisky one night after we'd sought refuge in the ship's snug bar from the icy deck. 'The Rossin House Hotel is one of the finest establishments in all of Canada! Mr Shears, the manager, is a personal friend of mine of long-standing.'

I can't believe my new-found chum truly thought that someone of my humble appearance would seek out a room at such a first-class establishment, but by then the whisky was working its familiar magic and I decided to follow his advice to seek a situation there. As a stranger in a strange land what did I have to lose? Having travelled a good 3,000 miles, I'd put serious distance between myself and the sorrows of home. Lying in my bunk that night, relieved that for once we were travelling across calmer waters, I fervently hoped that more tranquil times would make for a smoother passage ahead as well.

After the grandeur of London, I found Toronto somewhat down-at-heel. Though it was by now late March, the Humber River was still dotted with ice floes and a chill wind cut through its muddied streets. Streetcars were less plentiful than in London and I was surprised to find that electric lamps and telegraph poles did not appear to exist. St James Cathedral dwarfed the surrounding buildings and, as I searched for cheap lodgings, my travels on foot took me past the self-same Rossin House Hotel.

My companion aboard The Idaho had been right: it was indeed a swanky, first-rate establishment. Just the type of place I'd probably get ejected from and wind up sucking pavement outside, I surmised. Within a couple of days, I'd unsuccessfully sought employment there as a porter. After two-and-a-half weeks cooped up at sea, physical work was what I craved, yet in the end I plumped for a job as a dry goods clerk at a large store in the city centre.

The wage was meagre, but enough to fund me a room down East in a Church Street lodging house run by a middle-aged Scotsman named McAndrew and his comely young wife, Sarah. At least, I told myself, it was a start and would prove a useful berth to rest my head afore I decided upon my next move. There must have been a couple of dozen lodgers squeezed into that abode. Most were young men like myself, newly-arrived immigrants from England, Scotland and Ireland all hoping for a slice of the fortune we'd been promised the New World had to offer. Apart from a married couple on the ground floor we were all single men employed as carpenters, bootmakers, saddlers and the like. The exceptions were one of my room-mates, a somewhat surly Englishman named William Page, and myself who shared the same occupation of dry goods clerk, much as I'd have preferred a more robust activity outdoors.

The other person living in the house was Mary Smith, a 16-year-old Irish servant girl who had a tiny room in the basement. With upwards of twenty persons sharing five chambers under one roof there was barely enough room to swing a cat. McAndrew was a somewhat humourless cove who seemed to spend more time drinking in a nearby saloon than he did at the boarding house. This must have played a part in making his young wife feel somewhat neglected.

Once, on returning home from an early morning shift at the store, I elected to investigate queer noises coming from a bedchamber opposite our own. Imagine my surprise when on peering round the door I observed a naked Mrs McAndrew cavorting on the bed with two of my fellow lodgers, both similarily unclad! None of the trio was the least bit abashed about my intrusion and the flushed and beaming lady of the house even enquired whether I'd care to lend them a hand, as she so delicately put it. The next thing I knew I too was naked, and engaged in what I can only describe as a frantic and faintly comic wrestling match on the large double bed, by now creaking alarmingly under the weight of four persons; and groaning about as much as Mrs McAndrew.

Despite our best efforts I have to say that our lusty landlady proved more than a match for each and every one of us. Indeed, once we were spent from our exertions she cheerfully enquired whether anyone was open to the idea of an encore! Saddens me to say that, once we'd gotten our breath back, we strapping fellows were forced to decline her generous offer. That woman's coy and demure appearance was truly deceptive. I subsequently learnt she went to great lengths to ensure she personally 'broke in' any young lodger who crossed the doorstep, in much the same way a skilled rodeo rider breaks in a young stallion.

According to Page, even young Mary was known to have shared Mrs McAndrew's bed and he once came back unexpectedly to find our landlady frolicking in the bathtub with the married lady downstairs! Talking of Mary, she was frequently the tongue-tied subject of joshing from us lodgers; and sometimes that joshing would take a vulgar, even sinister turn. When returning home intoxicated some of the fellows were not averse to crudely propositioning her. Once, when a rather stout hotel porter became somewhat indignant and threatening at having his advances rebuffed, I elected to give him a slap in the face to shut him up. Truth be told I struck him more than once, leaving him sprawled insensible on the stairs.

Far from defending my actions, Page called me a fool for getting so riled, adding that I had the type of temper which'd prove my undoing one day. I was taken aback by his response as I invariably regarded myself as a sound fellow who stood up for others. At what point, I asked myself, had I become a bad fellow? That night I lay awake deliberating whether McAndrew had taken exception to the kerfuffle and might be minded to throw me out onto the streets like a whipped cur on the morrow.

As it happened I needn't have troubled myself. The portly porter had been so drunk he appeared to possess no knowledge of our brief confrontation on the staircase which had left him nursing a somewhat fat lip.

In that first letter home, I took considerable delight in telling John that I had found myself a good situation in one of the best shops in the city. I assumed it was what he, and Mother particularly, would be pleased to hear. It was important, I decided, to put on a cheerful front if only for Mother's sake.

John had told me in his last letter she'd become hysterical on learning I was sailing for America, certain that I would suffer the same fate that had befallen Tom and Frank. Thank God that Mr Francis had been on hand to calm her.

He was a good man who through fate had inherited so many of the grievances that dogged dear Mother even though he himself had suffered his own fair share of sorrow. If I'd still believed in God I'd have earnestly prayed at that point that Mother and I would meet up again in this old world.

The weeks passed and with the onset of summer the temperatures rose. My hours were long and opportunities for drinking with gay abandon scant, but by now I was easing up on the liquor and feeling much chipper as a result, it has to be said. My moods were not quite so black, I slept better than I had for a long time and those terrible nightmares I kept having about the loss of The Avon grew less frequent, thank God.

Maybe those vigorous afternoon sojourns I was now having with my landlady helped! I had never afore come across a woman like Mrs McAndrew whose carnal desires greatly exceeded my own. After a month or so at the Church Street lodging house she'd even taken to calling me her prize bull. At first, like all young bucks who think they're the bee's knees, I was flattered. Yet as time passed those other fellows assured me that was her pet name for each and ev'ry one of them too. It was plain to see why Mrs McAndrew's husband spent so much of his time downing liquor in the nearby bar. The poor beggar just couldn't face going home knowing how much youthful zest his frolicsome young wife possessed!

By summer, however, I was ready to move on, spurred by thoughts of greater employment opportunities in the United States. Chicago was the nearest US city to Toronto so that August I said goodbye to my store job and climbed aboard a train bound for The Windy City via the shores of Lakes Erie and Michigan.

Chicago may have been a boom town, with immigrants flooding in from all four corners, but people in Toronto had warned me of its grubby reputation and they were right. Too many souls had arrived there in too short a space of time and the city sewers were overloaded. T'was built on a low-lying flood plain and, don't ask me how, a few years previous the Chicago council had somehow elevated the entire city by four to five feet using some kind of jacking process. It was said that a five-storey hotel was raised in this way without even closing for custom! I had to doff my hat to American know-how on hearing that.

The 1850s had seen a number of riots stirred up by the Know-Nothing Party who were opposed to Catholics, immigrants and liquor. Fortunately, they were no more by the time I rolled up into town. I may not have been a Catholic, but as an immigrant fond of his liquor I very much doubt we'd have gotten along. When I reached Chicago I decided to stick with what I knew best, electing to seek work with horses. On only my second day in the city, I spotted a vacancy for a coachman employed by a wealthy solicitor. As luck would have it, Dr Theodore Russell was of Welsh descent. He clearly took a shine to Chicago's newest New World immigrant and took me on without even bothering to interview any other applicant.

The work was basic and quite monotonous on occasions, but naught I couldn't handle. Dr Russell was a widower who lived alone in a fine townhouse apart from an elderly male servant called Mottram, Mrs Frobisher, a middle-aged cook of somewhat waspish nature, and a young domestic help called Annie. Having taken up residence in a tiny attic room which was to be my quarters for the next two months, I was lying on my bunk taking stock that first afternoon when my ears were drawn to the sound of a young woman singing in the garden below. 'Oranges and lemons said the bells of St Clement's; you owe me five farthings said the bells of St Martin's ...'

My curiosity was aroused and, peering from my eyrie, I caught sight of a comely, dark-haired girl of about eighteen hanging assorted items of washing out on a long clothes line. Must be Annie, the servant girl, I surmised. Completely oblivious to her audience of one, she carried on singing while shaking out sheets and blankets, pausing only briefly to flail at the insects fluttering around her head.

'When will you pay me? Say the bells of Old Bailey; When I grow rich, Say the bells of Shoreditch ...' I stood and watched, enchanted. There was something so sweet about

107

watching this young girl sing a nursery rhyme she'd probably learnt on her mother's knee.

'When will that be? Say the Stepney …'

At this point I could no longer resist the temptation to add my own two ha'pporth. Taking care to remain concealed from Annie's sight, I suddenly burst forth with my very best baritone, delivered with the same might and passion I'd have reserved for the congregation back home at Brynhenllan:

'I DO NOT KNOW!!! SAY THE GREAT BELLS OF BOW!!!'

The effects of my surprise intervention were truly comical. Annie gave a start and looked wildly around her, up and down, this way and that, finally turning full circle as she frantically sought to detect the hidden owner of that mystery voice. 'Who's there?' she called out in alarm, 'will the rascal who has the sauce to spy on me whilst I undertake my daily labours please reveal hisself this instant!'

By now I was furiously biting my lip in a bid to quell the mirth that rose within. I momentarily considered completing the rest of the rhyme, but knew I'd only dissolve into hopeless fits of laughter if attempting to do so.

'T'is I,' I finally answered, breaking my concealment by leaning on the sill and hanging my head out of the window as she glanced quizzically upwards, one pale hand shielding her face from the rays of the fierce summer sun. 'And may I take this opportunity to compliment you, good miss, both on your singing and the diligent manner in which you are undertaking your laundry duties?'

'Why, who're you sir?' she stammered. 'An acquaintance of Dr Russell? Beg pardon, sir, but to whom am I speakin'? I ne'r so much as lain eyes on you afore.'

'Well, you'll be seeing me oft from today,' I told her. 'I am an employee of Dr Russell like your good self. He has just engaged me as his new coachman and I commence my duties on the morrow.' Annie visibly relaxed at this revelation. 'Oh, sweet relief,' she replied, 'for an instant I thought the manner o' your speech indicated I was addressin' a true gentleman of real merit an' importance!' It was such an unexpected riposte of no little wit that I just had to laugh. Glancing back down I saw that she too was now grinning. But Annie hadn't finished saying her piece. 'Instead of jus' standin' there and gawpin' from your lofty perch you git yoursel' down here this instant,' she commanded.

'Now I've always bin led to believe that many hands make light work, or do I take it that a gentleman of yo' position will not lower hisself to assist a lowly domestic help in such duties?'

'And I've always been led to believe that too many cooks spoil the broth,' I shot back. Annie need not have worried. I made my mind up there and then that she and I would get along famously. The Windy City suddenly did not seem such a queer and foreign place. Without further ado, I hastened down to the garden to formally introduce myself.

Annie McBride was a dark-haired beauty of tender years who, somewhat to my initial dismay, put me much in mind of Elizabeth, who I was still fervently trying to forget. I'd come to find that Annie was a kind, sweet girl, a couple of years my junior, with a ready sense of humour as I'd discovered that very first time we'd met.

It stood her in good stead at Dr Russell's fine abode for he sometimes acted somewhat pompously, was very demanding and ruled the household with a rod of iron. Yet not for the first time in my life I found first impressions can be wrong. I came to regard my new master as hard, but fair, and the more I got to know him the more I grew to like him for all his various quirks.

My own duties consisted of driving, grooming, feeding and exercising Dr Russell's grey mare, Mollie, a gentle, sweet-natured, if somewhat lazy little horse. Her chief task in the morning was to tow her master's handsome trap through the crowded streets of Chicago to Dr Russell's office a good mile-and-a-half distant, and in the evening tow it all the way back.

I always had to make my services available to Dr Russell, but as he was in law chambers much, my situation oft meant a considerable time lounging about. One afternoon, with my master holding court with some solicitor chums of his at the opening of a new hotel called The Palmer, I wandered into a nearby saloon more through boredom than anything.

I'd barely settled down at the bar with my ale when I was hailed by a fellow drinker sat at the far end. It was mid-afternoon and we were the sole patrons. 'You sound like you're from England, friend,' he said, having invited himself over to join me. 'Pray tell me your business an' for what length of time you bin in these parts?' The man, wearing a stetson and sporting a fine pair of Dundrearies, looked in his late thirties with a balding, greying pate and red drinker's nose. He seemed amiable enough, I thought cautiously, if slightly intoxicated. Judging by the way the bartender stonily ignored him I guessed he'd been perched on that barstool for some considerable time, putting the blessed world to rights.

Normally, when questioned about my origins, I'd say I was from England, as I'd found that few in those parts had ever seemed to have heard of God's Own Country. This time, however, I decided to reveal my true origins. 'Wales?' he answered, 'aye, I know Wales. I once sailed in a ship that docked in that mighty port of Cardiff.' And to my great surprise, as well as that of the bartender, he promptly launched into a couple of rather tuneless bars of Ar Hyd Y Nos, that old Welsh melody.

His name was Titus King and he'd originally hailed from Whitechapel in London, a place where I'd cavorted much. He'd left the East End many years previous for a life on the waves. The mariner's life brought him to America, where at the end of the North v South war he signed on with the US

Army as a cavalryman. Said he served three years afore doing a flit; in other words, deserting or taking 'The Grand Bounce'.

'Yep, I was a snowbird who took flight,' he said raising his whisky glass to his lips. 'That's what they call them soldiers who sign on for Uncle Sam over the cruel winter and skedaddle off to mine gold out in California once them snows thaw.' Even now, he said, three years on, he was afeared the army would come looking for him. 'I was in The Seventh Cavalry under General George Armstrong Custer,' he said, downing the remains of his glass, and tapping a sideburn with a shaking forefinger. 'The feller wasn't right in the head. Do you know what he did to deserters?' I shook my head. 'The bastard strung 'em up, that's what. A good few fellows must have had their necks stretched during my time as a bluecoat.

'A snowbird could count hisself lucky if he got the letter 'D' branded on his hip by a red-hot iron. Just gettin' his wings clipped, you might say. A soldier need only be late on parade and Custer could have him hung up by his thumbs for an hour or more. We buck privates hated and feared Ol' Iron Butt, as we called him. Not that you could ever question the man's courage, I have to say.'

I bought Titus a drink and listened some more. He told me how he was there at the Battle of the Washita River in November 1868 when Custer's Seventh attacked a sleeping Cheyenne village at dawn. What he saw, he said, made him finally resolve to quit the US Army. 'I never had no sympathy with them Indians,' he mused. 'Hell, I'd seen what they could do to others of their kind let alone our boys in blue once they gotten their hands on 'em. Scalps lifted, noses and privates chopped off, eyes left hanging outta their sockets, tongues severed. But what some of Custer's men did at the Washita was beyond belief. Them papers was full of what a great victory it was. Just the sort of thing folks wanted to read. What they didn't say was how Custer abandoned Major Elliott and 18 troopers to their hideous fate at the hands of them barberous hordes.

'When the fight was done we heard Elliott yell: 'Here goes for a brevet or a coffin!' and saw him and his boys take off after some fleein' Injuns only to run into an ambush a few miles downriver. We found their frozen bodies some time later. All of 'em chopped up like so much raw liver.' His voice trailed off for a few moments. 'With Indians you'd expect that kind of butchery; they's savages, right? But trust me, son, them bluecoats did a lot of things you'll never read about.'

Despite King's slurred speech and increasing use of profane language, my interest was piqued, even if what he was relating was somewhat sobering. The thought of becoming a soldier had never truly left me: it had first been awakened in my early childhood by stirring tales of Francis Batine and The Charge of The Light Brigade. Now, listening to Titus King ramble on in this dingy backstreet Chicago saloon, the notion of taking up arms surged back again with a vengeance, even if much of what he was saying made me feel more than a tad uncomfortable.

I knew already of Custer, whose dashing deeds during the North-South conflict had been diligently reported by the newspapers back home. And I also knew that he'd been sent West to take care of those red men following the Fetterman fight of 1866 when around eighty bluecoats lost their scalps on the Bozeman Trail out in Wyoming.

Lt Fetterman, who'd boasted that with eighty troopers he could ride through the entire Indian nation, was lured into a trap by a bunch of mounted decoys and his force slaughtered to a man. The thing that stuck in my mind was newspaper reports of a bent and mangled bugle lying in the red snow. Bugle boy must've gone down wielding it like a club. Elliott can't have been the smartest chicken in the coop 'cos he'd repeated Fetterman's blunder two years later.

'Anyways, we came down on that village like a thunderclap,' said Titus King, slamming his fist down on the bar. 'Dawn was about to break an' thick snow lay all around. Them Injuns never knew what hit 'em, we charged through that village like a blue cyclone shooting at anythin' that moved, be it man, woman or child.

'T'was all over in barely enough time for a man to light his pipe. Them Injuns that wasn't killed was rounded up as prisoners. Custer had reckoned the quicker we took them squaws and their little ones hostage the quicker the braves would lay down their arms, and he was right. He took a big gamble and Custer's luck paid off. I'm told them Injuns still call that sonofabitch Son Of The Morning Star after the fight on the Washita. He who attacks afore dawn.

'I won't lie; when it was all over we felt light-headed, drunk on a queer kinda joy,' he belched. 'Kinda like the feelin' you get when you sink two or three whiskies on an empty stomach, I guess. Sure, we was happy to be alive oursel's, but winnin' a big fight like that sends you kinda crazy for a while; leastways it did us.

'Some of the boys dragged this old Injun round the back of a teepee and caved in his skull with their rifle butts; said spillin' his brains all over the place was back payment for them Injuns slicin' up Fetterman and his boys. They took a big chance 'cos if what they did had gotten back to Custer he'd have strung 'em up there and then. Like I said, for a while them sergeants and officers had a real job tryin' to get a handle on some of us men.'

At this point King started coughing and wretching so violently that his barstool creaked and shook and I noticed he'd brought up flecks of blood; I hurriedly ordered a glass of water along with more whisky for us both.

He took a sip from his fresh glass and fell silent for a bit. 'I'm not proud of what I did,' he said gazing moodily into his glass. 'Some of my troop got hold of this young squaw, real fresh little thing she was. Bound an' gagged her an' took her back into the woods,' he continued hoarsely. 'I went in them trees with the intention of stoppin' 'em pleasuring themselves with her but when I saw what was goin' on thought I'd get a piece o' the action myself. I'll hold my hands up and admit I lost all reason. Hadn't had no woman in a long time. What's that they say? To the victor the spoils? That was how we saw it.'

He downed his whisky in a single gulp and sat there staring into space. 'So was that why you left the army?' I enquired. 'Because of those things that happened at the Washita?' 'I guess you could say the Washita was the last straw,' he replied. 'I'd been gettin' real sick of the whole Goddamn soldiering business and the Washita kinda made my mind up for me.

'Come the spring once the snows had melted I had a few greenbacks in my back pocket so struck out on my own. Still don't feel safe, though. Know deserters who was picked up years later. I'm always lookin' over my shoulder 'cos I feel Custer's forever on my tail.'

Titus King belligerently demanded I stay for another whisky, but being at my master's beck and call I made my apologies and explained I had to get back to my station. I'd just risen to my feet when he suddenly lunged across the bar and seized my arm.

'Don't you ever let them Injuns take you alive, son,' he implored, eyes wild and staring. 'Blowin' your own brains out will be a whole lot easier way to go. Don't yous ever forgit that.'

Prising myself free from his grip with an effort, I thanked him for his advice and company. Joining the army was something I could never rule out even if, knowing my luck, I'd end up being commanded by a madman like Custer. But joining up would be very much a last resort, I decided.

Still, most of the talk of Custer around Chicago was admiring; think I read somewhere he came from nearby Michigan. Most folks seemed to appreciate his attempts to control those Indians way out West and the Washita was still a big talking point nearly three years on. Titus King's experiences had given me food for thought, yet the Indians had now been herded back onto their reservations and the newspapers were all saying the wars of the Great Plains had been consigned to the pages of history. As I tipped my hat to the barman and stepped out into the street, I could hear Titus King singing an Irish quickstep which in time would come to be very familiar. . .

'Let Bacchus's sons be not dismayed,
but join with me each jovial blade,
come booze and sing and lend your aid,
to help me with the chorus:
Instead of spa we'll drink brown ale
and pay the reckoning on the nail,
for debt no man shall go to jail
from Garryowen in glory.'

Peacock & Goddard
3, South Square,
Gray's Inn
London WC
December 9, 1904

Dear Sirs,

James deceased

We annex copy of a very unsatisfactory letter which we received this morning from our correspondents in New York. We fear that it is useless to expect any good result from their inquiries now and do not think that communication to the British Consul would bring about any result. We are of course sorry for this but do not know of any other course to adopt. Yours truly

Peacock & Goddard

Messrs Eaton Evans & Williams
7 Wall Street
New York
Dec 8, 1904

Dear Sirs,

We are in receipt of a letter from one R L James residing at Opelika, Alabama, who refers us to Wm J James, residing at Bloomburg, Texas, as possibly having some knowledge of Wm B James, the subject of the inquiries.

The last letter from Wm B James to his brother was written from Opelika in April 1875. Wm J James, now in Texas, lived at Opelika at that time, and in that year went to Texas.

We have written to Wm J James asking for such information as he may have. Yours very truly

Owen & Sturgess
Messrs Peacock & Goddard
Grays Inn
W8

***

Arthur Nicholas sat nursing a cup of tea in his mother's parlour, listening to Mari and her best friend, Maggie Bowen, reminisce about a young man of his own age and from his own village who had blazed his trail West all those years ago. Mari had readily agreed to another interview, as she'd rather grandly put it, somewhat acidly asking Arthur that now he had a young lady friend whether he could actually still remember his way to Dinas Cross as his home visits had grown so infrequent? 'Once you've gone through Lower Town, you head up Newport Road onto the flat and Dinas is a mile or so distant,' she'd told him sarcastically when their paths had crossed at Fishguard market.

Arthur had grown accustomed to such comments and in actual fact always looked forward to his return visits. And not just for mam's tea and cake on this occasion for Mari had thoughtfully invited along Maggie, a former schoolmate of WBJ's, who had known him and his fellow siblings from Peniel.

'Oh aye, William Batine James,' said Maggie, a wicked smile playing on her lips. 'He was a bit of a wild one, that boy.

117

Always up to mischief. No wonder I carried a bit of a torch for him!' The two women started to chuckle as Arthur manfully sought to steer them back onto the subject at hand. 'Yes ... now then, Will ...' she finally reflected, sitting up straight, clearing her throat and striving to ignore the knowing looks Mari was throwing her way. 'Got thrown out of Peniel for cutting up rough in front of the teacher, I seem to recall. Can't say for sure 'cos I was off with the fever that week. From what I was told by others, he shouted and cursed at Mr Thomas and he and his brothers, Frank and John and their little sister Ellen got up and marched straight out of the class without so much as a by your leave. Never went back too. All those Jameses were pretty wilful, see?'

'Sounds like Will was a bit of a boy who could throw his weight about,' observed Arthur.

'Aye, that he could too,' replied Maggie. 'Had a real temper on him, but always looked out for the little ones, mind, and not just his own kith and kin. Those James boys were kept on a tight leash by their father, you have to remember. Real strict he was. Deacon at Brynhenllan. After Mr James died, they did go off the straight and narrow, I suppose you could say. Least Tom and Will did. Mr Thomas, the schoolmaster at Peniel, and Will didn't like one another one bit, to be honest. Come to think of it, I think Will hated the man for some reason. After Will left school, he got work as a carpenter down in Narberth and I know for a fact that Mr Thomas took great pains to stay out of his way when he came back home. Will worked for a few years down there and popped back every so often 'cos he was seeing this girl from Newport. Quite a dish she was, too, though with a reputation as being a bit of a handful. Later Will moved down to Llanelly where he got himself a situation as a ...'

'Commercial traveller?' interrupted Arthur, feeling very pleased with himself.

'How did you know that?' asked both women in unison,

looking at him in surprise.

'It's something I deduced from his letters,' explained Arthur, feeling he was finally starting to get somewhere. 'That knowledge does not bring me any further towards my ultimate objective in locating WBJ, but I'm starting to think he may have pursued a similar line of work in the southern United States of America.'

'You could well be right,' pondered Maggie. 'That boy was good with words as well as with his hands,' she added, giving her friend a playful smack as Mari again started to titter. 'You'd oft see Will down on Newport Sands with his horses during the summer months,' she went on. 'He'd gallop them up and down the beach and then take them into the sea for a paddle. Will reckoned the briny had magical healing powers and would ease any strains and niggles the mounts picked up. The faces of beachgoers when he rode those horses into the waves were a pretty picture, I can tell you! No-one else round here trained horses that way.' Maggie paused momentarily in her recollections. 'Did you hear about the time Will rode across the ice-bound Cleddau to escape the constables?' she asked.

'Indeed I have,' replied Arthur, meeting his mother's amused gaze. 'I suppose it's fair to surmise that his pursuers were too wary to follow in his wake?'

'Indeed that was so,' answered Maggie. 'Daring fugitive rides steed across ice-strewn river'; said the headline in The Haverfordwest Telegraph. 'Course, Will wasn't named in the paper; but all here in Dinas knew it to be him. His brother Tom was less fortunate that night and ended up having his collar felt along with a few others. But Will James wasn't bad, you know, just full of devilment. He only got into trouble for the occasional bout of fisticuffs. Seldom was the fellow who started trouble but always was the one to quell it, if you see what I mean? My brother Reginald knew Will well and liked him even if he did find him pretty queer on occasions. The

119

two had gone on their first foxhunt together as young boys when Will cut up pretty rough like he had at Peniel.' Maggie's demeanour had grown steadily more serious.

'Are you able to enlarge on that at all, Mrs Bowen?' prompted Arthur.

Maggie drew a deep breath. 'From what Reggie told me later the boys were among a group of horsemen chasing a fox with hounds,' she said. 'Will's own father was among the riders. After the dogs finally cornered the fox and killed it, blood was daubed on the boys' faces as was the custom with tyros. Reggie said Will suddenly started screaming in front of everyone; told them they were all a bunch of butchers, he did, asked how would they like to be hunted down and ripped asunder and that he wanted no further part of it. Caused a wholly frightful scene and galloped off all on his own.

'All present were left shocked and flabbergasted and pretty much decided to call a halt to the day's hunting at that point, though Reggie remembered Mr James going chalk-white with fury.

'Will told Reggie some days later he'd never go hunting ever again. Said something about it being an unfair contest 'twixt a wild animal, a pack of dogs and a bunch of armed men on horseback. Reginald didn't quite understand what Will was getting at, but seeing as he respected Will reckoned it'd be wise to leave sleeping dogs lie.' Maggie slowly shook her head, a quizzical expression on her face. 'No-one could truly fathom that boy,' Mari chipped in quietly.

'Now I don't want you thinking Will was in any way bad company,' Maggie told Arthur. 'He may have had some pretty queer ideas, but most times t'was good sport having him around. And Dinas Cross hasn't been quite the same ever since he slung his hook, isn't that so, Mari?' Arthur's mother grinned and nodded.

'Probably the last time I bumped into Will was when he was coming out of the Freemasons,' related Maggie. 'Said he was working as a commercial traveller down in Llanelly and passed on his regards to my family. I remember being taken aback at that.

'In what way?' asked Arthur. 'Well, Will being such a good horseman I really would have expected him to be working as a blacksmith or saddler or something along those lines,' Maggie answered. 'Told him that as well.' 'And what was his response?' pressed Arthur. 'Said he wanted to try something a bit different and get himself fixed up with a job that paid more money. I reminded him that when he was young he'd tell people he'd ride the winner of the Grand National steeplechase at Liverpool; and all the menfolk here in Dinas said they'd take out wagers on him and win pots of money!' And Mari and Maggie chuckled again.

Mike Lewis

CHAPTER 7

Chicago had grown to become the young nation's second largest city, and one of the largest in the world. It was certainly the biggest in the West; and assuredly the most filthy. Dr Russell told me the city had been constructed upon a prairie bog, hence the fact its inhabitants were invariably plagued by mosquitoes. 'The Windy City' was the name it was best known by, but it was also termed 'Slabtown' and 'The Mud Hole of the Prairie' for reasons that quickly became apparent to its newest citizen.

There were times when I coaxed a reluctant Mollie along streets so thick with mud the poor little mare could scarce wade through. Comical signs proclaiming 'Fastest route to China' or 'No Bottom Here' were placed to warn people of the sludge, though as a coachman I never found them very amusing. The city was sprawled along the shores of Lake Michigan and Dr Russell told me its water had once been so polluted that finding small fish in drinking water had been commonplace! And the weather veered from one extreme to t'other. Baking hot in summer; brutally frigid in winter and the wind ... well, you could never escape the infernal wind.

Work, however, was plentiful despite the huge wave of Irish and German immigrants that'd rolled into town and my own lot had improved considerable since Toronto. I had a job I could do in my sleep and a steady wage plus a roof over my head.

The more I got to know Dr Russell, the more I came to admire him. Despite being an educated gentleman he was not above having regular discourse with the likes of me; oft

123

complimenting me on my standard of reading and writing. I think he was surprised at the extent of my learning. I also guessed he was somewhat lonesome as his only son was living way back East and the sole contact they seemed to have was the occasional letter, as rare as hen's teeth.

Once in a while he'd summon me to his parlour for a nightcap of port or brandy and regale me with tales of his profession, the court cases he'd been involved with and their outcome. Must have been the first person I'd met up to that point who didn't believe in hanging on the grounds that the wrong person could get strung up. His well-reasoned views made me reconsider my own thoughts on the subject.

He and I once engaged in a spirited debate on the Hereafter. Dr Russell, who was non-religious, said he considered the idea of an afterlife, presided over by some old fellow with a long, white beard in the sky, a veritable hoot. 'It would be the telling sign of a mature and advanced society were we to universally reject such a preposterous notion without question,' he declared, twirling the brandy around in his glass and inviting a response by fixing me with a challenging stare.

Perhaps it was down to the drink, but I found myself, the fallen Welsh Methodist, mounting a trenchant, if not passionate case for life after death, even though deep down I did not subscribe to it myself.

'The eternal sleep, in my view,' said I, 'is nay different than alighting from one cab, crossing the street and hailing another. One way or another, all of us go on in a differing form.' In my mind's eye I could picture Elizabeth nodding approvingly. 'Oh, come, come, William my boy,' Dr Russell replied, 'where in Heaven's name is the scientific evidence for such conjecture? And pray tell me where precisely William Batine James dwelt prior to his own dear mother giving him life?'

I replied that I obviously had no recollection as, prior

to that point, I did not exist. 'Which just goes to illustrate the essence of my argument,' crowed Dr Russell triumphantly. 'As you did not exist prior to your birth, so you will not exist once you are no more!'

'With all due respect, sir, you're overlooking one important detail,' said I, embolded by drink. 'Once born, we are all endowed with souls. And once death comes calling and our physical being is but a mere shell, our souls will continue forth.'

'Bravo! Spoken like a true Welsh Methodist!' roared Dr Russell, as he raised a glass in salute before rising to his feet a tad unsteadily to retrieve the brandy bottle from a handsome cabinet. 'You can take the boy out of the chapel, but you cannot take the chapel out of the boy! Remain right where you are seated whilst I replenish your glass, William, for I am enjoying this conversation.' Dawn's rosy fingers could be spied by the time the pair of us finally repaired to our beds.

The thought of my own death and the manner in which I would meet it was ever-present. Even as a child I seemed to think of little else. Now, though I was a full-grown man, those morbid feelings still lingered. I always imagined Tom met his watery end staring death full in the face and oft wondered whether, on the day of reckoning, I'd do likewise. I could not rid myself of the bleak notion my own demise would be swift and sudden; my precious time on Earth all too brief. I simply could not countenance petering out on my death bed, aged, sick and infirm.

As I've stated previous, Elizabeth, who held challenging and forthright opinions on just about everything, and was ne'er shy in voicing them, fervently believed in life after death. She also opined that those souls who had newly departed were not averse to sending back signs to their grieving loved ones. On one occasion, she recounted how she had followed the trail of an overpowering stench of carbolic soap to a grandfather clock in Penfeidr which had formerly been owned by her own dear grandfather. The old gentleman, who'd passed away in Fishguard the previous day, was an obsessive bather who'd always reeked of carbolic soap and had quite evidently, she stoutly maintained, made a brief return to Penfeidr to check up on his cherished clock!

Whilst I myself had little truck with the conventional view of Heaven, I did like the notion of God manifesting Himself in different ways and surroundings. God is all around, I suppose you might say. In a field of golden wheat or amid a flowing river or even upon a mountaintop in Newport, Pembrokeshire, come to that. There would be a great deal worse places to end up than on the summit of Carningli, I'd surmise.

And should God indeed turn out to be some all-seeing being, I'd reason, then I'd welcome an audience with Him when my moment arrived. In view of the ill fortune and number of tragedies I'd experienced, I would, in all probability, take him strongly to task and launch a debate every bit as robust as the ones I enjoyed with Dr Russell! For that one reason alone I'd truly welcome the day of reckoning.

Dr Russell could possess a jolly sense of humour. Once, on learning of my previous occupation in Toronto, he treated me to a fair rendition of 'The Gay Young Clerk In The Dry Goods Store', a popular ditty of the day. One night, he asked me of my own family back in Wales as well as the circumstances that had led me to America. Although I deemed it wise not to give full chapter and verse, I did inform him of the deaths of my father and five siblings.

'Ah, William, you must endeavour to maintain contact with your remaining family as when all is said and done they are the foundations which anchor you to this world,' he remarked. 'Even if you do indeed decide that your future lies here in America you must endeavour to visit the old country whilst your mother still lives.' He was right, of course. Yet something was stopping me from writing home again.

Perhaps I was waiting until my circumstances had improved to such an extent that Mother and John would be proud of me. The job of a coachman was a couple of notches up from that of a dry goods store clerk; yet it was not a situation I could see myself pursuing indefinitely. T'would do for now, however.

Moreover, as time went by I could see I'd kindled the interest and curiosity of young Annie McBride, whose visits to my cramped little attic room grew e'er more frequent. I have to admit that she was increasingly in my thoughts as well. Even her disclosure that she was engaged to a young clerk who worked in an office next door to Dr Russell's did not faze me unduly. I consoled myself in the knowledge that my time in Chicago would be brief in any case.

I still had no idea where my destiny lay, but thought California just might be the place for me, even if such a distant location meant a perilous journey through hostile Indian territory.

At first, Irish Annie, as I took to calling her, knocked on my door on the pretence of offering me some fresh oranges and apples she'd bought from the street market. Said she reckoned I looked pretty run-down and that she fretted over my health and well-being. 'Ne'er in my wildest dreams did I envisage being mothered by a mere slip of an Irish girl,' I'd tell her.

As we got to know each other more we'd oft meet up in the nearby park, usually when Dr Russell had retired to his bed for his customary afternoon nap, and always when Annie knew her young fellow would be up to his neck in paperwork back in the office. In the past I'd have tried to get her to share my bed, but this was different: she was a sweet girl who'd shown me kindness and friendship and, indeed, was pledged to another. Such considerations would not have prevented me from pursuing her in the past, however. Maybe I had changed more than I knew?

127

We fast became friends, two somewhat lost souls striving to escape their mutually troubled pasts. Annie started to confide in me and I to her; to a degree, anyhow. She'd oft call me 'Taffy', a name that tickled her much after I disclosed that some English fellow in a downtown bar had addressed me so. 'Taffy was a Welshman, Taffy was a thief,' she'd chant mockingly, remembering the old nursery rhyme her late father had taught her as an infant. 'Taffy came to my house and stole a piece of beef; I went to Taffy's house, Taffy wasn't home; Taffy came to my house and stole a marrow-bone.' She told me how she'd been born in a slum in Kilkenny and how her father, a saddler widowed when the girls were small, had elected to bring her and her sisters to America in search of a better life.

Her father died of yellow fever barely a week after setting foot on American soil and the deaths of her sisters soon afterwards left Annie an orphan who was sent to the workhouse. One of her sisters had gone out for a walk one day and ended up being fished out of the river. Annie said t'was ne'er found out how she'd gotten there.

She ne'er went in to great detail about this period of her life, but hinted that her time at the workhouse had been greatly troubled and that she couldn't wait to see the back of the place. Over the past few years she'd had a number of different situations as a domestic servant, cleaner or waitress. At 17, she told me, she'd been about to marry a young coachman such as myself, but he'd fallen in front of a cab whilst intoxicated and died of a fractured skull, mere days afore their wedding. I thought that this background of tragedy accounted for her strong Catholic faith. Turned out she'd always been an ardent church-goer who prayed much.

Once, on becoming very upset thinking she'd lost her rosary, she frantically begged me to help her search the house from top to bottom. To her great relief, we'd eventually found the rosary in the coal bunker where she'd dropped it whilst going about her daily chores. Annie told me that throughout her misfortunes her faith had given her great comfort as it had remained the one constant in her life. I could understand that, though some folk no doubt felt the same about an old pair of slippers.

Aye, Irish Annie may only have been nineteen years of age, but she'd seen plenty and suffered much during her short time on Earth; no wonder those clear blue Irish eyes of hers bore a somewhat haunted look. We'd oft slip into her little second floor room or my eyrie in the attic to talk, as we could always rely on the fact the household was quiet for certain periods; with no impropriety taking place whatsoever. The fact what we were doing was strictly forbidden; house staff were discouraged from fraternising with each other under any circumstances; made our secret meetings all the more thrilling.

Annie was a clever girl who, had her family circumstances been different, might have made good for herself. I set about learning her to read and write and over the course of the next few weeks seemed to make some headway. She enquired whether I'd ever been a school teacher and seemed surprised when I said I hadn't. When I asked her once what she most wanted from life she said she just wanted to be happy, have a roof over her head, a decent fellow to care for her and never have to hunger again.

When she then asked me what I wanted, I said I'd just settle on being happy; it'd make a welcome change from the cruel twists and turns fate had subjected me to in the past, I reflected darkly. 'Ah, Will,' she'd replied, catching me offguard, 'in order to be happy a man has to first like hisself. An' from where I'm sittin' youse plain don't.' At the time that didn't make much sense to me, but looking back it sure as Hell does.

As I came to find out, Annie could see things in me that up to that point no one else had spied; not even Elizabeth and

I'd thought that girl could read me like a book. For as long as I could remember I appeared to have been labouring under some giant weight; I can only describe the feeling I sometimes had as like being borne down by some great rock on my back. There were some days the load seemed manageable, others when I feared I was slowly being crushed to death.

It put me in mind of a painting that had hung in the parlour at Pencnwc of Atlas holding up the celestial heavens; 'cept unlike him I was buckling under the strain. The best way I could describe it was it was akin to having a large and very heavy cloak around the shoulders which sometimes I feared would stifle me.

As the days and weeks passed, I realised that the burden I shouldered seemed considerably lighter when Annie was around. Instead of wallowing in self-pity, which was always a great fault of mine, I began to think how fortunate I'd been to find her.

Yet Annie was engaged to be married. She and her young fellow, Frank Ellis, were saving up for the wedding which would take place early in the new year. She told me he was a gent, really quiet and polite and treated her like a lady. 'Not at all like me then,' I'd replied, and she'd laughed. I wasn't too surprised she liked the idea of married life and children. Annie had lost her own family all too soon, after all. She said I'd get an invite to the wedding celebration. I had to act like I was grateful when in truth I was thinking a trip to the quack dentist to have all my teeth pulled would be preferable. I was surprised at how upset the thought of her marrying made me feel.

Once her sisters were gone, Annie had no living kin, none that she was aware of, leastways, and on leaving the workhouse she'd wandered into a servant's job at the home of some wealthy doctor in a monied part of the city. That situation ended when he came home intoxicated one night and endeavored to force himself upon her. Annie fought back hard, smashed a chamber pot over the wretch's head, scratched his face and ended up running into the street in a state of part undress.

She told me she didn't even trouble herself reporting the matter to a nearby police constable, knowing full well that it'd be her word against that of the good doctor. 'That's jus' the way it is, Will,' she said to me sadly. 'Some things'll never change. The likes of you and me just ain't got no voice. An' you may think youse Welsh is under the heel of them English, but jus' you try bein' Irish. We folks is at the bottom o' the barrel. Sure as Hell it's a tough old life, but youse gotta keep fightin', Will, you just gotta keep fightin' … Having spent the next week or so living on the streets, she'd eventually taken the job of a waitress in a cafe. That was where she'd met Dr Russell, a friend of the proprietor and one of the establishment's best customers. A few months later, he'd ended up offering her a situation.

She told me he was a good master who was very fair-minded. One of the things she liked about him was that he did not expect her to share his bed; an arrangement, she said, that would've been unfamiliar to most of the young girls she knew working as servants in the homes of Chicago's rich gentlemen.

Afore too long I found myself unburdening myself to her when she pushed me on my past. I told her about my family troubles, my experiences in Narberth, Llanelly and London and why I'd left Dinas, stopping short of the reason I could never go home anymore. E'en told her about Liz Penfeidr and some of what had gone on between the two of us. What I liked about Annie was that, like Elizabeth, she was not afeared to speak her mind. Instead of speaking ill of Elizabeth and rallying to my defence like I suppose most women would've done, Annie said she felt sure Elizabeth must have had just cause in leaving me. I wasn't expecting that.

What's more, she even went as far as saying she wouldn't mind meeting up with Elizabeth one day so, as she put it, 'we could swap tales 'bout the queer Welsh feller fate saddled us both with!'

'Are you truly tellin' me the whole story?' she asked me once, accusedly. 'Youse musta wronged that gal and wronged her bad. From what ya tell me, Will, that poor gal was plain head-over-heels in love with youse. I don't reckon she's done gone and woke up one morning an' just thought to rid herself of youse.' Despite all my stubborn protestations to the contrary, Annie trenchantly maintained there were pieces of my past I refused to acknowledge. 'Ain't ne'er met no-one as plain mule-headed as you, Will James!' she'd exclaim in exasperation.

Once, when we met up in the park one afternoon, Annie pointed out a distinguished-looking gent clad in a top hat and business suit, feeding the ducks.

'That, my dear Will, is Dr Theophilus Gordon, distinguished man o' medicine and a pillar o' respectability in town,' she said flatly. 'He's also the fella who tried to have his way with me when I was a servant girl of 15.'

As I listened in silence she went on to recount how Gordon had visited the workhouse with the select purpose of finding a young servant girl to employ. She'd found him courteous, highly-educated and well-mannered and had been delighted to subsequently receive his offer of employment. 'T'was my chance to finally rid myself of the workhouse,' she said. 'Landsakes, I'd have jumped through a flamin' hoop to git away from that accursed place; the smell of disinfectant, death and piss lingers with me still. It'll do so for evermore.' Yet Annie's hopes of better days had been cruelly dashed when a drunken Gordon attempted to take her by force. There was an icy look in those blue eyes as she recalled the stench of his sweat, the saliva on his lips and his clutching, pawing hands all over her small young body.

But Annie was nothing if not a survivor. She'd managed to douse Gordon's ardour with the aid of that conveniently-at-hand chamberpot, which she'd shattered over his head. Although she endeavoured to make light of the episode, 'he hadn't done reckoned on my wild Irish temper!', it was evident she'd been left with inward strife in the same way of some hollowed-out, dead-eyed soldier who's seen too much of battle. Matters were not helped by the fact Gordon lived just two streets distant and she'd see him going about his business most daily. Whenever he noticed her, she said he'd barely suppress a sneer and curse her under his breath. On one occasion, he'd even enquired whether she'd now found employment as 'a dollymop, although even such manner of occupation would be above the likes of you'.

He was clearly a loathsome fellow, as well as a hypocrite who lived a secret life, that much was plain. But what made my blood boil and temper seethe uncontrollably was not merely the fact he'd attempted to take little Annie by force; it was because, to his family, acquaintances and colleagues in the medical profession he was an esteemed man about town. A pillar of respectability, as Annie herself had called him.

Why was such a cruel fellow living in wealth and comfort while good people like me and Annie were by comparison forced to live like stray dogs fighting over scraps? I asked myself. Not long afterwards, unbeknown to Annie, I made a point of familiarising myself with Michigan Avenue, and more specifically, the rather grand townhouse with the red door where I was quick to establish Gordon lived.

I told myself that the reason I was there was to meet the good doctor simply to ask him whether he was in the regular habit of attempting to choke young servant girls who had the temerity to rebuff his advances. Merely to put the frighteners on, if you like, perhaps even instilling enough fear to persuade him to hand over a few much-needed dollars which I'd then pass on to Annie? A form of compensation you might say. T'was the sort of insane scheme I'd ne'er have contemplated back in Dinas, but here in Chicago, where no one knew me, it seemed fair sport. O'er the coming weeks, I started to hunt this odious individual. Whenever work allowed I would always make the point of returning towards home via Michigan Avenue, knowing that I would eventually find out what Dr Theophilus Gordon had to say for himself, yet I could not bring myself to go up those steps and announce my presence by using the bronze lion's head door-knocker afixed to that red door.

In the end, when our paths finally crossed, I gave him no time to speak. One sweltering evening in late September, whilst walking down Michigan Avenue on my way home to groom and feed Mollie her evening oats, I caught sight of a familiar portly figure wearing a top hat and swinging a cane, making his way slowly down the pavement before me. I knew in an instant that it was Gordon, having seen him about the place once or twice.

Glancing around quickly, I noted that the street was quiet, as most residents were probably now already ensconsed in their parlours, doubtless having enjoyed a hearty supper. Perhaps, I thought back afterwards, Gordon was partaking a post-supper constitutional on that fateful evening? If so, how unfortunate for him . . . As I approached my unsuspecting quarry, like a mountain lion stalking its prey, I raised my hat and wished him good evening. The old fraud was in the act of reciprocating when my right fist connected full on his face, a swift nose-ender, sending him sprawling backwards on the sidewalk with a half-cry.

In a thrice I was upon him like a rabid wolf; my fury knew no bounds. Leaping astride that paunchy figure I drove my fist again and again with great force yet cold deliberation into those soft, well-fed features intent on pounding them into the type of mush they'd served me aboard the Idaho. By the time I was done I hoped that those well-heeled solicitors and barristers he mingled with would ne'er recognise them e'er again. At first Gordon seemed to have been rendered quite insensible, but then began coughing and spluttering and, as I paused and drew back, exhausted by the number of blows I'd dealt him more than anything, he slowly sat groggily upright, his face a mask of blood, uncomprehending piggy eyes wide open with fear, pain and shock.

Turning to his side, he coughed violently and spat a few teeth out onto the paved stones followed closely by his supper. By now I knew I had done enough and t'was time to skedaddle, besides, a couple of dogs were barking excitedly and looking back down the street in the gathering twilight I could see figures emerging to peer tentatively from doorways. Raising myself to my full height, I stared down at Gordon for a few instances as he lay dazed on his side, attempting to feebly prop himself up on his elbow. Yet I felt no pity; nor was I yet done. Taking a mighty swing of my right leg I smashed my hobnail boot as hard as I could into that cultured face; the thump and crunch of shattered teeth seeming to echo down the gaslit street.

The coup de grace sent him flat on his back totally insensible and with that I took swiftly to my heels as urgent voices sounded after me. Legging it down the street and round the corner to cries of 'Stop thief!' I made good my escape, and tore along for a fair while, ducking down alleyways and doubling back on myself afore finally escaping the shrill of police whistles by seeking refuge in a spit and sawdust saloon in the centre of town.

Regaining my breath and attempting to ease my pounding heart I strode across to the bar and bought a large whisky afore raising a toast to the absent Irish Annie. 'Hey, bud, you coulda least have checked ya boots afore comin' in,' protested the landlord. Looking around I saw I'd left a bloody trail of prints all across the floor. Might the unhappy landlord blow the whistle on me and ensure I'd now be buckled?

Apologising profusely, I told him that a butcher's job was my trade and promptly cleared up the mess I'd left in my wake with the aid of a large piece of sacking.

Ne'er did I tell Annie of what I'd done, not e'en when she said Dr Russell had informed her that some ruffian had attacked and badly injured Dr Gordon in the course of an intended street robbery. Said if such lawlessness continued on the streets of Chicago he'd have no option but to relocate to New York or Boston. I knew I could count myself well fortunate not to have committed murder that night. Had I not been disturbed, I'd have pounded Gordon's head into that pavement like a hammer smiting home a six-inch nail even if it would've meant a certain date with the hangman had I been apprehended.

And, despite the shadow of the noose, I'd have felt no different had I stamped on a cockroach ...

CHAPTER 8

The events of the night of October 8, 1871 will forever remain engraved on my mind. Much wearied after a long day, I was grooming Mollie in her little stable beneath the house whilst looking forward to retiring to my attic room and a night-time feed of bread, cheese and a sausage. It was the Sabbath, a muggy day during a warm fall, and Annie had already retired to her own quarters on the second floor whilst Dr Russell tinkled the ivories in the lounge. I always enjoyed hearing him play piano as it signified a peaceful end to the weekend. As I brushed down a contented Mollie, herself quite wearied from the day's exertions, I could hear the familiar sound of 'The Blue Danube' meandering from the parlour above. As I worked on, idly wondering what Annie was up to, I'd become aware of a faint smell of burning, as if someone had lit a bonfire close by, but paid little attention as the stench of smoke and burning fuel was all around us daily.

But as I was platting Mollie's pretty mane I froze on hearing shouts of alarm from outside. They were most urgent and plainly nearby, so, abandoning my labours, I elected to go and investigate. Walking out into the narrow lane running past the back of the house I gasped aloud on catching sight of a huge black plume of smoke, not more than 50 yards distant, heading inexorably in my direction. It was a fire of unbelievable proportions greedily devouring wooden house after wooden house afore my horrified gaze. How in Heaven's name could I not have been aware of it afore?

A couple of men came running down the lane towards me, one I recognised as a fellow coachman from the neighbouring street. 'By Jaysus, mate, please rouse all and sundry,' he gasped in an Irish accent. 'There's not one moment to lose! We're headin' down to the courthouse to summon the fire brigade.' The Irishman's words drove me into action; dropping the brush in my hand I raced back through the stable, where ditzy Mollie stood munching her oats without a care in the world, into the basement and up the stairs. 'Fire! Fire!' I yelled, 'all out into the street this instant!'

A bemused Dr Russell appeared in the parlour doorway. 'Hold steady, my boy,' he said. 'I am sure t'is nothing the city's fire brigade cannot handle. This unseasonably hot weather has seen them fighting fires all week.' 'Beg pardon, sir!' I exclaimed. 'This fire is by far the biggest I've ever seen. T'is spreading really fast and we ourselves are directly in its path!' Dr Russell had started to reply, when I shushed him by putting my forefinger to my lips, something I'd never ordinarily have dreamt of doing to a gentleman of his standing. We both paused for an instant and listened.

Outside, the cries of terrified people were growing louder and louder, but at that moment the two of us became aware of another far more ghastly sound. T'was the roar of mighty flames coupled with the cracking of timber and shattering of glass.

Though we were not to know it at that instant, we were almost at the heart of what would become known as Chicago's Great Fire. And by now those rampant flames had stormed into the adjacent street, consuming everything that lay in their path while advancing with the howl of a tornado. Quickly retreating to from whence I'd come, I tumbled back down the stairs to the basement and out into the stable. On reaching Mollie, still steadfast that nothing would come between her and her damn oats, the acrid stench of smoke struck my nostrils like a fist and a glance outside told me the fire would fast be upon us.

I simply couldn't comprehend the haste with which it

had spread; those deadly orange tongues had darted through those wooden houses faster than a fellow could run. More and more terror-stricken people were now legging it past the stable door; frantic women clutching bawling infants to their chests, a distraught elderly lady with arms wrapped round her whining pet dog. At that instant it seemed Mollie finally became aware of her own predicament. She started to whinny and stamp her hooves as I was in the very act of untying her.

Leading her out into the back lane, I could by now feel the scorching heat of the flames less than thirty yards distant and gaining in ferocity by the instant. Mollie was starting to buck and rear when a hearty slap on her backside sent my little mare cantering down the road alongside hordes of fleeing townspeople; As I stood there helplessly watching her go I could only hope blind instinct would guide her to a place of safety. Turning back towards the house an awful thought suddenly sent me stone-cold with dread. Annie's room was on the second floor; had she managed to get out?

Back in I charged again, pounding up those stairs, heart hammering in my chest so hard I thought it'd explode. Dr Russell was emerging absent-mindedly from his study, carry-case in hand. 'God in Heaven!' I cried. 'Why are you still here, sir? The situation is dire and we must fly. The fire is upon us. Have all and sundry fled the house?'

'I have seen all flee, all but young Annie,' he replied. 'I have shouted up the stairs time and time again and hope and pray she has made good her escape. Where in Heaven's name are the blessed fire brigade?'

Afore I could reply there was an explosion of glass from upstairs and a tremendous groaning of floorboards as if the house was about to split in two: there was no mistaking it; by now an uncontrollable monster, the fire had ensnared the house firmly in its jaws. Thrusting Dr Russell in the back forcibly towards the stairs, 'you must get out now, sir!', I turned to head up the steps for the first floor, only to stop in

139

my tracks at the sight of a great wall of flames bursting forth across the landing afore me.

Heat singed my face and scorched my eyebrows, sending me toppling with a half-strangled cry backwards. I screamed and screamed for Annie fit for my lungs to burst, yet the roar of the fire, the sound of falling timber and the spreading smoke all but drowned out my cries.

What to do? I had to get through the flames come what may and a plan, borne of desperation, sprang into my mind. Tearing back into the hall I seized Dr Russell's navy trenchcoat from its stand. Draping it over my head and shoulders I once more approached the stairs which even now were fast becoming enveloped with flames.

Taking a deep breath I ran headlong into their midst; reaching the first floor landing with a supreme effort, coughing and choking. The black smoke all around me was so thick I could not have seen my hand in front of my face even if I could have extended it from within the trenchcoat. My way forward was blocked and as that chilling realisation gripped me I heard a mighty groan from above: instinctively I turned on my heels in the stark realisation that the roof was about to cave in. Feeling my way with my feet, I managed to grope my way back towards the burning bannisters, scorching my hands as I gripped them. I felt no pain, instead I was filled with an overwhelming urge to survive as a huge crash to the back of me signalled that the roof had indeed collapsed. No one beyond that point could still be alive, I knew.

Back down I stumbled, just about making out my own feet through the smoke on the precarious ascent. Gasping a lungful of smoky air on reaching the ground floor, I next plunged down the basement stairs and into the stables, now also well alight. There on the floor lay Mollie's discarded nosebag and a few scattered oats. Tottering out into the lane, all my strength suddenly abandoned me and I felt my legs go asunder. 'Don't just stand there, get some fucking water over him!' I heard someone cry.

Attempting to drag myself up on all fours, I realised that the trenchcoat that had afforded me invaluable protection moments earlier was now itself ablaze; I managed to wriggle free from its grasp just as a bucket of water, hurled by a wild-eyed youth still in his Sunday best, doused me from top to tail. Shaking my head, I retched violently, fighting to clear my lungs of the smoke that clogged them. My hands felt like they were on fire and I gazed in horrible fascination at my red-raw fingers which now resembled a row of split sausages.

The heat was getting more fierce and blind instinct told me I had to escape down the lane along which Mollie and countless numbers of our near-neighbours had previously fled. Struggling to my feet, I felt a strong, sinewy arm grip me around the midriff. 'Run for your life, lad; this is no time to dally!' said a man's terrified voice. Whoever he was jolted me back into life and I began an ungainly stumble down that lane along with all else.

But what of Annie? Had she been in her room as I feared then she must surely have perished. Why was my first thought for the horse and not that dear girl? If the fire had indeed claimed her, I'd be as much to blame for her passing as I was for Tom's, sent to the bottom of the ocean along with Frank because of the curse his own brother had maliciously wrought upon him. The rest of the night passed in a daze; having wandered from street to street, fruitlessly searching for Dr Russell and the rest of my fellow domestic staff, I ended up taking a ride in an omnibus transformed into a makeshift ambulance transporting the injured and the homeless to another part of town.

Later, in a church that became a refuge, a kind nurse bandaged the hands I had burnt in my doomed efforts to reach Annie. When I told her of my failed attempt at rescue she smiled sympathetically and, thrusting a Bible under my nose, suggested we both should pray.

'Spare me a sermon!' I cried, roughly pushing her aside. 'The fact I still live is not through God's way, but through my own frantic efforts! Would that your God have saved poor dear Annie McBride as she faced her fiery end!' I was benumbed with shock as I began to fully contemplate Annie's dreadful fate. I could have roused her sooner and made good our escape from that stricken house. Instead, by tarrying in the stable, I'd left her to those flames. The more I pondered events the more I could not countenance the fact that my first thoughts were for my blessed horse rather than Annie, when she was trapped and helpless. I blathered away to that poor nurse, probably making little or no sense, until having downed a meagre bowl of thin soup I fell silent and brooded for hours. In time I drifted off into a restless sleep.

Once my eyes were closed the flames rose again afore me and, as I fought to regain consciousness, the reproachful face of poor drowned Tom, green, bloated and distorted, swam once more before my tortured eyes. Awakening with a start, I saw the dim light of dawn alighting the giant stained glass window. I must have returned briefly to slumber 'cos next I saw Annie screaming and flailing her arms as the fire enveloped her; I could not revisit sleep again after that. I seemed to spend the next week in a state of near-paralysis, no doubt brought on by shock. I was frequently wracked by violent coughing fits which brought up lumps of ghastly black pleghm, the aftermath of my desperate dash through the inferno which had engulfed Dr Russell's home.

A doctor who examined me on the third day opined that I'd damaged my lungs by inhaling that choking black smoke and advised me to rest much. I, like so many other hapless souls, had lost all my worldly possessions short of the clothes on my back and even my woollen shirt, riddled with holes caused by flying embers, had to be discarded. Moreover, I had also lost my well-paid occupation with little prospect of finding another situation which paid a comparable wage. At least, I thought sorrowfully, I had escaped with my life, unlike poor abandoned Annie whose mortal remains or what was left of them remained buried in the charred skeletal ruins of Dr Russell's once-grand townhouse.

With nowhere to go and with no idea what had become of my employer, I remained at the shelter as the days slowly turned into weeks. Some of the nuns caring for us homeless would occasionally distribute newspapers to those who could read and from them I learnt that the great conflagration, unknown in modern times, had claimed around three hundred poor souls, destroyed four square miles of the city including the entire business district where Dr Russell's office was located, and left more than 100,000 residents homeless; of which I was now one. The fire had laid waste to much of central Chicago and somehow leapt the main branch of the river, consuming the near north side.

Help flowed in from far and wide. Although I was not to know it at first, Chicago became the recipient of a huge relief operation with tonnes of food supplies, clothes and fuel shipped in not just from all over the United States but from other parts of the world as well.

As I slowly began to recover and regain my lost strength I was unloading some supplies from a coach one morning when I glanced down at their origin and my heart skipped a beat. That tinned soup had emanated from Swansea, Great Britain, a gift of aid from my very own little country many, many countless leagues distant. My heart went out to those freemasons of that great port who had organised such a generous relief effort on behalf of bereft strangers in a distant foreign land. 'Chwarae teg, a diolch yn fawr i chi gyd,' (Fair play, and thank you very much indeed) I muttered under my breath. At that instant, and for the first and only time, I felt acute home-sickness for Yr Hen Gwlad.

As for the cause of the deadly firestorm all kind of rumours abounded. A badly-injured domestic servant in the shelter claimed it had begun in a barn near DeKoven Street after a cow knocked over a lantern while being milked. The Chicago Tribune reported a group of men playing cards in a barn were the true culprits. Maybe that was just newspaper talk but, whatever the reason, all and sundry agreed that, fanned by strong winds from the South-west, the flames had spread with rapid suddenness as much of the city's houses were composed of wood; my own narrow escape from being burnt alive bore stark testimony to that.

The drought-like conditions we'd experienced for several weeks had contributed to the flames taking hold so speedily; that and the fact firemen acting on erroneous information had been dispatched to the wrong location had combined to trigger a disaster on a scale never previously witnessed.

I remained at the shelter as winter gained its icy grip. Although I always had one spartan meal a day, a watery chowder that had ne'er seen neither a morsel of fish nor shrimp, my health remained fragile and it was not until the approach of Christmas that I set about seeking employment.

Trouble was, around 100,000 other homeless souls were all in the same boat. You'd spy an advert in the newspaper for a vacancy in a household and on arriving find a queue of applicants stretching down the street as far as the eye could see. All coachman situations seemed to have been taken while the demand for general labourers was virtually non-existent. I reasoned that in time there'd be a huge need for such workers; a quarter of Chicago would eventually need re-building, after all. But 'til then I'd have to go on living from hand to mouth and existing on the charity of the aid shelter. It was a prospect that filled me with despair. I think that had I somehow come into money at that point I'd have unhesitatingly booked my passage on the first ship back to Liverpool and taken my chances back in the old country.

I was in a dire state. At turns feverish, then dry as a

bone, beard haggard and unkempt, borrowed clothes worn and torn, plus I knew I stank like something a cat had dragged home. I was also bedevilled by a hacking cough, putting me in fear it marked the onset of consumption that had torn such a gaping chasm in my family; my mood as black as pitch. If I were to die now, I thought bleakly, no-one from home would know I was gone. I'd be buried in some pauper's grave I'd share for all eternity with a host of other unfortunates. Just like that drowned mariner who'd washed up at Cwmyreglwys in the aftermath of the Great Storm of 1859.

What on Earth would Elizabeth think if she could see me now? I pondered. This time last year the future had been so alive with promise and I truly felt the love we had for one another would last for all eternity. How quick and cruel can the wheel of fortune change! Here I was, not just down and out in Chicago, but pretty much bereft of all hope as well. . . I was not yet to know it, but fate was about to deal me a better hand; and one which would in time change my life forever.

Snow lay several inches deep on the ground as I trudged disconsolately along Grand Avenue on a bitter late January morning with the temperature almost 20 degrees below. Why bother? I asked myself as I'd set forth from the relief shelter on what I knew in my heart would amount to yet another fruitless attempt to find a situation. Wearied from my exertions and in exceedingly low spirits, I finally slumped down on the icy boardwalk, huddled into a corner outside the entrance to a gaily-lit saloon.

I lay slumped there in my borrowed tatty overcoat that wreaked of piss for some time, trying to muster sufficient vigour for the long tramp back to the shelter. It was no more than a mile distant, yet the way I was feeling it may as well have been in San Francisco. As I sat there staring dully at the endless parade of carriages and cabs clattering to and fro, a couple of well-dressed and well-fed passers-by tossed a few coins into my lap. Those fellows assume I am a homeless

145

beggar, I thought. While I might not be actually begging, I was truly homeless, and likely to remain so.

At that moment I noticed the long dark dress and boots of a young lady pause in front of me and then swivel slowly in my direction. Were yet more copper pieces about to be tossed in my direction? I pondered. Raising my head slowly I was startled to see she was peering intently down at me through the snowflakes swirling about her bonnet. We met each other's gaze and suddenly I ceased to breath. There, with a mix of joy and astonishment written all across her sweet face stood Annie, who I'd felt certain had suffered a hideous death in the great inferno!

For a few instants, neither of us spoke; just gazed at one another in silent wonder. After what appeared an interminable period it was Annie who found her voice first. For an instant she'd looked about to swoon. 'Holy Mother of God, is that really you, Will James?' she asked. 'Yes, yes, 'tis I,' I replied, struggling weakly to my feet. 'I … I thought you were lost … I thought I'd lost you in the Great Fire!' 'And I thought I'd lost you too!' she cried, blinking back tears.

There, on that bleak, windswept boardwalk, with impatient townspeople bustling past on either side clutching their top hats and bonnets as they leant into the biting wind, Annie and I shared a warm and lingering embrace. 'It's like you've returned from the dead,' she sobbed, both hands on my breast. 'And yet this is no apparition afore me. I thought I'd seen the last of you, Will. Dr Russell and I was sure you hadn't gotten outta that house alive!'

Joyfully reunited, the pair of us instantly repaired to a nearby café, Annie insisting on footing the bill once she realised the parlous financial as well as physical state I was in. 'Oh Will, jus' look at the state o' them clothes,' she said, her eyes the very picture of concern. 'I could feel them ribs o' yours through 'em. Youse look a sick man, well down on his luck. Please let me take care o' you, I beg.'

She bought me coffee, eggs and bacon and once I'd devoured that lot instantly ordered a second helping with a deft snap of her fingers. When it arrived Annie brusquely dispatched the waitress back to the kitchen having loudly taken her to task for failing to ensure my plate bore enough egg and bacon.

I couldn't help grinning when the somewhat flustered girl returned. My helping had now miraculously grown to include two fried eggs, four rashers of bacon and one considerably large sausage to boot! As the warm food started to thaw my innards, it was as if my lifeblood had started to circulate again for the first time in months. I felt renewed and replenished although I remember fearing that I was somehow still trapped in some cruel nightmare and that at any moment I'd awaken in that bleak shelter and find that Irish Annie hadn't really escaped the fire after all ...

But this was no dream. Annie really was sat afore me in that snug café; that old familiar smile on her lips. I was suddenly reminded with a pang of sadness that she was due to be married. Prior to the fire I'd been starting to think she might indeed be the girl for me; my feelings on seeing her back from the grave now confirmed that.

It transpired that she'd managed to escape the Russell residence through a back entrance after she'd heard him raise the alarm. Briefly reunited with her master in the street outside, she'd then watched in horror from a distance as the conflagration had seized hold of the townhouse, dragging it down in a fiery explosion and, they both assumed, burying poor old Will James with it.

Annie told me that Dr Russell had checked into a hotel in the aftermath of the disaster prior to heading back to Washington DC to stay with his son and convalesce. Mollie had turned up grazing on a common some miles distant a couple of days hence and was now employed in pulling the cart of a dairyman on the south side of the city. Annie herself had quickly found new employment as a domestic help and nanny to a nice family living in some style off Grand Street.

Words could ne'er do justice to the sheer joy I felt on seeing her again. As I drank my coffee and caressed her gentle face across the table I felt a huge weight on my shoulders lifting. T'was as if the horror of the Great Fire had ne'er happened. Then I came crashing back to earth on remembering that she was planning to get betrothed to that young clerk, Frank Ellis.

We met in the Harbord Cafe the next day and the day after that. On each occasion Annie happily insisted on paying for my food and drink as well as handing over a big box of her delicious flapjacks I'd always relished. She also revealed that Dr Russell had instructed her to pass on my address should our paths ever cross as he intended to pay me a handsome reward for what he said was my gallant and selfless conduct during the fire. 'You gotta regain your health, Will, and we gotta find you a job,' she'd say determinedly. Annie knew as well as I did that with so many rendered jobless, as well as homeless, such a task would not be easy.

'You thought o' signin' up for the army?' she asked unexpectedly on the third day as I tucked into a hearty repast of meat, potatoes and dumplings. 'Youse sure have a way with horses, Will, and I reckon you'd make a mighty fine cavalryman.'

I told her that I'd indeed considered the army as an occupation, although deemed it wise not to mention the awful tales Titus King had related about his time as a bluecoat. At the time I'd met that broken-down old soldier, thoughts of joining the army had receded to the back of my mind. Now I found myself clean out of choices. Perhaps, I thought, if Annie wasn't about to give her hand to another in marriage I might feel different about signing up? One way or another, I'd now never know for sure.

Annie told me of a US Army recruitment depot not

two blocks away from where we sat. I resolved there and then to pay them a visit and consider offering my services to Uncle Sam. Being so down on my luck did I even have an alternative?

Caring as ever, Annie insisted on lending me some money for clothes, adding with a playful frown that the US Army would most certainly not wish to employ someone so clearly resembling a hobo. I had to admit she most definitely had a point. I looked more like some half-starved chimney sweep than a would-be defender of the Land of the Free.

Soon afterwards, clad in fresh attire, I duly presented myself at the depot which Annie had said was in 'Brinmow Street'. Imagine my surprise when I found it located in Bryn Mawr Street; a discovery that coming so soon after the surprise of discovering the origin of that crate of tinned soup made me experience another glow of warm nostalgia! I was clearly not the first Welshman to tramp the streets of The Windy City. A sound portent, I hoped.

An appointment was duly made for me to see the officer-in-charge on the Monday morning. I spent much of the weekend at the shelter lying in my blanket weighing up the pros and cons of joining up. What would I be getting myself into, I wondered? T'was oft said that a soldier was a fellow too proud to beg, too dumb to steal and too lazy to work. But after a while I concluded I simply had no choice. Besides, I was fed up with hungering.

I duly presented myself at the depot on the Monday armed with two recommendations attesting to my fine and upright character. One had been supplied by Dr Russell a few months earlier, the other supposedly from Annie herself, 'cept as her writing was really limited an aid worker at the shelter kindly completed it on her behalf, like.

Upon arriving, I met a bunch of officers afore finding myself being interviewed by Captain Samuel Young, of the 8th US Cavalry, a tall distinguished-looking gent of traditional military bearing. Had you seen him wearing civvies on the street you'd have just known he was a cavalryman. After the interview, he said he was confident I had what it took to become a member of the famous US Seventh Cavalry.

Then came the medical performed by an army surgeon. I was made to walk briskly around the room several times. Then I had to hop, first on one foot and then t'other. How in Heaven's name this would make me into a good Indian fighter, I cannot say.

Following some acrobatics, the surgeon, a dour Scotsman with a white moustache, placed his hand on my chest and checked my heartbeat which, he said, was the slowest he'd ever heard. Despite all I'd gone through in the past three months, he then pronounced me as fit as a hare. I was next made to stand to attention while the surgeon examined my head, eyes, ears, mouth and nose and checked for any abnormalities. I was then made to stretch out my arms at right angles to my body and told to touch my shoulders with my hands, to place my hands together over my head and to turn my head and cough while the stern-faced surgeon checked for hernia.

He also studied my fingers and thumbs for dexterity as well as my chest capacity and looked over my legs to determine whether they were sturdy enough to carry my bodyweight. By now I was starting to feel like one of those prize heifers at Cardigan Show which I'd oft frequented in my youth, but the surgeon was not yet done. Finally, I had to bend over and grab my buttocks while he checked for haemorrhoids, an extremely important test considering all the hard hours riding a potential cavalry recruit faced.

Having passed the necessary hearing and eyesight tests, I was deemed fit for service, swore my duty of allegiance to Uncle Sam for the next five years, assigned to The Seventh and handed my fine new blue uniform there and then. Thirteen dollars a month to risk my life in the line of duty didn't sound like much to me, yet at least I'd be getting fed three times a day. That'd make a pleasant change from wondering where my next meal was coming from.

And like old pissed-up Titus King afore me, I'd soon be discovering at first-hand what General George Armstrong Custer, 'The Boy General' so beloved by all those newspaper folk, really was like. I could only hope King had exaggerated. The Seventh were a new regiment, having only come into being in 1866. They told me in Chicago that work was about to commence on Fort Abraham Lincoln, The Seventh's new regimental headquarters on the banks of the Missouri near a little settlement called Bismarck, deep in the heart of Dakota Territory. All the talk in town had been of waging war against the feared and hated redskins, but when I asked Young about the likelihood of action he said I'd arrived too late at the party.

'Poor Mr Lo is purty well licked,' he said, winking at an overweight sergeant who'd sat in on my interview. 'Most of them tribes are purty much back on them reservations, nowadays. If you wanted to trade bullets with them redskins way out West, boy, you're nigh on five years too late.'

As I was to discover, 'Mr Lo' was how soldiers oft referred to the red man. It was a cynical reference to a popular poem of the day which began: 'Lo! The noble savage'. For reasons I could ne'er fathom, 'John' was also a name many whites, soldiers included, used to address Indians. Anyway, I was then informed that The Seventh, the pride of the US Army since Custer licked those Cheyenne at the Washita, was a colour-coded regiment.

Noting my puzzled frown, Young explained that Custer had insisted on its formation that each troop would ride horses of a different colour. His thinking was that should a soldier become separated from his mount during the fog and confusion of battle he'd be more able to spy his comrades. As I came to appreciate, only Custer, who thought of combat morning, noon and night, could have come up with an idea like that. I was informed it dated back to the Civil War days which founded Custer's reputation. Simple, yet highly effective. Company B would ride coal-blacks, Company C roans, Company D chestnuts and so on. I was told I was being assigned to Company E, the Gray Horse Troop, who were currently stationed down in South Carolina on reconstruction duties. That was fine and dandy by me. I didn't give a bear's backside what colour mount I rode as long as it had four legs, was fit and spry and could get up to a fair old gallop.

The captain said that much of these duties down South consisted of rounding up moonshiners and breaking up their illegal distilleries as well as trying to keep a lid on the Ku Klux Klan. They had, he said, become mighty pesky in the years since the Rebs took such a kicking in the North-South war.

That fellow ne'er spoke a truer word. I was soon to find out that a lot of those folks in the Deep South treated negroes worse than a dog. Most lynchings down in those parts were blamed on the Klan, a really bad crowd who were well and truly riled the blacks had been given the vote.

The Klan were riding a big wave of popularity since war had ended six years back or so and plainly viewed us bluecoats as an army of occupation, which I suppose in a sense we were. 'If you're lookin' for some excitement, James, I can assure you that some of them rednecks will provide you some,' grinned Young. 'Judgin' how some of them folks behave down thar it's as if the Goddamn Civil War never happened.'

Annie and I arranged to meet under the big clock outside the rail depot prior to my departure. I was in a queer mood; made queerer by the fact she'd told me she'd be getting married that very Saturday. Standing outside the depot we were a bit stiff and formal at first; both a little tongue-tied, neither quite knowing what to say. 'I'm sure you'll make a good wife,' I said, putting my hand tenderly on her shoulder and trying to sound jocular. 'Just as long as you rein in that wild Irish temper of yours. Wouldn't want to be in poor Frank's shoes if you don't!'

'Can't say for sure, Will, but Lord knows I'm ready to try real hard an' make damn sure I make this work,' she smiled. 'Frank Ellis is a good man who thinks well o' me and has real ambitions. God willin', we'll one day end up livin' in a fine new town house on Burnside with lots of little ones runnin' 'bout the place.' I returned her smile, while at the same time thinking what a lucky fellow Ellis was and how, not that I'd ever have admitted it, I'd give what precious little I had just to be in his well-polished shoes at that instant.

I'd grown really fond of Annie. I could tell my feelings were reciprocated by the sparkling look in her eyes as we joshed with one another; and we'd joshed each other much. Others had noticed and remarked on it too. I fell serious for a moment. 'You know that I wish you and Frank every happiness, Annie. You deserve it more than anyone in the world. I really hope he treats you right 'cos, believe you me, a girl like you only comes along once in a fellow's lifetime.'

Annie glanced down and blushed. I could see she was starting to breath heavily. 'Betcha said that to quite a few gals in your time, huh, Will?' she replied with a brief smile. 'Indeed I have,' I responded. 'Difference is, I never meant a damn word of it 'til now … I'd never lie to you, Annie. Never in my life. You just remember that.'

Annie was looking as if she was about to cry. 'You've bin a good friend to me, Will,' she began, swallowing hard … 'and, who knows? If them cards had fallen different then maybe we'd have …' she broke off with a start as a mighty train horn screeched from inside the station. 'I have to go, Annie' I said simply, straightening up and, extremely foolishly in retrospect, offering her my outstretched hand. Annie surveyed my arm with a bemused look on her face for an instant afore smartly smacking it aside.

Afore I knew what was happening she had thrown herself at me and wrapped her arms around my neck in a tight and passionate embrace. I couldn't help but notice her chest was heaving wildly. We kissed fiercely and remained entwined for some time; passers-by must have assumed we were long-time sweethearts. Trust Will James to not only leave this special girl behind but also leave her to another, I thought bitterly. For crying out loud, would fate ever deal me a decent hand? Such a harsh twist of fortune could only happen to me!

Extracting myself with difficulty from Annie's clutches, I saw she was crying and my feeble attempts to console her proved futile. 'You ... you take good care of yourself now, do you hear?' I said, hearing my own voice break slightly. 'I'll write you soon from South Carolina with my forwarding address. Now if that doesn't give you good incentive to learn to read and write I don't know what in Heaven's name will, sweet Annie McBride!'

'I promise, Will, I promise,' she exclaimed, attempting a smile. 'But listen to me, Will. One day I knows you'll find the right gal. She may even be waitin' for you down thar in South Carolina for all I knows. One day, Will James, youse gonna make someone real, real happy ...' I couldn't find no words after that. All I could manage was a brief dumb nod of my head. And even if I'd found my tongue I wouldn't have trusted myself to say no more.

I snatched up my tiny battered suitcase, planted a quick kiss on Annie's cheek and turned and headed onto the station platform. My feelings were red-raw and even as I peered down the platform at the waiting train I wondered if I was doing the right thing. Has a man ever deserted The Seventh Cavalry on the way to his first post? I asked myself. When I reached the train carriage and turned to look back, Annie had followed me down the platform and was stood a few yards off to the side, white handkerchief pressed against trembling red lips.

For one insane moment I thought of darting across, throwing my arms around her, going down on bended knee and asking her to marry me there and then and to blazes with all those sour-faced railroad clerks stood looking on. Instead I smiled broadly, attempted what I hoped would look like a nonchalant farewell wave and climbed aboard.

But in the next instant, as the whistle harshly sounded to signal the train's departure as I took my seat it unleashed a huge wave of sorrow. I buried my head in my hands and wept, unheeding the curious looks of my fellow passengers. 'Thar, thar, young man, am sure you'll be seein' that purty gal o' yours agin purty soon right enough,' said a kindly middle-aged lady sat opposite, patting me gently on the knee.

I just looked up at her with streaming eyes, totally mute and wholly distraught. Dear, dear Irish Annie had meant far more to me than I'd ever possibly imagined, I now knew. Why on Earth did I ne'er tell her precisely how I felt? And to think it had taken the Great Fire to make me realise how much I cherished that girl … For many weeks I thought I'd lost her and then as if by some Heaven-sent miracle I'd found her again. Now, just as my feelings towards her had begun to rage like a forest fire, she'd been wrenched from my arms once more. And this time for ever.

Moments later as we clanked slowly out of the station, I could just make out the top part of Annie's arm waving slowly as we rolled past. Whether I liked it or not, I thought desolately, Chicago town and Irish Annie were already both part of my past. Another stop on my railroad of life was now firmly behind me.

Mike Lewis

CHAPTER 9

My first stop on travelling South from Chicago was Jefferson Barracks in the little town of Lemay on the banks of the Mississippi down in Missouri. I was supposed to be there for basic training which turned out to be so basic that all I ever seemed to do was march round a poky parade ground with a bunch of other bored and confused greenhorns for three weeks solid. There were no marksmanship tests or nothing which was a shame as I fancied myself a fair shot. Some of my fellow new recruits didn't look strong enough to mount a horse, let alone fight an Injun. How they got through the army medical God only knows.

Truth be told, most seemed to have trouble just sitting in the saddle as we trotted around the parade ground while this big, evil-looking sergeant bawled at us all the while as he sat with his feet up on the sidewalk chomping on a toothpick. And t'was true what they said about army chow. You wouldn't feed it to a hog. Hardtack, or 'wormscastles' as we called 'em, was supposed to be some kind of biscuit, but t'was like no other biscuit I'd encountered previous. It possessed the look and feel of a house brick, but most likely lacked the taste of one.

You had to soak the damned stuff in boiled water if you didn't fancy breaking your teeth and it was so full of worms that if you threw it out onto the yard it'd probably crawl right back. And don't talk to me about the stringy, barely-cooked helpings of rancid beef that were shovelled onto plates dotted with dumplings resembling bullets. Aye, army grub was a damn sight worse than the slop that had at least kept me alive in that Chicago aid centre. All in all, I was mightily relieved when I was told after three weeks I'd be travelling down to Unionville, South Carolina, to hook up with the Gray Horse Troop the very next day. 'You be sure to send us a letter now lettin' us knows how youse get on,' grinned the evil-looking sergeant, his foul-smelling mouth showing a line of broken teeth.

On the morning of February 26, I found myself sitting in the corner of the carriage of an East-bound train so cold I could see my breath. I was dressed in the civvies I'd bought with Annie's money having been told to skip wearing my new uniform on account it might attract some unwelcome attention from fellow passengers.

'Them Rebs, you might say, ain't too fond of our troops since we gave 'em a whippin', so chances are they won't take too kindly to some jumped-up young bluecoat who don't know his ass from his elbow,' Young had said.

'Them folks always seem to have a kinda hungry look in their eye,' he paused for effect, more for the entertainment of the lieutenant snickering in the background than anything, 'an' they're liable to look at you like you're a hunk o' raw meat!'

The train ride East took me through towns like Louisville and Charlotte, places which would become familiar over the next couple of years. I'd boarded the train South of St Louis along with some Southern fellow who, when I told him I came from England, claimed he'd worked as a horse groom for some monied family near London a few years afore.

A small, wiry little cove of about thirty with a thick mop of unruly light hair and full beard, he introduced himself as Will Hambert. When I returned the introduction he looked at me with a spark of sudden interest in his eyes. 'James, you say? Now that's kinda interesting. You wouldn't be no kin of the one and only Jesse James, now would ya, boy?' he said with a sudden cackle, as if t'was the funniest utterance ever.

I'd no need to ask him about the one-time Confederate bushwhacker, having read of his bank raids and hold-ups in all the papers. What I was not aware of 'til then, though, was that I was now venturing into that noted outlaw's backyard. I shook my head in response. 'Nope, not as far as I know,' I replied, 'but I hear that him and those Younger boys have well and truly stirred things up down in these parts.' 'They sure as Hell have,' beamed my new companion. 'Them damned Yankees may have won the war, but as long as we have the likes of Jesse and Frank James raisin' Hell, old Dixie's still alive and kickin'!'

And with that he proceeded to cup his hands to his mouth and give me a demonstration of the so-called Rebel Yell, much to the obvious annoyance and stern-faced disapproval of our fellow passengers. I'd heard the chilling Southern war cry once afore, as it happened. I'd been in a Chicago saloon when some intoxicated old Reb sat screeching in a corner had a pint pitcher whacked over his skull for his pains. Left him bleeding from the head like a pig, yet the crazy son of a gun still hadn't held his tongue.

The Rebel Yell itself came as a surprise; sounded to my ears more like the call of an angry buzzard. Yet had I been a young Union soldier at Gettysburg seeing hundreds of those maddened Johnny Rebs charging down on me opening their throats, I'd have more than likely soiled my pants.

I smiled to myself. Having told Will Hambert I was seeking work on a farm near Unionville, I wondered how he'd respond if he knew the true nature of my business there. It was possible I'd end up having a hand in the arrest of some of these old bushwhackers he so plainly admired.

Although he probably would've denied it, I marked Hambert down as a Klan supporter, maybe even a Klansman himself, as the longer we talked the more ugly his utterances became. When he described blacks getting the vote as 'an

outrage' as 'them folks ain't no more than animals', I decided
I'd heard enough. I myself didn't have any quarrel with the
blacks. Those fellows I'd met in Cardiff docks seemed right
enough and the few I'd come across in Chicago treated me a
damn sight better than a lot of white people, it has to be said.

So, explaining I'd already had a long journey, I pretended
to dose off with a copy of the St Louis Tribune draped o'er
my face. Listening to Hambert continue to rant to himself
I silently thanked those army staff back in Chicago for
insisting I dress in civvies on the journey South. Ne'er mind
the Indian-strewn Great Plains, I thought, I'd be meeting
more than my fair share of hostiles down in Dixie.

Although I'd rapidly wearied of the conversation with
Hambert, it got me thinking how fortunate I was to be able to
read and write in English. In spite of all, I suppose I had the
hated Welsh Not to thank for that, though I well recalled the
manner in which Elizabeth would spit out those two words
in absolute fury.

A person unable to read might ne'er have known about
the cruel deeds of Jesse and Frank James and the fact they
could be, for all I knew, lying in ambush for the very train
we were riding in. While Will Hambert seemed to view those
James boys as Robin Hoods of the South, I knew them from
newspaper reports as trigger-happy, ruthless outlaws who
wouldn't stop at shooting any poor soul who got in their way.

I also knew that a lot of innocent people had been
killed at the hands of the James-Younger Gang having got
caught up in the crossfire; and these were dirt-poor Southern
folk like those outlaws themselves. That just didn't sit right
with me.

Unionville turned out to be a non-descript little
farming town full of rednecks. I'd seen much poverty in
Llanelly and London, but here it was a whole lot worse. In
Unionville t'was commonplace to see three or four people
sat astride the same horse and whites seemed just as bad off

as the blacks. E Troop, my new company, were stationed just South of the town, garrisoned with B Company, the Black Horse Troop. Welcoming me to Unionville, the words of one of the company sergeants were less than encouraging. 'Well, I sure hope this kid lasts longer than Stump,' he gestured over to a watching corporal. I duly found out that Pvt Byron Stump had died of disease the week afore, just 48 hours after arriving as a new recruit.

Three companies of the Seventh had been dispatched to Unionville when martial law was declared two years previous. I learnt that eleven local blacks had been rounded up and jailed after a one-armed Confederate war veteran was shot dead. Word spread quickly around town and a mob of men, women and children had stormed the jail, chased away the sheriff and his deputies, seized the suspects, dragged them out into the main street and stretched their necks one by one. Martial law was declared the next day.

The barracks were alive with tales about the hostile locals. 'Damned Yankees' was one of the more repeatable insults thrown at us by resentful townsfolk. Riding through Unionville you'd be liable to have all manner of things flung at you ranging from a bucketful of piss to a Bowie knife or a flurry of snowballs in the dead of winter.

Nothing summed up local hatred of federal troops better than the sad death of one Pvt Cushman the previous year. The young trooper had fallen hard for a Unionville girl, only to have his dreams of matrimonial bliss ended by the diagnosis of syphilis. After brooding upon this for a time in a local saloon, the anguished Cushman blew his own brains out in a fit of melancholy. Now Cushman had been a God-fearing farm boy from New York State and his commanding officer somehow gained permission for him to be laid to rest in the local churchyard. What the Unionville folk did was bury the young fellow in the remotest part of the plot; well away from respectable Southerners, like. 'Those two-faced bastards buried Cushman facing South,' one trooper snorted, in between vicious spits of tobacco. 'That ways they'd made sure he'd be faced away from the North come Judgement Day.'

Oh aye, how those townspeople hated us Yankees. And the feelings us bluecoats had for them was mutual. We were only ever allowed into town in groups, ne'er on our own, and dust-ups with the locals were still commonplace.

I must confess that after a while I found the way they held us in such contempt a tad wearing. A greenhorn like myself had played no part in the North-South conflagration that'd pitted blue against grey, countryman against countryman, brother against brother. Though I suppose, looking at it rationally, a lot of Unionville folk had probably lost kin to bluecoat bullets. Their feelings of hate were directed at the uniform and all it represented rather than the dumb young Welsh fellow wearing it. At least, that's what I liked to think.

So Unionville remained our station for the next twelve months. And they were twelve pretty long and monotonous months, I confess, when time just seemed to drag. The worst period was when I was put on extra duties as a hospital attendant for two whole months. Don't know what I could e'er have done to deserve that. Must have looked the wrong way at one of those mean-minded sergeants, I suppose.

Working in the hospital was a job we all feared and hated as the prospect of contracting some deadly virus was high. People back up North would have been taken aback at the high incidence of disease among troops. During my time in hospital I saw fellows die of yellow fever, scarlet fever, cholera and consumption. There were no end of ways for a fellow to exit this life. The stench of death, vomit and disinfectant drew painful reminders of those harrowing weeks leading up to Father's death. God in Heaven, his sad passing now seemed several lifetimes ago.

I learnt that the rate of sexual disease always shot

up when we were based down South. The Northern Great Plains were pretty much bereft of women; leastways, the type of women a decent fellow would wish to consort with. Any unmarried woman in the vicinity of a fort was likely to be diseased. Aside from those laundresses of Fort Lincoln and the women on the hog ranches of Whiskey Point on the opposite bank of the Missouri, you never so much as spied anyone of the fairer sex who was available, shall we say. The officers' wives, of course, were strictly off-limits even if, as I was to discover later, one or two did seem to take more than a passing interest in us buck privates.

It was a damn sight different down South with Unionville and its fleshpots just a short ride away. And while most of the local menfolk seemed to go out of their way to show their disdain for these invading Yankee bluecoats, some of the womenfolk had an eye for a strapping young fellow in uniform. It's fair to say that attention from Southern women was a rare treat for what we fellows of the lower ranks grew to regard as a pretty tiresome and unrewarding situation. Yet there was oft a price to pay; followed by a swift appointment with the regimental surgeon.

I hadn't been in Unionville long afore I had my first real trouble, and it was served up by a fellow trooper, not one of those evil-looking fellows who still toted the grey Johnny Reb uniform in their dreams at night.

Pvt Riley was viewed as the troublemaker of E Troop; a fellow who oft settled arguments with his fists and was generally deemed as someone to steer wide of once he'd partaken of a few bevvies; which was pretty much ev'ry night. For some reason, he seemed to take a dislike to me and on one occasion when me and the boys were sat drinking in a downtown saloon came up very drunk, stuck his scarred and whiskered face in mine and, unleashing a stream of foul oaths, demanded that we go outside to settle our differences like men.

He was so intoxicated that I think he mistook me for some other fellow. And I don't know what exactly were the differences he was referring to, 'cos up til that night I couldn't recall ever exchanging one single word with the oaf. 'Why bother?' I enquired to his offer of a street fight, 'why let the rain spoil my fine new uniform when we can settle our differences right here?' With that, rising in an instant and stepping quickly forward, I snapped a sharp punch to his face which caught him unawares and sent him staggering back.

All present sprang to their feet, our table getting knocked over, beer flying all around. Riley hadn't been expecting such a riposte, but numerous bouts of fisticuffs in the pubs of Dinas and Newport and fairgrounds of Narberth and Haverfordwest had taught me that he who smites the first blow oft prevails. And sometimes it could only take one punch.

Riley next rushed at me with clenched fists, foaming like a mad dog, which is precisely what I'd hoped. Ducking smartly under his wild left swing I unleashed a second blow at his ugly visage, straight and true. Riley's nose split, spurting claret, and the force of the blow again sent him hurtling backwards several feet, only the bar itself keeping him upright. Taking a couple of swift paces for'ard, I let fly with the right once more, the heaviest blow I'd thrown up to that point, finding the point of his jaw and sending him toppling sideways like a falling tree. Riley landed quite insensible on the sawdust and beer-strewn floor with a force that cracked a floorboard and sent bottles crashing off shelves.

'Boy,' I heard one old fellow say softly behind me. 'That young Yankee sure knows how to use them fists o' his.' Riley was just like one of the many loud-mouthed braggarts I'd previously encountered, but unlike a lot of those kind of fellows he never knew when he was licked. Although I'd seen him off in that first kerfuffle I felt pretty sure there'd be another and, as usual, my instincts were proved right.

About a fortnight later, a group of us had gone into town and Riley had once again got steaming drunk to the point he'd been thrown out onto the sidewalk at two different establishments. Believe me, a fellow had to be really intoxicated and objectionable for that to happen in a town like Unionville.

Wearied from a long day, I'd gone ahead back to camp and was dead asleep in my blanket when I was suddenly awoken by a sharp blow to the face. Hands clawed and gripped at my throat and I was yanked, half-conscious, from my berth.

Trying to clear my head I saw Riley's enraged features pressed right up against my face. He was in the midst of yelling a stream of wild oaths and threats when, seeing my opportunity, I lunged forward and sank my teeth hard into his conk, causing him to squawk like a prairie chicken and unleash his grip. As he tottered backwards, clutching his snout and howling, I straightaway threw three hard punches to his unguarded breadbox in quick succession, right ... left ... right, doubling him up and taking the wind right out of his sails. 'Urghhhh!'

I followed these with a mighty big blow upwards, beginning from somewhere down near my ankles, to send him crashing down heavily, spreadeagled on his back. Afore Riley could move I leapt atop him knees first, an old street-brawling trick aimed at busting a fallen man's ribs. Knowing what a lunatic I was up against, I was intent on beating him senseless afore he could wreak any further havoc.

But old Riley was possessed with the strength of half-a-dozen men as, locked together, we wrestled, spat and clawed at one another in the dirt while all those young bluecoats remained glued to their beds, cowering under their blankets. None of those gallant young soldier boys wished to get involved in what they felt sure was a fight to the death.

After a couple of minutes of fierce grappling, with

Riley still cursing wildly and loudly questioning my parentage, he somehow ended up face down on the ground with me perched high on his back; all I needed was a saddle, bridle, spurs and bit and I'd have been sat pretty. I punched him again and again in the back of the skull, so hard and with such fury that I felt sharp stabbing pains shoot up my arms as my fingers bust. Unable to use my fists no more, I seized the fellow's shock of greasy black hair instead and slammed his head again and again into the rock-hard ground. 'Ugh! Ugh! Ugh!' grunted Riley, though he was not yet done.

Spying out the corner of my eye an iron poker lying next to the wood stove I snatched it up and, ramming it under the fellow's chin, repeatedly wrenched it upwards with both hands in an attempt to choke him senseless. 'Ngrrhhgh! Ngrrhhgh! Ngrrhhgh!' gurgled Riley yet, Heavens to Betsy, still the fellow struggled! Withdrawing the poker, I was raising it above my head with both hands just as Riley glanced around to see what was happening. As he did so I brought the poker down hard on his cranium with every last ounce of strength I still possessed, like a blacksmith's hammer smiting an anvil. DONG!

The metallic clang of iron on skull must have been heard the length and breadth of Unionville, a mile or so distant. Brought me to mind of the chimes of Big Ben back in London! That finally did the trick, thank God. Old Riley was out cold and didn't stir from his induced slumber for a good six or seven hours. The poker fared little better; it was left as bent and misshapen as a cucumber. When I spied Riley's sullen visage the next morning it gave me grim satisfaction to see a set of teeth marks on his nozzle and a poker-shaped line of blue bruises down the front of his ugly face; almost as if the force of that mighty blow had carried clean through his thick skull. Most likely it was caused when I'd repeatedly driven Riley's dumb head into the ground.

Thanks to that marble-headed mucksnipe I was unable

to attend all my duties for a while on account of my broken fingers, swollen fat as plums. The fact I'd well and truly licked Riley again made no difference to his dealings with me. Despite being part of the same company, we remained sworn enemies and when he was in drink I was always wary lest he pulled his six-shooter out.

On arriving at Unionville, I'd quickly found out that e'ery soldier seemed to have a nickname. Discovering I hailed from Wales, some of my English-born comrades took to calling me 'Welshie' or 'Taffy' at first, but after my little dust-up with Riley they'd settled on Calamity James.

Much later, when we were stationed back down in the Deep South, John Ogden and 'Irish' Tom Eagan, two of the fellows I got to know best, sometimes addressed me as 'Jesse', a reference to my namesake, Jesse James, who was still causing no end of trouble in the Southern states around those times. No-one else did though and the nickname never really stuck. Perhaps I should have bade them to call me Ishmael.

***

Arthur Nicholas pulled up his collar and buried his hands in his pockets as he trudged up Prendergast Hill from the centre of Haverfordwest, striving to steer a path around the vast puddles of mud on the road before him. Occasionally, a passing cart or carriage would plough through the mess, causing the lone pedestrian to take evasive action in order to avoid a spattering.

In spite of these attempts, Arthur looked down in growing dismay as a steady pattern of mud made his best office trousers increasingly resemble those of a farmhand. Yet onwards he strode, purposefully leaning forward into the wind and rain; taking a mental note of the numbers of the houses he passed. There, as anticipated, was the Bull Tavern; the Prendergast Cafe a little further on. The waft of coffee and cake as he strode by almost persuaded the young solicitor to duck inside for some respite from the elements, but Arthur was a man on a mission: today he had made an appointment to see WBJ's sole surviving sibling: his elder sister Mary, a 65-year-old widow who lived with a grandson at No 95, Prendergast.

Mary Lloyd, a small, grey-haired, petite lady with a slight stoop, welcomed him warmly into her tiny terraced home. On enquiring whether he preferred conversing in Welsh or English (Arthur opted for the latter), she insisted on serving him tea and welshcakes despite his protests to the contrary. 'Shame my grandson Tom isn't here to meet you,' she added. 'That boy is the spitting image of our Will, he is.' Mary said she had been greatly intrigued by Arthur's compulsion to find her lost brother, although she held out little prospect of his quest proving successful. 'I don't know, Mr Nicholas,' she said doubtfully, 'I personally question whether dear William still lives. Had he indeed survived this long in America I find it hard to believe he would not have maintained contact with his only surviving sister after the Grim Reaper laid waste to our family.'

As Arthur sat in Mary's small parlour nibbling welshcakes and sipping tea, she told him a little about herself. 'I married James Lloyd, a dairy merchant from this place, at Dinas Church back in October 1862,' she said. 'Mr Lloyd was a good 25 years older than I, but t'was a good marriage and he a good husband. I bore him eight children and we had a good life through working hard and enjoying the rewards.

'We worked and resided in west London during the 1870s and three of our children were born there. Aye, looking back, those were indeed the best days of our lives. We never planned on staying, though. We wanted to come home as we felt Pembrokeshire was a better place to raise the little ones. After a while we both tired of the stench of London, as well as its grime.'

The hardship, she continued, had descended on her husband's death in 1892. Mary had been forced to sell their large farm of Greenfields on the Cardigan Road and had decamped a short distance away to her current modest abode. 'A different life entirely,' she conceded. 'But I'm getting older now and material possessions no longer seem as important. All my siblings died young and their passing made me appreciate my own good health.'

Her memories of WBJ were disappointingly few. 'Will? He was what our mam would call a bachgen drwg (naughty boy),' she smiled. 'Always up to mischief, always getting into trouble, although at heart he was a good boy who'd have given you his last farthing if he had one. You have to remember, Mr Nicholas, that I was ten years older than Will, a considerable gulf in age when you are young. And Will must have been only about six or seven when I left Pencnwc for a servant's job and never really went back.

'Will left home for Narberth when he was 15 or 16 and I saw precious little of him for a long time after. When Mr Lloyd and I moved up to West London to work at Portman Market Will sent us a telegram from Llanelly saying he was moving up as well.'

Mary paused, raised a hand to her mouth and coughed. 'When Will turned up on our doorstep it was the first we'd seen of him in quite a few years,' she said. 'How did he seem to you?' Arthur wanted to know. 'Oh, he was pretty much the same old Will,' she said. 'Happy go lucky and with an eye for the ladies although he told us he had a sweetheart called Elizabeth back in Newport and that their romance was very strong.

'Seemed to write to him every blessed day, she did, and he to her. Then they parted company and ...' Mary's voice trailed away and her smile faded. 'And he took it badly?' Arthur enquired. 'Yn anfodus, wir,' (Unfortunately, yes) she nodded. 'Very, very badly, I'm afraid. He started drinking much and staying out all night. My husband had employed Will as a market porter to help give him a leg-up in London but he started not showing up for work, which was not like him at all. We were both terribly worried about him.

'Will told me that Elizabeth was the great love of his life and that he'd never get over losing her. I thought of telling Mother of my concerns, but she'd just buried my two younger sisters and I had no wish to add to her burden.

'Soon after him and Elizabeth finished, Will suddenly announced he was sailing to America to start anew, as he put it. I begged him to write and let us know how he was, but apart from one short note we received from Toronto we never heard anything more from him from that day to this. To this day I earnestly hope he'll get in touch, but after all these years I think it highly improbable.'

'A difficult question to put to you, Mrs Lloyd, but how would you describe Will as a person and what do you think he might be doing now?' asked Arthur intently. As his investigation progressed he was starting to feel more and more like one of those detectives he enjoyed reading about. Mary sighed and looked down at her hands on her lap. Arthur noticed she was gripping her left hand with her right very tightly. He suspected this conversation was becoming somewhat harder than Mary had anticipated.

'Like I said, Will was a bit of a boy who got up to a fair amount of mischief,' she said guardedly. 'But at heart he was good as gold. The thing about the young Will was he didn't like school at all. Hated being reminded of his time at Peniel. I'm sure something really bad happened there. Tom, my eldest brother, tried to drag it out of him but Will flatly refused to even talk about it, he did.

'As his big sister I was pretty sure Will must have had some bad beatings but, not being that close to him, I could never find out if that was indeed the case. There again, Tom was much closer to him, yet he never got nowhere either. As for what he's up to now it'd have to be something to do with horses, I'd imagine.'

Arthur then told her what his mam had said. That despite always landing up in scrapes WBJ would invariably find a way of getting out of them. Mary laughed, her earlier pensiveness seeming to vanish. 'Your mam, bless her, ne'er spoke a truer word,' she chuckled. 'Our father was fond of saying that if you threw Will into the most tempestuous sea, he'd always bob to the surface like a cork; and that boy didn't really know how to swim. Splashed so much folk oft thought he was drowning!

'Oh aye, Will always knew how to survive all right and, while most of the time I think he may be no more, sometimes I think he is still out there somewhere. Will being Will, he'd only get back in touch if he truly wanted to. He was not known as 'Will o' the Wisp' for nothing, you know!'

Mary paused, raised two fingers to her lips and seemed momentarily lost in thought. 'There is someone else you really should talk to,' she told Arthur. 'Someone who might have a better idea of what Will got up to in America and might even be able to shed some light on where he dwells now ...'

Trying to hide his rising excitement, Arthur clasped his hands together and leant forward in his chair expectantly. 'Elizabeth, that girl from Newport I told you he was seeing while staying with us in London,' she went on. 'Like I said, Will was terribly fond of her and they were together for some time. Everyone thought they would end up getting married. They would have made a handsome pair, for sure.'

'Didn't you say that when they parted Will took it really badly?' enquired Arthur. 'Bearing that in mind what makes you think they could still be corresponding?'

'I'm not saying they are now, but Elizabeth might have information that I don't,' came the reply. 'Like I said, those two were very close for a time. I well recall Will saying Elizabeth had been his rock around the time our sisters

Ann and Ellen passed away. She helped pull him through, apparently. He said he didn't know how he'd have managed without her. She was called Elizabeth Morgans, but I don't know what name she goes under now. I know she still lives in Newport having married a master mariner and that they have a number of children.

'I came across Elizabeth at my brother John's funeral at Brynhenllan last year. First time I'd seen her in more than thirty years. We had a brief conversation afterwards, wished each other well and then went our separate ways. Had Elizabeth still been in touch with Will I imagine she would have imparted such news to me as his sole surviving sibling, but you should still speak to her.'

While Mary was talking, Arthur recalled more than one reference to 'my sister-in-law from Newport' in the WBJ letters. Of course, those letters were written in Victorian times and in the custom of that period WBJ might simply have been being courteous. Arthur, however, couldn't help thinking there was more to it than that. Who was this woman, he wondered?

He assured Mary that he would indeed track down the erstwhile Elizabeth Morgans, even if she could not remember her married name. 'If you do, please be sure to pass on my best regards to her,' she said, 'but there is something important you need to know first ...' Arthur cocked his head to one side. Mary paused again, pursing her lips, as if unsure whether to impart such personal family information to this earnest young stranger sat before her. 'Oh, why not?' she asked eventually, as if addressing herself, 't'is common knowledge back home and t'was an awful long time ago anyway ...'

Looking across at her inquisitor she took a deep breath and said: 'Before Elizabeth and Will got together she was seeing my eldest brother, Tom. Then, after she and Will parted company Elizabeth went off to Cardiff and married

Tom, without her parents' consent, I understand. A few days after that Tom set sail for China aboard The Avon and the ship was lost with all hands in the English Channel; Frank, my youngest brother, among them.'

Arthur was shocked at this revelation, although coming from Dinas he was only too well aware of the grim mortality rate among local mariners in the last century. 'How terrible,' he muttered. Mary nodded. 'The poor girl came back to Newport a widow, after just a few days of married life. Shut herself away in the family farm of ... Penfeidr, I think it was called. Very big farm out there on the Cwm Gwaun road. Took her an awful long time to get over it by all accounts.

'The loss of The Avon affected so many families locally, although ours was hit hardest, of course. It was Frank's first long sea voyage and it was Tom who'd signed him up. I think what persuaded Frank to go was that Tom really wanted someone from our family to be there in Cardiff when he married Elizabeth. So Frank agreed to attend the wedding before setting sail with his elder brother and the two of them never came back.

'Growing up, Tom had always been something of a firebrand. One of those fellows who'd act on impulse without so much as a thought for the consequences. But at the time of his death he'd straightened himself out and had so much to live for; he'd just got married having gained his master mariner's certificate and was very close to taking charge of his own ship which is what he'd always wanted. Yet there you go, Mr Nicholas, none of us know what's around the corner, do we? Life is what happens to you when you're busy making other plans ...

'I must have next seen Elizabeth a year or so afterwards. The poor girl had suffered much. I didn't know her family but heard her father had greatly disapproved of her marriage to Tom. She told me she'd locked herself away for months, stricken with grief. My sister visited Elizabeth often, bless her, kept insisting she speak to her and encouraging her to come out and in time, I suppose, helped her get straight.

'Some time later, while they were out together in Newport, Elizabeth had a bit too much of the drink, got very upset and confessed to my sister she'd never stopped loving Will. She said they'd made a pact to meet up as spirits atop Carningli Mountain once they'd both passed and that she couldn't wait to join him in eternal life. She said she just knew he'd be sat up there looking out for her if he passed first.

'My sister was greatly troubled and told me she feared Elizabeth might try to do away with herself. Elizabeth gave up the drink completely soon afterwards, I believe, and her life has worked out for the best. I gather she now lives in one of the finest houses in Newport. After all that went on she deserves every happiness, I'm sure you'll agree.

'Yes, you really should contact Elizabeth, I think she'd be glad if you did. And by all means tell her t'was I who suggested you get in touch.' Mary was now on her feet, her hand extended. 'It's been a pleasure speaking with you, plesur iawn, (a big pleasure) but now I must busy myself and be off to the shops,' she smiled. 'Pob lwc! (Good luck!) I wish you all the very best with your continuing enquiries, young man. I do hope you are successful and establish the fate of my dear brother.'

Arthur had enjoyed conversing with this kind and friendly widow and as he left Mary's home he thought how thrilled she would be if he did indeed succeed in tracing WBJ or, at the very least, discover his ultimate fate. For all the ongoing attempts to find WBJ out in the American Deep South, the young solicitor had a growing hunch that a breakthrough in the case might be made closer to home; and that the former Elizabeth Morgans, who he had now established was 'the sister-in-law from Newport' in the WBJ letters, could well provide it.

CHAPTER 10

Our soldiering duties down South were in the main helping US marshals in arresting those who'd fallen foul of internal revenue laws and trying to prevent blacks from being strung up by night-riding Klansmen. Those hateful fellows preached the word of Christ, yet their work was that of the very Devil. The first time I saw a Klan rally, honest to God, I could just feel the hairs on the back of my neck stand up. All those silent marching figures clad in hoods, colourful masks and pointed hats that brought to mind the dunce's hat at Peniel; they left me more spooked than even those eerie death songs our Indian scouts would sing. If this was what religion did to some people then I was well off out of it, I decided. No wonder those wretched negroes feared and despised the Klan so much. Rounding up Klansmen and running them out of town was some relief from the monotony of raiding illegal distilleries, I suppose, but it was not what we'd signed up for, for the princely wage of thirteen dollars a month.

As time passed it became obvious that the old hands of the regiment were starting to itch for a return to the Great Plains. From what we kept hearing, and newspaper reports bore this out, Mr Lo was back to his usual tricks in Montana, Dakota and Wyoming Territories; killing a few settlers here and there; thieving horses and cattle, driving homesteaders off their properties, burning ranches to the ground and generally making something of nuisance of himself. Much of the barrack-room talk centred on the Seventh going back up North to settle what we regarded was unfinished business with the Sioux and Cheyenne. As things worked out we wouldn't have long to wait.

One thing I learnt quick as a new recruit was how much soldiers loved to bellyache. The army had just replaced the Seventh's tried and tested seven-shot Spencer carbines with single-shot breech-loading Sharps. This had not gone down well with a regiment whose more experienced officers and men had used the Spencer to great effect against gray troopers in the North-South war. While dropping a Spencer butt first could set off a disastrous discharge which no doubt caused many a luckless trooper to have his foot or some other part of his anatomy blown off, a lot of our officers were reluctant to give them up.

Although the Sharps were said to have an effective killing range of 500 yards, their rate of fire was said to be four shots per minute at best, much slower than the old Spencers. The big problem with the Sharps, the first weapon in The Seventh I ever fired, was the flashback. The sharp front breech block cut through the paper on the inserted cartridge for ignition by the percussion cap. After a time, loose powder would get ground between the breech and the block and could cause an additional burn when fired. The powder could foul the works so much that the lever couldn't even be forced back into position.

A regular beef in the barracks was that the US Army were having to deal with a penny-pinching government as well as Mr Lo on the Great Plains and our Klansmen friends down South. By the time of my arrival in Unionville all of the Seventh's Gray Horse Troop were equipped with . 50 caliber Sharps and . 44 caliber Colt pistols. Like it or not, the Spencers were a thing of the past. As soldiers we had to make the best of our lot and just get on with it. The Seventh was always afflicted with a high rate of desertion; at one point one in five troopers who'd signed up for Uncle Sam were said to have taken flight as snowbirds once the winter snows on the plains had gone.

The horse assigned to me was called Scout, a sturdy little gelding of six years of age whose previous owner had done a moonlight flit when the company had shipped out to Kentucky the previous year. I wanted to rename Scout 'Soldier', the name of Father's faithful old Shire Horse back in Pembrokeshire all those years afore, 'til I surmised that by persistently shouting the horse's new name I'd unwittingly cause mass confusion in the mounted ranks! So Scout he was and Scout he would remain. He wasn't by no means the biggest horse in the regiment, but in time I'd come to appreciate he had a really big heart. Best mount I ever rode by a country mile.

Finally, in March of 1873, the regiment was ordered out of the Department of the South and back to Dakota where Fort Abraham Lincoln, our brand-new headquarters, was under construction. I and my fellow Gray Horse Troopers assembled at Memphis, Tennessee, that spring, full of expectation at what the coming months would bring. From there we marched to the little town of Cairo where, by all accounts, the Klan had been even more troublesome than down in Unionville. Here we boarded a northbound train, horses, equipment, provisions, the lot. The long rail journey took many days as we had frequent stops en route to feed and water the horses, but eventually we arrived in the town of Yankton, Dakota Territory.

This was my first visit to the northern plains which stretched as far as the eye could see, whilst above us hung the biggest sky man had ever laboured beneath. The landscape was so vast we might as well have been a column of ants crawling across it. You could lose my own little country many, many times over in this huge, hostile wilderness, I thought.

As I was to find, the weather of the plains could change faster than a woman's moods. It was while loitering in Yankton, waiting for our wagons as well as for the ice to clear on the Missouri, that we were struck by the worst-

ever blizzard we'd ever encounter on the plains; and in early
May as well! I ne'er forgot that storm. We were camped on
the outskirts of town over by the rail road tracks when the
blizzard hit and conditions were so bad that night that, with
no sign of any lull, our officers gave the unprecedented order
for every man to take their mounts into town and try and
find what shelter they could. Had they not done so scores of
soldiers and their horses would have froze to death.

Once in Yankton, some of the enlisted boys landed on
their feet and were put up in some of the town's best hotels
and treated to some decent chow, all at Uncle Sam's expense!
A few other fellows ended up as guests in the homes of
sympathetic Yankton townsfolk while still others, including
myself and my good friend, Pvt John Ogden, made do with
bedding down in a large stable attached to the Tavern In
The Town, while what became known as 'Custer's Blizzard'
howled and raged outside like a thousand wild beasts.

Though there were times the groaning timber supports
made us fear the whole stable would crash to earth around
us, there was enough dry straw inside to keep us warm as
cats. In addition, the plentiful supply of beer supplied by the
innkeeper, a one-time Union soldier, and his two sweet young
daughters certainly helped as well! Those kind people even
laid on fine breakfasts of eggs, bacon, grits and oatmeal each
morning. Aye, it was good to be in Dakota Territory after a
year living amongst murderous rednecks!

There was another thing I'd remember about Yankton:
that was where I first clapped eyes on the redoubtable General
George Armstrong Custer. He was tall and slim, a spare,
lithe, sinewy figure with bright, dark, quick-moving blue eyes;
florrid complexion, light, wavy curls, high cheekbones, firm-
set teeth, probably weighing around 170 pounds, and very
energetic. Sort of like those hummingbirds you'd sometimes
spy flitting from flower to flower in the Deep South. Aye,
I thought to myself as I surveyed him carefully, the type

of fellow completely incapable of staying still; not e'en for an instant. He wore a close-fitting blue cavalry jacket, high Wellington boots slightly above the knees, the type very popular among cavalry officers, Spanish spurs and golden aiguillettes; plainly the sort of fellow who went to some considerable lengths to ensure he stood out in a crowd, like.

Sometime later, when we were garrisoned at Lincoln, I remember one of the company sergeants warning me to always make sure I was doing something in Custer's presence 'even if it's only doin' up your Goddamned bootlaces', otherwise Ol' Iron Butt would bawl me out. If there was one thing he hated more than doing nothing it was seeing his troops doing nothing. It was said that Christmas Day was Custer's least favourite day of the year as it just meant idly lounging around the fort listening to music concerts or performing plays and suchlike when he'd far rather be out on the plains hunting Indians.

So now, as I gave a weary, sweating Scout a much-needed brush-down and bag of oats, here in front of me was the famed Boy General of the North-South conflict; the dashing cavalier whose stirring exploits had so enthralled thousands of Union-supporting newspaper readers. From what I can recall he was wearing his hair long, a tawny shade of yellow, something like old Buffalo Bill used to wear. He also toted a big, wide-brimmed western stetson, which I found out later was an old Confederate hat aimed at protecting his pale skin from the sun, and a long, twirling military moustache, which so many of his officers, at least the ones who would go on to become members of the so-called Custer Clan, would copy. In short, he looked the epitome of the bold, daring young cavalry officer that readers of the Northern press had come to expect. No wonder they hung on his every word and deed.

On leaving Yankton, the entire regiment set off on a 500-mile overland march, up the East bank of the Missouri River to Fort Randall and Fort Sully afore arriving at our final destination of Fort Rice. The further North we marched the more our spirits rose. We had a wagon train behind us and a flat-bottomed steamer keeping apace along with the column which must have stretched back for a mile or two. Spring had arrived on the plains and we troops would ride in columns of fours through vast carpets of colourful wild flowers, mosses and grasses, marvelling at the wondrous birdsong resounding all around.

General Custer and his better half would parade at the head of the procession, with a few scouts thrown out in front, of course. Flankers were posted out wide to increase our chances of detecting any hostiles, while a full company brought up the rear behind the wagons. The Seventh Cavalry on the march must have made an impressive sight. That long march North would remain one of my happiest memories as a US cavalryman.

At Fort Rice my fighting reputation was further enhanced. One evening a bunch of us, including a sergeant from F called Mason, were off duty and heading towards the sutler's store for a bottle of beer or two and maybe a game of checkers or whist.

I viewed Mason as something of a blowhard, e'en though he ne'er took a backward step. He was one of those fellows who always had some sort of beef or other and if there wasn't no trouble to be found could always be relied upon to stir up some. The following year he'd be reduced to the rank of private for gross neglect of duty on the Black Hills expedition only to re-enlist in '75 and get assigned to E. That fellow always seemed to harbour a grudge against Hohmeyer for some reason.

As we approached the store three or four Ree Indian scouts were loitering outside, conversing in their native tongue. As Mason drew abreast of the first, a young brave of perhaps 16 or 17, he turned on his heel and, with no warning whatsoever, slapped the fellow hard across the cheek with his open palm. Don't know who was the most taken aback, us or those Rees. Shocked as Hell, the young Ree staggered back on the sidewalk clutching his stinging face and then cried out in perfect English: 'What the Hell was that for? I didn't say nuthin!' The scowling Mason was unrepentant. 'That was for what you was thinkin',' he hissed. It was so unjust and uncalled for that I just had to speak up. For an instant I felt I was back in Peniel. 'What in God's name is wrong with you?' I heard myself demand to Mason. 'Those Rees are good people and when we pick a fight with the Sioux and Cheyenne they'll be on our side once the shooting starts. Why in Hell's name can't they converse in their own tongue?'

Clearly rooting for a fight, Mason now turned his hate-filled face towards me. Stepping forward, head cocked to one side, so close that we were now little more than a foot apart, he cupped his hand to his ear and enquired sarcastically: 'What's that you say, Welshie? Best speak up now 'cos I'm a little hard o' hearin'. 'You can hear me well enough, so now hear this,' I replied coolly. 'You apologise to that young fellow; maybe even offer to buy him a beer. All of us can then go inside to slake our thirsts and just forget that this unfortunate little misunderstanding e'er took place.' For an instant no-one moved nor spoke; just stood there eyeing one another up and down.

The atmosphere was tight-taut as it always is afore all Hell breaks loose. The other fellows were standing back to see how it all played out as were the Rees, one of whom I noticed with alarm was stealthily sliding a hand towards his holster. That fool Mason could get himself shot here, I thought. And maybe a couple of us as well. At first I thought the mule-headed ruffian had seen the folly of his ways and was ready to back down. Couldn't have been more wrong. 'No fuckin' immigrant trash fresh off the Goddamn boat tells me whadda do,' he snarled. 'You just made the biggest mistake o' your life, Welshie. Am gonna spank you a damn sight harder than your momma ever did, boy. You'd best start sayin' your prayers.'

This was the moment to pull a trick I'd come up with as a street-fighting young buck. When an adversary squared up close spoiling for a fight I'd misdirect my gaze over his shoulder and suddenly widen my eyes, all startled, like. The ruse worked every single time, believe me. My opponent would turn his head back sharply, afeared someone was stealing up on him from behind, afore snapping it back my way. Trouble was, he'd turn straight into my right hand travelling at the speed of an oncoming freight train. And it'd slam right into his jaw, sending him down instantly insensible.

While I knew damn-all about physics, it seemed that the twisting of the head directly into the punch heightened the effects of the knockout blow. Even a moderate punch thrown in such circumstances would render a fellow senseless, I reckoned. Everyone who fell victim to my 'goodnight punch', as I called it, was dispatched straight into instant slumber. I demonstrated the technique to Tom who duly used it to drop a drunken six-foot tar who'd pulled a knife on him in a tavern down in Cardiff docks. That sly little ploy dug me out of trouble no end of times.

And so it proved at Fort Rice. Mason was the perfect patsy, as they'd have said back in Chicago. I threw a fearful look over his shoulder which he fell for hook, line and sinker. He shot a look behind and turned his dumb fool head back just as I drove home the nose-ender to end all nose-enders. Not even a .44 caliber bullet fired point blank from a Colt would've had such a startling effect. Mason's head jerked back violently and he crashed heavily to the sidewalk on his back senseless, feet twitching, raised fists frozen in a fighting stance. The young Ree he'd slapped jumped backwards off the sidewalk in shock. 'Holy Christ!' exclaimed Ogden. 'You sure carry some fuckin' dynamite in them fists o' yours, James!' Later that night he'd jest I could make a handsome living as a prizefighter on leaving the army; with him pocketing most of the takings as my handler and manager!

Two of the boys hoisted Mason up and bore him back to barracks where he lay dead to the world for several hours. Me and the rest got on with our evening. Even treated that young Ree and his chums to some beer as it happened. Yet it wasn't a case of me sticking up for some poor defenceless Injun. I just hated seeing people picked on for no reason. In truth, I'd have acted no different had I seen something similar played out on the streets of Cardiff or London. The way I saw it there were good Injuns and bad Injuns, just like there were good and bad white people. The fact they were Rees that Mason picked on made no difference to me. A few of our fellows came up afterwards and patted me on the back, saying they'd always known Mason was an ass and that he'd get what was coming to him someday. Couldn't recall them saying that afore though! Queer to relate, but me and Mason always got on pretty well after that.

After being stationed at Fort Rice for only a few weeks, we found ourselves on the march again on what was termed the Yellowstone Expedition, the aim of which was to survey a route for the Northern Pacific Railroad along the Yellowstone River. The expedition was under the overall command of Colonel David S Stanley with Custer as his second-in-command. Stanley's column consisted of over a thousand cavalrymen, infantry, and two artillery pieces and hundreds of mule-drawn wagons. We must have been a grand old sight as we headed out of Fort Rice as the band struck up 'Garry Owen' on June 20. Although I wasn't to know it at the time, my first engagement with hostile Indians after 18 months as a cavalryman in The Seventh wasn't far off.

Captain McDougall, our troop commander, told us our job was mainly to provide protection for a bunch of surveyors employed by the Northern Pacific Railroad. These fellows were working deep in hostile territory and the thought of those fearsome red men sitting up in those hills overseeing their daily labours was giving them the jitters.

As we headed up the North side of the Yellowstone West of the Powder River in Eastern Montana it seemed to rain every blessed day. Then, only a few days out of Rice we were hit by the most violent hailstorm that caused half our cussed mules to stampede and brought our march to a complete standstill. What happened to the so-called 'Custer's Luck' the papers were always mentioning, we wondered?

Now a mule may be one of the most ill-tempered creatures known to man, but on this occasion I almost felt sympathy for the dumb brutes as they took a shellacking from hailstones the size of apples. Their pitiful braying lasted for hours as we sorry band of soldiers, all soaked through ourselves, did our damnest to round them up. It was times like this when I questioned my decision to take Annie's advice and call in at that army recruitment depot in Chicago.

Annie, sweet Annie … I'd occasionally wonder what had become her. Although she couldn't read or write herself she'd made me promise to send her letters from the Deep South. Yet both my letters to Chicago had gone unanswered. That troubled me a great deal. She must have settled happily into married life and had no wish to correspond, I guessed. Maybe she was even a mother by now. The sight of my comrades opening their envelopes for news from home always made me reflect on the lack of my own. As one of the few fellows in the company who could read and write I was oft called upon to read a letter from back East to some homesick trooper or occasionally write down their thoughts for those loved ones eagerly awaiting their soldier's return.

We hadn't pushed very far West of Missouri when we started coming across buffalo in ever-increasing numbers. We troopers were particularly pleased to see those strange, lumbering, shaggy fellows as they afforded us the opportunity to beef up our slim rations of hardtack, biscuits and bacon with some fresh buffalo meat. Trouble was, breaking away from the wagon train to hunt those varmints was strictly forbidden although, in the early days of the march at least, little groups of soldiers would peel off from time to time. Woe betide anyone if word had gotten back to Custer, yet he spent much of his time riding with his scouts way out in front of the column mapping the way ahead.

We must have only been out of Rice for about a week when I shot my first buffalo calf. Me, Tuttle and a fellow named 'Wild Bill' Torrey, who was also seen as a decent shot, had broken off from the column with a couple of Ree scouts. We'd known a herd was a few miles West as Eagan and some other boys from E had gone hunting the day afore. When they returned shame-faced and empty-handed Hohmeyer told them caustically that too many fellows in E Troop couldn't hit a Goddamn barn if they were standing inside it. The three of us vowed to make our first sergeant eat crow.

As we rode out the Rees told us that while buffalo were still plentiful, whole herds were being wiped out by white hunters shooting them up for pure sport. Some of these great frontiersmen would shoot the buffalo from a train, or the 'iron horse' as the Indians called it. So many were being killed that whole areas of the plains now stank of rotting meat. Indians depended heavily on the buffalo and our Ree scouts reckoned their mass slaughter was Washington's way of trying to bring the hostiles to heel. 'They're tryin' to starve 'em into surrenderin'', was what they said. Round about this time, General Sheridan, a Civil War and Indian plains fighter of considerable infamy, had opined that 'The only good Injun is a dead Injun'. Most folk back in Chicago seemed to readily adhere with those sentiments.

Now I'd detested fox-hunting as a boy as the odds seemed so unjust. As the five of us headed out onto the prairie, though, I reasoned that the odds were greatly in favour of the buffalo and our growling bellies told me we were more than justified in trying to land ourselves some fresh buffalo steak. Breasting a hill, we caught our breath at the sight of around one thousand of the beasts grazing peacefully down below; and the scouts reckoned this a small herd! Couldn't believe how close we'd gotten without them detecting our approach.

We were stealthily approaching a mere couple of hundred yards distant when the Rees suddenly shot past yelling and whooping, giving us no choice but to spur our mounts on in their wake. At last the great herd started to move, and as four thousand hooves gathered speed the very ground seemed to shake beneath us.

The instructions the Rees had given us were simple: always be mindful of a cow protecting her calf and under no circumstances take a tumble else you'd end up squashed flat as a saucer. Riding furiously, I drew a line on a large cow, her calf running alongside. As I'd been warned, she veered sideways right towards us, prompting Scout to skip aside nimble as a cat. What a horse, I thought to myself. Most mounts would have been shoulder-charged to Hell. Out the corner of my eye I could see either Tuttle or Torrey screaming and shouting as they rode down a magnificent bull. Which of us would land the prize this day?

Following some of the most thrilling moments I'd ever experienced on the back of a horse it turned out to be me! I rode back to camp with my calf looking and feeling like the cat's whiskers. That night I was the most popular fellow in E as our company cook fixed up our first feast of buffalo meat. After watching the meat spitting and blackening in the firepit I duly observed the magical effect of hot food on shrunken bellies. Almost as if it by-passed the digestive organs and went straight into the bloodstream. The boys were laughing and jesting again for the first time in many days. They were so impressed with my marksmanship that I couldn't find it in me to confess I'd been lining up the buffalo cow that instant I'd pulled the trigger. Her poor calf had somehow gotten in the way just as the orange flame had sprung from my Sharp. I can tell you that the hump of a young buffalo is as tender and as tasty as the finest steak served up in any one of Chicago's swishest hotels.

As we pushed deeper and deeper into Indian territory, however, the opportunities to hunt buffalo as well as game such as prairie grouse, grew fewer and fewer. Every so often I'd experience the deep thrill of spying my first hostile Indians in the distance. Oft one lone brave, sometimes two, you'd see them keeping a wary eye on us from some distant knoll or hilltop no doubt taking note of our progress. As the column trundled nearer they'd mount their horses and ride off. We never took up the pursuit as our orders were to only molest Mr Lo if he molested us.

A lot of our fellows laughed and jested about who would get the most scalps when we finally caught up with the Sioux. I always found such conversation queer as we had Crow, Ree and Arikara scouts as part of our column. Moreover, I found the practice of taking scalps stomach-turning and I know full well I wasn't the only bluecoat who felt that way, though few would e'er admit it. The sound of a scalp being lifted made a distinct plop, I was told. I was ne'er tempted to take an enemy's hair and e'en if I had been just knew I'd end up spilling my guts. Our Crows, Rees and Arikaras weren't averse to taking Sioux and Cheyenne scalps. Everyone seemed to go round scalping one another.

All three tribes were traditional enemies of the Sioux, but I always got the impression they perceived them to be superior fighters and were grateful for the protection being part of such a large train afforded. The Rees, Crows and Arikaras were always a tad jumpy when there were Sioux around.

Saddlesore and increasingly weary, we pushed on and on through territory very few white men had seen, crossing the flooded Little Missouri River and into Montana Territory

187

afore reaching the Yellowstone. Custer then led us and C Company along a rough trail to the mouth of Glendive Creek where the steamboat The Far West was awaiting. Being a sign of the civilisation we'd left far behind, boy, was she a sight for sore eyes! In addition to key supplies, the boat had bought a stack of mail from Lincoln much to the delight of those officers and troopers lucky enough to have some folks to write to.

Sat there feeling a bit left out, I got to thinking I had to write home again soon. In the past I'd told myself there was no point as I was always being kept on the move, but in the winter we were due back on permanent station at Lincoln. Aye, I told myself, I felt that would be a more preferable occasion to send home another dispatch from this strange land. In truth, I'd just felt no great compulsion to write. On arriving at Toronto, I felt it best to keep contact with the family to a minimum, if only to try and forget the trials and tribulations of the past couple of years.

Lately, I'd arrived at the conclusion that this approach appeared to be working: out of sight, out of mind, I suppose. My thoughts had not been of Elizabeth for a long, long time and that was how I wished it to remain. That girl had been sat inside my head for way too long and I had no wish for her to take up residence in there again. Yet I again found myself wondering what she was doing now.

Having set up a supply depot and left a couple of companies of troops behind to guard it, we were ferried across the Yellowstone to its North bank. On we pressed West until after about a week the column met the steamship Josephine a few miles above the mouth of the Powder River. Man and beast alike were grateful for the supplies of forage and extra clothing she bought. That night, we were suddenly awakened by the sound of gunfire at the edge of camp. Turned out a couple of pickets reckoned they saw some mounted Indians snooping about and let loose a few rounds to scare them off.

Soon after setting off the next day our scouts came across the trail of ten Indians, easily identifiable as their horses were unshod, heading up the valley.

By now every soldier was in a high state of readiness and anticipation. Can't speak for the others, but my belly felt as if a mighty river eel was wriggling inside it. We sensed some sort of confrontation would not be long in coming and a soldier's inkling could always be relied upon. On Sunday, August 3, we awoke to the call of Reveille and the glorious sight of the sun rising like a fireball in the East. Feeding Scout his morning oats, I gazed at the distant hills bathed in orange and wondered a touch morbidly if there were any among our party who wouldn't live to see it sink into the West. I chased such thoughts from my mind as it did no good to dwell on them.

I was in a state of mild excitement, true, but afeared of death I was not. A soldier always thinks that it'll be the other fellow who gets it, ne'er himself. As luck would have it, Company E remained with Stanley's column on a tributary of the Yellowstone that day and saw no fighting. But as I'd feared, for some of our band it would indeed prove to be their very last day on Earth. We did not learn the full story of the day's events until sundown; must have been too far away for the sound of shooting to carry. Turned out that Custer had taken Troops A and B to scout out West when they were attacked by a large force of Indians and forced to hole up in a wood.

The shooting went on for a few hours, neither side giving ground. Sometime in the afternoon tragedy occurred. Our head vet Dr Honsinger was a somewhat stout German fellow of about fifty years of age who always wore a blue coat and buckskin pantaloons. Being a vet, he was particularly fond of horses and his own mount received more loving care and attention than e'en Johnny Ogden's Sky Dancer, the most fleet-footed mount in E Troop.

Sometime in the afternoon they left the column to ride down to the river, Dr Honsinger telling a camp guard that his horse was near-begging for a drink of water. The vet was the last fellow you'd have expected to take a risk like that but I suppose he felt the needs of his horse came first. Augustus Baliran, the sutler, who I knew a bit, went with him. The pair were learned fellows and good chums united by an interest in fossils which they'd seek out and gather on the march whenever the opportunity afforded itself.

Hohmeyer told me later it appeared that Dr Honsinger and Mr Baliran had elected to take a chance by riding on their own down to the river, thinking there were no hostiles in the vicinity. Had they been aware that Custer and two companies of The Seventh were trading bullets with a few hundred Indians just a few miles further West they would have assuredly stayed right where they were. What troubled Hohmeyer the most was that a Ree scout, who spoke no English, had set off after the pair and tried to stop Dr Honsinger by grabbing the reins of his horse, pointing to the West and saying: 'Indians, Indians'. Honsinger could by now hear sporadic shooting coming from that direction, but assumed it was Custer's men out hunting. 'No, no, cavalry, cavalry,' he told the anxious scout and, pulling his bridle free, rode on with Mr Baliran to be joined a short while later by a couple of malingerers from Yates' F Company.

As the little band approached the river, totally unaware they were in mortal danger, a force of Indians, concealed in some trees, surprised them at the base of a bluff and both men, along with Ball, of F, were shot from their saddles and killed. The other fellow, Brown, made good his escape and rode at speed back into camp screaming like the hounds of Hell were on his tail: 'Everyone back there is killed!'

At first we feared the worst and assumed Custer had fallen victim to some fiendish Indian trap and perished along with his entire troop as had Fetterman and his band a good few years back. Turned out that Brown was referring to Dr Honsinger and his dear friend, whose bodies were even now more than likely undergoing dreadful mutilations at the hands of their evil slayers. At about the same time Custer brought the impasse to an end by ordering a mass charge which drove back the Indians. Although his men gave chase for three or four miles, their mounts were no match for the smaller and faster Indian ponies and they'd eventually abandoned the pursuit.

The boys were pretty sorrowful that night about what had happened. Dr Honsinger and Mr Baliran had been easy meat served up on a plate for those hungry redskins. 'It should never have come to pass,' McDougall kept saying, head in hands, over and over again. Neither of the deceased were fighting men; they weren't even armed, for God's sake. And both were well known to us troops. Me and Hohmeyer had bought a bottle of whisky from Mr Baliran that very morning. Ended up raising several glasses to him and Dr Honsinger with Eagan and some of the others that night. The boys from F told us both bodies were unmutilated, although Mr Baliran had two arrows sticking out his back. It seemed that Dr Honsinger's gallant horse had managed to convey him almost to the top of the bluff before a Sioux bullet brought him down. We were relieved to learn the poor fellows had not been butchered.

Hohmeyer surmised the Indians had been disturbed by Brown's panicked flight from the scene of the ambush. Of Ball there was no sign, but Brown had seen him take a bullet in the back as he'd made a dash for his mount, after relieving himself in some bushes. Dr Honsinger and Mr Baliran were buried side-by-side at the foot of the bluff where they fell, but Custer ordered there should be no headstones. Said he didn't want no hostiles digging up the bodies and hacking them to bits, which is what Injuns did, or so we were told.

He was really mad about what happened and gave

some of the officers a stern dressing-down. Yates was given a particularly hot time, by all accounts. Custer told him Dr Honsinger and Mr Baliran should ne'er been allowed to have left camp without an escort. I suppose it was a warning of the dire peril that could await us all in the land of the red man where the spectre of death lurked around every corner. Hohmeyer told me that night that if the Sioux caught him alone out on the prairie he'd have no hesitation in blowing his own brains out rather than face being tortured to death. 'Always remember, James,' he said, 'to save the last bullet fo' yourself.' I was reminded of the conversation I'd had in that Chicago saloon with Titus King many, many moons afore.

Falling into the hands of the Sioux was every trooper's dread. There was always much talk of what those red devils were capable of. One fellow related how he'd seen an Indian shirt made entirely of white women's scalps. In the same teepee, he said they found the long chestnut locks of another woman which must have been four feet long. Though it'd happened seven years back he said he still couldn't drink it off his mind. What I couldn't countenance was that some soldiers took Injun scalps as well as chopping off fingers and noses. I felt sick when I learned that the practice of cutting out squaws' private parts had been commonplace just a few years previous and was apparently still not unknown.

As it happened, I had little o'er a week to wait afore I had my first taste of Indian warfare. In the early morning hours we were roused from our slumber by the sound of our camp coming under fire from a big bunch of redskins across the river. This was a tad unusual as Mr Lo didn't often attack after dark, but by dawn bluecoats and redskins were taking potshots at each other from several locations.

My marksmanship had improved much so I wasn't too surprised when Custer chose me as one of the twenty sharpshooters he posted behind trees along the riverbank. Poor Tuttle must have been just five yards away to my right when that bullet bore its way clean through his brain. Shortly afterwards we were confronted by a couple of hundred warriors charging across the Yellowstone in an attempt to over-run the camp. T'was a real test of our Sharps. We stood our ground and blasted away as those Indians yipped and howled like incarnate fiends. As I worked my heated carbine as hard as I could, I could feel a river of hot sweat running down my back, but strangely no fear. T'wasn't no time for that; we just had to do our utmost to stop the enemy reaching the camp and engaging us in hand-to-hand conflict. And none of us wanted that.

Drawing a bead on a big Sioux warrior wearing a war bonnet in mid-stream about 150 yards from my position I let fly and watched in grim satisfaction as he toppled from the back of his mount into the foaming waters of the Yellowstone, which were by now turning crimson. Urged on by our sergeants, we continued to fire round after round into those rampaging hordes who were by now attacking from all sides. Afore long, we sprang to our mounts stationed behind with the horse-holders as bugles signalled a counter-attack. Across the river we streamed, roaring like thunder as those Indians who moments afore had seemed on the verge of gaining the upper hand turned tail and fled.

Spurring Scout on, I galloped past Hohmeyer whooping like a madman and firing wildly at the fleeing enemy with my Colt. He shouted something I didn't catch, but anticipating his displeasure at the reckless manner of my riding, I pulled back hard on the reins. Shooting at moving targets with a Colt from horseback was a waste of ammunition anyhow. We must have chased Sitting Bull's warriors for a good eight miles or more afore pulling up. Although those Indians outnumbered us two-to-one, they had, as some old hands had predicted, decided to skedaddle once The Seventh charged.

We didn't escape unscathed. Apart from losing Tuttle and three others we had three wounded, including Lieutenant

Braden, who had fought so gallantly, only to have his thigh shattered by a Sioux bullet which sent him tumbling off his mount.

Back in camp afterwards it was widely thought he wouldn't make it through the night. He did pull through, although his soldiering days pretty much ended there and then on the banks of the Yellowstone. We had no idea how many Indians we'd potted; many bodies were washed downstream and estimates of Indian dead varied from man to man. While I took no pleasure in seeing those Indians dying, I reckoned it had been either us or them; and I'd much rather it was them. As Captain Benteen liked to tell us: 'You sons of guns are paid to get shot at by the Government.'

I was quite pleased with how I acted for the first time under fire, even if I'd gotten a tad over-excited when we chased the enemy out across the plains. I was also pleased with the way Scout responded to my entreaties, but unlike his greenhorn rider that doughty little horse had seen it all afore. Feeling slightly giddy as we rode back I remembered Titus King's recollections of how he felt after the Washita. I reckoned that the rush of blood to my head wasn't down to the joy of killing; rather it was my grateful soul rejoicing that, unlike Tuttle and those other unfortunates, I'd still be around to watch the sun slip down behind those purple Western hills.

CHAPTER 11

F Lynchon
Dakota Terr
January 1/74

Dear Brother

I am once more going to trouble you in the hope you will answer these. If you do not wish to correspond with me please let me know to save me sending to you so often. This is the last letter I am going to send you if you don't reply.

Please give my best love to Mother and Mr Francis hoping that they are in good health as I am at present. I am not going to send you a long letter this time.

I wish you a happy new year and many of them. Tell Mother not to trouble about me and tell her to send to me.

Please give my best respect to my sister-in-law and to Mr Morgan and Capt Vincent hoping they are all in good health. I have no more at present.

Please answer these few lines if you can spare time. I must wish you good by this time. Excuse these few lines and all blunders.

Yours
W B James

Once the regiment arrived near Bismarck in September I wrote John my first letter in a very long time. Two months passed without hearing anything back so in early November I wrote him again and still no reply was forthcoming. I was not best pleased. In fact, I was well-nigh furious with my only brother left on the face of this good Earth. After all, I reasoned, it was not as if I wrote him every month or so. Assuming the letters were reaching their destination the very least he could do was respond. So I'd wrote him again on New Year's Day and when I threatened not to write ever again unless I received a reply I truly meant it.

Less than a week after my dispatch a rare letter from Mother brought yet more grim tidings from home. Captain David James, husband of my elder sister, Elizabeth, had been lost at sea when The Barbados sank on passage from Glasgow to Quebec in November of 1872. I would have sent my condolences to Elizabeth direct, but the memory of the bitter manner of our unhappy parting and the hurtful things she'd uttered was still all too raw, e'en after the passage of three years. When I'd run into her on what proved my very last night in Dinas the woman had given full vent to her long-dormant fury; in truth, she'd laid into me without mercy.

Unlike Ann, Elizabeth had always liked and respected Liz Penfeidr. When I'd introduced them in the Royal Oak at Newport one night Liz Penfeidr had jested that she was striving her utmost to keep me on the straight and narrow. 'Then I trust you'll fare considerably better than I,' Elizabeth had replied, archly. 'I've been endeavouring in vain to do so for nigh on twenty years!'

During our drunken quarrel at The Ship Aground, Elizabeth had viciously berated me over what she said was my ill-treatment of Liz Penfeidr, accused me of heaping shame on the family through my wild ways and rounded off by saying how I'd always been such an immense disappointment to long-dead Father. Now I'd still been stiff and sore from that beating I'd suffered outside The Grenadier in London, yet Elizabeth's harsh tongue inflicted far more hurt than any punch or kick. Over time I'd reflect on her words again and again; particularly what she'd said about the way Father viewed me ...

With the winter snows arriving early, we'd spent a wretched couple of months camped out in our pup tents on the west bank of the Missouri five miles downriver from the wild frontier town of Bismarck while we waited to move into our new wooden barracks at the fort. It was not 'til November 1 that we finally got a proper roof over our heads and most of the boys were wracked with coughs and colds and all manner of afflictions by then.

As we were to find, fort life could be pretty humdrum in the depths of a long and bleak Dakota winter. Our time was taken up by drill training, horsemanship trials and yet more drill training. Sometimes on fine days we'd play baseball or company tag, like a bunch of children in a playground. Anything to keep the blood moving, muscles loose and our minds alert. 'Zig-zag, James, zig-zag!' the watching Hohmeyer would down his clay pipe to bellow from the sidewalk and I'd duly oblige. Being the most fleet-footed in the company I relished giving the other fellows the slip. Most were like fish out of water if they weren't on the back of a horse anyway.

Away from the parade ground we'd chop wood, haul water, tend the company vegetable patch or take on sentry duty. It was all just killing time, I suppose. Killing time until we were told to go out and kill some more Indians. At night we'd play checkers or poker in front of a roaring wood stove or write letters in the dim flicker of a kerosene lamp which cast eerie shapes on the walls; letters that in my case did not seem to be reaching their recipient.

Tom Eagan was viewed as the strong man of our company; he'd been a labourer back in Ireland and boasted a pair of biceps as wide as hams. One arm-wrestling contest I had with him entered regimental folklore. Hohmeyer timed our grim struggle at a shade over 14 minutes as the pair of us sweated, grunted and groaned like a couple of sweethearts locked in rapturous embrace, exhorted all the while by our fellow troopers several of whom had laid sizeable wagers on the anticipated outcome. Half the fellows were on Eagan's side; the other half on mine. I won through in the end when an exhausted Eagan finally surrendered. He reckoned afterwards he'd have had to broken my arm in order to prevail. He was probably right about that, but I was so stiff and sore afterwards that it was as much as I could do to raise a tankard to my thirsty lips.

Eagan had family in America who'd fled the potato famine back in Ireland. I'd sometimes help him compose a letter for a sister back East. Once, whilst drunk, he told me his real name was Hagan, for reasons he didn't specify and I knew better than to enquire. Many troopers had signed up using false names as some, myself included, had somewhat colourful pasts. What irony that I'd concealed my own enlistment from my family yet was one of the few to sign up under their real name!

Brown, another acquaintance who in time would also gain his stripes, was a sturdy, good-looking fellow from Maryland who must have been the only trooper in The Seventh who'd worked as a candy maker previous. He'd good-naturedly shoulder jests that in the event of running out of bullets he could always offer Mr Lo a tin of toffee or jar of jelly beans as a peace offering. Like me, Brown had signed up in '72 planning on serving just one enlistment. He'd have had more than his taste of adventuring by then, he reckoned, and instead of hunting Indians would go back to making confectionery. All manner of waifs and strays found a home in The Seventh.

The only bit of real excitement that winter came when

an occasional party of hostiles would creep up a gully near to the sentry posts, unleash a few arrows and then skedaddle back out onto the plains again. We'd loose some bullets in their direction but never could tell if we hit anything or not. On one bright moonlit night a big, grey timber wolf loped into the fort, burst into the enlisted men's barracks and dragged a petrified trooper from his bunk afore being shooed out the door by the rest of the boys. Luckily the critter wasn't rabid, and most wolves were.

Soon after we moved into our winter quarters an infantryman called King was shot dead by a character named Spotty Whalen in a row over a girl at the Dew Drop Inn at Whiskey Point across the Missouri from Lincoln. Whiskey Point was the red light district of Bismarck and was where we soldiers would spend our downtime once we'd gotten paid.

The night after King's death a bunch of our fellows took the wooden skiff across the Missouri with vengeance in their hearts. They showed up outside the hotel where King had met his end and tried to force their way inside. The owner of the hotel, a somewhat desperate character called Mullen, came out shooting and when the smoke cleared he lay dead as did Trooper Dalton, of L, while a bartender was badly wounded. The Seventh Cavalry band and most of the command turned out for Dalton's funeral the next day. The Bismarck Tribune duly reported the tragic occurrence under the headline: 'Bismarck's First Baptism of Blood.' Small wonder the town quickly became known as 'The Wickedest City In The West'.

Whiskey Point itself consisted of fifteen saloons and at least as many hog ranches. On one wild night of debauchery I got through three of those women at the Dew Drop for a main course and still managed to have Cigar Susan, one of the fort laundresses, for dessert when I'd gotten back! God knows I suffered a really bad dose of the lice afterwards, though. The following year the entire area was destroyed by a large flood which, some of the more God-fearing members of the Fort Lincoln command contended, was quite clearly an act from Him above.

Maybe it was the boredom of those long winter evenings in the barracks with the snow lying deep outside that got me thinking of home again or, if I'm honest, Elizabeth. I realised with a shock that three years had passed since we'd parted. I'd done so much in that time and I wondered if she had too.

While I dearly wanted to know how Mother and John were faring, that blessed Morgans girl was once again back in my mind. I eagerly awaited John's response and the fact none appeared aroused my considerable displeasure which grew with each passing week. There was another reason I was in an ugly mood when I penned that letter on New Year's Day: one I'd sent to Annie in Chicago had arrived back unopened a week or so previous. On its front, next to that dear girl's name, someone had scrawled in pencil one dreadful word: 'Deceased'.

This terrible revelation hit me like a sledgehammer. I gazed numbly at that envelope for an awful long time oblivious to all the barrack room chatter and laughter. Poor Annie was no more and I wondered how she'd met her untimely end. Should I write back for details or would that serve only to increase my agony? The mere fact she was no more was enough. I knew from the newspapers that disease was rife in Chicago in the aftermath of the Great Fire and reckoned that was what had claimed the life of a girl who had shown me nothing but true kindness and compassion when, God knows, I'd been at my very lowest ebb.

That night as I lay listening to the snores of my comrades, I found myself shedding my first tears since the day when Annie and I'd met for the last time beneath that large clock at the Chicago train depot. Annie dead at the age of 21; t'was just too sorrowful to contemplate. She'd survived that terrible voyage from Ireland to settle in Chicago and then lost members of her family one by one. Now, having finally found happiness with Frank Ellis, and being able to look to a future which held much promise, her young life had been cruelly extinguished. Was the gypsy curse at play again? I wondered bitterly. The mere fact most of those close to me seemed destined for an early grave would indicate that it was.

Tossing restlessly in my bunk, the eerie howls of wolves and coyotes sounding out on the prairie, I yearned to turn back time so I could once again be with Annie and tell her what she meant to me. Life was so fragile, I reflected. What was it Liz Penfeidr used to say? All of us are just passing through. That queer and mysterious girl ne'er spoke a truer word. And she oft said that the only question that truly mattered was where our souls went once our bodies were mere dust.

I remembered then how we'd both liked to think our souls were bound for the summit of Carningli, the Mountain of Angels, and how I'd faithfully promise to await her on the bench-shaped rock where I'd once hewn our initials with a large knife. Our time on Earth was very short and once we were gone what was left? A moss-covered tombstone in the unkempt corner of some forgotten graveyard that no-one would care a fig about. That was the ultimate fate of us all. My mind harked back to that happy Christmas of 1861, the last time us Jameses were all together at Pencnwc. In a hundred years from now there'd be nothing to show any of us ever walked this Earth, I thought mournfully, save a bunch of ruined, overgrown gravestones at Brynhenllan for passing dogs to cock a leg over.

***

One evening Arthur arrived back at his Lower Town lodgings to find a note from his sweetheart, Louisa Perkins, awaiting him. Small, dark, petite and God-fearing, Louisa had always been far more interested in matters of the church than the subject of WBJ. Sitting in the Royal Oak one evening she'd disclosed that Arthur's mention of the atrocities committed on both sides during the Indian Wars left her feeling quite sick. Whilst voicing strong sympathy for the fate of the Indians, Louisa had also expressed the heartfelt hope that the Boer War, which had finished a couple of years before, would be the last major conflict afflicted on their generation. 'The evil that men do,' she'd said, with an emphasis on the word 'men'.

So, knowing her lack of enthusiasm for the WBJ story, Arthur was considerably surprised by Louisa's curt note stating her mother wished to speak to him about 'Will Pencnwc' as a matter of the utmost urgency. He had only met Mrs Perkins on a couple of brief occasions previously.

A few days later Arthur found himself walking down the hill from Fishguard towards the small village of Goodwick and the tiny white-washed fisherman's cottage where, Louisa, an only child, resided with her parents.

There, Mrs Perkins, a consumptive-looking lady of about fifty who appeared older than her years, had warmly welcomed him into their modest home, explaining that her mariner husband, Caleb, was away at sea. Arthur had been somewhat baffled by her approach and, when pressed, it became obvious that Louisa was similarly puzzled even though she had related Arthur's great unresolved quest to her mother. 'Louisa tells me you're endeavouring to find the whereabouts of a Mr William James, from Dinas Cross?' enquired Mrs Perkins, over the inevitable cups of tea and plates of welshcakes. 'I do so hope that you will be successful in your quest as both myself and my dear husband owe Mr James a very great debt that no amount of money could ever repay.'

As Arthur and Louisa, sitting alongside one another on a red couch, listened keenly, Mrs Perkins proceeded to relate the events that unfolded one fine summer's day down in Fishguard Lower Town about 35 years previously when she was aged 14. 'A group of us girls from Goodwick had decided to go swimming off the quay,' she recalled. 'Although, if I'm really honest, we were more curious as to whether there'd be any boys about the place.' Arthur and Louisa exchanged amused glances. 'There was me,' Mrs Perkins went on, 'my elder sister Mary, Lynda Tremadog and little Rosie Morse, whose father had sadly been lost at sea the week previous, from what I remember. I was the best swimmer of the group, or at least thought I was. Mary and the rest could barely swim a stroke by comparison.'

As Louisa's mother paused briefly to take a sip of tea her demeanour grew more serious. 'Although the wind was getting up and the others wished to go home I dived in for one last swim off the quay,' she related. 'I swam out a fair way, fully intending to climb out and dry myself on my return. That was when I got into trouble. My right leg was seized with cramp at about the same time I took a mouthful of sea water; then I realised the current had seized me in its grip and was pulling me out. I was suddenly overcome with great terror.

'I started flailing for the shore with all my might, shouting to the others I was in need of urgent assistance. Though I was close enough to the quay to see Mary's horrified face, I knew in my heart that I lacked the strength to reach it.

'I kept swallowing more and more seawater. By now waves were breaking over my head and my strength was fast fading; in between my head bobbing under the water I could hear the cries of the girls screaming for help. I must have been going under for the umpteenth time when I distinctly remember thinking I'd breathed my last and that I'd never re-surface. As I slid below the waves the faces of my sister and my dear mother and father appeared before me.

'Then, just as I abandoned all hope and resigned

myself to my fate, strong hands seized me under the arms and I felt myself borne upwards. I thought at first I was in the embrace of a mermaid. As my face broke the surface I took long, deep grateful gulps of the sweetest air I had ever breathed. Coughing and spluttering, I became aware that I was being hauled back to the quay by a young man who, it later turned out, had been working on a boat on the far side of the Gwaun and had dived into the water on being alerted by the girls' cries. I was panicking something awful and he had to reassure me. I told him I didn't want to die and he replied: 'You will not die here this day, cariad; I will not let you. But you must assist me and kick hard for the quay with all your might.'

'After what seemed an eternity we reached the quay and these other boys pulled us up. I was crying my eyes out and feeling quite poorly and my saviour stayed with me for some time whilst I expelled the water from my lungs. Then he insisted on walking us all to the nearby Dinas Arms where the landlord, a friend of his he said, gave me some whisky. A hot toddy I think they called it. I had never consumed alcohol before and, indeed to goodness, the drink went straight to my head!'

Louisa and Arthur both chuckled. That certainly sounds like Will to me, thought Arthur. 'The other thing I remember most clearly is the young man asking me where I lived,' Mrs Perkins went on. 'When I told him I was from Goodwick he replied that had he known that he'd have thrown me straight back in and left me to drown!' Arthur and Louisa both burst into laughter in which Mrs Perkins herself joined. 'Aye,' she grinned, after a few moments, 'all present were quite tickled by that. Goodwick and Dinas Cross people weren't supposed to get on, see?' 'I suppose we should all be grateful that Will James evidently did not allow his prejudices to govern his actions that day,' observed Arthur. 'Indeed we should,' nodded Mrs Perkins.

'As I got the drink down me I asked Mr James when he'd first learnt to swim which prompted much laughter from his watching companions. He replied that he was more happy on the water than in, but was open to the idea of having swimming lessons from me if I so desired! 'You could not have picked a more unlikely fellow to pull you out,' was what he said. 'When I go in the sea I'm not so much swimming as drowning!' We went home that night and Mary told our parents. All she could relate was that I'd been saved by one of a group of young men from Dinas Cross; and that his name was Will Pencnwc. A few days later I came down with a nasty case of pneumonia and was poorly for some considerable time.

'It wasn't until the spring that my father and I rode up to Dinas Cross, fully intent on finding my rescuer and thanking him personally. Father was ready to give him a reward. When we arrived we found the James family had left Pencnwc several years previously and that Will himself had gone overseas. So, sadly, we never got the chance to express our deepest gratitude, which is why I was so interested to learn from Louisa of the nature of your enquiries.'

Arthur then briefed Mrs Perkins with the bare facts of the WBJ case with which her daughter was now well familiar. 'I trust you will be successful in your undertaking for I still cherish the hope I may yet be able to thank Mr James in person for his gallant actions all those years ago,' she said quietly. 'You see, Mr Nicholas,' Mrs Perkins continued, 'Mr James did not merely save my life that day. As far as I'm concerned he also saved our Louisa. And every time I look at the face of our dear sweet daughter, the most precious thing me and my husband have on the face of this Earth, I tell myself that without Mr James' timely intervention she, quite simply, would not be.'

Louisa's mother uttered those words with such heartfelt and naked emotion that Arthur felt tears suddenly prick his eyes. Turning to Louisa he saw her swallowing hard. As their eyes met Arthur noticed a single tear making its way slowly down her cheek. 'Indeed,' said Mrs Perkins, her voice trembling slightly, 'I am not blessed with overtly good health and the time I have left on this good Earth may well be short, but even after 35 years I earnestly hope that I may one day get the opportunity to personally meet Mr James. That is why I wish you God speed in your noble endeavour, Mr Nicholas.' Arthur nodded solemnly, again turning to look at a teary-eyed Louisa. 'Oh, Arthur ...', she sniffed. 'Pray do your utmost to find him.' Arthur took hold of her hand. 'I give you my word that I will move Heaven and Earth to do so,' he replied.

An hour or so later, Arthur and Louisa sat in their favourite corner of the Royal Oak and raised their glasses to WBJ. As he gazed tenderly across the table at Louisa and reflected on her mother's poignant words of gratitude, Arthur realised that he, too, was deeply indebted to WBJ for his heroic deed on that far-off day. If WBJ did still live and Arthur was successful in tracing him then how fitting that this long-lost son of Dinas would inherit the keys of Llanwnwr. And through his own diligent efforts as well! The William Batine James case had now ceased to be a job of work, he acknowledged. Mrs Perkins's surprise revelation meant it had now become deeply personal.

Sitting there with a contemplative Louisa, Arthur knew he was now compelled to see it through to the very end, whatever that end might be ...

CHAPTER 12

A big talking point that winter was the discovery of gold in The Black Hills of Dakota. These were sacred Indian lands, out of bounds to us whites since the Laramie Treaty of '68. The discovery of gold changed all that. Afore too long, gold-hungry prospectors and miners with dollar signs in their eyes were turning up in the Black Hills all eager for a piece of the cake. The gold rush was further fuelled by Indians occasionally showing up with little bags of gold which they'd hint they'd found in Black Hills country. More than likely they probably lifted them from the body of some poor unsuspecting miner along with his scalp, but whatever the gold's origin it helped turn the trickle of interlopers into that fine country into a raging torrent.

Afore too long talk about Custer heading some kind of expedition into the Black Hills became widespread. There was always some kind of rumour going around Lincoln, what with so many fellows dawdling their way through the long winter waiting for something to happen, but this was different. The papers got wind of just what precisely was in the air afore any of us soldiers.

> **F A Lincoln**
> **Nr Bismarck D T**
> **April 11/74**
>
> Dear Brother
> In answer to your kind letter of this day I was glad to find by your letter that you and Mother are

in good health. I was glad to hear that you are in a good situation at present I hope you will do well. You mention in your letter about coming home. I shall come home to see you but I can't mention the time if God will spare my life. Dear Brother don't trouble about me as long as I have my health I am all right. I hope we shall meet again in this old world. Please give my best love to Mother and tell her that I shall come home to see her some time. If you go to Llanelly mind and call with Mr Thomas, draper, of Hall Street, and give Mr Humphreys my compliments and call with Mr C Evans, London House and H J Howells, Hall Street, they are the best customers in Llanelly. I am not going to send you long letter this time I will send soon again. Dear John, I am going to ask you if you can send me your card de visit. I shall send you mine in my next letter. I shall wait to hear from you soon. I hope you will write oftener. I shall answer your letters by return. I must conclude this time. Please give my love to Mother, Mr Francis and sister-in-law at Newport. Please excuse this short letter and all blunders. Good night and goodbye at present.

Your Dear Bro W B James

Please send back soon and mind your card de visit

Your Dear Brother

W B James

John's first letter in a very long time gave me a much-needed buck in spirits. He apologised for not keeping in touch, but insisted two previous letters sent must have gone astray. I was pleased to hear he was working as a commercial traveller in Cardiff, covering much of south Wales and was therefore happy to pass on details of some of my old customers. I urged him to send me his carte de visite in his next letter and

I would send him mine.

I ended up getting a carte de visite when we were stationed down in Alabama. Myself and young George Walker had gone down to the studio of an Opelika photographer named Crim. We'd had to run the gauntlet of a bunch of n'er do wells loitering on the sidewalk, one of whom had spat a wad of baccy right at my feet. Knowing the pair of us were well outnumbered, I elected to let it pass.

My photograph showed me in uniform so I could scarce send John that. After all my diligent efforts to conceal my situation over the past couple of years there was no way I'd be dumb enough to send him a carde de visite of me sat there in my Seventh Cavalry finery! Poor Mother would have had a fit. When we arrived back at Lincoln I got Goff, the post photographer, to take a picture of me wearing a bowler hat and somewhat threadbare suit that left me looking like some down-at-heel bank manager. This was the carte de visite that I'd dispatch home to John.

That June, following six months of humdrum garrison duties and routine escorts, we finally set off as part of a major expedition under the command of General Custer. And for once we of the rank and file pretty much knew our destination: the Black Hills on what was planned on being a 60-day expedition.

We must have marched around 400 miles West; a long column with our army wagons four abreast and a huge herd of beef cattle trailing the train: the picture of a modern army on the march. The higher we got the cooler the air became and while we had to remain alive to the possibility of a surprise Indian attack, nights around the campfires were pretty relaxed. Ev'ry night there'd be a band concert and The Seventh regimental band would always play the 'Garry Owen'. Other tunes they played was 'The Mocking Bird' and 'The Blue Danube' which reminded me of those nights spent grooming Mollie in her little stable in Chicago while old Dr Russell played the piano in his study above. My mood inevitably darkened as I contemplated the fate of poor sweet Annie now, due to unknown causes, no more than a corpse in the ground.

The officers would oft gather for a sing-song round the piano; the lamentful 'Shenandoah' and more lively 'The Girl I Left Behind Me' both being popular. Us enlisted fellows would sometimes run through a few songs of our own. 'When Johnny Comes Marching Home', 'Annie Laurie' and 'Little Footsteps' were ones we favoured, but one night I couldn't resist giving the boys a rendition of 'Hen Wlad Fy Nhadau', that new hymn Uncle William would sing after a few ales down at the Cross in Dinas. And I sung it pretty much note-perfect in my long-neglected baritone, even if I say so myself. No-one understood the words, of course, and I thought I'd get a joshing, but McDougall said afterwards it was one of the finest hymns he'd ever heard. They'd have been as pleased as punch to hear that back in Ramah Chapel!

As we went further into the high country, our surroundings began to change. We found ourselves riding through grass which reached up to our stirrups, surrounded by a paradise of wild flowers.

T'was hard to believe what potentially dangerous territory we were getting ourselves into and, oh, what a pleasant change it made from those blisteringly hot days on the plains when you were constantly having to spit just to clear your lungs of choking dust.

One of the expedition's aims was to provide protection for miners and prospectors against the Indians, although us troops did some prospecting ourselves whenever we could. Many's the time I heard a fellow soldier state how a sizeable gold nugget wouldn't just buy him out of the army, but also set him up for life. I suppose all of us were to a degree affected by gold fever. We'd borrow a couple of pans off the company cook, grab some picks and shovels and off we'd go.

And we found gold too. Alas! It was only a couple of specks.

Custer had given permission for a number of newspapermen to accompany the expedition. E'ery night he'd invite them to his tent for supper and no doubt regale them with tall tales. The discovery of gold must have come up because, come August, Lonesome Charley, who was said to be Custer's favourite white scout, was ordered to ride one hundred miles South West through hostile territory with dispatches telling the world the Black Hills' secret. By the time we returned to Lincoln having covered close on 1,000 miles it seemed that gold was all anybody wanted to talk about.

To be truthful I felt sorrow for the Indians. Under the Laramie Treaty these were their lands, yet by announcing those hills were full of gold Custer was more or less advertising free entry to the world and his wife. On the one hand The Seventh were supposed to be safeguarding the interlopers already there, while on the other opening up the front gate for many more to join the party. It troubled me that the Indians were being manifestly double-crossed.

Queer as it may sound, it got me thinking about my own upbringing and how the speaking of Welsh was outlawed in school. We'd been made to feel guilty and afeared of using our own language, though what was done to us just did not even begin to compare with what was happening against the Indians who were being forced to give up their sacred lands as well as their whole way of life. 'They took our land and made it their land,' as uncle William used to say.

The effects of that glorified picnic of an expedition, as Hohmeyer would refer to it, were felt the next spring when a whole army of miners set march for the Black Hills, stoking the resentment and displeasure of the Indians even more. We lit the fuse on a powder keg when we went in there, no two ways about it, and the consequences would come back to bite us like a rattler on the arse.

Something queer awaited me back at Lincoln. A letter

211

addressed to me, yet the writing on the front came not from John or Mother but by some unknown hand. Studying the stamp-mark I noted with puzzlement that it had come from Chicago. What on Earth was this? I asked myself, tearing open the envelope in haste.

> **Chicago**
> **Illinoy**
> **July 28, 1874**
>
> My deerest Taffy
>
>   Yoo haf bin misinformd. Am verrie much alife.
>   Your deer luv
>   Annie

I could scarce believe my eyes. Months afore I'd been informed that Annie was no more; now here I was being told she did in fact still live. What devilment was at play here? Was I the victim of some cruel trick? If this letter was indeed her work, why in God's name had Annie not included her address so that I could respond? What was the true meaning behind this sparse message? Lying back on my bunk in shock my immediate suspicion was that it was some dastardly sleight perpetrated by some despicable miscreant who, for reasons unknown, would be taking fiendish delight at my distress.

But re-reading the letter I suddenly spied something which made me sit bolt upright with a cry of joy. The letter, I had not at first noticed, was addressed to 'Taffy', darling Annie's pet name for me. She and only she referred to me by that name; no-one else in the whole wide world! Moreover, its inclusion was a sure fire sign that the letter could only have come from Annie herself, as no-one else would address me such. Gazing across our quarters from the edge of my bunk I decided that the use of Taffy was a secret code, letting me know the letter did indeed come from Annie. Even if she would not, or could not, disclose her actual whereabouts.

I lay back once more and tried to fathom what it all could mean. I was now convinced that Annie had either written that letter, or got someone to write it on her behalf. But why the lack of forwarding address? Why so cloak and dagger? Although the queer missive begged more questions than answers I began to fear she was in trouble of some kind. And yet, whatever her circumstances, she'd clearly felt compelled to let me know she still lived and that I was foremost in her thoughts. Though a married woman, she had even addressed herself as my dear love! What had transpired in Chicago I had no idea, although I sensed it was not good. Yet the fact Annie was still out there filled me with tremendous joy and hope as well as much frustration. When would she write again? I wondered desperately. Next week, next month; a year from now? Would I end up going to my grave vainly awaiting another letter?

I spent the rest of that summer waiting and hoping for a further missive like some lovesick schoolboy enchanted by his first love, but naught whatsoever turned up. Towards the end of September, no more letters from Annie having arrived, six troops, including us men of E, were re-assigned back South to the Department of the Gulf to perform constabulary duty for the rest of the year.

We'd mixed feelings about the deployment: on the one hand it meant missing the harsh plains winter and more opportunities to meet members of the fairer sex; on the other the type of duties we endured in the Deep South made time crawl like a cockroach across a barn floor. All soldiers dislike change and soon after arriving in the little town of Greensboro we were told the Sharps rifles we'd finally got used to were being phased out in favour of single-shot Springfields, although we'd have preferred, to a man, a repeater like the old seven-shot Spencer. At the same time we were assigned .45 calibre Colt pistols and sabres. Those breech-loading Springfield carbines could fire a .45 copper-cased cartridge over 1,000 yards with an effective range of 250 and were said to be really accurate. Had a bitch of a kickback, though, which could easily bruise chin or shoulder. And later I'd find that some greenhorns would struggle to reload them.

Some of our officers, the very ones who'd bemoaned the demise of the old Spencers, were by now well and truly converted by the Sharps even if they felt a seven-shot carbine would be preferable in battle. As usual the thoughts of us fighting men held no merit. We just had to accept a decision drawn up by some desk-bound pen-pusher in Washington.

Greensboro
Alabama
Nov 1/74

Dear Bro

Just a few lines to know if you wish to correspond with me, if you don't please drop me a line but I don't suppose you do but the least you could do is to inform me so please give Mother and Stepfather my best respects hoping they are in good health. I hope these few lines will find you all in good health as I am at present.

This is the last time I am going to write to you if you don't reply so I must wish you all good and hope we will meet in Heaven above.

Goodbye for ever
Yours truly Brother
W B James

> If you wish to reply to me I will give you my address.
> I don't suppose you will write to a Brother in a strange
> country so far from home. Out of sight, out of mind.
>   Address
>   W B James
>   Post office
>   Greensboro
>   Alabama

I was feeling pretty low when I penned that letter, but again felt justified in bitching to John. I was halfway through my five-year army enlistment and in all that time I could count on the fingers of one hand the number of letters I'd had from him. In truth, the overall tally was much less. So here we were in 'lil ol' Greensboro' as they called it down there, getting the predictable hard looks and mean stares from the menfolk and the usual coy smiles from the pretty young womenfolk. No wonder those old Rebs wished nothing but ill upon us. Seeing how deep the wounds ran, I couldn't help but wonder for how many years the bitter after-taste of the North-South conflict would linger.

Only a few years previous a federal soldier stationed in the town was shot dead in a row over unpaid fruit outside a store and his comrades had been on the cusp of lynching the culprit when their commanding officer unexpectedly showed up. The day we arrived in Greensboro was the day I saw my first Ku Klux Klan handbill posted on a building in the main street. 'Dare not wear the holy guard of our mystic brotherhood save in quest of BLOOD', it began. The order was said to have come from the 'Great Grand Cyclops'. 'Let the guilty beware,' it continued. 'Everywhere our brotherhood appears. Traitors beware!'

Couldn't make head nor tail of it, if I'm honest. Not for the first time I concluded that if the worship of God drew the likes of those robe-bearing lunatics to church then I was decidedly better off without it, although the Klan by now seemed pretty much done.

Soon after Christmas I was among a party of troopers under Captain Craycroft who captured 15 distillers in the North-East of the county, seizing their stills. One big fellow with the stature and bulk of a grizzly bear, and covered in about as much hair, lunged at our officer as we burst into their cabin. Almost without thinking I swivelled on my heels and dealt the attacker a swift blow to the jaw. He went down pole-axed and lying there on his back quite senseless emitted a loud snore! Not for the first time I was grateful for my fistic prowess and Craycroft seemed mightily impressed too.

What happened that night may even have had a bearing on my promotion to corporal towards the end of the month. Intoxication was a big problem in The Seventh and it paid for a man to know how to use his dukes. I was also appointed overseer of post stables which carried a fair weight of extra responsibility. I now had two stripes on my arm, sixteen dollars in my pocket each month and, best of all, could order those idle buck privates around! Having served on the bottom rung of the ladder for three years, Corporal William B James had a mighty fine ring about it, I thought. What a great shame, I reflected, that Annie wasn't around to share my good fortune as well as my higher pay.

I celebrated my promotion with some of the boys in one of Greensboro's many saloons. Finally, after downing a few too many beers, and hearing myself claim kinship with Jesse James, I decided to quit while I was ahead and head back to camp. If only I'd obeyed my instincts! As it transpired I did not make it back 'til dawn on account of being waylaid by a lady named Matilda Mae.

It was one of those really steamy Alabama evenings with crickets chirping, thunder growling increasingly in the heavens and lightning illuminating the shops and bars of downtown Greensboro. And suddenly there she was: standing in a doorway porch watching the cascading rain, clad in a long violet dress, strawberry red bonnet on her head, grinning like an alley cat. 'Well, hello soldier boy,' she purred. 'Ah, reckon if ah don't getcha outta them wet clothes real soon you're done bound to catch ya death of cold out thar!'

Well, I hadn't had no female company in an awfully long while. The wild night that ensued was worth whatever it was I paid, yet would have severe repercussions in the form of an acute case of the clap. It'd be several weeks before I regained full health. Like I said, I should have gone straight back to camp.

Matilda's back was a mass of scars. Said she'd been subjected to cruel mistreatment by some drunken Yankee soldiers when Union troops invaded Greensboro at the end of the North-South war. Went on to say atrocities committed on Southern womenfolk had been rife, 'but it were ne'er spoke about'. I was taken aback by what she said. I'd been led to believe Lincoln's bluecoats had been on a Holy crusade to free slaves so had God on their side. From what Matilda was saying plainly not all of them did. Soon afterwards Company E had moved on to the little town of Opelika, a place packed with wild saloons all busting at the seams with thirsty railroad workers labouring on the new line.

It was a mightily dangerous place; guards on passing trains would tell passengers to lie flat on the carriage floors when passing through in case of stray bullets fired from the street. Most nights we'd be awakened by distant gunfire back at camp. Aye, Opelika was very different to sleepy Dinas Cross where just about the only sounds you'd hear at night would be the barking of the dog fox down in the cwm or a pair of brawling tomcats settling their differences out on the farmyard. Life had been hard back home, I acknowledged, and after Father's death became a damn sight worse, but just about the biggest peril walking those Dinas Cross streets was being mown down by a passing horse and cart. In Opelika a fellow could get himself killed very easily and the women were as deadly as their menfolk. When one of our fellows got into a quarrel over payment with one of those rough and ready saloon gals she'd stuck a Bowie knife in his balls.

A happier memory was of the afternoon I happened across a negro gospel choir singing in the open air. Ogden and the rest were heading for the saloon when I dawdled to listen on the main street. The hymn I think was called 'I am Coming, Lord' and the singing unquestionably the finest I'd heard in a long time. In truth, it'd not have been out of place at an eisteddfod back home. After they were done I was pushing my way through the saloon's swing doors when they started singing the hymn again. 'Cept this time t'was in Welsh!

Couldn't believe my ears. Having paused in mid-stride I turned quickly on my heel, went back out and stood there listening on the sidewalk in silent wonder. No, I'd not been imagining things. Those young blacks were stood in that street singing 'Arglwydd Dyma Fi' as if their very lives depended on it. As I stood there transfixed I seemed to suddenly get some grit blown into my eyes. Leastways, that's what I'd have told my fellow troopers had they come out to find me.

After the choir had finished the hymn and I'd joined in the applause I sought out the conductor. The kindly young fellow was more than happy to hand over a hymn sheet; said they'd learnt the Welsh version from an old pastor the previous year and had no real idea of what they were singing! The Welsh version differed from the English and I'd begun to translate for his benefit only for some folks in the crowd to commence to heckle this interfering bluecoat, so deemed it wise to take my leave and let the choir get on with it.

Belatedly rejoining my comrades in the saloon, I reflected on how queer it was that Yr Hen Wlad kept surfacing unexpectedly; a bit like one of those huge catfish we'd occasionally spy on the Southern rivers. Back in

Chicago, Dr Russell had informed me of the existence of a Welsh language newspaper which he pronounced 'Uh Drick'. I finally came across a copy of Y Drych in an Alabama saloon of all places. While seeing Yr Hen Iaith in print inevitably stirred warm and nostalgic memories it was not the same type of Welsh spoken back in Pembrokeshire and, if I'm honest, I found some parts nigh on incomprehensible. Nevertheless, I gauged enough to read of an inquiry into the discovery of a British brig, the Mary Celeste, out in the Atlantic with n'er a soul aboard as well as Disraeli winning the General Election.

As a corporal, the extra pay was greatly appreciated. Yet t'was not enough to extricate me from the hole I'd dug myself in over the previous few months. I was finding more and more that army pay just didn't stretch far enough, leastways to cover my losses at the poker table. Card games were all we soldier boys seemed to do in our spare time, and what started out as good sport fast became a habit. This was pretty dumb conduct for someone on sixteen bucks a month and soon after our return South I found myself having to beg or borrow money from Hohmeyer, Ogden or Eagan; a dollar here, a dollar there. Trouble was, I obviously had to repay them and afore long my debts were mounting up. Now that I was a corporal I was well aware that I should be setting a better example.

>
> **Opelika**
> **Alabama**
> **April 21/75**
>
>
> Dear Brother
>
> Just a few lines to inform you that I am in better health than I have been for the last three months. I hope and pray that I will be able to attend business soon. I have sent you two letters and have had no answer to them. I don't know what is the reason that you don't answer my letters. I send you one from Greensboro and one from here and had no answer whatever. I hope you will answer this one. I am going to ask you one favour if you can lend me a little money. If you can spare some I shall feel obliged if you will send them at once. I hope I shall be able to pay you back soon. If you can spare me some please send a check on my bank. I have no more to tell you at present only wish this letter will meet you and Mother in good health. Please tell Mother I am going to write to her soon. Please give my best love to Mother and Mr Francis and all my friends. Enclosed you will find my card de visit hoping you will send yours to me. Goodbye at present.
>
> Yours truly Bro W. B. James
>
> I hope to hear from you soon and pleased to register the letter.

I hated writing that letter to John, but in truth I was getting a tad desperate. I wasn't the only soldier in The Seventh to pick up a gambling habit; Lt Calhoun, who was married to Custer's sister, was said to lose a load of dollars pretty much every night. But Calhoun's pay was a damn sight more than mine, that was the big difference. One of the boys, Hiley, an Englishman with a cut-glass accent who, when soused, would claim he'd been born of noble stock, was said to have fled to America due to gambling difficulties back home. He and I shared many a night at the sutler's store in Lincoln engrossed in games of poker that seemed to stretch all night. I suppose we both lost far more greenbacks than we won. Anyway, I felt that passing a begging bowl in John's direction was wrong and pretty much an admission of defeat. As his elder brother I should be helping him out, I reasoned.

In the end, after a couple more sleepless nights, I knew t'was my only option. John, the last I heard, was earning good money as a commercial traveller and t'was I, after all, who'd directed him down that path and passed on the names and addresses of potential customers. Plus I'd pay him back, of course. As it happened, I could have saved myself the time and effort in writing that last letter 'cos I ne'er heard a thing back. Hell would have to freeze over afore I wrote John again, I vowed.

On becoming corporal I'd treated myself to a new fire-arm, a Winchester 66 rifle which enabled its user to fire several shots without having to reload. Although the single-shot Springfield carbine remained The Seventh's weapon of choice, a few of my comrades toted privately-owned guns.

While the practice wasn't widespread it was allowed. Custer, for instance, had a number of private weapons including his favourite Remington sports rifle. Nicknamed the 'Yellow Boy' 'cos of its brassy receiver, the Winchester was a handsome weapon which constantly drew admiring glances from my fellow troopers. While I had no real beef with the Springfield I felt a repeater would make it easier to fell a buffalo as well as affording better protection in the event of a prolonged dust-up with Mr Lo. That queer note from Annie may only have consisted of a couple of lines, yet had instilled in me a burning desire to live. Now I knew she was still out there I vowed to take whatever steps were necessary in order to stay alive. And one of them was arming myself with that repeater rifle and .44 Henry cartridges.

Just afore we left Opelika that old James temper almost landed me in the soup again. There was an awfully big dust-up in a saloon 'twixt a bunch of us troopers and a few fellows we knew to be members of the Klan, 'cos we'd arrested them a few months previous. Their leader was a one-eyed hulking brute named Culpepper who had this enraging habit of spouting quotes from the Bible when drunk, which was forever and a day.

After I'd helped smooth things down and was getting some of the boys to clear up the broken chairs and tables, Culpepper came barging up out of nowhere and, for reasons known only to himself, began trying to goad me. I'd warned him to back off a couple of times when he called me a dirty Yankee heathen and I suddenly felt something snap inside. I'm neither dirty, a Yankee, nor a heathen, I thought. For some reason I was suddenly gripped by huge anger.

Just as Culpepper launched into a slurred recitation of the 23rd Psalm I spun round and whacked him hard on the conk. He dropped back into a chair, nose clean broken judging by the amount of claret, but still wouldn't hold his tongue. Vowing to make him eat his words, I snatched the Bible from his hand, tore out a handful of pages and, seizing his scalp and jerking his head back, proceeded to thrust them down his gullet like some old maid would stuff a goose.

Culpepper was struggling and pleading and grunting like a hog as, laughing dementedly, I rammed more and more paper down his throat, his groans becoming e'er more muffled 'til two of the boys grabbed my arms and hauled me off. The sight of old man Culpepper sat there blinking in shock, nose pouring blood and snot, mouth stuffed with pages from his Bible, gave some of us real fits. But Ogden told me later he'd feared the old buzzard had been about to choke. Said his face had turned as blue as our uniforms.

He also said I was lucky a sergeant hadn't been witness to what went down as I could have been looking at a court martial for inappropriate conduct. The next morning I felt pretty foolish if not downright ashamed by what I'd done. T'wasn't as if I had any real reason for it, either; more through plain devilment and frustration, I suppose. Once again I'd lost control of myself. And me with a pair of stripes on my arm now as well. What's more, I knew I couldn't blame the demon drink for what I'd done even if it had been to such an obvious ratbag like Culpepper. Not a drop of liquor had passed my lips that night yet I could have gone ahead and smothered the life out of that old sonofabitch and still slept like a new-born infant back at camp afterwards.

By now ten months had passed since that queer note from Annie. It was just as well I'd been kept busy else I'd have gone clean out of my mind dwelling upon it. Ogden told me to forget her as she'd probably gone and found herself another better-paid fellow, which was pretty much the worst piece of advice he could have given. 'Us boys can have our pick of most any woman in town an' you jus' sit thar with a face like a Goddamn bloodhound,' he said.

Sometimes, when I'd get really maudling, I'd think of running off to Chicago and scouring every street until I found not so much the girl I'd left behind me, more like the girl who'd slipped through my fingers. Yet it'd be useless, I knew. Chicago was a pretty big place and there was no way of e'en knowing whether Irish Annie still resided there, anyhow. Besides, if I did do a flit knowing my luck I was just bound to get caught and what folly would that be? Throwing away a job that paid well just when my discharge was coming into sight. Although Annie's note had fair bucked me up, I oft wished I'd never gotten it. To have my hopes raised, then shot back down again was slowly killing me inside.

We were recalled to Dakota Territory that May, ending

up being stationed near Fort Randall on the Missouri River with Companies A and H, and later that summer at Wounded Knee Creek. Our duties consisting of throwing out miners and unauthorised persons from the Black Hills; even though it was Custer's bragging about gold that had drawn them there like bears round a honeypot in the first place. As the plains winds started to chill and winter approached we again returned to Lincoln; prior to a three-month stint at Fort Totten, where I turned the head of an officer's wife.

I'd been showing off some of my riding skills to the boys, leaning out of the saddle at full gallop to pluck a red bandana out of the dirt and suchlike, when I'd caught her eye. If I'm honest, I'd seen her watching me from the sidewalk afore starting my act. In truth, Enid Douglas, who was married to a frequently absent lieutenant, had been shooting me meaningful glances for a number of weeks.

The finest-looking woman at the fort by a country mile and one indisputably possessed with the most spectacular bosom, Mrs Douglas's romantic life was the subject of much speculation and discussion in the barracks. The boys had even laid wagers as to who would be the first lucky fellow to have their wicked way with her as rumours abounded she was free with her favours. Anyway, that afternoon we got talking and when she told me her husband was away on detached duties in Washington, I could pretty much guess what was coming next. But I was wrong.

'I'm told you are a good baritone,' she said, much to my surprise and disappointment. 'My husband's unfortunate absence and those of others mean we're looking for baritones for the concert we're holding this Saturday.' So, knowing it was ne'er a good idea to ignore the wishes of an officer's wife whether her husband was at his post or not, I readily agreed. Choir practice would make a pleasant change from checkers and whist, I decided.

Striving to ignore the knowing looks and winks of

my fellow troopers, I followed this true English rose back to the officers' quarters where she handed me a large hymn sheet. 'We'll be singing a collection of hymns,' she said. 'Are you familiar with any of them?' It so happened that I was, but it was the hymn on the back of the sheet that caught my eye. T'was something I'd oft sing in the tavern with a few other Welsh boys who worked down Portman Market in West London. Ne'er in my wildest dreams had I thought I'd ever get the opportunity to sing it again. 'Think it's only fair ma'am, that I give you a little demonstration,' I said. 'For all you know you've been the victim of some enlisted man's jest and my singing may resemble the caterwauling of a tomcat.'

'I am confident I have not been misinformed but, by all means, corporal, please be my guest,' she smiled. And so I cleared my throat, closed my eyes and began to sing …

> Hark I hear the foe advancing
> Barbed steeds are proudly prancing
> Helmets in the sunbeams glancing
> Cymru fo am byth
> From the rocks rebounding
> Let the war cry sounding
> Summon all at Cambria's call
> The haughty foe advancing
> Men of Harlech on to glory
> See your banner famed in story
> Waves these burning words before ye
> Cymru fo am byth!

When I finished and opened my eyes, she was slowly pacing up and down, hands clasped behind her back. After she hadn't spoken for a few moments I started to think she'd been unimpressed with my efforts and that maybe the choir could fare without me after all. When she finally swung round to face me I saw, to my shock, that her eyes were moist.

225

'That, corporal, was the most beautiful singing I've heard in a very long time,' she said quietly. 'Have you ever performed professionally?'

'Not apart from singing for my supper back in London, ma'am,' I replied truthfully. 'They taught us well in chapel as children and I suppose you could say that the old voice has kept the wolf from the door from time to time.' She had just started to say that London was her home town when there was a timid knock on the door. 'Come in!' she called and the door opened to reveal a young Negro servant girl. 'Beggin' ya pardon, ma'am,' she said. 'Judy an' me was outside when we heard that singin'. We's thought Lt Douglas was home from Washington.'

'I'm afraid not, Mary,' replied Mrs Douglas. 'Lt Douglas still has matters to attend to, but our choir has, in Corporal James here,' she said gesturing in my direction, 'a more than capable replacement baritone.' After Mary had left, Mrs Douglas told me that my manner, poise and bearing were more those of an officer than an enlisted man. She also said it was obvious I'd had a good learning from the way I spoke. 'Tell me, corporal, the meaning of these words at the end of the hymn' she asked, pointing at the hymn sheet. 'I assume I'm right in surmising that they are, in fact, Welsh?'

'Yes indeed ma'am,' I replied. ''Tis an old Welsh marching song,' adding saucily, 'a tad more stirring than any of those English songs you'll hear those tone-deaf officers render!' I oft overdid the insubordinate bit, I confess, but just couldn't help myself sometimes. Besides, past experience had taught me that should any officer's wife express amusement at such sauce, then I could always count on their complete and undivided attention. She started to laugh, and, not for the first time, I thought what a handsome-looking woman Enid Douglas was. Well-spoken and slim, aged in her mid-thirties, brown hair piled high, and clad in a blue dress laced with yellow flowers. I pulled up my sleeve and proudly showed her the tattoo I'd had done down in Opelika, complete with my initials beneath.

'Oh my, a red dragon,' she said, stroking my arm. 'The flag of Wales, my country,' I replied. 'The tattooist said t'was the first he'd ever done. Did a capital job as well, don't you think, ma'am?' 'That he most certainly did,' she replied with a deep breath while continuing to stroke my arm, only by now her fingers were slowly making their way up my muscled bicep ... 'Mmmm ... I am certainly glad I made enquiries about you, Corporal James,' she replied, airing herself with a fan in the other hand. 'I had an instinct you were a good singer and my instincts,' she paused at this point looking at me up and down, 'as usual have proven correct. That hymn you sang was so ... so ... stirring and red-blooded and ... well ... for want of a better phrase ... manly ... it would truly not be out of place at our concert.'

I realised that Mrs Douglas, by now looking somewhat flustered, was fanning herself quite feverishly. She was also breathing heavily. 'However,' she added, her brown eyes flashing wickedly as she stopped her caressing, 'in order to establish beyond any reasonable doubt that you will indeed be an asset to our choir I do require you to undertake some private practice with me here tonight ...'

'It'll be my pleasure, ma'am,' I replied. 'But why wait so long?' And with that I placed both hands on her heaving bosom, took hold of that blue dress laced with yellow flowers and, in one deft movement, tore it asunder. 'Oh, Mercy me!' she gasped ...

In an instant we were in the bedchamber, relieved of all garments. As we embraced and fell onto the large bed she was panting that she was sorry, didn't know what devil had possessed her and that she'd never sinned against her husband afore. On hearing this I threw her across my knee and duly administered a good spanking to her hind quarters which had the desired effect of arousing the good lady to ever loftier heights of excitement. Corporal punishment, I suppose you might say!

Then, ordering me to tie her wrists and ankles to the bed iron with scarves, she got me to sing Men of Harlech again, only really softly due to the servants next door. I'd bound her fast, she was moaning heavily and I was just preparing to mount up when, to my complete and utter dismay, my private practice was rudely interrupted by the trill of a bugle from outside on the parade ground. Unbeknownst to me, The Seventh's commander, Colonel Sam Sturgis, had turned up unexpectedly and we were now being summoned for an impromptu troop inspection!

There was simply nothing else for it. Having frantically retrieved my uniform and donned it in unseemly haste, I darted from the bed-chamber leaving an aghast Mrs Douglas trussed up like a turkey at Thanksgiving, strictly forbidding her from moving prior to my swift return. Imagine my discomfiture when McDougall duly ordered me to give Sturgis and his wife a lengthy display of my horse-riding skills!

Dusk was falling afore I finally returned to the Douglas quarters eager to complete the Welsh conquest of England. Yet hark! On approaching the bedchamber I was halted by the sound of voices from within. Peering around the door, I saw Mrs Douglas still in the starfish position; bound by wrist and ankle and naked as a jaybird. The one difference to the scene, and a highly significant one at that, was the presence of her servant Mary who was diligently engaged in freeing her mistress from her bonds.

'Pray make no mention of this to Lt Douglas, I beg,' I heard Mrs Douglas say. 'I have succumbed to temptation and sinned before God, dear Mary, and the Lord Almighty has been swift in his admonishment!'

Fortunately for me, the pair were so preoccupied that I was able to slink off sight unseen. I should have heeded the words of dear Father who'd always lectured me on the perils of leaving a job half-done, I ruefully reflected, and Mrs Douglas would undoubtedly have had much explaining to do had her husband arrived home unexpectedly.

Back at the barracks, the boys were greatly astounded as I related all. When I somewhat mischievously went on to announce that, given the compromising circumstances and the obvious suspicion over what had transpired beforehand, Mary the servant girl was, in fact, the rightful recipient of the Mrs Douglas wager, their jaws plain hit the floor.

Considering the havoc I'd unwittingly wrought, I wasn't too surprised to receive a note the next day saying that 'due to unforeseen circumstances' there was now no longer a place for me in the choir. Maybe Lt Douglas had indeed come home unexpectedly, I surmised. Can't say I was too disappointed and thinking back on what his wife said about my singing made me feel like a dog with two tails!

T'was while we were stationed at Fort Totten, or Fort Totty as I'd forever refer to it, that long-running rumours of some kind of spring offensive against the Sioux became rampant. The US government had, it seemed, finally tired of the Indians breaking out of their reservations and President Ulysses S Grant plumped for a military solution.

The Black Hills gold rush was pretty much inevitable in my book. After the financial crash of 1873 – the Panic of '73 the papers called it – it was obvious those bigwigs on Capitol Hill would cast their eyes around hoping for some kind of quick financial fix. To them the Black Hills held rivers of gold. The fact that those lands had been given to the Indians carried no weight whatsoever.

It didn't pay to express such views back in the barracks. Most of the talk there was of fighting redskins, rutting with their squaws, who would claim the most scalps and speculation over the romantic life of that Calamity Jane who was always in the newspapers.

Yet the government's handling of the Indians continued

to stick in my craw. While I was scarcely a saint, and oft went hot and cold thinking of all the bad things I'd done, I liked to think of myself as a man of my word. Every dollar I borrowed from Hohmeyer, Eagan and Ogden was duly paid back, for instance, even though I'd had to scrimp and save like billy-o to pay off all my debts. If I made a promise to some fellow o'er a handshake, I'd never dream of breaking it. That was just the way we'd been raised by Father and Mother; religion didn't come into it. The fact Washington had promised those lands to Sitting Bull and his band and had now reneged on the Laramie Treaty troubled me more and more. But when I tried to speak to Ogden about it I could see he and I weren't singing from the same hymn sheet. Or even the same hymn book, come to that.

'Why worry your head 'bout a bunch o' cut-throat savages, Will?' he replied. 'We're soldiers, not politicians, for Christ's sake; let them learned fellers on Capitol Hill attend to their political affairs an' leave us boys o' The Seventh attend to the fightin'.'

A line from that old Tennyson poem I remembered from childhood popped into my head. 'Ours is not to reason why, ours is to do and die,' I muttered to no-one in particular, although judging by Johnny's blank expression he was unfamiliar with the works of the Poet Laureate. He was right, though. If the common soldier questioned every order he was given then precious little soldiering would actually get done. Not for the first time I reminded myself that I was now less than a year away from completing my five-year enlistment. Some of the other fellows, including Ogden, were on their second.

'Sure beats herdin' cattle on the folks' farm back in Massachusetts,' he'd say. 'Guess I just ain't cut out to be no farmer. Thar's jus' one way to milk a cow; one way t' plough a field an' one way t' plant a Goddamn crop.'

And while I understood such sentiments perfectly

well, I'd now had more or less my fill of army life. Despite being promoted to sergeant on my 27th birthday I was by now firmly of the opinion that twelve more months would be more than enough and then what? A return to the old country and the sedate life of a farmer in the lush green fields of Pembrokeshire? No, I was still pretty sore with John and, in truth, Elizabeth as well, so a push way out West and an opportunity to see what places like California and Oregon had to offer held more appeal. One way or another, I decided, I'd have to resolve my future come discharge time in February. There'd still been no further word from Annie and by now I doubted there e'er would be.

As we'd anticipated, in April we were returned to Lincoln to prepare for the expedition against the Sioux. There, E Troop were to a man disappointed to learn that McDougall, who we all greatly admired, was being transferred to Company B. His popularity was evidenced a couple of years previously when e'ery man of E put their names to a letter expressing our dismay at the fact he would not be accompanying us on the Black Hills expedition. As things turned out, McDougall ended up retaining command after all, so all was well. But there was to be no turnaround this time. We were informed that Lt Algernon Smith would be our commander. It was a decision we neither welcomed nor desired.

Assigned to us from Company A, Smith was a US Army veteran who'd sustained serious injury during the North-South War. Related to Custer through marriage, he was part of what we fellows called The Custer Clan, that tight-knit little bunch of officers who curried Custer's favours and who would go out of their way to stay the right side of him. I suppose my attitude towards Smith was one of mild contempt following an episode that occurred on the Black Hills expedition when he was quartermaster.

One night after the wind got up a couple of mules got

loose, strayed into camp and, being dumb mules, ended up entangled in the ropes of the headquarters tents, braying and thrashing about. For this Smith ordered one of the teamsters, a fellow named Roberts, to be trussed up like a hog to a wagon and left there for some hours. This seemed a great injustice. It was through no fault of Roberts that those mules got loose in the first place. The poor devil almost died of thirst and was never the same again. And this was the doing of the officer who would now lead us into our long-awaited showdown with the Sioux and Cheyenne. I felt uneasy and thought me and my companions in the Gray Horse Troop deserved better.

Smith's devotion to Custer went way beyond laughing at the General's jokes and joshing with him like a schoolboy while out on hunting trips; the son of a gun even donned buckskins to make him look just like his hero, although Custer carried the look off with a sight more style. In fairness, Smith, who was called 'Fresh' by Custer for some reason, was not the only officer of The Seventh to cultivate the Custer look, but he went a sight further than all the rest, for sure. Full of devilment on the Lincoln parade ground one morning I pretended to mistake him for Ol' Iron Butt himself.

'Begging your pardon, sir, I thought you were the General,' I saluted hastily, seemingly coming over all embarrassed at my apparent folly, like. You could tell from the smug expression on Smith's face that he was as tickled as a prize pupil singled out for special praise by his schoolteacher. The fact he swallowed my ruse so easily made me feel bad at having sport at his expense even if he remained blissfully ignorant of that fact.

I don't think Nettie, his wife, stood watching her husband adoringly from the porch of the Custer residence, was quite so easily fooled, though. She may have glimpsed the smirk on my face when Smith wasn't looking 'cos I could feel her suspicious glare bearing down on my back from a range of twenty paces. Mrs Smith clearly worshipped the ground her husband walked upon, was very ambitious on his behalf and no doubt looked forward confidently to the day when he'd take over command of the Seventh.

As usual we were given precious little notice of when we'd be setting out. Smith told us it would probably be in mid-May, but even he seemed uncertain. As the days slipped by expectations arose throughout the fort. We sensed that in a way what would unfold in the coming summer was what we had spent our time preparing for. The Yellowstone and Black Hills expeditions and all that rigmarole down in the Deep South were nothing but mere dress rehearsals for what awaited us out on the Great Plains. What we did know was that Sitting Bull had led hundreds of Indians off their reservations into the wilderness seemingly far beyond the reach of federal troops. The Seventh would be part of a combined force commanded by Generals Crook, Gibbon and Terry which would be dispatched to find them.

An air of melancholy hung over Lincoln as we prepared for departure. One night, while returning from the stables having overseen our mounts' night feed, I ran into Smith and his wife engaged in earnest conversation outside the officers' quarters. Whilst neither seemed aware of my presence I was close enough to observe Mrs Smith's face glistening with tears.

Eventually, May 16 was given as the date we were moving out. The Seventh would be part of a massive column heading West with the objective of finding the runaway Indians and escorting them back to where Washington reckoned they belonged. While we had no idea where they were holed up, and therefore no idea how long we'd be away, the general view among the ranks was that we'd find those Indians had skedaddled into the Badlands, that queer country of broken hills, buttes and canyons a couple of hundred miles distant. What sport we'd have steering our wagons and beef cattle

233

herd through that Hellish terrain, I thought grimly.

The day afore our departure, I was bawling out some of our fellows over their lamentable attempts to pack down some mules when a wagon appeared on the rough track along the bank of the Missouri leading to the fort. As it approached, work seemed to slide to a halt as we realised it contained a group of women all craning their necks expectantly as the wagon drew ever nearer and they peered curiously around their new surroundings. The wagon drew up outside the officers' quarters where its female cargo disembarked. There were about half-a-dozen of these curious new arrivals gazing about the parade ground and barracks, striving to ignore all the stares and catcalls they were getting. Then I remembered we'd been due to receive a fresh batch of laundresses that day. No wonder our fellows were acting like dogs on heat. Apart from those rough creatures who inhabited Whiskey Point, the fort laundresses and officers' wives, you never got to see no woman. During those harsh plains winters when the darkness seemed to last eternally we'd grow so bored we'd hold dances where soldier would jig with fellow soldier; that's how bad it got.

Ordering the men to continue their packing duties, I glanced up and was struck by the sudden realisation that one of the ladies had detached herself from the rest of the group and was now advancing slowly towards me. As she got nearer I could see she was young and pretty, small and dainty, her hair encased in a bonnet. She was clad in a narrow-waisted long yellow dress and bore what appeared to be a searching look on her face. I glanced behind me at first, thinking her gaze was set on someone else. Then my heart stuttered as it dawned t'was I who was the object of her obvious curiosity.

The woman continued to walk slowly towards me; finally halting less than ten yards distant. At that point she slowly and deliberately raised her hands to untie the ribbon of her bonnet from beneath her chin. As I continued to watch, she, with a pale and freckled right hand, dragged it from her head, allowing dark masses of curly hair to tumble forth. And it was Irish hair ... My heart, which had started to pound fit to burst, now seemed to have stopped completely. There, standing afore me with a look of sheer joy and wonder in those blue cornflower eyes was Irish Annie McBride!

'Holy Mother of God, Will James,' she breathed, 'please tell me that is indeed you?'

For a few seconds I found I'd no voice; it seemed that the hustle and bustle around us had retreated so much that we were now the only two people standing on that blessed parade ground. 'Yes, yes 'tis I,' I replied hoarsely. 'But for so long I thought ...'

'You thought I was no more; that I'd breathed my last, but you was betrayed by false information,' came the reply. 'I seem to make a habit of comin' back from the grave, huh, Taffy? Guess we both do.'

Mike Lewis

CHAPTER 13

Haverfordwest
December 9, 1904

Arthur Nicholas read and re-read the letter from London he'd just opened and thumped his fist on the desk in frustration, the sharp report causing his two colleagues to jump slightly and look over enquiringly in his direction. What might have been a lead in the search for WBJ had proved just another blind alley; at least in the considered opinion of Peacock & Goddard. A William J James had been traced who formerly lived in Opelika in 1875. He was very unlikely to have been a Pembrokeshire farmer's son, thought Arthur despondently, and the New York-based solicitors had more or less ruled out an approach to the British Consul. What was always going to be a daunting challenge had over the preceding eight months begun to increasingly resemble a wild goose chase.

'Don't want to sound discouraging, like,' said Arthur's kindly old colleague, Clifford Thomas, 'but old Mr Eaton set you a well-nigh impossible task on tracing this Mr James in my honest opinion.'

'You never spoke a truer word, Mr Thomas,' replied Arthur, 'you never spoke a truer word. People who knew James tell me he was always hard to button down. He was, apparently, not known as 'Will 'o the Wisp' for nothing. Yet had I known just how slippery a customer I was dealing with then I might have been tempted to leave this particular wild goose well alone.'

Arthur, however, remained intrigued about the character

of the man he sought. He was, in fact, starting to revise his theory that James had gone out to Canada and then America as a commercial traveller. From what his mam, Mrs Bowen and Mary Lloyd had implied, WBJ was clearly something of a maverick and adventurer. Would the relatively humdrum existence of a commercial traveller be sufficiently engaging for an individual with a daredevil glint in his eye who tended to buck authority, thrive on danger and live by his wits?

Again and again people had remarked on James' remarkable ability on horseback; and from a very young age to boot. Arthur now found it hard not to conclude WBJ was working with horses somewhere in the Deep South; as a blacksmith, farrier or coachman, perhaps? Only that week he had heard another WBJ tale to add to his growing collection. Another friend of his mother's had recalled walking up Cwmyreglwys Hill in the direction of Dinas one evening sometime in the late 1860s when she saw a horserider trotting down the hill towards her. As the figure came nearer she realised that what she had initially taken to be a particularly tall rider was in fact WBJ. Having lengthened the reins of his steed he was guiding the animal down the road whilst standing erect in the saddle.

'Looking back, it could only have been William,' she'd told Mari. 'As we passed one another he raised his hat and wished me a good evening as if such a mode of transport was commonplace! I later found out he'd gone and done it for a wager. More than likely had a quart of ale inside him too!'

Arthur could not resist a smile. Even if his quest for this man was destined to fail he had at least garnered some interesting yarns with which to entertain his fellow drinkers the next time he dropped in at the Freemasons Arms. Instead of placing his faith on the half-hearted efforts of solicitors based on the other side of the Atlantic who he suspected were more interested in the pursuit of a pay cheque than an actual missing person, Arthur had gradually come to believe that the key to the WBJ mystery lay much nearer home. He had one more card left to play; one more person still to visit. The former Elizabeth Morgans; the somewhat mysterious woman who WBJ had courted prior to her tragically brief marriage to his elder brother.

Arthur had grown increasingly intrigued by the 'sister-in-law from Newport' who popped up so regularly in that clutch of letters he now knew off by heart. The news of her earlier relationship with WBJ explained his frequent mention of someone whose marriage to his elder brother had been cruelly ended. For the first time, Arthur would be meeting someone who knew WBJ intimately and the young solicitor had an intuitive feeling that Elizabeth would be able to shed some light on her one-time paramour's ultimate fate. The net, he kept telling himself, was closing in.

After some initial enquiries, Arthur established that Elizabeth Evans, as she was now known, lived with her second husband, Captain David Evans, at Spring Gardens near Newport Parrog. As Mary Lloyd had said, it was one of the finest properties in the town. As the Evanses were clearly well-to-do, Arthur was not too surprised to find the captain's number in the Newport phonebook.

For all Mary's assurances he was still unsure how Elizabeth would greet his approach. No doubt he would have to ask some hard and rather personal questions and discreet enquiries had led him to believe that the one-time Elizabeth Morgans was a formidable, rather prickly character by all accounts. Taking a deep breath, Arthur dialled the number for the Evans residence and sat back in his office chair waiting to be connected ...

***

Annie and I continued to stare at one another as if in a trance. Ne'er afore in my 27 years had I been so astonished;

yet it was a joyous astonishment that rose up within me like a fountain to such an extent I feared I'd faint with happiness on the spot. I remembered the deep lasting sorrow that flooded my being on seeing that stark, single word 'deceased' written on the letter that was returned to me at Lincoln. The thought that poor little Irish Annie was no more had struck me very hard; maybe as severe a blow as any I'd suffered afore. Then came that queer little note stating that she still lived, shorn of any explanation as to where she might be. Now here she was standing on the parade ground of Fort Abraham Lincoln, for Heaven's sake!

T'was an even bigger shock than our last unexpected encounter in Chicago. For an instant I half-expected to be shaken from my slumbers by Hohmeyer's boot slamming into my belly, but, no, I was indeed awake and fully conscious and that really was dear darling Annie standing smiling shyly afore me.

'Sgt James!' Smith's sharp and sarcastic bark returned me to my senses. 'Once you've stopped admiring the merchandise that wagon's brought in we'd be most obliged if you cared to join us and resume your duties!' More by sign language than anything, Annie and I pledged to meet up later, once our respective chores were done on what would be my last night on the banks of the Missouri for several weeks. Our time together would be cruelly short, I thought numbly.

By the time we finally did carry out our secret rendezvous, around the back of the quarters all at the fort had christened Laundress Row or Suds Row, the heavens had blackened and the prairie wind was starting to moan. Finding some shelter from the pattering rain, Annie and I shared a warm hug before she related all that had befallen her since that now-distant day she'd seen me off from Chicago railway depot, a newly sworn-in private in the US Army.

She told how she'd fallen pregnant almost instantly after her wedding to Frank. Alas! The union had not proved a happy one and right from the start her new husband exhibited hitherto unknown jealous and possessive qualities. Moreover, the firm Frank worked for began experiencing some financial difficulties and the worse the situation grew, the more he'd drink and when in drink, she explained, he'd knock her from pillar to post.

As she continued I felt that old, familiar burning anger rising within me like a spring tide. The thought of my beloved Annie being at the mercy of a violent drunk filled me rage and nausea. At that instant I wished Annie had never told me her woes as I'd already begun to plot how I could somehow make a trip back to Chicago on some excuse for the Army, when in actual fact my objective would be seek out Annie's now-estranged husband and exact violent and terrible retribution. One day I would again meet up with Frank Ellis, I thought coldly.

In my more philosophical moments I'd come to accept that I was an oft violent man with an oft vicious temper; but slapping some drunken and lecherous hotel porter in the mouth for propositioning a teenage servant girl was one thing; beating and punching your pregnant wife and kicking her down a flight of stairs quite another. 'That was when,' Annie whispered, 'I lost the child.'

I could not stop myself from lashing out at that point; the nearby wooden porch post taking the full force of my fury. To my instant regret the sharp crack of splintering wood made Annie flinch violently and prompted a couple of mule-skinners scuttling past in the worsening downpour to turn and glance quizzically in our direction. The blow also opened up a large gash across my knuckles which began to bleed freely.

Wincing in pain and feeling extremely foolish, I placed my damaged hand in an armpit and apologised, realising full well that the punishment Annie had endured from her husband had shaken her to the core.

241

'Believe me, Will,' she said, shaking her head and smiling sadly, 'violence ain't no answer. You don't meet violence with violence. When is you boys ever gonna wake up to that fact?' Meeting violence with violence? But I've been doing that all my life, I thought uneasily. Life on the frontier was a constant fight for survival and I could not envisage living any other way.

The fraudulent one-word notice of her apparent death was easily explained. Annie said she had received and read my first letter from Unionville, only for Frank to fly into a great rage on discovering its contents. She did not have to tell me of the terrible price she'd paid for that missive of mine; I could still see the pain and terror mirrored in her wide eyes.

'In a way I was dreadin' gettin' another letter from you,' she went on, voice trembling. 'And then when it came ...' Annie glanced momentarily away and out into the inky wet blackness of the increasingly wild Dakota night with a shudder. 'I took even more of a beatin'.

'That was when he wrote that I was deceased on the envelope and sent it back to Lincoln by return. He figured that was the last we'd ever hear of you, as did I; 'cept I didn't wanna believe it. That was why I sent that note sayin' I was still alive. Was too afeared to give our new address. Life continued purty well much as afore; Frank was okay some of the time, mean and sullen on others. He'd still beat me ev'ry so often, but ne'er as bad as when I got yo' letters. They'd got him thinkin' that it was youse, not him, that was the feller fur me, I guess.'

'Well, am I?' I blurted out, surprising and at the same time appalling myself with the directness of my enquiry. 'Am I truly to believe you've been carrying around a torch for me when all this time I thought you were lying dead and cold in the ground?'

Annie let out a deep sigh, wrapped her shawl tighter around her small body and gazed up at me as the moon

242

briefly emerged from behind a cloud, its light illuminating her sharp cheekbones and delicate features.

'Tried and tried, Lord knows how hard I tried, but I've just never gotten over youse, Will James,' she said softly. 'All that time I spent with Frank I was secretly yearnin' I could be by your side. I'd wonder what youse was doin'? Who youse was seein'? Whether youse was alive or dead? Heard about that big fight with them Injuns up on the Yellowstone and wondered if youse still had your scalp.

'Then I recalled the day youse signed up when youse said youse was a feller who could come back from the dead an' that there weren't no Injun on the whole o' the Great Plains that could kill ya. Many's the time back in Chicago I wished to declare my true feelin's, yet how could I when I was gettin' betrothed to another feller?

'I kept tryin' to tell myself that the US Army needed you more than me; that youse was just some passin' Fancy Dan I'd get over in course of time and that I was just another Sally-Ann t' youse.

'Truth is you'd somehow gotten inside my head and I just couldn't damn well git youse out. Youse was perched inside there like some Goddamn Irish leprechaun; 'cept you is Welsh, o' course. Guess in the end youse was plumb near drivin' me crazy.

'One day I found myself headin' into the self-same army depot where you signed up. Said I was the sister of William B James, of E Company, Seventh Cavalry, and was there any way they knew your current whereabouts? Officer in charge was real helpful, said E Troop was headin' back to Fort Lincoln real soon. Then he enquired whether I'd be lookin' for work in the next month o' so as they was plain runnin' out of laundresses at Lincoln.

'Thought he was jestin' at first. Couldn't believe my luck. Put my name forward and when I called back later they'd told me I'd been taken on. Youse gotta give me dues for that, Will. How in the heck was I ever gonna hook up with youse otherwise?'

Annie suddenly shot me a warm smile. 'Youse a good lookin feller', with a kind, brave an' noble spirit few possess, but that sure as Hell weren't what drew me to you in the first place.' She then grew solemn. 'Within days of our first meetin' I could see that youse was an unhappy feller who bore a burden somethin' awful. I saw and can still see that sadness in yo' eyes.

'Dear Will, what in Heaven's name happened in yo' past that could've left you so? The tragedies that befell your family was terrible indeed, but so many of us have known such sorrow, myself included. I'd wager that something in your past dwells deep within yo' soul an' despite all efforts to rid yourself of it stays wedged within the core of yo' very bein'.'

I stared beyond her into the blackness for what seemed like forever. Above us forked lightning danced through the heavens as thunder growled and satanic black clouds spewed forth torrents of giant hailstones which began to clatter upon the wooden roofs of Laundress Row. Returning my gaze into Annie's own, my mind seemed to be backtracking along a path through forgotten courtyards, neglected and overgrown. It was as if I'd armed myself with a sickle and was striding along some dimly-remembered route; compelled to continue while at the same time being afeared, if not terrified, of what I would find.

To my rising astonishment, I found myself beginning to recall vague shapes, sounds and smells of a past existence that I'd buried deep within the darkest corners of my mind. This winding trail, I sensed with a gut-wrenching certainty, was leading me back to those dark and wretched days at Peniel; a time of dread and horror and fear. Squeezing my eyes tight shut, I once again could feel the malevolent one-eyed glare of Thomas peering down upon me from above those half-moon spectacles. At that instant I swear, on my dear Mother's life, I could even detect the smell of the starchy frilled shirts he wore; the stench of alcohol on his breath.

'School,' I said simply, as Annie continued to look piercingly at me through eyes masked in shadow. 'My ... my schoolmaster, Thomas, was a very bad man,' I stammered, feeling my face flush scarlet for no plain reason. 'He'd beat and strike us children at the merest excuse. He was a staunch advocate of the Welsh Not rule, which decreed that we children should be beaten for using the mother tongue we used among ourselves and within our homes. Those who fell foul of him would be caned across their backsides and forced to bear the sign of the Welsh Not around their necks the following day ...'

Annie's face was a mix of pity and revulsion, but she'd nowhere near heard half of what I had to say yet.

'Thomas was especially harsh on myself. The first time he beat me was when I must have been about ten or eleven after he'd heard me speaking Welsh to my sister in the playground. A few weeks later he caught me speaking Welsh again, but this time he said my second offence carried a far more dire punishment ... he ordered me to stay behind once school ended at 4 o'clock ...'

I took a deep breath and looked at Annie with pleading eyes. Blind instinct was screaming at me to halt and turn back from that path now leading me to the very place which still held so many hidden fears and terrors. Instead, and solely through Annie's gentle promptings it must be said, I struggled onwards, towards what I sensed was fast becoming the point of no return.

'T'was a thundery day in November,' I recalled. 'Night was drawing in and the rain and hail were buffeting the school roof just as they are on this wild Dakota night. All my fellow pupils had departed to their cosy homes by the time Thomas picked up his cane and led me by the hand to the small alcove at the back of the classroom. He told me that as I'd now broken school rules on two occasions I was to be the recipient of a more severe punishment, but one he hoped would set me on the path to eternal righteousness.

'You have to remember, young James,' he said, 'that Welsh is the language of the past and English the language of the future. Your development and those of your peers are my prime consideration.

'My most fervent wish is that you all get on in life. You must think of English as the carriage or train which will carry you forward and convey you to places and situations far beyond your wildest imagination.'

'He ordered me to bend over the small altar afore which he would pray several times a day. While he'd beaten me there afore, on this dark, oppressive afternoon it was different.

'It was just him and me, and remembering the pain of my previous lashings my young self felt nauseous to the stomach, anticipating the pain he would unleash now there was no other soul present to witness it ...'

I broke off at that point, and stared down at my boots, sickened at the thought of what I was now so close to revealing to Annie, who by now had brought her own face so close to me our noses were almost touching. What in God's name would she think of me? I asked myself. Would she consider me any less of a man?

I drew in another breath, to try and combat my growing feeling of faintness and the humming in my head, and struggled on. 'He caught hold of me from behind, undid the buckle of my belt and pulled my trousers down,' I said more evenly than I'd expected.

'He then bent me over the altar, saying that what he was about to do was for my own good ...'

By now the roar of the storm overhead was being replaced by the heightening buzz in my ears. I was continuing to feel light-headed while a tightness in my chest made it difficult to force my words out. 'He ... he ... pushed himself onto me and … and … I can still recall his hot breath on my neck.'

I looked up. 'I beg of you dear Annie please believe me when I say that there was nothing whatsoever I could do to stop him …' At that point a flash of lighting brought her face into sharp focus and I could see her staring at me with a look of sheer and utter horror.

'He … he … was grossly indecent towards you,' she whispered at length. 'There was nothing I could do …' I repeated helplessly. 'I was ten or eleven you must remember. I didn't really know what was happening apart from the fact I was in acute pain.

'And even if I had known, Annie,' I said, my voice rising, 'what the Hell could I have done? I was ten or eleven years old for Heaven's sake!

'After that first occasion Thomas did it quite a few more times, always on the pretence of having heard me speak Welsh, even when I ne'er. The man said I needed purging, that was the word he'd use. Aye, he took me over that altar … again and again and AGAIN, he did!'

Annie's eyes were tight shut and as I started to shout and curse and rage she held me as close and tight as if suckling an infant. Barely five foot and weighing next to nothing that girl clung on with a strength I ne'er knew she possessed. I could feel the tears in my eyes now, but there was no going back.

'He ordered me not to tell another soul,' I babbled, 'that no-one would believe me and that if I did tell he'd punish me all the more. He said he held the power and the glory and I had none. He said our family would suffer eternal damnation if I told …'

Annie had heard enough. 'Please don't, Will,' she said softly, 'youse don't have to tell me no more.'

'And you know what he also got me to do?' I continued, as hot tears mingled with the rain now alighting on my face. 'He … he …'

'Please Will,' she implored,' youse don't have to do this!' 'He ... he ... he got me to recite Yr Arglwydd Duw, The Lord's Prayer, in Welsh, while he was having his way with me,' I spat, as great, uncontrollable wracking sobs began shaking my body so violently I felt it would break asunder.

'Ev'ry time he did it I had to say those words so that I would gain forgiveness from God, he said. And you know what, Annie? To this day I cannot recite The Lord's Prayer in my native tongue! Nothing, not one damn word beyond the first bloody line! Yet I can recite it in bloody English! No wonder God wants no part of me!'

Annie was still clinging fast, shushing me and shushing me as she strived to quell the tempest that lashed and tore at me from within. 'And after I'd finished the prayer,' I said, dropping my voice to no more than a hoarse whisper, 'then he'd beat me with the cane.' 'Dear God,' replied Annie incredulously. 'Having been indecent towards ya he'd beat ya even then?'

'Yes!' I shouted dementedly. 'And can you see not why? Is not the answer as plain as the face you see afore you?' Annie raised trembling hands to her open mouth as her face finally crumpled. 'I had broken the Welsh Not!'

CHAPTER 14

We parted shortly afterwards. Annie wanted to try and smuggle me into her quarters but we both knew the risk was too great; her having only started work that very day. How we both yearned to spend what would have been our very first night together. Yet we had to get our heads down afore it got too late and leave our goodbyes 'til the morrow. No further words were needed in any case. I stole back to our quarters like a man barely awoken from some fiendish nightmare. Only mine was all too real, and at that instant seemed to have befallen me only yesterday.

When I got in, the barracks was full of gaiety and laughter as the boys contemplated what the next morning's great push West would bring. A myriad emotions left me unable to partake in such discourse and my sullen muteness finally led a concerned Ogden to enquire whether all was well. I muttered something about having some gut rot after chow and lay down exhausted on my bunk striving to ignore the good-natured joshing over the new young laundress with whom the fellows had seen me conversing.

'You have to hand it to Jesse,' chuckled Eagan. 'That feller was quick off the mark as far as that young fresh was concerned, t'be sure.'

Eventually I placed my pillow over my aching head and sought a blessed sleep that just would not come. I'd wager a pretty penny that the torrential rain and hail on the roof coupled with the excitement of our impending pursuit of Sitting Bull and his band made slumber nigh on impossible for most anyone in those barracks that night.

As fortune would have it, the dreadful storm that struck forced the postponement of our march for an extra day. Following breakfast next morning we were told we'd be leaving on the morrow instead. The storm had blown over and the fort was once again swarming with activity as hundreds of soldiers, scouts and cussing mule skinners busied themselves for the off.

As for myself I was more than grateful for the delay. After baring my soul and God knows what else to Annie the previous night I'd been in no fit state to ride a damn horse, let alone head off into the Montana wilderness to fight a bunch of redskins. Plus I had a package to dispatch home to Wales.

I was pretty shaken up about the awful secret Annie had drawn out of me. T'was as if some part of my brain had locked those dreadful experiences of Peniel into some hidden cupboard. Somehow, she'd not only managed to help me find it; she'd also given me the succour to summon up the strength to find the key. While what I found there had been truly terrible, I was greatly relieved to have finally unburdened my soul, even if I wasn't quite done with confessing yet.

On that damp, misty morning at Lincoln I walked tall. Afore long, I found myself more or less back to my old self, barking out orders to the slothful privates and joshing as usual with the likes of Hohmeyer, Ogden, Eagan and Brown. Yet the jests we threw freely at one another were disguising the lingering anxiety I still harboured.

I managed to grab a few words with Annie down at Laundress Row as we troops fixed lunch. We again arranged to meet once our respective duties were done that night. I felt a huge warmth and growing love for her and held out the fervent hope that the two of us had a future together. Maybe, I thought, she's going to be the one who saves me.

Yet what cruel irony, I brooded, that I was about to embark on a summer-long foray into dangerous Indian territory just as dear Annie had once again come back into my life. Against that, what a fortunate fellow was I to have such a beautiful young girl watching out for me! Not for the first time I was deeply indebted to that little Irish princess who'd befriended me all that time ago back in Chicago. What on earth she saw in me I could not guess, yet I knew one thing for sure: having lost Annie on two past occasions I was sure as Hell not going to lose her a third time. Yet how would she respond when I'd tell what transpired on that God-awful night on the cliff top path? The last time I'd ever set foot in Dinas and the reason I could never go back.

That evening, Annie seemed quite low and finally broke down and wept as she reflected on my tortured confession of the night afore. She said I'd undergone a grave ordeal which had scarred me to the very soul. She also reckoned it'd cost me my religious faith. Annie begged me not to turn my back on God and that time would eventually heal all wounds. She was so utterly sincere that I just couldn't find it in my heart to say I'd rejected God just as I'd rejected brother John and the rest of my family back in westernmost Wales. The lack of interest from home had led me to conclude that I had to live my life alone and that life would have no place for Christian worship. Besides, I had prayed to God on countless occasions and ne'er once had He offered succour.

Anyway, I still had one last grim secret to impart. Annie asked me what become of Thomas and, there and then, I made up my mind to tell her.

'T'was the winter of '70 and I'd gone back to Dinas Cross,' I told her. 'I was feeling very low as my sisters hadn't long since died and Elizabeth had left me to marry Tom. Our brother James was on his death bed.

'Can't recall exactly, but I'd been drinking in some of the pubs around Newport that night. Hunched in the corner of the Castle Inn on my own, I started thinking of Peniel and my childhood suffering at the hands of Thomas. Sometime later I found myself on the path above Newport Sands, eyeing those seafront houses and wondering where he dwelt. Feeling somewhat poorly I'd continued walking along the cliffs to gather my thoughts and to clear my head of the drink more than anything. T'was a wild and windy night.'

Sitting opposite me on a bench in front of Laundress Row, Annie reached out, took both my hands and drew them towards her. While there were other folks about, bluecoats among them, to me it mattered not. I just had to get this off my chest. 'I can't remember how long I'd walked, maybe a mile or two, but I started feeling better and elected to start back,' I recounted. 'I hadn't gone far when I saw a man slowly coming along the path towards me from the direction of Newport.'

'I paused and looked at him and, as the full moon came out from behind a cloud, I saw that by some peculiar trick of fate it was Thomas himself. It might have been pre-ordained that he and I were there at that point, and he and I alone ...'

I fell silent and as my breathing increased apace, Annie clutched my hands tighter. 'So what ensued, Will?' she asked. 'I went up to him and introduced myself, and said he would remember me from those days at Peniel.

'He looked perplexed and said he'd taught hundreds of village children and professed not to recall me. I could see he was lying by the uncomfortable look on his face; the more he spoke and the more I began to rage the more afeared he became until he began to shrink away from me.

'Oh, Will ...' Annie was staring at me in anguish as if she knew where my recollections were heading. 'You see, that's what angered me more than anything,' I snapped, 'the fact he claimed he had no knowledge of me after all that he'd done. To my mind I felt that admission made me seem even more cheap and worthless than I felt already.'

'So what did ya do?' she enquired warily. I took a very long breath before continuing. Once again I seemed to have pushed horror-laden events to a place I assumed I'd never bring myself to go to ever again. 'I seized him by the collar and shook him like the rat he was,' I snarled. 'I told him he'd better start praying to his God, as no one else could spare him now. The fellow was crying and pleading ... I think ... I think he knew what I was going to do e'en afore I knew myself ...' Annie had raised her head and, like me, her breaths were now coming thick and fast almost as if she'd been running. Having got this far I may as well tell her the whole frightful yarn now, I thought.

'I ... I started throttling him and backed him up towards the edge of the cliff,' I continued. 'His glasses had fallen off and his one good eye was as big as a dinner plate; ne'er in all my life had I known anyone to look so afeared. All he kept saying was 'Peidwch! Peidwch!' (Stop! Stop!) Which only served to enrage me all the more.'

'But why?' asked Annie. ''Cos he was using Welsh, can't you see!' I cried. 'And yet he'd been only too happy to beat me and the other children for speaking Yr Hen Iaith! T'was one rule for him and to Hell with the likes of us!' Annie fell silent again.

'So afore I flung him from that cliff top do you know what I made him do, Annie?' She shook her head slowly, a look of sheer dread written all over her face. 'I got him to recite Yr Arglwydd Duw, The Lord's Prayer, word for word, line for line, just like he'd done to me all those times. Then I dealt him a fearful blow which sent him over.'

Annie took in a sharp breath as if unprepared for my admission. 'By Jaysus ...' she whispered. 'Somehow, he managed to cling on to the edge for a time, gasping and pleading,' I went on.

'I leant down and offered him my hand and for a brief instant I could tell he thought I was going to haul him up; only that was never, ever my intention. Instead, I slowly ground my boot onto both his hands one after t'other.

'The last word he uttered was the word 'Please!' before

I unleashed a hearty kick to his face which sent him tumbling backwards and downwards. I heard him let out a loud grunt as his body bounced off the rocks before striking the waves below. Gazing down at the cove, I could eventually just make out the outline of his body; it seemed to be floating face down as the current dragged it out towards the Irish Sea. I stood vigil on that cliff top for some time until it started to rain.

'Then I turned my collar up, picked up my hat from whence it had fallen and strolled back to Newport as if naught had happened ...'

God knows how many minutes we sat there in heavy, oppressive silence. As time passed, my fear that Anne would recoil from the grip of the murderer she now knew me to be grew. Had she known of my guilt would she have e'er taken pity on me in the first place? Would she have fled in the opposite direction as fast as her legs could carry her on that sunny summer's afternoon we'd first met back in Chicago?

We carried on staring at one another dumbly. My secret was finally out. My whole outlook on life, approach to people and, indeed, entire character had been bent and shaped by those events at Peniel. The revenge I'd committed years later was anchored to me more firmly than any ball and chain. I dragged my eyes from her face, dropped my gaze and stared hard at the ground.

'Ne'er happened, Will ...'

Those three words crashed into my brain like a breaker unfurling upon the shingle at Aberfforest Beach in the dead of night.

I frowned disbelievingly at them as if they'd been delivered in some foreign tongue. I looked up to see Annie was shaking her head slowly. 'Ne'er happened, Will. You ain't no murderer ...'

'But ... what is this you say?' I replied with an effort. 'I was there, was I not? I was there and you weren't. I attacked him and threw him off that cliff top. I watched his body drift out to sea. Oh, how I now wish it had ne'er happened, but it sure as Hell did! So what in God's name do you mean, Annie?'

'I mean, Will, that youse ne'er met Thomas on that cliff path, youse ne'er beat him to within an inch of his life an' youse sure as Hell ne'er threw him off that cliff top,' she said calmly. 'All that you've said was in yo' head. Youse sure wanted it t' happen. For years you've bin thirstin' for revenge. Youse wanted to inflict as much pain on that piece of shit as he did you. So night after night, where ever youse was, you'd lie there an' go through what would've happened had you come across him.

'Lord have mercy 'pon you, Will,' she went on. 'Youse sure a damn sight more mixed up than I e'er could know. That's what's makin' me so sad. Doncha see why youse get these thoughts? You're still blamin' yourself for what happened as if it was in some ways your own darn fault.

'You've had it goin' round your head all these years and it's done gone and festered, Will, like some great big open sore. Relivin' it agin and agin and agin ain't doin' youse no good. Nuthin', and I mean nuthin' youse or I can say or do can change what happened way back then.

'Forget Peniel, Will. Don't let what happened stay with you the rest of yo' days. Leave it be! You're the kind of feller who sticks up for ... what's that damn word ... the underdog, ain't ya? People need someone like ya t' fight their corner.

'You've got a good learnin' and for all I knows you could end up becomin' a teacher and maybe protectin' kids from some evil bastard like Thomas.'

Aye, I thought, gaining instant succour from her wise words. Thomas had not just robbed me of my childhood innocence, he'd also committed a great betrayal. Children look up to their teachers. Leastways, they should.

A good teacher, and there were no doubt many, could

change the course of a child's life just as someone downright evil could plant a seed that if left unchecked would sprout a poisonous weed. That, I now knew, is what had happened to me and through no fault of mine. Dinas Cross, my home village and the place which had held so many happy childhood memories now conjured up only black thoughts of evil and an unquenchable desire for revenge.

'I went back just that once after Elizabeth and I parted,' I told Annie softly. 'By then I was working in London and lodging with my sister and her husband near Paddington. Elizabeth was due to join me but my sudden rages and propensity to use my fists must have done for her. In time she chose my brother o'er me and, with hindsight, I cannot attach any blame to her.'

Then I ran back over what Annie had just said. That the events of the night I wreaked my terrible revenge on Thomas had merely existed in my tortured mind. 'But how can you say that it was not so?' I cried. 'The memory is as fresh to me as if it happened yesterday. Every last damn detail! While it pains me to say this, Annie, you know not whereof you speak!'

Annie let out a sharp exhalation of breath and looked down at the hands she had been tightly squeezing. Glancing up quickly she then looked me straight in the eye: 'Youse told me youse was out of your mind with drink,' she began firmly. 'Said you'd gone up on that cliff top that dark and stormy night, right? And who should come along at that very instant in the early hours of the mornin', but Thomas hisself. Real convenient, huh? The man you'd hated all them years just out for a lil' stroll in that weather and on that night?

'Youse truly reckon anyone would have been dumb enough to go out walkin' them cliffs at that hour, Will? With a gale blowin' too? And in the dead o' winter? Only a drunken madman would've gone up there that night, doncha think?' she went on, glaring hard at me. 'An' one Hell-bent on destroying hisself.

'Youse dreamt up that attack whilst in a drunken stupor and when youse awoked thought it was real. O'er the years you've done gone and convinced yoursel' it truly happened. It ne'er did, though a big part of you sure wanted it to. You may be a madman, Will James, but you sure as Hell ain't no murderer.'

I sat there, struggling to piece together the fragments of that demented night. The reckless carousing in Fishguard, the barmaid I'd bumped round the back of the Royal Oak, then more frenzied drinking down at the Ship in Lower Town. The wild horse ride back to Dinas and the spot of drunken bother I'd got into at the Freemasons.

Then that ugly confrontation with my sister Elizabeth and awakening in a puddle outside The Ship Aground. How I got there I knew not. Might I have been waylaid and knocked insensible? Finally I'd ended up at The Sailors Safety at Pwllgwaelod, from there weaving my unsteady way to the cliff path. Yet in my fevered head I'd come across Thomas on leaving Newport, a couple of miles distant. I knew for a fact I'd barely staggered a half-mile out of Pwllgwaelod before passing out through the effects of drink. What Annie was saying rang straight and true. The act of murder I thought I'd committed could not have happened once I'd weighed it all up. It was well-nigh impossible. My supposed revenge on Thomas was nothing more than a trick of my drink-addled mind. And to think I'd been bearing the guilt of his supposed demise around with me like a lead weight for these past five-and-a-half years.

Not only had Thomas escaped scot-free after what he did to me and God knows how many other young unfortunates; he'd continued to blight my life and cast a shadow I laboured under still. 'What's happened to youse is as plain as the nose on yo' face,' Annie continued. 'You suffered terrible as a mere child, at the hands of someone

257

who shoulda looked out for you.'

'He defiled yo' body and wrecked yo' soul, but that don't mean it can't be mended again, Will. It's poisoned your mind, made youse the angry feller you is today. For all I knows even helped decide you t' join the US Army 'cos that way you git to kill folks without havin' your neck stretched.

'Like I says, youse may not knows it, but youse reckon that what happened in that schoolhouse is somehow down to you, the ten or eleven-year-old you, that is. It's made ya bitter an' twisted; it's made ya damn well hate yo'self which is so tough for me t' witness.

'Don't you see it explains all the drinkin' and the fightin' and the whorin'? An' why youse turned your back on the good Lord? But what it don't do is make you a bad man, Will. You're a good man who's suffered real bad. An' you're still sufferin'. Life will get a whole lot easier once youse just learn to like yoursel'.

'As God is my witness, nuthin' youse coulda said or done coulda stopped Thomas doin' what he did. He can go rot in Hell while you an' me git on with our lives. When all is said and done he's no more than somethin' you'd scrape off the soles o' them cavalry boots o'yours ...'

Annie looked down, paused briefly and took a deep breath. 'Ne'er told no one this afore, but back at the workhouse I was ... interfered with,' she went on, matter of factly. 'Guess I was seven or eight at the time. This doctor was supposed to look at us kids ... yet did things t' me I didn't understood. He was so big and I was so little; so little I guess I didn't know what he done was wrong.'

Annie raised her head. 'Went on for a few months then he left. Heard later he got the fever and died. But y'know, Will, I dreamt about what he'd done fo' years after. Kept seein' his cussed face when I slept. Got so bad that for a while I was too damn scared to rest my head. Just dinna wanna sleep no more. Got over it in time, though. Same as you'll get over this.

Jus' remember, Will, that whatever don't kill youse will sure make you stronger'.

I was overwhelmed with sympathy for Annie. I also felt sick to the stomach. As if she'd not suffered enough in her life, I thought, and there'd been no one at the workhouse to offer her protection. Yet I also knew she had indeed emerged defiant and unbroken. She'd become a strong woman. T'was a reminder that I was not the only soul to have suffered such an ordeal. There was Annie and, no doubt, many, many others. Far, far more than I could ever begin to contemplate.

Annie then said she loved me. I told her I loved her also. What's more, I meant it more than anything I'd said in my whole damned life. I also thought long and hard about what she'd said about the effects of Peniel with which I'd unknowingly wrestled for so long. My sudden rages, my frequent recourse to fisticuffs which oft spilled over into sadistic violence, my contempt bordering on near-hatred for religion; the cruel and cavalier way I'd occasionally treated women. Trophies to be won, used and then discarded.

There'd been times in the past when I'd behaved truly badly. Drink, I reflected, hadn't helped, though I could scarce blame everything on the bottle. I thought again of that dreadful night in Newport, when Elizabeth and I were thrown out of the Castle. Yet that had nothing on what had happened later; when I'd struck her hard across the face with the back of my hand.

I had wilfully, if unsuccessfully, also endeavoured to bury the memory of all what had happened that night after we'd departed the inn. Elizabeth had berated me all along that unhappy walk back towards Penfeidr. What demons so possessed me that I would lash out at the girl I loved? But lash out I had and poor Elizabeth had been sent reeling back into the brambled hedge by the ferocity of the blow.

T'was no use burying my burning face in my hands; try as I might I just couldn't erase the memory of the look that crossed her features; not one of fear, but one of sheer contempt and disgust which somehow made what I'd done seem all the more terrible. What was it she'd said on raising her hand to her reddened, throbbing cheek? 'Damn you, Will James!' she'd spat. 'May you and your kind rot in Hell for all eternity! Neither you nor any other man will lift a hand to me ever again!'

Without even knowing it, I'd begun to behave like Thomas and others of his ilk. In preying on those less able to defend themselves I too had become a monster. I'd joined the ranks of lowlifes who strike women. How in Heaven's name did that happen? At what point had I become bad? A familiar wave of shame swept over me as I recoiled from the awful recollection of something that was by now several years distant. Looking down at my hands I saw they were shaking. At times such as this the self-hatred remained as acute as ever. Elizabeth had once said that unless I learnt to curb my violent temper I'd end up swinging on the end of a rope.

I now recalled that arrest of those distillers in Alabama under Craycroft. He'd praised me for flooring that fellow who'd sought to attack him. But after the captain had gone upstairs another of the moonshiners had given me cause to force him into the side of the cabin, elbow driven firm across his throat. He'd turned beetroot-red and, eyes bulging, had started to retch when my companions intervened. A forerunner to the Culpepper incident, I suppose.

One, a Scottish fellow who later deserted, said they'd feared I'd been on the cusp of killing the fellow. Luckily for me, Craycroft, who valued me highly, had not borne witness to what I'd tried to tell myself was but a fleeting loss of self-control. 'Cept it wasn't. No matter how hard I tried to justify it, there was no denying that I possessed some kind of trigger which caused me to go off like a firecracker whenever it was pulled.

But could I honestly pin the cause of my unhappiness and anger to Peniel? Or was I simply an evil and violent man? Elizabeth had evidently come to her senses and realised she couldn't become betrothed to someone who would so freely raise a hand to her. Poor drowned Tom had his faults, I knew well, but I recalled him saying on more than one occasion that any man who struck a woman was a coward who deserved to be horse-whipped 'til he bled.

What were Tom's true feelings towards me? I contemplated. Did Elizabeth ever reveal to him my violence? Did he go to his grave detesting the brother who'd vied with him for Elizabeth's hand in marriage? Indeed, was it my ill-will, my malevolent thoughts that had somehow conspired to send him and Frank to their doom? These past five years I'd managed to convince myself that this unfortunate chain of events were all down to Elizabeth when, in truth, they were all down to me.

I desperately hoped she'd get the package I'd had sent that morning. Unburdening myself to her was one way I felt I could move forward and go on to leave the army, marry Annie and we could then put all behind us and forge a new life in Chicago as man and wife. 'An' youse sure in Hell weren't to blame for your brothers drownin',' Annie's voice broke into my thoughts. 'Them boys was mariners. They knew them risks full well. Guess youse could say their luck plain ran out. And it's high time you forgit that gypsy curse, too, Will. Didn't stop you an' me survivin' the Great Fire an' from hookin' up again, first in Chicago and now in Fort Lincoln, huh?'

Still trying to come to terms with what Annie had said about what hadn't happened on the cliff path, I was aware of my heart starting to beat faster. I was flooded with the type of relief a frightened child feels on awakening from some hideous nightmare to find his own dear mother hunched over him. In short, I felt I had been given a second chance. I was not the evil person I'd thought I was. An evil sin had been committed against me when I was very young. I was not the sinner; t'was I who'd been sinned against. Aye, I'd contemplated murder to exact revenge, but where would that have led me? To an appointment with the hangman. The anguish and shame that would have heaped on Mother would have been indescribable.

'What youse wanted to do to Thomas was natural,' said Annie, as if reading my thoughts. 'Trouble is, took over yo' life. Made you angry an' that anger oft comes out when you's drunk; an' sometimes when you're sober as well, Will.

'Pity is that what Thomas did has affected yo' dealins' with pretty much everyone you've ever crossed paths with since. Includin' Elizabeth an me. And yet at the end o' the day youse wasn't to blame one bit for what happened. That's what I find real unjust.'

'I've dreamt of killing in cold blood for years,' I reflected sombrely. 'Night after night after night. What I've lost sight of is that the greatest robbery in life is to rob life. I guess we must both be grateful I ne'er got the chance to act out those thoughts.' 'Youse say that, Will, yet here you is in the US Army,' she replied. 'You gonna think about robbin' life agin when you next line up some Injun in yo' sights?'

'Believe me, if I could, I'd take flight tomorrow,' I said truthfully. 'I'm done with soldiering; I'm done with killing. I just want to live like normal people. I don't want to follow Custer on his damn quest for personal glory.

'What'll it mean to people like us if that fellow ends up as President? Pretty much damn all. Instead of hunting Indians I'd much prefer to stay back here and bake flapjacks with you, Annie. If there was a chance of the two of us getting a one-way ticket out of here, I'd seize it with both hands and the US Army wouldn't see me for dust.'

'Then why don't we, Will?' she implored, cupping my face tenderly in her hands. 'Just you an' me. We can sneak outta here one night, jump on the train at Bismarck and be back in Chicago in no time at all. Or maybe pick up a pony and trap and strike out West. You know me, Will, I ain't the kinda gal who spooks easy, but I've gotta mighty bad feelin' about this campaign. Padre reckons there's a whole lotta Injuns out there an' I jus' keep thinkin' it'll all end bad.'

'Padre said the same about the Yellowstone campaign of '73 and the Black Hills expedition of '74,' I replied untruthfully. 'As for you and me doing a midnight flit, it'd make no sense. Custer would send some troops after us and they'd find us. It'd be just you and me, Annie, all alone ... out on the prairie. And even if we made Chicago we'd end up looking over our shoulders for the rest of our days. We don't want to spend our lives living like a pair of outlaws.

'I'm getting out of the army in February; I've just got to get through the next few months. We may hit trouble out West, but nothing we won't be able to handle. We'll be over a thousand strong and armed to our very teeth. There's not a cat in Hell's chance of those Indians taking The Seventh.

'Remember Annie, this'll be the last army expedition I'll ever undertake. Winter will soon be setting in when we get back. Pretty much the worst thing that could happen to me then is getting bitten by a horse or having Jack Frost nip my ears.'

'Remember I told youse back in Chicago that the likes of you and me ain't got no voice?' she asked. 'Well, from where I'm sittin' an enlisted man in the US Army gits treated lowest of the low.

'You fellers are seen as no more than slaves, at the beck an' call of some high-falutin' officer who apart from yellin' orders don't even lower hisself to speak to ya. The common soldier is jus' sent out there as cannon fodder in battle; t' be used up, chewed up and spit out like a wad o' baccy.

'An' even when death comes a-callin' youse don't count for nuthin'. You still ain't got no voice. Just some unmarked grave way out on some lonesome prairie or on some river bank in the high country, t'be forgotten and known only to God alone. You lose your life servin' this country, Will, and there'll be no grand parades back East for you and fellers like you. No Fancy Dan speeches or nuthin'.

'This country will soon be celebratin' its 100th birthday and it's the likes of you boys in the Gray Horse Troop who've done made it what it is. And whatcha goin' git for it if you don't git yoursels' killed? Some shitty piece o' metal to fix on yo' chest on the fourth o' July an' an army pension that ain't worth five cents? It's all for nuthin', Will. All for nuthin' …

Annie didn't have to say those words. I'd already reached pretty much the same viewpoint. Hearing it from her lips, though, made me resolve to leave the army first chance I got. The reason I'd ride out with the rest of the boys on the morrow wouldn't be to claim a few Indian scalps, assist Custer's bid for the White House, help safeguard wagon train routes for settlers or those newly-laid railroad tracks. I'd be riding out for the rank and file: the enlisted men of E Troop, for the past four years the only family I'd possessed.

Like all families we'd had our fair share of trials and tribulations, fights and quarrels, but, unlike my own blood relatives, I thought bitterly, we'd stuck together through thick and thin. As we would again this one last time. Apart from Annie, those fellows of the Gray Horse Troop were all who mattered to me. And I would not, could not, leave them now.

'I have to ride out on the morrow, Annie,' I told her softly.

'Ah know,' she replied.

I thought then of something Elizabeth oft said. 'Seize the day', she'd tell me, 'as you know not what the morrow may bring.' Irish Annie had given me another chance, I reasoned. And I just had to grab it with both hands. God knows I'd made enough dumb decisions in my life. I sure as Hell wasn't going to make another. 'Once we've settled up our business with Mr Lo, I'll break away from the column on the trail back to Dakota,' I told her. 'I'll be well done with the Seventh by then. I'll get a letter or telegram through to you from Bismarck; we'll arrange to meet up in Chicago and to blazes with the consequences.

'We'll just have to take our chances, Annie. I'll grow a full bushy beard, we'll call ourselves Mr and Mrs Batine and lie low like a couple of bears in mid-winter. Lord knows, won't be the first time I've e'er had to make myself scarce!'

Ne'er had I seen Annie show such joy. She closed her eyes, then laughed delightedly and e'en clapped her hands. 'Youse can set yousel' up as a coachman agin,' she beamed. 'We'll track down Mollie an' buy her back from that dairyman, an' youse can git to treat me to a slap-up meal at the Harbord Cafe for once!'

Annie said she was still in touch with Dr Russell, adding that the cash reward he'd offered arising from my actions during the Great Fire would sure come in handy. The smile abruptly died on her lips. 'Mr Custer sure ain't gonna be happy at ya quittin' The Seventh,' she said. 'Whatcha reckon he'll do if he catches up with ya?'

I glanced over at the lights of the magnificent Custer residence twinkling on the other side of the parade ground as memories of a thousand midnight flits back home in Dinas Cross came flooding back. I turned back to Annie with a wide grin. 'Mr Custer's going to have to catch me first,' I replied.

'So where'll we meet up in town?' Annie wanted to know. We both thought for an instant and then said as one: ''Neath the big clock outside the rail depot!' Annie was chuckling at the prospect. 'Best not be late else I'll be left lookin' like one of them gals what hang round on street corners!' she giggled. 'I'll be stood 'neath that clock singin' Oranges and Lemons. An' I still ain't givin' up on that townhouse on Burnside with lots o' lil' ones runnin' 'bout the place, y'hear?'

Then Annie paused and her eyes narrowed ... 'Youse best not keep me waitin' thar, Will James ...'

'And you'd better be sure not to dally yourself, Annie McBride …'

Sat there on that bench at Laundress Row, I felt blessed by some miracle. I could ne'er undo the past, I knew, yet by spilling out my soul to Annie, my heart was gladder, my step lighter. I resolved to consign the events of Peniel to history. To strive to become the best person I could possibly be.

I then apologised for pulling the wool over her eyes. I'd been afeared she'd have taken offence at what she'd regard as my deception. I needn't have troubled myself as she didn't see it that way. She told me that when she'd said she loved me, she'd waited five long years to deliver those words. 'E'en,' she'd added with a short laugh, 'e'en if youse a bit cracked and broked. I figure I can put you back together agin. They may not been able to fix ol' Humpty Dumpty, but I reckon I can fix ol' Will James!'

Annie kept saying the past mattered none, that the future was all that counted and that she'd sit there ticking off the days at Lincoln until the faithful Scout carried me back to safety. She'd do her utmost to write me as oft as she could as it'd be mighty good practice for her.

As I'd anticipated she then asked how long we'd be gone. I told her I didn't know and that it all depended how far West old Mr Lo had fled. Shooting the breeze in the barracks that morning most of the boys reckoned we'd be away a good four to five weeks, especially if the Indians were hiding out in the Badlands like our scouts reckoned they were.

Didn't quite know how far distant the Badlands were, but they had to be a good two or three hundred miles from Lincoln, for sure.

Whether the Indians would return meekly to their reservations or decide to cut up rough and make a fight of it no-one knew, but most of us sensed there'd be a dust-up of some sort, not that I admitted as much to Annie. Being the troublemaker he was, I reckoned old Sitting Bull would've stirred his braves up good and proper.

Sitting Bull's mere name was the subject of much mirth in the barracks. Some of the boys had taken to referring to him as Slightly Recumbent Gentleman Cow. From what I read in papers like the Bismarck Tribune and the Chicago Inter Ocean, he was a renowned medicine man, revered by many tribes of Indians. He hated whites with a passion.

Given what had happened in the Black Hills, where the US Government had more or less served notice of eviction on tribes of Indians who'd long considered the area as Holy ground, I could understand his bitching. Seemed to me Washington were sick to the back teeth of those pesky redskins and plain itching for a fight. As usual, it would be up to us soldiers to go in and deal with the repercussions of the actions of a bunch of aged fellows up on Capitol Hill.

Despite being knocked up, I slept very fitfully again that night, the faces of Elizabeth, my long-dead brothers and precious Annie floating afore me. And to think the two of us still hadn't spent one single night on Earth together. I'd reach out for Annie as I slumbered; yet she was always just beyond my flailing grasp.

I suppose I wasn't the only one of us bluecoats who had a restless night. Time and time again I'd awake suddenly, thinking I'd heard the sound of Reveille, only to realise that blasted bugle had sounded only in my dreams. Guess in a way I was quite literally raring to go, like a lot of the eager young bucks tossing and turning in their rolled-up blankets around me. As my brother James had said long afore, akin to a mariner bound on a long voyage, I already had one foot aboard ship.

At 4am, we were finally awoken to a damp, foggy morning. Those accursed rains had turned the whole of Fort Lincoln and its surrounds into one vast muddy swamp and men, horses and mules all shivered in the cool damp morning air.

Ahead of us lay several hours of hard toil afore we even broke camp. With a column made up of hundreds of soldiers, scouts, packers and mule-skinners, along with the wagon train, horses, mules and beef cattle, progress would be slow. Smith told Hohmeyer that Custer had decreed we should take three Gatling guns and a cannon, on the grounds the number of Indians he expected to encounter was considerable. I surmised they were bound to slow the pace of the march. There were times I took issue with the orders of Old Hard Ass, and this was one of them.

From what I knew about the Badlands it was such gnarled, twisted and rugged country that a troop of cavalry could toil their guts out there all summer and still not manage to drag one damn Gatling through. No, I decided, those Gatlings would more than likely prove surplus to requirements and our Springfields, Colt 45 revolvers and sabres would have to deal with whatever the enemy'd throw at us.

As we mounted troops were organised into marching formation, word spread among the ranks that scouts who'd arrived back the previous night brought news that Sitting Bull's warriors were amassed along the Little Missouri River around 150 miles Westward. The talk was of around 1,500 lodges and a force in the region of 3,000 braves. When Smith addressed the troop, he said t'was likely there'd be heavy fighting inside a fortnight. General Terry had said that we'd return to Lincoln just as soon as Sitting Bull and his fellow hostiles were herded up, but there was always the chance they'd fight to the death. On the face of it, the fellows appeared to welcome this news, although beneath all the bravado and tough talk I could hear the sound of guts churning.

'Can't wait to see the look on Mr Lo's face when them Gatlings open up,' grinned O'Connor a tad nervously. 'He'll be damn well wishin' he had a darn sight more than some lousy bows and arrows.' I didn't have the heart to tell him I guessed the Gatling guns wouldn't be accompanying us into battle. Given Custer's renowned impatience, I reckoned he'd find their progress way too ponderous. Yet, by now an old hand myself, I knew the importance of talking up prospects ahead of an anticipated fight. Your average soldier needs a damn sight more assurance than your average fellow and the ride out of Lincoln was scarcely the time and place to piss on Custer's parade.

I wondered then how Annie was faring and what she was doing. Despite the early hour, I guessed she'd already be hard at work on laundry detail; up to her elbows in shirts, pantaloons and socks. Part of me earnestly hoped she'd be among the families who'd gather at Laundress Row to see us off. Another part of me hoped that she wouldn't as the past couple of days had been so raw and upsetting I still wondered whether I'd even be fit to carry out my duties.

If luck was on our side, this expedition would be over quicker than the last two and we'd be back on station in four weeks or so. Well, five most likely. Although Annie meant the world to me, I told myself that my befuddled brain would clear somewhat the more distance I put 'twixt myself and Lincoln.

Finally, after what seemed forever and a day, we were ready to move off in columns of fours. With a commanding, theatrical wave of his hand, Custer, milking the moment for all he was worth, signalled the bugles and the familiar sound of Boots and Saddles filled the air.

Orders were bawled and, as if one single body, we troops mounted our expectant steeds in unison. Even Scout, normally as cool as a mountain spring, was snorting and prancing as if he couldn't wait for the off. Then 'Forward, March!' commands echoed down the lines. The regimental band, mounted on their white horses, struck up 'Garry Owen' and, amid clattering hooves, jangling spurs and clanking equipment, we were off on what was for me and some of the other Custer veterans our second foray into Yellowstone.

Scanning the expressions around me, I was struck by the contrasting attitudes of the men of E. Old hands such as Hohmeyer, Ogden, Eagan and myself were pretty stoic about what lay ahead; we'd been through this sort of thing afore. But the company greenhorns, and there were a few, laughed, joshed and generally horsed around as they laid wagers on who'd get the first Injun scalp. I suppose the stirring sound of the band, the sight of the huge column stretching forth and hordes of teary-eyed womenfolk snivelling into their handkerchiefs must have turned their heads. Yet I knew that most of them had ne'er set their eyes on one hostile Injun; let alone experienced any action.

I found myself grinning as, from way down the line, I heard Brown bellowing a string of profanities to get some of these young valiants to shut the Hell up. Then Brown himself suddenly went mute. Some uppity officer must have told the free-cussing corporal to hold his tongue due to the close proximity of wives and children.

So off we marched, dozens of Indian scouts under the command of Lt Varnum leading the way. Several of these fine fellows were beating upon small skin-covered drums and singing their war chants which were pretty monotonous and melancholy, in stark contrast to the gay tunes of the band. Riding in silence now, we first passed the Arikaras' log cabins, their squaws and children singing their peculiar songs outside, and then the officers' quarters where several wives including Mrs Custer had assembled.

I'd never really liked Smith's wife, nor she me, but when I saw her bury her head on her husband's shoulder and sob piteously, a lump unexpectedly rose in my throat. What sorcery had Annie unleashed upon me? I pondered. I found it hard to imagine such a sight would have affected me like this only a week or so back. But then, I reflected, much indeed had transpired over the past 48 hours and both myself and Annie were still trying to fathom it all out. Finally we came to the string of unkempt cabins of Laundress Row that also housed the wives and families of us enlisted men. Some of the women, most of whom were weeping, came forward to give their husbands, who remained mounted on their steeds, an awkward hug.

The children, well the boys anyhow, were stood stiffly to attention, toy guns made out of sticks slung over their shoulders in homage to their fathers. Some of those proud little urchins even gave us the salute which Ogden and myself solemnly returned. Then I caught sight of Annie as our grey mounts drew abreast. I was riding on the outside of the column so she was able to stride right on up to me. Unlike the other women, she was not crying; maybe she'd used up all her tears over the previous two nights, but no woman had ever looked at me the way she was looking now. I was nowhere near prepared for what came next. T'was as if I'd been struck by lightning.

Raising her right hand to take mine and clutching her rosary in her left she bowed her head towards Scout's grey flank as if in prayer then said in a calm, low voice: 'Most everyone I've ever been close to on this Earth are now dead an' gone. My parents, my sisters, uncles and aunts, dear friends ... the sweet young feller I was 'bout to get betrothed to, workmates back in Chicago. E'en the kind gentleman who gave me shelter when I was homeless.'

She looked up. 'Youse and youse alone, Will James, are all I have left in this old world. Youse are the one I hold most dear. You were my past, you're my present and I pray to God, oh, how I pray to God above, that youse will also be my future. I ask of you just one thing today, Will, and that is that youse promise with every ounce of your soul that you'll come back t' me ...' Annie was by now gripping my hand so fiercely I could feel her nails digging into my skin. All the while she was speaking in low determined tones so no one else could hear. But I could hear e'ery word she uttered and they made

271

the hairs on the back of my neck stand to attention. 'You leave my life, I'm better off dead,' she whispered.

When she fell silent I came over all tongue-tied, like, and struggled for a fitting riposte. 'Fear not, you know me, I am a fellow who can come back from the dead,' I said at first. I regretted uttering it even afore those words were out of my mouth. Way too trite; so I tried again. 'I promised you all those years ago in Chicago that I'd never lie to you,' I began, 'so I can't sit here and tell you it doesn't pain me deeply to leave you now. You must truly believe me, Annie, when I say you have my word that once this is all over I will indeed come back; if God will spare my life.'

'God will!' she whispered fiercely. 'Do you wanna go to Heaven or would you rather not be saved? What happened in the past has bin and gone. T'is done! All that now matters is you an' me and our future together. I knows your take on religion, Will, but youse must have belief if the Almighty is to guide ya home safe.'

Taking a deep breath, I nodded dumbly. The intensity of that instant was so great that any further words would have been nigh on meaningless, anyhow. Besides, I seemed to have lost use of my tongue. All around us, wives and children were crowding around their menfolk, hugging, crying, laughing or jesting, yet the surrounding clamour seemed to melt into the background. And my blessed girl was still not done. 'Do you swear on your mother's life that you'll come back t' me?' Annie demanded, her gaze ever more steely. Not getting an instant response she repeated, with even greater urgency: 'Please tell me, I beseech you, do youse swear on your own mother's life, Will?'

'Aye! Aye, I swear on my dear Mother's life!' I exclaimed. I'd never known Annie to behave so.

My blurted response seemed to satisfy her because she nodded. 'Indeed, thy will be done,' she answered. 'On earth as it is in Heaven. You always was a man of your word ... I pray, Will,' she continued, reaching up to caress my cheek, 'I hope and pray I'll see your face again.' Still dry-eyed, not having shed a single tear, she finally released my hand and, giving Scout an affectionate farewell pat, turned swiftly on her heel to head back to her work quarters without so much as a backward glance. I remained bolt-upright in the saddle staring after her as if surveying a phantom; glancing down at my hand I saw she'd drawn blood.

When I looked up again she was standing in the doorway alongside a middle-aged laundress known to all as 'Old Mrs Nash'. Bunching her fingers to her lips, Annie, still solemn and unsmiling, blew me a kiss. That's when I felt tears prick my eyes: Old Mrs Nash looked so old and Annie so young …

'Forward, ho!' came Smith's bellowed command, abruptly breaking my reverie and making both me and my mount jump. Wrenching myself away from Annie's unwavering gaze with a supreme effort, I spurred Scout forward as the band struck up the jaunty strains of 'The Girl I Left Behind Me' …

Mike Lewis

CHAPTER 15

Bloomburg
Texas
Dec 16 1904

> **Messrs Owen & Sturgis**
> **Attorneys At Law**
> **No. 7 Wall St, NY**
>
> Gentlemen,
>   In answer to yours of 9th instant I have to say that the only James living at Opelika, Ala, in 1875 were D B James and B C James, my Brothers. I left that country in 1873 and went West returning to this country in 1898. On enquiring I find I have a nephew still living in Opelika. I am now 70 years old.
>
> Kindly
> Wm J James

Arthur Nicholas was making his way to Newport aboard the Cardigan omnibus having been dissuaded from walking to Bwlchmawr and picking it up from there by the array of discoloured clouds billowing forth from the West.

        As the bus left Lower Town, the horses bearing the strain of the long haul up the Newport Road, the driver cursing and making full use of his whip, passengers stared curiously at the sight of one of the first automobiles ever seen in town pulled in at the side of the road, black smoke belching from its interior. Judging by the number of irate letters in the columns of the County Echo, the town's few automobile drivers pretty much dreaded the steep ascent up Newport Road where their brand new vehicles invariably gave up the ghost. Not that the omnibus driver showed any sympathy. 'Nothing wrong with horse power, boys!' he shouted gleefully, whilst urging the horse bus past the sorry spectacle parked up on the left.

Arthur recognised the disgruntled automobilist as Mr Cornock, a retired greengrocer, who lived at Spring Hill, Dinas. Standing there, hands on hips, he was a picture of silent fury, distainfully eyeing his prized machine with a face as red as the flames now billowing from beneath its bonnet.

Half an hour later, having stopped off at his mam's home to collect his bicycle, Arthur stood and scrutinised the line of graves before him in Ramah cemetery at Brynhenllan. Here was John James, father of the clan, who died on June 17, 1863. 'Oh spare me that I may recover my strength before I go hence and be no more,' read the inscription.

Alongside stood the tomb of both James girls, Ann and Ellen, and their brother James; their mother, Ellen and brother John Clement lay adjacent. Of elder brother Tom and youngest brother Frank there was no mention. Arthur was not normally one to linger around graveyards, he found them all too depressing, particularly since the death of his own father who now lay at Macpelah cemetery at Spring Hill on the other side of the main road.

Studying the dates on the James gravestones, he noted that Ellen James, by a strange quirk of fate, had died on June 17, 1885, 22 years to the day after the death of her husband. Checking his watch, Arthur observed with a slight feeling of apprehension that his appointment with Elizabeth Evans in Newport was now little more than one hour away. As the appointed time drew near Arthur had been feeling increasingly nervous about their meeting. Elizabeth herself had answered the telephone when he'd rung the house and once he'd explained the nature of his call there had been such a long silence at the other end of the line he'd assumed she'd placed the receiver straight back down.

When Elizabeth had at last responded, her tones were precise and measured. She had merely stated a date and time that would be convenient for the young solicitor to call round before the line went dead. At least, thought Arthur, she had not turned his request down flat.

That night Arthur had a strange dream. He was sitting in a corner of The Ship idly gazing across at a group of men conversing at the bar. Arthur had been so absorbed in his own thoughts he had not initially noticed one of the group break away from the others and slowly pace across the bar towards him.

Gazing up with a start, Arthur stared at the tall, grey-bearded middle-aged man standing over him. The stranger wore a large broad-brimmed hat which shielded his features in the dimly-lit tavern. 'I'm James,' he said, extending a hand. 'I hear you've been seeking me.' Then Arthur awoke with a violent start which sent Mrs Canning's large ginger tomcat leaping off the foot of his bed in alarm. The cat turned and gazed indignantly at him with large green startled eyes.

***

Out onto the prairie we marched, us cavalrymen resplendent in our blue shirts, broad felt hats, cavalry boots and blue or buckskin pantaloons. In our web belts and saddle pockets we each carried a hundred rounds of ammo for our Springfield carbines and Colt revolvers and, knowing several days, if not weeks of hard riding lay ahead, rode with lengthened stirrups to avoid fatigue. The Gray Horse Troop were reputedly Custer's favourite so we weren't too surprised to find ourselves the lead company of a column that must have stretched back almost two miles, riding just behind Old Iron Butt, his good lady and his sister who'd been allowed to accompany us a little way.

Whilst always a somewhat reluctant soldier, I'd grown fond of E Troop. Smith would sing the praises of what he called our esprit de corps, which I think meant we stood shoulder to shoulder, or something like that. We carried a tad more experience than the other troops, got on with each other well enough and, Company F apart, were the best turned out troop in the entire regiment.

Those fellows of F were not known as the Band Box Troop for naught. No matter what hardships were encountered out on the march they always stayed looking spruce. Yates, their commander, had much to do with that. He was one of those officers who seemed bound for the top and was already being spoken of as a potential successor to Custer once he headed off back East to launch his bid for the White House, as was generally supposed. As for the likelihood of Yates taking over the Seventh, I guessed Smith and his better half would have much to say about that.

The one company you had to watch out for was I, under the command of Captain Keogh. He was typical Irish, born to fight and brave as Hell; the type of fellow who would shirk at naught.

Fighting, drinking and chasing women were what he lived for, though not always in that order. There were Irish a-plenty in the Seventh; Garryowen was our marching song, after all, and most seemed to be under Keogh in I. Ne'er had a conversation with the fellow though I eyed him with caution and swear he did the same to me. Walking across the Lincoln parade ground one day I'd seen him approaching from the opposite direction. As we passed I'd saluted and we'd both eyed each other up and down warily like a pair of suspicious alley cats, neither of us speaking.

Keogh was, by all accounts, a formidable fighting man

and pugilism played a big part of his troop's physical exercise routines. When in drink he'd bellow that he could lick any man in the Seventh. Going by those searching looks he oft shot my way I guessed he'd gotten wind of my own fistic reputation, yet couldn't quite bring himself to take me on. Had he done so I'd no doubt whatsoever that I'd have put him on his back readily enough. Yet, being Keogh, I'd more than likely have had to kill him to keep him down; and that Irish sonofabitch would still have gotten up even then. Like so many Irish you could tell from Keogh's eyes he was a killer whose up-and-at-'em approach to life was readily followed by those fellows serving under him. If there was a dust-up in some local saloon near where we were stationed you could bet your bottom dollar that Company I would be in the thick of it.

Nope, those fellows weren't known as 'The Wild I' for naught. Given that Annie remained back at the fort I was hugely relieved that Keogh and most of I Troop weren't too.

The first camp we made was really pleasant. It was a good campsite with plenty of dry wood in supply which meant we could light up our campfires, having dug the toilet trenches known as sinks first. Then, as sergeants, it was down to me and Ogden to supervise our new recruits' first night routine.

Having checked the site for rattlers, we'd put up the officers' wall tents and feed and groom our horses afore seeing to ourselves. Then we'd oversee the company's greenhorns as they fried their bacon followed by hardtack in the grease afore pouring the whole mix into hot water to make it all a tad more inviting. Following bugle calls, Tattoo and Taps, me, Ogden and Eagan would settle down in our pup-tent. As first sergeant, Hohmeyer had his own further up the line; our three other corporals, Brown, Meyer and Mason, my one-time adversary, shared. We talked for a while afore getting our heads down, all of us well aware sleep would be hard to come by in the days and weeks ahead.

Ogden and Eagan both held their usual calm demeanour, but Ogden told us he felt old Hohmeyer was more jumpy than normal. A big family man, he'd been uncharacteristically quiet on the first day's march. Ogden put his silence down to Hohmeyer missing his wife and children. Though sometimes testy, Fred was always approachable so I resolved to try and pin him down for a parley first chance I got. The biggest bellyache in camp that night was that we'd only got our greenbacks once Lincoln was long behind us. Those officers were really cunning and, knowing how an enlisted man's mind worked, they'd decided there was not a hope in Hell of us being paid afore leaving the fort.

Their thinking was that had we been paid prior to leaving a lot of the fellows would have jumped straight on that wooden skiff and rowed across the Missouri to Whiskey Point to blow their earnings on beer and loose women. And they were dead right, of course. I suppose the instructions, which can only have come from Custer, spared many a bad head the next morning and so rid us sergeants of the unpleasant task of rousing a bunch of ill-tempered drunkards.

As it was, we were given two months' pay at that first camp, minus hospital and laundry fees and other deductions. As First Sergeant, Hohmeyer was entrusted with keeping the company pay in a leather pouch. There'd be no need for any greenbacks where we were heading.

It proved a far from peaceful night. In the early hours we were roused from our beds to tackle a huge prairie fire which threatened to engulf the whole camp.

There was Custer, wild-eyed with concern, bellowing orders at us half-awake fellows already frantically beating at the flames with gunny sacks, shovels, boots, pans, kettles and buckets of water from the nearby river, in fact anything we could get our mitts on. Custer treated us in his customary manner, i. e. like dirt, a fact that was not appreciated by us, although we'd grown accustomed to his testy nature by now.

During the smoke, noise and confusion, I heard derogatory remarks aimed at the leader of the Seventh coming from the darkness around me. It took about three hours afore the fire was put out, leaving us just an hour or so for sleep afore the dreaded Reveille, which we all hated with a vengeance, sounded at 2:40am.

For three weeks we marched, oft in the most dire weather the prairie could throw at us. Gales tore at our tents and sudden downpours left us soaked and shivering. Finding good firewood was always tough and many a time we had to make do chewing a few scraps of raw bacon at night.

The officers ate quite well, though, thanks in the main to the deer and grouse the scouts shot while out hunting. On warm nights Ogden, Eagan and I'd sleep outside, trying to ignore our rumbling bellies while smoke arising from the line of officers' tents told us they were cooking venison or beef steaks on their Sibley stoves. Aye, the difference betwixt an officer and an enlisted man was as wide as the Mississippi; and it was way too wide in my opinion.

The infantry marching with us fared even worse. On a good day we could get through twenty miles yet these poor fellows were having to keep up in boots no man should have to wear. At least we had horses, although a fair few riderless cavalrymen accompanying the column also had to keep up on foot. Having to walk in cavalry boots, their feet resembled mashed-up pieces of raw steak by nightfall. That was the price paid for not having enough mounts to go round. Treating fighting men in such a way was sheer folly in my estimation.

Two weeks out, when we were just West of the Little Missouri in the Badlands, we had our worst day since leaving Lincoln, on the back of three days' bridge-building in our efforts to get across them. We awoke to a terrible wet morning, breakfast consisting of raw bacon dipped in vinegar and sprinkled with salt. No wonder the fellows were belly-aching. Back at Lincoln there'd been much speculation that this was where we'd catch up with the Indians; now we were here there wasn't so much as hide nor hair of them to be seen. Tempers frayed as we awaited the officers' stoves to cool so we could break camp and when we finally got moving several wagons became bogged down in mud. We managed to cross the Little Missouri, but progress remained dreadfully slow and when we finally camped around 2pm it was clear there was a coming storm.

The ensuing rainstorm so chilled us to the bone that some of the fellows elected to sit round a campfire in their ponchos with their backs to the wind rather than lie shivering in dripping wet pup tents. When we rose at 3am there was snow on the ground and a few hours later came the order that there'd be no march that day. That was just as well 'cos it went on snowing for several hours; most of the officers holed up in their tents leaving us enlisted men huddled around the campfires trying to ride out the storm. While not as savage as the Custer Blizzard of 1873, it was another reminder of how the treacherous plains weather could turn in a heartbeat. As overseer of post stables I spent much of my time with the horses who were having a real hard time of it. Our hunched-up greys, Scout among them, were the picture of misery as they stood forlornly, heads drooping, as the snow continued to pelt down.

Around me the air rang with the curses of men struggling in vain to light a campfire so they could at least get some hot food down them. Aye, the day was quite Hellish and we still hadn't seen one single hostile. Hohmeyer told us that night that our Arikara scouts had taken the storm as a bad omen that some disaster would befall us. Hardly made for cheery camp-side conversation. Already it seemed that ought that could go awry was sure to do so. A couple of days later, having left 'Snow Camp' behind us, we crossed into Montana Territory, our eyes scanning the horizon ahead for any trace of our elusive quarry.

We'd left Fort Lincoln for getting on for three weeks now, and early optimism for a quick return was disappearing fast. To think I'd told Annie to expect us back by around June 10, even if I hadn't truly believed it myself. I was a tad disappointed not to have gotten a letter, but knowing the trouble she had writing, and the fact she'd require some assistance, I realised I'd just have to bide my time.

I was not relishing this expedition though. The Black Hills excursion of '74 had been pleasurable; my best time in The Seventh. And even the Yellowstone expedition of '73 when we lost poor Tuttle on the banks of the Yellowstone had seemed a doddle compared to our present undertaking. Added to that I now shared Ogden's concerns about Hohmeyer. He'd been unusually distant and reticent ever since we'd set out. When pressed on what was troubling him he just wouldn't come clean. I reckoned he'd had bad news from his folks, maybe his children were sick or something, but try as I might Fred just wouldn't elaborate. Simply said we had a job to do and just had to get on with it.

I understood he might be worried about his folks, a lot of soldiers get like that from time to time, but troubled myself over the effect his distracted state of mind might be having on the rest of our fellows, a lot of whom were looking to our first sergeant for guidance and assurance. Eagan even opined, in his soft Irish brogue, that Hohmeyer just didn't have the belly for fighting no more. I couldn't rid myself of the grim feeling that, when push came to shove, all of us would find out if that was true soon enough.

One night I was awoken by one of the worst nightmares I'd ever had. An Indian, face contorted with rage, reared up to the side of me, raised tomahawk poised to strike. Awake in an instant, I sat bolt upright in my blankets, awash with sweat. I looked wildly around our cramped tent, the sleeping forms of my comrades on either side. Thank God it had just been a dream. But hardly had that thought entered my head when suddenly the tent flap was torn open and the self-same Indian sprang through the opening, features enraged, death in his eyes and that damn tomahawk raised above his head about to fall. 'Sweet Jesus!' I exclaimed, sitting bolt upright again. I'd thought I'd awakened when in reality I'd still dreamt. Considerably shaken, I knew it unlikely I'd return to my slumber, so I left the tent to go and check on the horses, standing quietly in a line like a parade of grey ghosts.

I stopped and inspected each one, noting with concern how thin and gaunt they were becoming, yet there was still no indication when our long march would end. As I continued my prowl around the camp, pausing only to exchanges greetings with the occasional picket, I was struck by the number of owl calls I was hearing. But were they owls? I asked myself. Could they not be Indians signalling to themselves in the darkness? I told myself that Hohmeyer's jitters just might be infectious and maybe I was starting to get just as skittish.

Temperatures remained bitterly cold as we pressed on, us cavalrymen hunched in our saddles, collars turned up, frost-nipped ears glowing scarlet and our breath small white clouds of bunched vapor. Over long marches, I'd learnt how to drop off to sleep in the saddle, Scout's plodding motion rocking me gently into a brief slumber. This might last mere instants but if it happened oft enough you truly did feel a tad more refreshed. Yet sleep was well-nigh on impossible now as we plodded through the biting wind across bleak, snow-covered terrain towards our rendezvous with Gibbon's column somewhere along the Yellowstone. Behind us the sullen ranks of infantrymen trudged alongside the creaking wagons in brooding silence, occasionally rubbing their ears vigorously to stop them dropping off through frostbite.

Around mid-morning we met up with some of Gibbon's Indian scouts who reported great numbers of Sioux South of the Yellowstone. Apparently a couple of fellows who'd broke away from the column to go hunting had been relieved of their scalps somewhere further upstream.

The news galvanised us weary troops: at last there was a real prospect of catching up with the red devils very soon. Beforehand I'd detected a distinct drop in spirits as the boys realised the further West we plunged, the longer we'd be away from our station. The fact we were now so far from civilisation reinforced feelings of lonesomeness and homesickness; I knew that was certainly true of me. When all was said and done we were interlopers in the land of the red man, after all.

Eagan kept saying he doubted the Indians would stand and fight, as evidenced, he reckoned, by their relentless flight in the face of our huge advancing column. On the other hand, Meyer, his fellow corporal, whose readily cheerful disposition was now but a distant memory, told me he'd never felt so depressed in his whole life. The fellow, I could not help but notice, was indeed as miserable as an old rook. Brown, in stark contrast, loudly offered to strike a wager with all and sundry that the coming fight would go down in history as Custer's greatest victory and that thanks to the writings of Kellogg, the war-mongering Bismarck Tribune scribe who was accompanying our expedition on his mule, we boys of The Seventh Cavalry would be remembered for e'er more.

Much as I wished to concur with Eagan's view that there would be no fighting, I wasn't so sure myself. Judging by what the scouts were saying, Mr Lo was massing in considerable numbers somewhere further West and with old Sitting Bull calling the shots I couldn't see those Sioux laying down their weapons and lining up readily for us to escort them back to their reservations. Even Mason, one of the more gung-ho members of our band, felt tangling with so many Injuns without the support of other regiments would be complete and reckless folly.

A mere 24 hours after our long-suffering mounts had

been up to their knees in snow, we found ourselves sweltering in soaring temperatures. We were hot as Hell and Terry was forced to quit the march with sunstroke, handing temporary command over to Custer.

This was bad news for the long-suffering infantry, who hated marching under Ol' Iron Butt. He seemed to regard those fellows as lower than vermin. The weather was hot, patches of snow dazzling and most of us were nursing headaches when we finally halted to make camp. Even there our misery continued as once we'd pitched our tents great clouds of mosquitoes made sleep damn near impossible.

Smith conferred with Hohmeyer that night and Fred later relayed the gist of their conversation to me, Ogden, Eagan and Brown. It appeared that having already travelled much further West than anticipated, we now had only around a week's worth of supplies left. Bacon, hardtack and tobacco was running low and while we still had the beef herd, the meat we were being fed was getting stringy. Smith said we'd be pushing on up the Powder River on the morrow, where it was felt the Indians were concealed.

After Fred had acquainted us with his intelligence, I took the opportunity to collar him away from the others as he headed back to his tent. Told him he hadn't seemed his usual self of late and asked after the family.

To my surprise, Fred opened up. Said he seemed to be feeling the grind of soldiering more than he used to, pointing out that, although still only 27, he was now on his third enlistment. I knew he didn't like Smith overmuch and now Fred let on he'd a few misgivings about our troop's second-in-command, Lt Jimmy Sturgis, as well. Still only in his early twenties, Sturgis was green as grass, fresh out of West Point and assigned to us while on detached duty from Company M. His father, Colonel Sam Sturgis, was the commander of The Seventh, so young Jimmy clearly had some pretty big boots to fill.

Hohmeyer was uneasy that such an untested young officer, 'as raw as an uncooked fish' was how he'd put it, had been given such a big role in a major push against the Sioux and Cheyenne. Bet his pa's influence had something to do with that. None of us knew the young officer, who seemed a tad quiet, though he appeared a decent enough fellow. Fred went on to say he felt the entire regiment was under-strength with far too few experienced officers and non-coms. Young Lt Reilly, of F, he snorted derisively, had barely learnt to sit on a Goddamned horse.

Although I could appreciate Fred's concerns it still seemed a queer thing to get worked up about. Hohmeyer was the kind of old soldier who'd roll up his sleeves, shirk at nothing and spit in the eye of the Devil. Besides, in all my army days there'd ne'er been a time when The Seventh was at full strength. Fellows would always be off on sick, or on furlough leave. Officers would always be deployed on other duties and such like.

Maybe Fred's own instincts were indeed correct: maybe after a few too many years of hard soldiering the job really was starting to lose much of its shine.

On and on we rode, across rolling plains of high grassland before beating a path down Beaver Creek. Leaving this valley the next day we hit country full of sagebrush, cactus, prickly pear and rattlesnakes. We had to watch out for those critters who were everywhere. The first duty that always awaited us on making camp was to clear the area of rattlers, usually by dispatching them with a spade, sabre or cavalry boot. Food being so scarce for us troops I heard of one fellow from M Company, Rattlesnake Jim, who'd fry them and eat them, then wear their skins around his neck! Anyway, within hours of leaving Beaver Creek we were again the picture of absolute misery. The country here was much drier, and our horses churned up great choking clouds of white, alkaline dust which clung to our sweat-stained faces despite our bandanas, burning our reddening skin quite badly.

Least we cavalrymen could allow our mounts to do the work, but for the rest of the column and the infantry it was another grim march to endure. A couple of mules died of exhaustion and when I groomed a sorry-looking Scout that night I found his fetlocks bloodied by prickly pear while cockleburs were dotted all around his tail and mane. Pretty much all our mounts were suffering the same way. By now we were deep in country no white man had ever seen. Conversation among the troops was long in the past as we all silently wondered when a battle would come and whether we'd be in any fit state to fight it. Lonesome Charley got it in the neck one day for mistakenly leading the column nine miles to the South.

Although General Terry always showed a concern for the welfare of us troops which Custer lacked, nothing pissed him more than taking the wrong route. All being well, we'd hook up with the columns of Gibbon and Crook at some point, so Terry could be forgiven for being in no mood to dawdle. A couple of fellows from Benteen's H Troop showed up that morning having been out all night after losing their way hunting. Sensing hostiles were in the vicinity many had given them up for dead. 'Cos of this Terry ordered that such hunting trips should now be curtailed and night pickets doubled, with orders to be particularly observant near dawn as this was when Indians were most likely to attack.

Campfires were to be put out quickly and, although officers' tents remained, at night us members of the rank and file slept on the ground by our horses, saddled and bridled and ready to mount up in an instant. The next day we completed an exhausting march of over 30 miles through rough and broken country to the Powder River. It may well have been the hardest day yet; several mules dropped from exhaustion and a few horses played out.

The river itself was a most welcome sight to hundreds

of weary, bedraggled soldiers. Fellows dashed to the river and jumped in fully clothed; mules and horses who had seemed at the point of death trotted into the swirling waters, the healing powers of which had to be seen to be believed. The Powder was to be our camp from which we would depart to meet the Indians, with what results remained to be seen. All of us were dog-tired that night, but as I settled down on my blanket, the faithful Scout chomping stolidly on his oats above me, my thoughts turned to Annie. I was hit by the sudden realisation that I was missing her madly.

Three weeks had passed since we'd parted, yet it seemed so much longer. I'd hoped against hope for a letter, yet knowing that mail brought forth by Indian scouts was strictly limited, I suppose I wasn't too surprised it hadn't come. As a sergeant, I could reasonably expect more privileges than the rest of the boys, so with that in mind I firmly resolved to dispatch a letter East at the earliest opportunity. Afore sleep came I found myself again reflecting on my disclosures to Annie back at the fort; as well as her reaction.

We rose at 5am on June 9 and within the hour the camp was bustling with activity as word spread Custer would be leading The Seventh up the Powder on a ten-day scout the following day. All around me carbines and revolvers was being checked, ammunition distributed and new pouches, blankets and ponchos issued.

We were told to expect Custer would only be taking his most experienced troops, with all greenhorns having to sit this one out. It was to be a speedy reconnaissance so we'd be travelling light which is why I spent much of the day overseeing equipment, dispensing with some and scanning clothing and blankets to assess what was truly indispensable. T'was a wearisome job, for sure, but nowhere near as bad as the task of those in charge of the mule-packing who had to contend with those snorting, braying and kicking sons of bitches who oft bucked so much that the water casks on their backs were frequently sent clattering.

Many of those mules took exception to being forced to take the regulation cavalry bridle in their jaws as well as having the somewhat unwieldy McClellan saddle deposited upon their backs. On several occasions, some poor infantryman was expelled high into the air when one of the critters decided to buck; the poor unfortunate coming to ground with a loud thud and a burst of derisive laughter from his watching companions.

Terry and Custer, we learnt, had spent the previous night aboard The Far West at the mouth of the Powder with the intention of hooking up with Gibbon and his Montana column. No doubt they'd be discussing how, along with Crook's column, they could join forces, form a circle of troops and corral the Indians.

Late afternoon, a furious thunderstorm broke, giving us troops, clad only in ponchos as we had no tents, an unexpected and inescapable shower. If the Almighty was constantly seeking ways of lowering the spirits of men destined to fight a great battle, then he was doing a damn fine job. A surprise greeted us the next morning with the news that Major Reno, not Custer, would be leading six companies of The Seventh, including E, on the scout. Custer's nose would have been well and truly put out of joint by that.

We were told to load up 12 days of supplies, 11 mules being designated to each company. This meant that, along with forage and equipment each pack animal faced carrying a load of over 200lbs, well more than they were used to. Packing and loading seemed to go on forever and once we were done, only the dumb brutes' heads, tails and feet were visible. It would have been quite comical if the mules' natural cussedness didn't get the better of them. Packed up to the gills and ready to go, those jackasses would simply pin their ears back and stand there stock still. Even a close-up report from a Springfield probably wouldn't have made those sons of bitches move.

The packers would respond with a stream of vicious oaths and ferocious lashing of sticks; the mules would answer with a kick of their heels or by unleashing a steaming river of piss. Suddenly, as if one, they'd dash forward together and generally not act up again for the rest of the day.

We started out mid-afternoon, six companies of The Seventh, along with one Gatling gun, a detachment of scouts and around a hundred of those pack mules. Well over one hundred men had to remain behind at the Powder, including a few boys from E, and their glum expressions as we rode out were a picture. Ne'er been a soldier alive who hates to miss out on any excitement. Our orders were to follow the Powder South and West. Already wearied by the long trek West, I can't say we were looking forward to several days' hard riding, but one thing was for sure: Reno would no way push us as hard as Custer, who looked really frustrated as he sat astride his horse watching us ride out.

No such luck. As it happened the scout turned out to be an awful slog even if we did find several Indian tracks leading Westward along the banks of the Rosebud. Our Ree and Crow scouts were plainly spooked by just how many Sioux and Cheyenne signs they were seeing. Some of the boys were pretty rattled too. I lost count of the number of greenhorns who kept coming up to me in camp and enquiring how I reckoned it would all play out; as if I had all the answers!

For what it was worth I felt as sure as I could be that there would be a kerfuffle of some sort, but reasoned that with the size of our column along with the combined armies of Gibbon and Crook, who we'd be hooking up with in a jiffy we hoped, we'd have superior fire power, even if we were outnumbered.

Aye, I thought to myself staring across at the row of Company I tents where groups of Keogh's men were lounging outside laughing and shooting the breeze, old Sitting

Bull will know he's met up with a pretty bad old crowd once The Seventh turn up at his party unannounced. I reckoned that when that happened those Injuns would scatter like dust in a prairie storm.

Every day of that Reno scout was purgatory; every Hellish day different and yet somehow stayed the same. We marched through some of the roughest terrain we'd ever come across: canyons, buttes, river valleys and ravines; all the while taking turns to pull that infernal Gatling gun along behind us.

There was no way, I thought bitterly, that Custer would have insisted on bringing this lumbering field gun if he'd been among those unfortunates having to drag it. Such weapons would spray death and destruction all over an open battlefield, true, but the twisted and hellish terrain of the Badlands was just no place for them.

As usual, we got precious little to eat and to think that one of the reasons I'd joined up in the first place was so I'd quit hungering. Lying in my blankets the rumbling of my belly would oft keep me awake; that and the wretched mozzies which descended upon us and proceeded to eat us fellows alive. All in all, those camps were well-nigh on intolerable. Yet lack of decent chow wasn't the only thing gnawing away at me. By now I was positively pining for Annie. I'd have gladly given a month's rations for a letter with a Fort Lincoln postmark. She'd promised to write, or leastways get someone to write for her, yet still nothing had turned up. I wondered if all was well with her?

What made me feel worse was that I hadn't been able to send a letter back. I'd tried on a number of occasions but always seemed tied up with stable duties whenever the call for mail came. There were only so many letters that could be carried back East on horseback, so the few lines I'd scrawled remained on scrunched-up paper in my saddle pocket.

We must have covered nearly 250 miles by the time we

met up with Terry and Custer on the banks of the Yellowstone just over a week later. Horses and men were played out, troopers exhausted from pushing and pulling that damned Gatling through gullies and ravines and canyons. The sun was ferociously hot and man and beast suffered cruelly.

When we finally camped just a few miles away from the rest of the troops on the Tongue River we found the ground littered with scores of gaily-coloured agates. Selecting one of a particularly brilliant green hue I pocketed it with the intention of taking it back for Annie. T'was the right-coloured pebble a daughter of the Emerald Isle would treasure. Some of the fellows carried carte de visites of their wives or sweethearts and while I'd never possessed one of Annie, at least I now had something to remember her by. Perhaps I should carry it next to my heart, I thought. It might even deflect an Injun bullet ...

We were really glad to hook up with the rest of the column. All of us were tired, hungry and in dire need of baths, clean clothes and shaves. But we'd barely had time to eat and spruce up when the order came to saddle up again. By 4pm, Custer was leading pretty much the entire Seventh up the Yellowstone, horses, mules and all, while the Gatlings were loaded aboard The Far West which then tracked us along the river. I know I wasn't the only trooper glad to see the back of them. I was less pleased to hear we'd been told to leave behind our sabres to be crated up and placed aboard the steamer. Custer, it was said, felt their rattling would give away our location on a night march. The sabre was the cavalryman's sole means of defence in hand-to-hand conflict. We'd just have to make sure not to let those red men get too close.

Rosebud Creek
June 21 1876
four days out of Little Bighorn

We camped on the south side of the Yellowstone feeling that things would pretty soon come to the boil. Can't speak for the rest of the companies but I can say that the men of E were pretty well cooked by now. It was no coincidence that the dozen or so mules that broke down at this spot had been among those pack animals which had accompanied us on the Hellish Reno scout. During an inspection of the mounts of the Gray Horse Troop I had concerns for up to a dozen and relayed my thoughts to Hohmeyer who I suppose passed them on to Smith.

There was an air of excitement in the air as The Far West, a welcome reminder of home, tied up on the South bank just across from us. A pontoon bridge was extended to shore and, as a number of soldiers stood guard, emergency supplies were unloaded for the forthcoming pursuit of the hostiles as well as a supply of mail. It was again hard and monotonous work, those bags were heavy and the dust they raised made the eyes itch like Hell, but Ogden and myself and a few other company sergeants had to make sure the fellows didn't slacken til sufficient supplies were humped to shore. Then and only then was the mail distributed to those who'd received letters. I was heading over to inspect our greys again when a shout from Hohmeyer stopped me in my tracks. 'Letter for Sgt William B James!' he barked.

> **Fort Lincon**
> **Dakoter Tertory**
> **June 15, 1876**
>
> My deerest Will
>
> Hop this leter gits to yoo bin tryin to git a leter out but bein a lawndres dont seem to carri much wait round heer am misin you reel bad them daze and nites seems to drag passed hows it goin out thar hop yoo keepin safe and getin nuff ta eet deer Will I wish I cud says I woz doin ok but in trooth am findin it reel hard the day yous rode out in that missed we was stood thar wavin an it luked like yous solder boys was ridin hi into them clouds leestways that was how it luked to us niver seen nuthin lak it afore sum folk reckened it was bad sine an that nun of yous boys wood eva cum bak alife thar I was stood wiv an offisers wive weepin and wailin on ma sholderan I was stood thar feelin jus as bad my frend Polly sed the doc told her it was sum kand of trik of the lite an missed an it dont meen nuthin I shaw hope hes rit bout that an ba the waze it woz Polly wat rote this leter 'cos her writin and spellin is purty good wel beta then man anihowse you beta make shaw yous rit me soon Will James els yool be seein ma wald irish tempa when yous git bak.
>
> ya eva lovin
> Annie

Ne'er was such a badly-written missive so joyfully received! I sat on that riverbank in a happy daze, reading it over and over. How gladdened was my heart to hear from Annie and to discover she was still not lacking in humour. And I wasn't unduly perplexed at that bit about us soldiers riding into the clouds. I remembered Fred hearing something similar from his wife, Mary, when we were two weeks out from the fort. She told him that as the column left Lincoln the sun shone on the mist and created the illusion that we were all riding into the sky. 'Like on a stairway to Heaven' was how she'd put it. As Annie had stated, most of the womenfolk stood watching that morning had been really spooked by what they saw as a bad omen that none of us would e'er come back. In fact, there'd been so much concern that Mrs Custer had held a meeting a few nights later to explain that it had all been down to some rare meteorological trick; though some of the womenfolk, by all accounts, remained jumpy.

Whatever the truth of it, my biggest concern remained Annie's welfare at the fort. While she was reasonably safe there from the perils of the plains, it was the amorous intentions of some of those soldiers we'd left behind that troubled me. I knew in my heart of hearts that Annie would be attracting her fair share of attention as well as compliments. Yet though I was troubled by the thought of her so much as speaking with another trooper, I tried my best to push such thoughts to the back of my mind. Besides, from now on I was going to try really hard to rein in my wild ways; and that included not taking a swing at some poor fellow who'd simply shot an admiring glance at my future wife.

Back in Dinas and Newport, Elizabeth had oft told me to grow up when I'd acted like a fool. Now maybe I was finally on the way to becoming that grown man at last. By now, I'd made my mind up that once I'd returned to dear old Chicago town, I'd seek out the best jeweller and buy Annie the finest gold ring a US Army sergeant's pay cheque could afford. I'd have dearly wanted all from E Troop to attend the wedding fandango, but now Annie and me were planning to do a flit that would ne'er happen.

While we were unloading supplies from The Far West, Custer, Terry and Gibbon met for a big parley aboard the steamer. When I wasn't re-reading Annie's letter by the light of an oil lamp, I was in the same boat as all those other troopers who spent the night trying to work out what would happen next. I barely got ne'er a wink of sleep as usual. Mostly on account of the mournful howling of one of Custer's dogs, muzzle raised to the starry sky. An eerier death howl I'd never heard.

The next morning, Smith told us to prepare for a long march which would start at noon. We were told to take 15 days' rations with us, which to me indicated the Indians weren't in the immediate vicinity, along with twelve mules. Each trooper would carry 100 rounds of carbine ammunition and twenty-four rounds for his pistol. While some bemoaned the absence of the Gatlings and sabres, I felt sure the Springfield would do its usual effective job. I knew that a few years previous a couple of hundred prospectors had fought off a large force of Indians in the same vicinity. If a bunch of civilians could do that I felt pretty sure that the heavily armed and greatly experienced Seventh Cavalry would fare e'en better. The Springfield was a lethal long-range weapon, designed for cavalry such as ourselves, though I myself was more than happy with my trusty Yellow Boy.

Once camp was established a surprise was in store. A mackinaw boat carrying a number of merchants pulled up on the South bank with a load of merchandise and produce to sell. I had to admire their pluck as well as their nerve at negotiating a long stretch of river from Bozeman through hostile territory. Some of us, including myself, bought straw hats to deflect the rays of the fierce sun; some officers even bought welcome supplies of fresh eggs whose cost was beyond the reach of the likes of us. Later that night, however, a couple of traders attached to the expedition set up a stall from which they dispensed liquor at one dollar a pint for the thirsty troops.

A lot of our fellows, perhaps fearing their time on Earth was short, seemed to down as much as they could.

Anticipating my heavy workload the following morning, I made do with my usual coffee. I suppose me and Custer, a long-time observer of temperance, must have been the only stone-cold sober fellows in camp that night. We paid for the boys' drinking the next morning as the packing of the mules was done in such a slipshod and careless manner that I took great delight in bawling them out, if only to see them flinch horribly and raise their paws gingerly to throbbing heads.

As evening drew in, a group of officers, Reno included, held a concert aboard The Far West. A group of us E troopers, including myself, Ogden and Eagan made our way to the bank and listened to the sounds drifting across the river. 'Lorena' was a song filled with want and longing that always turned me melancholy. In the past, whenever I heard a rendition I'd think of Elizabeth; now I thought only of Annie.

'The year creeps slowly by Lorena,
The snow is on the grass again
The sun's low down the sky, Lorena
The frost is where the flowers have been
But the heart throbs on as warmly nowadays
As when the summer days were night;
Oh, the Sun can never dip so low
As down affection's cloudless sky.'

Soon afterwards we heard the unmistakable melody of 'Shenandoah', my own personal favourite, followed by 'Annie Laurie' and a few others. Ogden reckoned that had I downed some beer or whisky I might have been emboldened to get up on that boat and treat those officers to 'that queer hymn' he recalled me singing.

T'was ne'er a chance of the strains of 'Hen Wlad Fy Nhadau', sounding along the Rosebud, though. The concert was strictly confined to officers, with us enlisted men left in the role of distant spectators. Maybe that Mrs Douglas should have had a word with those fellows about my voice and told them what they were missing! I was sure she'd have given me a good reference. The concert finally gave way to a poker game which, by all accounts, stretched long into the early morn and proved one of the stiffest ever played on the rivers. I suppose the prospect of getting killed caused some of those officers to get a tad reckless with their greenbacks.

Afore I drifted off into an uneasy sleep, I became aware of a sinister noise from down in the Indian quarters where the Ree and Crow scouts were housed. You could hear them singing their death songs, having their death pow-wows and beating their tom-toms. 'Them Injuns is like dogs,' yawned trumpeter Moonie. 'They can sense death a-comin' a-ways off.'

As sleep was again hard in coming I got up to head out to the sinks; on my way back I was greeted by Hohmeyer who was clutching a small leather pouch in his hand. 'There you are, Will, I was just comin' lookin' for you,' he said, with that somewhat troubled air I'd grown to know so well. 'I knows you won't mind me askin' one l'il favour. You're a good man, Will, who over these past few years has proved hisself a good soldier. You're an honourable feller as well and for that reason I'd like to entrust you with these.' If only Father could have heard these words, I thought. Puzzled, I opened the pouch, and found myself looking at carte de visites of Fred's wife and children and himself along with some pencil sketches he'd drawn on the long ride from Lincoln. When I looked up quizzically he said: 'I'd like you to see that Mary and the l'il ones get these, just in case I don't make it through the next few days.'

I returned his gaze for a few instants, not really knowing what to say. 'I'm sure you'll make it, First Sergeant, there isn't a bullet nor arrow that's been made that'll stop old Hohmeyer,' I said eventually, striving to keep the tone light.

'Besides, you'll be carrying all our pay in that leather bag of yours; you're way too valuable a fellow to shed his life-blood out here in this God-forsaken wilderness.'

'Maybe, maybe not,' he replied with a thin smile. 'Anyways, I'd sure like you to take it, just in case.'

'It'll be my pleasure, Fred,' I answered, addressing him by his Christian name for the first time in my life. 'But, believe me, you'll have so many yarns to tell those children of yours when you get back to Lincoln that they won't need bedtime stories no more.'

Hohmeyer said naught, but smiled quickly again before turning on his heel and melting back into the darkness. I stood stock-still for some time, staring after his retreating figure, trying to make sense of what this veteran of the Washita battle and countless other dust-ups with plains Indians had just said.

And in that instant, I suddenly wished I was back at the Powder River depot …

CHAPTER 16

Arthur paused in front of the magnificent sea captain's house affording spectacular views of the sands and breakers rolling beyond Newport Parrog. The whole scene wreaked affluence, from the well-manicured garden and immaculate flower beds right down to the automobile garage in the drive. Arthur reflected on how he seemed to be seeing more of these strange wheeled contraptions on local roads with every passing week. This was where Elizabeth Evans had lived with her second husband for around thirty years. This was also where she'd raised a family. Striving manfully to ignore his growing discomfiture, Arthur walked up to the door, noting the fine silver horseshoe adorning it, and raised the knocker. As he announced his presence, he noticed an attractive teenage girl taking down washing in the large garden eyeing him curiously.

The door opened to reveal a well-dressed, good-looking lady of around fifty, with high cheekbones, her dark hair tied back in a bun as severe as the look on her face. Her large brown eyes instantly locked enquiringly on to Arthur with such a fierce intensity that made him briefly avert his gaze.

'Mrs Evans?' he asked, raising his bowler.

The woman tilted her head back imperiously. 'Yes indeed, t'is I, and I gather I must be addressing Mr Nicholas of the Haverfordwest solicitors office, am I not?' Arthur nodded his head. 'In that case,' the one-time Elizabeth Morgans replied, shaking his proffered hand, 'you had better come in before that rain cloud spills its contents all over your good self, as well as my fresh laundry.'

She led Arthur through a house awash with maritime paintings and maps, fine ornaments and ornate furnishings, to what she said was her husband's study, pausing briefly to instruct a young servant girl to immediately provide a pot of tea, jug of milk, bowl of sugar and two cups of her best china.

Having gestured at Arthur to take a seat, she sat down on the opposite side of a large desk in a high chair that, Arthur noted, perched her above him. He felt uncomfortably under scrutiny. A bit like a naughty schoolboy summoned to the headmaster's study. 'Cymraeg neu Saesneg (Welsh or English)'? she brusquely enquired. Arthur found himself apologising that he'd prefer to converse in the latter. Still severe and unsmiling, Mrs Evans placed her elbows on the desk, leant forward, clasped her hands together and studied her young visitor for a few moments before finally speaking. 'So,' she began at last, 'you wish to speak to me about a former acquaintance of mine called William Batine James who, I'm given to understand, stands to inherit the farm of Llanwnwr out on Strumble Head; if you do indeed manage to locate him, that is.' Arthur confirmed that this was indeed the case.

'Very well,' nodded Mrs Evans, 'but before we begin I will first need your absolute assurance that this conversation is private and anything that I may say to you must not go beyond these four walls.' Arthur hastily assured her that, as an apprentice solicitor, he was honour-bound to observe such confidences. 'That's good to hear,' replied Mrs Evans briskly, 'as, for me, the past is pretty much a closed book to which I rarely, if ever, return. I am a happily married woman, with three grown-up children and I obviously have no desire to say anything about my former life which may in any way embarrass my dear husband who, I might add, is away attending business in Swansea at present.'

'You have my word that anything we will discuss is for my ears and my ears only,' replied Arthur earnestly. 'Very well,' repeated Mrs Evans. 'Now that we have reached an understanding you are welcome to proceed.' And with that, having taken delivery of a tray of tea and biscuits, she folded her arms and sat back in her wicker chair. A nervous Arthur had not rehearsed his questions beforehand; in actual fact there were not that many to put to her. Yet he began with a query that occurred to him quite spontaneously. Why was Mrs Evans willing to speak about a man who she had lost contact with well over thirty years previously?

Elizabeth, whose haughty demeanour made it appear she was looking down her nose at Arthur, eyed him stonily at first before finally speaking. 'An interesting question, the answer to which is actually very simple,' she said, a slight smile forming on her lips, much to Arthur's relief. 'In a strange way, I like to think William James has played a part in what you see around you,' she said, opening her arms and gesturing at the impressive surrounds with both hands, 'for reasons,' she continued intriguingly, 'that will shortly become apparent. As you have evidently done your homework, Mr Nicholas, I am sure you will know that as a young woman I stepped out with Will James for a time before leaving him for Thomas, his elder brother, who was subsequently lost at sea the very week we were betrothed.'

Arthur confirmed he was aware of the facts and had started mumbling his regrets for the loss of her first husband when she silenced him with a wave of her hand. 'Please, there is no need, and whilst I do appreciate your sympathy it was a very long time ago when all is said and done. Yes, what happened to us was indeed tragic and I thought my life was over for a while, but Tom was just one of a number of mariners from these parts who went down with their ships,' she turned her head to gaze through the window out upon Newport Bay and let out a sigh.

'His youngest brother Frank, just eighteen, died alongside him. The grim loss of life at sea among merchant

303

seamen was, and remains to an extent, one of the great scandals of our times. All those young lives sacrificed …' she turned back to Arthur slowly shaking her head, 'I suppose that's the inevitable result when profits are low and risks are high, don't you agree, Mr Nicholas?'

Arthur nodded awkwardly. He then asked her, as he had previously his mother, Maggie Bowen and Mary Lloyd, what sort of person WBJ had been? Elizabeth's brow furrowed and she was quiet for some time as she again switched her gaze in the direction of the seaward view, plainly coagulating her thoughts. Arthur became aware of her fingers lightly drumming on the desk. When they stopped, he suddenly realised with a shock that there were tears in those eyes. Elizabeth suddenly released a half-stifled sob. 'I'm sorry, you will have to excuse me,' she said, raising a white handkerchief to her face abruptly.

As Arthur sat frozen to his chair, appalled, she rose swiftly and hurried from the room without another word. Arthur remained rooted to the spot uncertain what to do. The heavy silence that descended was punctured only by the loud ticking of a grandfather clock in the hall. While Arthur felt terrible to have unwittingly caused Mrs Evans such distress, he was somewhat nonplussed by her reaction to what had seemed, on the face of it, a fairly mundane question.

Being a diligent young man, he had taken the trouble of asking a few people in Newport what Mrs Evans was like beforehand. To a man they had described her as a steely, feisty, even fearsome character who did not tolerate fools lightly. Yet a question concerning WBJ's character had evidently reduced her to tears.

Arthur must have sat fidgeting at that desk for a good ten minutes, although it seemed more like thirty, before he detected the rustling of Mrs Evans' skirt approaching from the direction of the lounge. She walked past him back towards her seat as Arthur stood up and started to apologise.

Red-eyed, but composed, Elizabeth shook her head and waved away his sympathies. She had clearly been crying and still clutched the now crumpled handkerchief in her right hand. The fact she made no attempt to disguise her obvious distress made Arthur suddenly warm to her. 'You will have to forgive me, Mr Nicholas,' she began. 'I ... I just wasn't quite prepared for the somewhat personal nature of your enquiries.' Straightening herself up in her chair and returning his gaze again, she instructed him to continue.

With some trepidation, Arthur again asked her to describe WBJ as a person. 'The boy with the thorn in his side,' she began, sniffing thoughtfully, while again gazing outside. 'Will was not the person most took him to be; and by that I don't mean he was dishonest or dishonourable or anything like that. In fact, the opposite was the case, if anything. He was so different to most fellows; someone who put the welfare of animals ahead of people, for instance.

'He told me he once had a terrible row with his father over what Will had perceived to be his ill-treatment of a horse. The quarrel had only concluded when Will turned on his heel and fled. His father had subsequently taunted him that this had been a sign of weakness, but Will told me he'd just had to depart as he'd been afraid of what might have ensued. He said he'd felt so angry he'd been on the verge of striking his own father. I believed him too,' she said, turning back to Arthur.

'Indeed, for a time I must have known him better than anyone, yet I would never, ever pretend to have understood that boy completely. He had a reputation for being happy-go-lucky and, yes, I suppose that was part of his character, but the few of us who were close to him, myself included, knew there was another troubled and much darker side to his personality.'

As Arthur listened raptly, she went on. 'Will was a restless soul who I always got the impression was seeking something even he knew not,' she continued. 'He had bad experiences at school, that I do know, although he never went into specifics. Strangely enough, Thomas, the schoolmaster he detested so, was buried here in Newport only the other week ...

'For some reason, the death of Will's father seemed to hit him far harder than his brothers and sisters, although it obviously affected the whole family hugely. Will religiously kept a little pocket diary at that time. On the day his father died, I saw there was just one brief entry. 'Someone,' he had written, 'should have stopped the birds from singing today.' Looking back, Will didn't have solid foundations after losing his father at such an important stage of his young life. I myself was fortunate in having a sound base, but Will, and other unfortunates like him, have their foundations built on sand. Yet I don't think losing his father was the sole reason for his problems, or even the main reason. Many families suffer the pain of losing one or both parents,' Elizabeth paused briefly to take a sip of her tea.

'There was something else that troubled Will,' she went on, 'something I could never quite put my finger on, although God knows I strived my utmost to find it. Like I said, that boy had a thorn in his side. As we're being very frank with one another I think it only fair as well, Mr Nicholas, that you should know that being with Will James wasn't all sweetness and light, I'm afraid. Drink brought out a dangerous side in his character which I witnessed on more than one occasion ...' she trailed off, seemingly unsure as to how far to proceed with her revelations.

'T'was what finished us in the end. We were having a real parrot and monkey time of it. When we'd arrange to meet I never knew which Will James was going to show up; that's how difficult it became.

'When sober he was the most humorous, kind and loving boy you could ever wish to have in your company. Extremely bright, decent scholar too, if one with a dislike for authority; indeed, I'd say his standard of reading and writing in English were the match of any university student.' Elizabeth's eyes narrowed. 'I suppose,' she observed witheringly, 'we have the Welsh Not to thank for that.' She took another sip of tea.

'You mentioned drink could bring out a bad side to him?' prompted Arthur. Elizabeth nodded. 'When in drink... ', she paused, looking fixedly at Arthur from across the desk, 'Will was the Devil in the flesh. None of us could understand why. In truth, it was because of my problems with Will that I took the vow of temperance when I was 22. I disliked the way the drink changed people.

'My father once told me Will was born the way he was, but I didn't think that then and I don't think that now. Somewhere along the line, for reasons unexplained, Will James got chipped and damaged, if not actually broken. As to why and how that happened I, like everyone else, can only surmise. What I would give,' she said, maintaining her unusually powerful eye contact, 'to know the reason or reasons that lay behind it.'

Elizabeth took another sip of her tea. 'I sometimes gained the impression that Will felt he was not worthy in the eyes of his father and that he somehow needed to prove himself,' she continued, leaning her head to one side. 'You have to remember, Mr Nicholas, he was sandwiched 'twixt elder and younger siblings and, I don't know, perhaps felt he'd been given short thrift by his parents. I know he'd had relatives who'd served in the army in years past and Will said on more than one occasion that he could think of no greater glory than serving his mother country; no worthier cause to die for. For a time he was wrapped up in the romance of being a soldier and defending our land from foreign invaders. The 1797 French invasion of Fishguard was still in living memory when Will and I were young, you have to remember.'

Elizabeth shrugged her shoulders. 'I may be guilty of

making something out of nothing but I've thought about what ailed Will much over the years,' she went on. 'I believe he carried a certain amount of guilt for the trouble and angst he'd occasionally wrought on his parents and yearned to somehow make amends; particularly as far as his father was concerned. He was always what we folks would call a bachgen drwg (naughty boy), you understand? And I have to say that I was always drawn to rebels. As a young woman t'was my one great failing.' Elizabeth smiled ruefully as she returned her cup to its saucer.

Arthur then asked Elizabeth what she thought Will might be doing now? 'A far easier question to answer,' she said, relaxing back into her chair. 'Something to do with horses, I'd wager. Indeed,' she nodded, smiling, 'I would wager quite a bit of my dear husband's money on that.' Sensing their talk was drawing to a close, Arthur fired one more question at her; a query he feared she would regard as impertinent. 'Do you still think of Will James?' he asked. Another very long pause. 'Indeed, I most surely do,' she eventually replied, rocking gently back and forth in her chair, a dreamy expression on her face. 'You could say that I think of Will Pencnwc whenever I look at our front door.'

Noting Arthur's puzzled frown she rose deliberately to her feet and, beckoning him to follow, led him back through the house towards the door through which he had entered her home almost a half-hour earlier. 'Don't tell me you did not notice,' she called back over her shoulder as they walked. 'And there's me thinking that you legal gentlemen were trained observers!'

Opening the door, she stepped outside onto the steps and indicated to her guest, with an exaggeratedly theatrical wave of her hand, her reminder of the long-lost WBJ. 'The horseshoe?' asked Arthur stupidly. Elizabeth nodded. 'The horseshoe,' she said. 'The horseshoe Will sent back to me from America with a letter.'

Staring at her in amazement, Arthur suddenly realised self-consciously that his mouth was agape. He shut it with an audible snap. 'Will was even more superstitious than I; he was convinced his entire family had fallen victim to a gypsy's curse,' she continued. 'He clearly felt this horseshoe would ward off evil spirits and, when I look around me,' Elizabeth again threw her hands out wide to illustrate the spectacular garden and breathtaking sea view, 'I think it has worked a treat and continues to work its magic, do you not agree?'

Arthur nodded. The house and garden were truly magnificent. Yet he was still reeling in shock at the horseshoe revelation. 'That letter from America you speak of, Mrs Evans, can you by any chance recall its contents?' he asked. Elizabeth's smile had now faded and, not for the first time Arthur felt he was pushing his luck. 'You don't have to ask me to recall what it read,' she said sharply. With that she turned swiftly on her heel and walked quickly through the hall before disappearing up the large staircase.

Arthur stood there, unsure whether his interview had been abruptly terminated in somewhat bizarre fashion. Had Elizabeth taken offence? Had she perhaps gone upstairs to summon the village constable by telephone and request him to escort this annoying inquisitor from her premises? In the little time he had known her Arthur gained the distinct impression this woman did not mince words. Plainly not a person to cross. As he loitered in the hall, Arthur was not terribly surprised to see a Women's Social and Political Union poster announcing 'Votes for Women!' hanging on the wall.

He could envisage Elizabeth at the head of a march for women's rights and no doubt giving police officers a sharp piece of her mind. Just as Arthur was about to go apologetically on his way, shutting the door gently behind him, footsteps echoed on the wooden stairs. As Elizabeth reappeared wearing spectacles that made her look older, Arthur saw she was looking down at a faded letter. She walked up and wordlessly handed it over. Glancing down, Arthur recognised WBJ's clipped, neat handwriting with which he had now grown so familiar.

F A Lynchon
Dakota Ter
May 16, 1876

Dear Elizabeth

Forgive me for contacting you after all this time but I wish to send you my sincere if extremely belated condolences on the death of your Husband, my dear Brother Tom.

Tom was twice the man I will ever be and I felt and still feel your loss keenly even though five years have passed.

I owe you a sincere apology Elizabeth for behaving the way I did for reasons that have only now become apparent.

I wish you all the health and happiness in the world and please accept enclosed as it will bless you with good fortune in the years ahead.

Please excuse short note and all blunders.

Yours Sincerely

Will Pencnwc

William B James

PS: Did Liz Penfeidr ever run down the slopes of Carningli like she said she would?

Neither Arthur nor Elizabeth spoke for a few moments as he struggled to digest the contents of the hitherto unknown letter. Arthur's mind was in a whirl. 'Lynchon', he now suspected, should actually be spelt 'Lincoln'. Had Will's normally good use of English for once let him down? Alternatively, could it not be a deliberate error on his part?

Something he dimly remembered from a school history lesson came back into Arthur's mind. He rubbed his chin, momentarily lost in thought. Could 'F A Lynchon' actually be Fort Abraham Lincoln? An idea was now beginning to form ...

'Your kindness and assistance in this matter are truly appreciated,' he said looking up at Elizabeth. 'Given the circumstances, I am fully aware it cannot have been easy for you to re-visit such memories. However, Mrs Evans, I beg to inform you that I have one last favour to ask.' Elizabeth gazed back at him coolly. 'May I please remove this horseshoe from its fittings?' asked Arthur. 'I have a belief that it will provide firm evidence to confirm my suspicions about what Will James was doing in America and may yet lead us to him even now. I truly feel we are nearing the conclusion of our search.'

Elizabeth put her hands on her hips and let out a long sigh. 'You wish to prise that horseshoe, which has been there for nigh on thirty years, off my front door?' she asked, exasperated. Arthur could only look at her with a pleading expression with which he hoped she'd sympathise. 'Well ... go on then!' she exclaimed. 'If you truly must! I suppose I had better make haste and go and seek out a screwdriver then, hadn't I?'

'Thank you Mrs Evans, I'm truly, truly grateful,' stuttered Arthur. 'I will, of course, ensure it immediately goes back to where it belongs.'

'Indeed you most certainly will and just thank your lucky stars Captain Evans is away,' Elizabeth's voice sounded from the interior of the house. 'He would never have permitted such tomfoolery. And if any ill-fortune befalls this household in future then I will know who is to blame!'

Moments later, Arthur was unscrewing the horseshoe from its fittings as Elizabeth looked on quizzically. Removing it gingerly, he turned the horseshoe over and quickly found the sign, created in a forge by a US Army blacksmith over thirty years previously, he had been seeking. Arthur looked up into Elizabeth's intrigued features, his heart racing, face aglow with triumph. His theory had this time been proved to be correct; and to think he'd thought at one point that WBJ had been a commercial traveller in the Deep South!

'I can now reveal to you, Mrs Evans,' he said, 'precisely what Will James was doing out in America at the time you received his letter.' Elizabeth's gaze did not falter. 'He was a soldier in the US Seventh Cavalry, Mrs Evans! And this,' Arthur added, thrusting the good luck charm under Elizabeth's nose excitedly, 'is a US Seventh Cavalry horseshoe!'

CHAPTER 17

The Ride to Little Bighorn
Thursday June 22, 1876

Dawn was starting to break when we were roused from our slumbers by Reveille. If we didn't catch up with any Indians today, we'd be getting pretty close, I reckoned. After the usual breakfast of bacon and hardtack, ammunition was doled out and we prepared to ride out around noon. Must have spent a good hour scribbling letters on behalf of various fellows for them to be sent back home aboard The Far West which was preparing to depart downriver. One or two even offered me a dollar for my troubles, but I shrugged them aside. What kind of fellow would charge a kindred soul for writing a letter which might be the last he'd ever send on this good Earth?

Trouble was, I spent so much time writing other boys' letters that by the time I'd checked out the horses and kit and everything found I'd precious little time to pen my own. I'd barely managed to snatch a few minutes down by the river when the order came to saddle up.

> ## Somewhere on the Rosebud
> ## June 22, 1876
>
> My dearest Annie
>
> Just a short letter to let you know that our hunt is nearing its end as we close in on Sitting Bull and his gang. The scouts tell us there's a fair few of the red men out here but nothing the fighting Seventh cannot handle.
>
> I trust you are in good health as I am and hope that washing all that laundry is not getting you down too much. What lots and lots I will have to tell you on my return.
>
> Please excuse short note and all blunders.
>
> > Your ever loving Will
> >
> > William B James

Could've kicked myself all the way to Lincoln and back. Those paltry lines were all I had time to scribble while an impatient mail rider stood tapping his foot aside me. I consoled myself with the thought that I'd write a much longer letter next time. Soon afterwards we formed in columns of fours along the flat of the Yellowstone's South bank near the Rosebud for Terry to conduct a parade review. The whole of The Seventh mustered over six hundred strong and the difference in demeanour of previously tired troops was startling.

The prospect of some fighting had raised spirits; e'en the horses pranced about with gay abandon as if they sensed the excitement that lay ahead. Scout, I noticed, was trembling slightly and covered in a sheen of sweat. I knew he was one of the fitter mounts and could only guess that the anticipation that abounded was getting to him too.

Clad in a fringed yellow skin suit, and wearing a greyish-white broad-brimmed felt hat, Custer rode his horse Dandy hither and thither, galloping the full length of the regiment to take his customary place at the head of the column. That fellow was born to be a soldier; he simply lived for occasions such as this. As the Gray Horse Troop trotted past Terry, Gibbon and Brisbin, Smith and Sturgis giving them the salute, Custer sallied into view again clearly wanting to cast an eye over his favourite company. 'May God go with you, gentlemen,' called Terry. 'On behalf of my fellow officers I'd like to wish you all the best for a successful pursuit and ultimate victory.'

As he did so, we heard Gibbon sing out: 'Now, Custer, don't be greedy, but wait for us!' Wheeling his horse while giving a wave of his hand Custer threw back his head and laughed. 'No, I will not,' he hollered back and rode off after his command. 'What the Hell did Ol' Hard Ass mean by that?' Brown enquired, out the side of his mouth. 'Either that he won't be greedy or that he won't wait for reinforcements when the moment comes, take your pick,' I replied shortly. 'Either way, we'll be finding out soon enough ...'

When we stopped to water the horses a few hours later Hohmeyer told me of a troubling discussion he'd overheard between Custer and his senior officers the night previous.

Fred was always good at eavesdropping on such pow-wows. He'd slink around the back of the tent and put an ear to the canvas. If challenged he'd swear blind that, as a first sergeant, he'd simply been going round inspecting the horses or checking up on the pickets. Anyway, the previous night Fred's heard Custer tell his officers that we wouldn't be taking Gatling guns towards the Bighorn Valley on the grounds they'd slow the march. No real surprise there then, this country and the enemy we were facing just weren't made for Gatlings. However, Custer had then gone on to say he'd turned down the offer of taking three companies of Major Brisbin's Montana Regiment along as well. He reckoned the Seventh could lick anything coming our way.

According to Fred, Benteen wasn't happy. 'I don't

care a fig for the Gatlings,' he'd heard him say, 'but I'd feel a damn sight better if we had the Montana Regiment along as support. From what the scouts are saying, this is the biggest force of Indians ever assembled on the Great Plains. I, for one, am sorry we're not taking Brisbin's boys along with us and I fear we will regret it.'

Custer's curt response to this, apparently, was: 'You have your orders.' Hohmeyer said it was obvious Custer wanted all the glory to go to The Seventh. Didn't want no-one else stealing his thunder.

The group of horsemen setting out from camp that morning bore little resemblance to that smart band of bluecoats who'd departed on this great adventure five weeks previous. Well over 300 miles of hard riding across rugged terrain in all weathers had left its mark.

The dark-blue flannel blouses that most of us wore had by now stained green or purple by rain and sweat. We sported an array of hats of all styles and covers. Many of us, myself included, were wearing those light straw hats bought from those traders on the banks of the Yellowstone. While hats such as these were technically against company regulations, Smith at least had the good sense to take on board the amount of time we'd been out in the field and was quite relaxed about our non-regulation headgear. No-one, least of all Custer, can have thought the hostiles would have proven quite so elusive when we'd departed Lincoln.

I found myself hoping that maybe we'd not be encountering quite as many Indians as the scouts had said, but all the trails they'd come across pointed to a force numbering several hundred; and those trails were getting fresher the further we pushed on up the Rosebud. In one abandoned Indian camp the embers of their campfires were still too hot to touch.

Custer looked the epitome of derring-do. His two brothers, Captain Tom Custer and young Boston, wore similar fringed buckskin jackets and pants to his own, as did a number of the officers, including, of course, Smith.

Custer wore his trademark red scarf around his throat, to make him more readily identifiable once the shooting started, I assumed, and that light-gray broad brimmed hat atop a head with hair cropped short afore leaving Lincoln. He must want to deny some Injun the privilege of lifting his scalp, I thought mirthlessly.

Listening to the chatter of the troops around me, I took some heart from the fact they'd seemed to have regained something of their vim and vigour. The mood of the fellows was eager, excited and confident. I was among the few who'd fought Indians afore, and the general feeling, among us E troopers at least, was that the fighting Seventh would just have too much in hand no matter how many hostiles were out there.

Together our ranks mustered over six hundred strong and we were being led by a commander who, like it or not, had led from the front and proved his mettle in battle time and time again. What's more, Custer was a fighting man blessed with extraordinary good fortune as evidenced by the fact it was said he'd had a dozen horses shot from under him during the North-South conflict, ne'er so much as suffering a scratch. Custer's Luck, as the newspapers called it, was again in evidence when The Seventh had attacked and captured that Cheyenne village on the Washita eight years back despite being well outnumbered. Hohmeyer and Ogden, both Washita veterans, told us they reckoned Custer might now deploy the same tactics and attack the sleeping hostile village at dawn. Such a battle plan had served him well at the Washita, they opined, so it made sense to follow a similar course of action.

What was of concern were the problems we were having with the pack train carrying our extra ammunition as well as supplies. With speed being so important, and the regiment pushing on in its eagerness to catch up with its quarry, the pack train was lagging further and further behind; a problem which seemed insurmountable.

All was quiet in camp that night; I suppose most of us were alone with our thoughts. Trumpet calls were forbidden as a surprise Indian attack could always be on the cards and we wanted to lie low for as long as possible, ideally right up to the very moment of attack.

Custer held a pow-wow with his officers in the tent, Smith later calling myself, Hohmeyer and Ogden for a briefing. He wasn't clear-cut, more or less stating that we would continue our pursuit of the hostiles until we found them, which could be at any time now. Custer, he added, had again expressed his complete confidence that The Seventh, and The Seventh alone, he had emphasised, could handle anything the entire Sioux nation could throw at us. I did think of asking Smith at which point we'd meet up with the Montana Column as well as Crook's column approaching from Wyoming, but knowing he'd more than likely chew my head off, dismissed the notion. Probably didn't e'en know himself, anyway. If anyone could have questioned him further t'was Hohmeyer, but he stayed mute and a newly-promoted sergeant such as I rarely, if ever, asked questions above his station.

Rosebud Valley
June 23 1876
two days out from Little Bighorn

We continued to head up the valley the next day, Crow scouts riding up ahead, Arikaras on the flanks. Benteen and three companies had been given the unenviable task of assisting the lumbering pack train to the rear. After a few hours, we came across an abandoned Indian village, the first of a number we'd encounter that day. The scouts examined pony dung, lodge circles and lodge pole trails to try and gauge the size of the big village that lay ahead. Rumours were rife among the ranks as usual, with estimates of Sitting Bull's fighting force ranging from a few hundred to several thousand. T'was another very long march afore we finally pitched camp along a plain on the east side of the river. Ogden remarked on how eerily silent the valley was, but being out in the wilderness hundreds of miles from civilisation what the Hell did he expect? The sound of rail roads, traps and stagecoaches? Guess he was, like the rest of us, getting a tad jumpy.

The endless waiting and anticipation was the worst part. Once we spied and engaged the enemy, I'd no doubt that such fears would vanish. We were professional soldiers and this was what we lived and trained for, after all. A horrible and grisly sight was in store for us on setting out the next day, which was again warm and sunny. We hadn't made too many miles when we came across another large abandoned Indian camp, where the scouts found the scalp of a white man hanging from the centre pole of a lodge. Who the poor unfortunate had been we could only guess, but judging by their concerned demeanour the Arikaras took this as a warning sign to us not to proceed any further.

We stayed mounted on our horses as Custer took a look round. As he did so, Color Sergeant Hughes drove the staff of his battle flag into the dry ground only for it to instantly topple. When it fell down pointing to the rear, Lt Wallace, seated a few feet to my left, remarked a tad too loudly for my liking that it boded ill for the General. While all and sundry knew Wallace to be superstitious, he was a somewhat rummy old cove who believed in doing dumb things like putting his socks on last, for God's sake, I was irked at his words. In truth, I'd have rebuked him in private had I held a similar rank.

Far from considering ill omens, now was surely the

time to be stirring the boys up and emphasising our strengths. I may not have been some high-faluting officer, yet I knew full well that talk of ill omens was most definitely not the way to stoke the boys' fires. I hoped that few of the other fellows heard what Wallace had said as no soldier should be afflicted by doubts on the eve of battle.

Onwards we rode, in two parallel columns in the vain hope of lessening the thick choking dust clouds thrown up by the horses. We stopped to examine Indian trails on countless occasions afore finally halting for what we called lunch around noon. We rested up here for several hours, Hohmeyer wisely telling us to get our heads down for a bit as there'd likely be little chance of sleep over the coming hours and days. On resuming the march towards sundown, we again came across the remains of several more large campfires, some of the fires smouldering still. One of the scouts told me the entire valley bore signs of hundreds and hundreds of trailing lodge poles signifying a vast number of Indians lay not far up ahead.

By now I'd surmised that what would shortly transpire would make the fight we'd had back on the Yellowstone in '73 seem little more than a skirmish. With the sun dropping in the sky and the cruel heat finally starting to ease, we bivouacked on the West side of the Rosebud having marched another 28 miles that day. We were dog-tired, hungry and thirsty as usual, having trekked and been in the saddle pretty much constantly for the past fifteen hours. The fellows were pretty quiet as they fed and groomed the horses, wolfed down their bacon and hardtack and rolled out blankets to get some rest using saddles as pillows. I bawled out one I caught eating some of the oats meant for his mount. Myself, Eagan and Ogden talked over events for a half-hour or so, seeking to determine what would happen next, which was always pretty much a waste of time as trying to read the minds of officers, and Custer's in particular, was damn near impossible at best.

Ogden said Hohmeyer expected us to attack the village at dawn either on the morrow or the day after that. He said it was obvious Custer would be looking for a repeat of the Washita. As we talked in low tones, I realised Eagan was taking no part in the conversation; on closer inspection I found the exhausted corporal had fallen asleep, head leaning on his sturdy arm. After what we'd experienced this past few weeks, were we really in any fit state to fight a battle? It was a sign for the rest of us to turn in although some of the fellows took the opportunity to freshen up with a quick bathe in the river. We can only have rested for an hour or so when Fred was once again shaking us awake with the news the command would be moving out at 11pm. The boys rather glumly downed a cold supper, kicked sand to douse the flames on the one campfire each troop were allowed to brew coffee, and prepared to saddle up once again.

After another officers' conference, a few of the younger ones gathered to sing a few songs, anything to try and lift the pensive nature that now enveloped the camp. They ended up singing a few bars of For He's A Jolly Good Fellow, no doubt aiming to buck up the spirits of our leader who'd seemed a tad detached in his thoughts over the past 48 hours or so. Thought this singing somewhat queer as we weren't supposed to make no noise. After they finished, a solitary quavering voice could be heard singing Nearer My God To Thee from another part of camp. Don't know who the Hell that was and all enquiries to find out came to naught. Looking back, it was pretty queer. Smith came up afore we moved off and outlined the plan. We'd march overnight, probably to a suitable ravine near to the hostiles' village where the whole regiment would hole up during the day prior to a dawn attack next morning.

Fred's instinct had indeed proved correct. Custer would be looking to repeat his tactics which had paved the path for victory at the Washita. We'd picked an ideal night as it was black as pitch, so dark that you could barely see your hand in front of your face. The pace was slow as we left the valley and visibility so low than a fellow had to follow the sounds of rattling carbines of those ahead. Some troopers were even forced to bang tin cups to guide those behind. The loudest sound was that of Keogh savagely cursing the exhausted mules the men of I were endeavouring to escort from the valley. When their packs loosened, the men cut them off as ordered and left them where they fell. The big fear, Hohmeyer told us, was that if we tarried the Indians would scatter to God knows where and we'd end up having to pursue them to the ends of the Earth. If that were to happen, I thought despondently, I wouldn't see Annie again until the fall.

My mind was wandering fearfully and for some reason I found myself remembering those passages from Father's book that had so gripped me as a child. Ahab, the sea captain had dragged the Pequod's crew to their doom on his ill-starred quest to find the great white whale. Would Custer, a fellow so clearly cut from the same cloth, in time lead us all to destruction on his own obsessive chase? Though I kept trying to keep a lid on my fears, there seemed portents of ill where e'er I looked. After about three hours of weary progress, we halted once more, the troops sliding off their mounts and laying down to try and grab forty winks there and then. I was no different, in fact I couldn't recall feeling so baked afore in my life, so having picketed Scout, I settled down alongside him, head again propped up by his saddle.

I was asleep in a heartbeat and what fantastical dreams I had! They say that on occasions exhaustion makes it impossible to dream but that was truly not the case now. Does extreme fatigue induce a degree of delirium within a fellow? I asked myself. In the hour or so I was in the Land of Nod, I found myself legging it down the long sloping hill leading into Cwmyreglwys. Turning right at its foot, I hared past St Brynach's Church and down onto the rocky beach where Tom, James and Frank were setting to sea in the little wooden skiff we'd built ourselves.

They were already some way out as I splashed through the shallows in their wake, spurred on by their waves and cries of encouragement for me to follow. Next I was back on Strumble Head, surveying the passing ships with their creamy wakes from up on high with dear old Spot again by my side. Hugging my beloved lost dog tight to my breast I felt sheer unbridled joy at seeing him again. 'Oh, Spot, where have you been?' I sighed. 'T'is 14 long years since I spied you last. Did it take you all that time to dig yourself free from that rabbit hole?'

On our visits to Llanwnwr, Grandfather Batine would take us to the place where the French army had invaded in 1797 and march us, our sticks over our shoulders, up to Frenchman's Field where he swore the body of a slain French soldier lay buried somewhere beneath the buttercups and daisies.

What happy times we children would spend at Llanwnwr where Grandmother Batine would treat us to a slap-up meal of roast beef or a leg of mutton. Our little bellies would be so full afterwards we'd have to undo our belts. Then, if the weather was bad, we'd spend the day in the farmhouse, us boys playing with Grandfather's old set of tin soldiers, riding his faded wooden rocking horse or enjoying endless games of hide and seek through the large, comfortable rooms.

Now I was coming downstairs to the parlour and hoisting myself into Grandfather's red rocking chair to gaze up at the fine oil portrait of Pegasus, the white winged horse, resplendent above the mantlepiece of the huge fireplace. Yet I was not alone, for there was a young woman standing with her back to me. As she turned slowly, I saw to my surprise that it was Elizabeth. She was clutching a letter in one hand, a horseshoe in the other and she was smiling. I was just reaching for a huge slab of roasted brown beef turning slowly on a spit when I finally stirred in my sleep, perhaps roused by Scout's nervous snorting.

Streaks of yellow were already appearing in the sky. We'd shortly be on the move. I sat up in my blanket, coughed a bit, shook my head blearily and was instantly wide awake. Probably 'cos of the dream, I now had that Welsh hymn Arglwydd Dyma Fi going round in my head. I thought that queer, having ne'er had the chance to sing it since seeing that negro choir perform back in Opelika, yet thanks to that hymn sheet I'd studied I could recall every blessed line. In fact, I found myself humming it as I fixed my meagre breakfast of raw bacon, hardtack and cold water. Despite my continuing lack of religious faith, I found it somewhat soothing.

Mi glywaf dyner lais,
Yn galw arnaf fi,
I ddod a golchi 'meiau gyd,
Yn afon Calfari.

Arglwydd, dyma fi
Ar dy alwad di,
Golch fi'n burlan yn y gwaed
A gaed ar Galfari.

Yr Iesu sy'n fy ngwadd,
I dderbyn gyda'i saint,
Ffydd, gobaith, cariad pur a hedd,
A phob rhyw nefol fraint.

Yr Iesu sy'n cryfhau,
O'm mewn Ei waith trwy ras;
Mae'n rhoddi nerth i'm henaid gwan,
I faeddu 'mhechod cas.

Gogoniant byth am drefn,
Y cymod a'r glanhad;
Derbyniaf Iesu fel yr wyf,
A chanaf am y gwaed.

CHAPTER 18

The initial euphoria Arthur experienced at Elizabeth's house had long since vanished by the time he caught the omnibus back towards Fishguard. Far from sharing his exultation on discovering what the horseshoe represented, she had fallen silent and pensive for an inordinately long time. Neither spoke for some moments and it was Elizabeth who found her tongue first. 'Would you please accompany me back into the house?' she asked, making it seem more of an order than a request.

Once inside, Arthur had light-heartedly observed that Elizabeth's suspicion that WBJ would have ended up working with horses had been proved spectacularly correct. All he received in response was a cold hard stare which shrank him into silence. 'Please don't patronise me, Mr Nicholas,' she'd snapped. 'You know as well as I do that The Seventh Cavalry under General Custer were annihilated by a huge force of Indians around thirty years back. T'was in all the papers at the time and cast a huge pall over America's Centennial celebrations, unless I'm very much mistaken.'

Nothing gets past this woman, Arthur thought. He did indeed recollect reading of Custer's fate, but following further discourse, neither he nor Elizabeth could be sure of the year. 'Custer was indeed vanquished,' he'd told her, 'but that does not necessarily mean Will James was present at the battle. Please don't leap to any premature conclusions, Mrs Evans, and allow me to make further enquiries so we can finally get to the bottom of this.' Arthur left Elizabeth standing uptight and anxious in her hall staring into space as he let himself

325

out. The look on her pale face frightened him.

He was making his way down the doorsteps when she spoke again. 'Mr Nicholas,' she'd said, in a small voice that suggested her earlier composure was threatening to vanish, 'might not Will James have been among those slain?' Turning swiftly on his heel and striding back up to her, Arthur placed a supportive hand tenderly on Elizabeth's shoulder. 'I beg you not to distress yourself, Mrs Evans,' he urged, 'until we are in possession of the full facts. I will do my utmost to gain answers to the questions we have and, rest assured, I will impart to you what information I unearth with all due haste.' Elizabeth could only manage a terse brief nod as an equally troubled Arthur finally went on his way.

Sitting in the omnibus heading back to Fishguard, Arthur realised he was still left with more questions than answers. What had WBJ been referring to when apologising to Elizabeth for behaviour 'the causes of which have only now become apparent'? Was this a dark reference to mental problems? Surely Elizabeth could have been able to cast some light on that? And what could that strange last line about Carningli Mountain possibly infer?

The revelation that WBJ had served in the US Army was a major step forward, but there was still no evidence as to what had happened to him in the 29 years that had elapsed since he'd dispatched that horseshoe from Fort Lincoln, if he still lived. Having established WBJ had at one stage served as a US soldier Arthur consoled himself in the knowledge that the fate of his fellow Welshman would surely soon be revealed, yet he was now strangely apprehensive at the thought of what he would unearth. In fact, he had the horrible feeling his search would not end well. Arthur knew from his school history lessons in Fishguard that The Seventh Cavalry, commanded by General George Custer had, as Elizabeth recalled, indeed been wiped out by overwhelming numbers of Indians back in the 1870s. He now had a sinking feeling in the pit of his stomach that her worst fears would shortly be realised.

This new revelation, he decided, would require further research as well as a letter to the US War Department who could confirm the fate of the lost soldier from Dinas Cross one way or another. Arthur hoped against hope that they could confirm WBJ's discharge from the army as well as some record of what occupation he had then pursued in civvy street.

A couple of days later, Arthur was sitting in Haverfordwest Library poring over a book on the Indian Wars published only a few years previously. As he had suspected, all 210 men from five companies who had rode with Custer at Little Bighorn on Sunday, June 25, 1876 had been massacred to a man, yet the remainder of The Seventh under the command of Captain Benteen and Major Reno had survived a few miles upstream following a desperate rearguard action. The following day saw Arthur dispatch a letter marked 'urgent' to the US War Department in Washington DC. How urgent they themselves would regard his query was a matter of conjecture.

That night Arthur dreamt he had left the Ship in Lower Town and was returning to his lodgings. Rounding the corner into Bridge Street he had looked up on hearing a horse snort and had been startled to see, about forty yards distant, a mounted horseman poised like a statue under the gas lamp just before the Gwaun Bridge. As Arthur approached tentatively, he could see the rider was wearing a broad-brimmed hat and carrying a rifle, which was thankfully not raised in his direction. He realised with a shock that he was looking at a US Army cavalryman of the 1870s. The man's headgear meant his facial features remained in shadow in the light cast by the street light. Arthur had halted and was standing expectantly before the spectral figure in anticipation of some response when he suddenly awoke.

Two nights later, Arthur dreamt he was astride a horse racing at full gallop across the Great Plains. On and on they charged on what mission Arthur could only guess. Perhaps he was carrying some message for The Seventh Cavalry? he thought. Eventually, Arthur pulled up at the sight of numerous campfires up ahead. He had found the regiment's location and would very shortly be coming face-to-face with William Batine James. Their meeting, Arthur thought, had been a long time coming and he had a host of questions to put to this long-lost son of Dinas Cross.

'Halt! Who goes thar?' shouted a picket. 'My name is Arthur Nicholas, of Dinas Cross, and I come bearing a message for William Batine James,' responded Arthur. 'William Batine James? Don't know no-one of that name,' came the suspicious reply. 'Pray tell me, friend, in which company does he serve?' Unable to give an answer, Arthur was struggling to think of a suitable reply when the picket, apparently upon conferring with an unseen superior, drawled: 'Hell, ya mean Will o' the Wisp? Come through an' I'll git one o' the boys to take ya over.' Arthur did as he was told and moments later, having dismounted, found himself following at the heels of a young private through the camp's main street.

Everywhere Arthur looked groups of troopers were lounging around campfires in the dim light cast by oil lamps. The murmur of low conversation filled the air, punctuated by the occasional burst of raucous laughter. Someone was playing a mouth organ off to the right. 'So these are the men of Custer's legendary Seventh Cavalry,' thought Arthur, excitedly, 'and very soon I will finally get to meet William Batine James in person!' The young trooper in front had halted. 'Thar's Will's tent over yonder,' he said, pointing to a tent pitched next to a line of horses. The soldier put two fingers to his lips and let forth a piercing whistle. 'Rouse yourself, Will!' he cried. 'There's some feller here from Dinas Cross to see ya!'

And then, to his great dismay and disappointment, Arthur awoke in his bed in Lower Town. He could not believe it. WBJ, he thought dejectedly, had eluded him yet again. The young solicitor did finally go back to sleep, yet he dreamt no more.

As it happened, Arthur did not have to wait as long as he'd anticipated for a reply from Washington. Almost six weeks after his letter to the US capital had been dispatched, a large officious-looking brown envelope bearing a US stamp and US Government postmark landed on his desk in the Haverfordwest office.

Its contents confirmed Arthur's dark forebodings. Instead of feeling pride in his long-running efforts at solving the conundrum Eaton had set 12 months previously and earning himself a pay rise in the process, he now experienced feelings of only depression and sorrow.

Department of War
US Government
Capitol Hill
Washington DC
April 30, 1905

Dear Mr Nicholas

I thank you for your enquiry of April 2 regarding the fate of William Batine James, late of the US Seventh Cavalry.

Please find enclosed a copy of a Final Statement of the aforementioned soldier which was signed by Lt Charles C De Rudio at Fort Abraham Lincoln in the presence of witnesses.

As you will see the statement confirms the death of Sgt James at the Battle of the Little Bighorn on June

25, 1876 and according to Lt De Rudio's testimony the body of the said Wm B James was supposed to be among those recovered and buried on the battlefield, but was not recognised.

I trust this information is of use.

Yours Faithfully

T Havelock

The statement of effects showed money that WBJ possessed or was owed by the US Government at the time of his death on that lonely Montana field.

Studying the stark, impersonal figures representing all WBJ had left behind him, Arthur noted he had deposited the sum of $20 with the US Paymaster on May 15, 1876, just two days before The Seventh rode out of Fort Lincoln. Had WBJ been saving money for the day he left the army, he wondered?

DUE SOLDIER

For retained pay under act of May 15, 1872 ... $50. 00

For clothing not drawn in kind ... $29. 33

For deposits with the USA Paymaster, September 7, 1875 ($8); May 15, 1876 ($20) ... $28. 00.

Proceeds of sale of effects (April 26, 1877) ... $20. 60.

DUE UNITED STATES

For tobacco ... $1. 14.

The above statement does not take into account basic pay due for the period May 1–June 25, 1876.

A wave of sadness struck Arthur. This was all there was to show for a young life cut short. The fact WBJ's body had not been identified on the battlefield meant he had not even left a gravestone for posterity. Later that day, Arthur found himself retracing his steps to Spring Gardens in Newport with a heavy heart. He had decided it would be improper to tell Elizabeth of WBJ's death over the telephone; it was the type of news he felt it his duty to pass on in person. He knew he'd be doing the same for Mrs Perkins later that week. Louisa, he thought disconsolately, would be heartbroken.

Elizabeth had taken the news stoically and with great dignity, although Arthur noticed that she'd gone quite pale. She'd gripped the bannister at the foot of the stairs so tightly her knuckles had turned white. This hardy woman was no stranger to grief, yet the news had evidently knocked the stuffing out of her. Elizabeth thanked Arthur graciously for his kindness and even offered him a cup of tea, but the young solicitor decided it was best he departed. 'I was prepared,' she'd muttered. 'I had a feeling it was going to end this way.' Then, to Arthur's alarm, she suddenly admitted to feeling quite faint and asked him to accompany her out into the garden.

There, as they stood among the rhododendrons and buddleias alongside an ornate fishpond, Elizabeth had steadied herself against an ash tree as she proceeded to take several long gulps of air until her pallor slowly returned to normal. Then Arthur followed her line of gaze towards the summit of Carningli rising spectacularly against an azure blue sky. Both remained silent for a while as they listened to the birdsong all around them. 'Someone,' Elizabeth said at length, her voice choking slightly, 'should have stopped the birds from singing today ...'

She then announced her intention of taking a walk up the mountain later that week. 'T'is many years since I went up there; yet there was a time when no weekend was complete without a stroll up Carningli,' she smiled sadly. 'T'is a truly mystical place, Mr Nicholas,' she went on, continuing to stare up at the rocky peak. 'T'is said fairies dwell at the top and anyone who spends the night up there experiences myriad strange dreams.'

Arthur then surprised himself by saying he would be only too pleased to accompany her on the hike. 'A very kind offer, young man, but please rest assured that I will not want

331

for company as I retrace the footsteps of my youth,' she replied.

As Arthur bade his leave and passed the front door on his way back to the road he turned one last time to admire the silver US Seventh Cavalry horseshoe afixed. 'I'm afraid I have one final question for you, Mrs Evans,' he told Elizabeth, 'and let me assure you now that I will not take any offence should you decline to answer; but what did that last line of the letter, with its curious reference to Carningli Mountain, signify exactly?'

Elizabeth smiled hauntingly as she stared at the horseshoe, her mind going back more than three decades to a time and place where possibilities seemed boundless and time stretched into infinity. 'A private joke from those days when Will James and myself were both young and foolish,' she said at last. 'I did reply to his letter, by the way. I never received a response, nor did I really expect to. I knew that letter was Will's goodbye.'

Elizabeth then turned to Arthur. 'May I be so bold as to enquire whether you are married, Mr Nicholas? Or perhaps have a young lady friend?' Arthur rather bashfully told her about Louisa, with whom he was becoming increasingly besotted. Elizabeth smiled warmly. 'Make the most of your youth, Mr Nicholas,' she told him. 'Seize the day as before you know it you'll find yourself far nearer the end than the beginning.

'Will James and myself allowed such days to scatter like kernels of corn blowing across a field. I must have shed an ocean of tears over that strange wild boy from Dinas Mountain but, you know Mr Nicholas, when I look back on those times I know that I have never felt more alive.'

Owen and Sturgess
Attorneys & Counsellors at Law
No 7, Wall St
New York
March 14, 1905

Messrs Peacock & Goddard
3 South Square, Grays Inn
London W8

Dear Sirs,

Replying to your favour of March 2 inst we have had a reply from Mr W J James of Bloomburg, Texas, in which he states that the only parties in Opelika in 1875 named James of whom he knew anything were his brother D B James and B C James. Neither of them is the party for whom we were inquiring.

We subsequently wrote to Greensboro, Alabama, from which place, according to the information you sent us, W B James wrote to his brother in November 1874, but as yet we have no reply to our letter.

Yours truly
Owen & Sturgess

Mike Lewis

CHAPTER 19

Little Bighorn
Sunday, June 25 1876.

We set off at a lively walk. As we rode, all and sundry were speculating what might ensue in low, earnest tones. I was plain done with talking myself; just wanted us to reach our place of concealment and get our heads down in preparation for the planned attack on what would be Monday, June 26. In truth, what I really wanted more than anything was a cold beer and a good meal of something other than bacon, beans and biscuits as hard as a dog's head. I reckoned that, God willing, my hurried letter would more than likely reach Annie's fair hand on the morrow. As today was the Sabbath she'd shortly be attending the morning service back in Lincoln.

Meanwhile, the boys were full of what they reckoned lay up ahead. 'Mark my words, this little foray will end as soon as we have tethered Sitting Bull,' said one old hand. 'If that is all, the campaign will soon be over,' agreed another. 'And Custer will take us all with him to the Centennial.' 'Of course!' answered a third. 'And we will take Sitting Bull to Washington with us; leading him up to the White House by a ring on his nose!' Bursts of laughter ensued, prompting me to hiss to all within earshot that noise had to be kept down. The last thing we wanted was to be spotted by hostiles and lose the element of surprise.

I'd plain forgotten about the Centennial on July 4 when America would celebrate its 100th birthday. It'd be a pretty big deal in Washington and no doubt there'd be a parade at Lincoln. Things were bound to get really wild across the river in Bismarck where the bars and whore-houses would be doing brisk business; not that any of us would be back in time to help shoot up the town.

We hadn't gone too long when the command halted once more. Word came down the line that Custer was again conferring with his scouts. Will this march ne'er end? I thought. I was starting to think we'd ne'er catch up with the elusive enemy. Sitting Bull was a medicine man; perhaps he's rendered all his red men invisible, I pondered, my queer thoughts probably resulting from an acute lack of sleep.

Soon afterwards Smith was summoned up front for a conference. He was only away a few minutes afore he came trotting back, an expectant look on his face; Sturgis alongside. Ignoring an attempt by Kellogg, the somewhat bothersome scribe, to strike up a conversation with him, Smith straightaway wanted to speak to Hohmeyer, myself, Ogden and our corporals, Eagan, Brown, Meyer and Mason, in private.

Heading down the trail a little way, the two officers halted beneath some cottonwood trees and, turning in his saddle, Smith said: 'There's been a change of plan, gentlemen. The scouts inform us that the enemy has discovered our location: accordingly, the attack on the hostile village will commence forthwith.'

I glanced across at Hohmeyer and saw his eyebrows shoot up in surprise. Ogden just there sat there in the saddle biting his lip, a thoughtful expression on his face. The corporals looked askance. What Sturgis felt I could only conjecture as he was giving nothing away. Yet what was about to transpire was something none of us had foreseen. O'er the past few hours we'd been readying ourselves for a dawn attack the next morning. Now, Custer, evidently having been spooked by the suspicion we'd been spotted, had decided to attack at once.

Looking over at Fred again I realised I knew him well enough to gauge his thoughts. This was indeed to be a repeat of the Battle of the Washita, but with two big differences. The number of hostiles ahead would greatly outnumber those encountered on that frozen November morning eight years gone. And the attack would not take place at dawn but at around midday, with the sun already high in the sky.

As usual ours was not to reason why, ours was to do and die. We returned in silence to the ranks who were then addressed by Smith. 'I have no doubt whatsoever that The Gray Horse Troop will acquit itself with great honour this day,' he ended up by saying. 'And may God go with each and every one of you.'

Beside me, young O'Connor was crossing himself, clutching his crucifix and mumbling in prayer. The battle that Custer had longed for was about to begin. The thought suddenly occurred to me that the likes of Annie and I had been fighting battles all our lives.

The hostiles' village, Smith told us, lay around fifteen miles distant in the Little Bighorn Valley. With luck, I reckoned, we could get there within two to three hours, maybe a bit less. Whilst watering a grateful Scout my attention was suddenly drawn to the sight of Bloody Knife, Custer's ornery old Arikara scout, performing some kind of sacred ritual while gazing up at the blazing sun. He was gesturing frantically with his hands and chanting so loudly that Billy Jackson, a half-breed scout of tender years, paused alongside me to take in the unsettling scene. As Jackson wheeled his horse away I saw there were tears in the fellow's eyes. Catching up with him moments later I enquired as to the meaning of Bloody Knife's queer conduct. 'He's sayin' he'll not see the sun go down tonight,' replied the young scout. 'He reckons both himself and Custer will be goin' home by a road they do not know.'

The sight of Jackson's teary visage struck me with

the force of a punch to the solar plexus. I got me an acute case of the jitters at the thought of Bloody Knife's stoic conviction of his own impending doom. How many of us will be travelling home by an unfamiliar road by sundown? I wondered. I decided there and then not to divulge Jackson's chilling disclosure to the rest of my comrades.

My thoughts turned to Grandfather Batine who seven decades previously had signed up for the Pembroke Cavalry in the years following the battle of Fishguard. What would he think of me? I pondered. Grandfather had joined up as he clearly desired to help defend our homeland from the invading French. By participating in an attack on an Indian village containing untold numbers of women and children was I not now cast in the same role as those French bastards who came to north Pembrokeshire to rape, loot and pillage? I fought to banish such thoughts from my mind. On the verge of a big fight this was one Hell of a time to question the part I was about to play in whatever was about to unfold.

More commands were bellowed as the column was arranged in battle formation. McDougall, our much-respected former commander now in charge of B, had uncharacteristically overslept and reported in late. As punishment, B Company was given the pack train escort detail. As we trotted past them their faces were as long as month of Sundays. One or two of the troopers were plain in tears at the thought of missing out on the fight, but we men of E were now fired up and ready and offered them precious little sympathy.

We moved out in columns of fours, fifty feet 'twixt each company. Smith rode at our head, young Sturgis alongside. I wondered what was going through his mind. A West Point military cadet just a few months back, here he was, second-in-command of E Troop at the cusp of what looked certain to be a pretty hot fight. He and others, myself included, I thought grimly, would be tested to the utmost this day. If

Sturgis felt any sign of nerves he wasn't showing them; leastways not yet. We'd find out his mettle soon enough once those Indians started loosening a few shots at us.

After nearly two more hours of riding word came from upfront that the Indian village was now just two to three miles distant and, from what scouts were reporting, the red men were on the jump.

The question in everyone's minds was would we be able to intercept them afore they scattered to all four corners of the plains? The thought of spending weeks tracking Indians in such wild country just did not bear contemplating. I, for one, just wanted to take care of business, round up the hostiles, escort them back to their reservations with a minimum of bother and saddle up for Lincoln as soon as possible.

Summer would be pretty much done by the time we returned and I sure as Hell wouldn't be spending another long winter back at Lincoln. I reckoned it'd be easy to peel away from the column on the long march back East. Maybe whilst undertaking picket duty at night. In truth, I was more troubled at the prospect of dying of thirst out on the parched prairie than encountering a wandering tribe of hostiles, or even a detachment of cavalry, come to that. Might it not be prudent to rest up in the heat of the day and resume my lone flight in the cool of the night? I pondered. If managing to hitch a ride on some steamboat I would contend I was a miner or prospector who'd gotten lost and had stumbled across a riderless US Seventh Cavalry mount as I tried to make my way back East.

Though catching a train from Bismarck would be too risky as the depot was always crawling with soldiers, I'd send Annie a letter from town letting her know of my planned date of arrival back in Chicago where we'd meet up again under that big old rail depot clock. Within weeks, I'd no longer be a bluecoat. Whenever I contemplated that fact I felt a huge surge of excitement and anticipation.

A plan was forming in Custer's mind and, as what happened at the Washita, he gambled on dividing his forces ahead of the attack. Now here was Benteen peeling off to the South West with upwards of a hundred men from D, H and K under his command.

I could tell from the wistful looks of some my comrades they were troubled by such a move. Knowing the strength of the enemy was considerable, was dividing the column at this point somewhat foolhardy? What their orders were we could only surmise, but hopefully Benteen and his men would catch up with us again sooner rather than later. If what the scouts were saying about the size of the hostile village was correct, we'd need every available man, for sure. My belly was by now all of a-flutter. Ne'er felt so nervous afore in my life.

Following yet another halt, Reno came riding down the line closely followed by three companies. Custer, it transpired, had ordered them to traverse the river at the foot of the valley below and charge the Indian encampment. I snatched a look at the faces of his men as they rode past, some openly grinning, the features of others pale, pensive, pinched and anxious. 'Give them sons o' bitches Hell, boys!' exclaimed Ogden as they trotted by. We sat there and watched them go, knowing our turn would be next. Taking my water bottle from the saddle pocket, patting Annie's green agate for luck as I did so, I raised it to my dry, cracked lips, ordering all around me to do likewise. Mouths were getting really parched and there was no way of knowing when we'd drink next.

'Well,' I said, raising my three-pint canteen in a mock toast, 'here goes the Gray Horse Troop.' Eagan suddenly pulled up alongside, offering me a swig from his own bottle.

'Try a little o' this, sarge,' he grinned. I knocked it back and almost gagged. Eagan's canteen was a-brim with neat whisky. I felt sure he wasn't the only trooper relying on a little liquid courage, mind.

Spluttering and wiping my mouth I became aware of

O'Connor offering me his hand. 'May God go with you, sarge,' he said solemnly. 'God speed to you too, son,' I replied, returning his handshake as the whisky burnt its way down. 'And if I so much as see you turn your back on those hostiles at any point I'll put a slug plumb between your eyes!' I said it with a smile and a wink, so he could tell I was joshing, but poor O'Connor didn't seem to appreciate my lame attempt at wit. He turned away with a set expression on his young face and fixed his sights dead ahead. The Adam's Apple bobbed in his throat.

The whisky must have taken swift effect as my raised fist and sudden yell of 'Ymlaen!' (Forward!) prompted a number of my companions, including Smith and Sturgis, to swing round in their saddles and gaze at me quizzically.

Within minutes we were trotting along a set of bluffs which afforded occasional views of the Little Bighorn some way below. I noted Scout was moving a tad wearily with some alarm; small wonder after what these mounts had been subjected to over the past few days and weeks, like.

I cared for the condition of the company's horses more than anyone and the fact they were pretty run down and hungry even afore the onset of battle angered me much. The sheen on their coats had long since vanished; their previously rounded forms angular and hollowed, eyes fixed in sunken sockets. I'd no time to dwell on that now as an urgent shout of 'Injuns up ahead!' broke my thoughts. Craning my neck I could see naught at first, but the column was gathering speed. We shortly reached a high ridge where moments earlier hostiles had been spotted, but by the time we'd attained its highest point Mr Lo had given us the slip once again.

Just then a distant bugle call sounding a charge drifted up towards us. Glancing down to my left I caught a brief glimpse of Reno's boys thundering down the valley of the Little Bighorn at full gallop; I must confess it was a stirring sight and a few of our fellows waved their hats and cheered, their mounts whinnying, pawing the ground and pulling hard on the reins in their eagerness to join in. 'Boys, hold your horses!' roared Custer, sensing our impatience. 'There are plenty of them down there for us all!'

The next instant a rider came galloping down from the head of the column. As he passed I recognised him as Kanipe, of C Troop. Ogden asked him what was up and Kanipe replied that he was heading back to gee up the pack train and to also try and find Benteen. Custer was evidently troubled by the size of the village. We knew the pack train carrying extra supplies including ammunition wasn't too far back, but given the awkward nature of the terrain they were traversing coupled with the cantankerous nature of those mules, how long would it take McDougall to reach us?

Then familiar sounds resounded from down below: 'Pop! Pop! Pop!' as Reno's men stormed the hostile village. 'Sounds like ol' Reno's winnin' the fight all on his own,' said someone. 'Jus' hope he leaves some of them Injuns for us,' came the reply. 'I fancy some scalps to take home for the old lady.' Might not the fight be done and dusted by the time we got down there? I pondered.

Soon afterwards we halted yet again as Cooke, Custer's adjutant, scribbled down a message at the dictation of the General. He then handed it to a trooper who took off like a bat out of Hell back from whence we'd come. Two hours must have passed since we'd last seen Benteen. It just had to be an order for reinforcements.

By now we could see the Indian village; leastways a portion of it. Teepees seemed to stretch across the valley forever and a momentary hush descended as we realised the size of our task. Turning in his saddle, Custer took off his hat and waved it triumphantly. 'Hurrah boys, we've got them!' he shouted. 'We'll finish them up and then go home to our station!' Some of the troopers cheered, though I noticed they sounded a tad less enthusiastic than afore.

Now we could spy Custer conferring with Yates, Smith, Calhoun, Keogh and Tom Custer. Afore we knew what was happening Smith rode up to say we would seek a fording of the river with a view to capturing squaws and children fleeing Reno's assault. I knew from Hohmeyer and Ogden's oft-recounted recollections that the capture of women and children at the Washita had led to masses of Cheyenne warriors dropping their weapons and surrendering despite outnumbering the Seventh greatly. I found myself now hoping we could take this great encampment with as little blood spilt as possible.

We followed Smith and Sturgis over the hills for a little while afore the moment we had been keenly anticipating finally arrived. Moonie sounded the Charge to send us plunging down a steep coulee towards the river; Yates and F, the Band Box Troop, in support. As we cantered towards the stream we could see the figures of Indians frantically scurrying along the far bank hither and thither; it looked like they were indeed on the run and that perhaps our undertaking would prove a damn sight far easier than I'd anticipated.

We arrived at the water's edge to come under sporadic fire from the opposite side of the river; at the same time Scout seemed to take a slight stumble and, looking down at the ground, I could see his forelegs sinking in mud. What had seemed a firm crossing point from afar was in reality very soft underfoot. If that was a concern it was but a mere trifle compared to the increasing hail of Sioux and Cheyenne bullets now zipping around our heads. And what we thought was the Northernmost point of the village only appeared to be its middle. There were so many teepees the valley appeared draped in a white sheet. What in Hell's name had we gotten ourselves into?

Things seemed to happen really quickly after that. Smith had splashed into the shallows to the right of me and I think was turning his mount to shout an order when he shook violently from the sudden impact of an Indian bullet. It pitched him forward on the neck of his horse with a loud gasp.

Turning Scout swiftly, I clutched vainly at Smith only to watch in horror as our commanding officer slid slowly out of the side of his saddle, landing with a splat in the growing quagmire of river mud and water churned up by our anxious mounts.

Springing from my saddle into the shallows I grasped him by the shoulders and turned him over; Brown arriving at my side the next instant.

Smith was soaked in brown water, his broad-brimmed hat upturned in the mud beside him. When his eyes flickered open briefly they had a milky, faraway look and although his lips moved no words came out. Above us I could hear Sturgis shouting at the boys to pick their targets and aim low, as the cascade of shots flying our way increased alarmingly.

Smith's eyes snapped wide open. 'Nettie?' he said. Between us, Brown and I dragged the stricken lieutenant to the bank.

He was a wretched sight indeed. That buckskin suit he wore, the one Nettie Smith had sewn so lovingly, was covered in clinging brown mud.

It was when we undid his buttons that we noticed the ugly red stain spreading swiftly out from under his pale blouse. Ashen-faced and sweating, Smith let out a deep moan and again made a futile attempt to speak.

Behind us things were hotting up as gunfire increased from the far bank. I now heard frantic shouts of 'Lieutenant! Lieutenant!' and one of 'Jesus, no!'

Brown was trying to get some water down Smith when Hohmeyer, having also dismounted, joined us at the wounded officer's side.

'Sturgis has been dropped as well!' he exclaimed. 'He is surely lost!' Horrified, I rose and looked back towards the river.

A body was drifting slowly downstream, face upward, arms outstretched. Just like that drowned mariner at Cwmyreglwys all those years ago.

As I watched aghast Torrey and Farrell splashed into the shallows on foot in a brave attempt to reach the fallen officer, only to come under heavy hostile fire themselves.

With bullets kicking up water all around they turned on their heels and dashed back to the relative safety of the bank.

There was naught that could be done. Sturgis was indeed lost and Smith in a desperately bad way. Dear God, I thought, Sturgis was the son of the Seventh's commander presently on detached duty back in St Louis. There'd be Holy Hell to pay for this.

Hohmeyer's urgent tones interrupted my thoughts. 'Don't you worry none, sir, we're gonna git ya outta here!' he barked at Smith, with a surety I hadn't expected. 'Brown! We'll put him on your mount and git him up to Dr Lord pronto!' Brown at first did not appear to hear, but continued to look down at Smith, who was by now taking deep and grateful gulps from the water bottle. Noting Brown's sick expression, I followed his line of gaze down to Smith's belly. I realised with a sudden chill that as fast as E Troop's commander was taking in water it was flowing out through the bullet hole in his belly just as quick.

T'was no time to lose. Betwixt us, Hohmeyer and myself manhandled Smith aboard Brown's horse, laying the semi-conscious man over its neck while the now-mounted corporal gripped the reins behind him. 'It's gettin' dark,' gurgled Smith. 'Oh, so very dark ...' Spurring his mount forward gingerly, Brown set off carefully up the bank, intent on carrying our commander to surgeon Lord who was now somewhere up on the bluffs ahead along with Custer and the other three companies.

Behind us things were getting e'er more serious; more

and more Indians were appearing and without anyone shouting orders some of the boys had taken it upon themselves to dismount and fire while struggling to control their mounts with their spare hands at the same time. This meant they were firing wildly all o'er the place. Someone yelled that two more fellows had been dropped, I'd no idea who and knew we'd be hard-pressed to attend anyone else who fell wounded. 'We're takin' one Hell of a whippin'!', cried Hohmeyer. 'We've gotta get outta here!' Turning swiftly he called on Moonie to sound Recall so those of us still living could remount and put distance 'twixt the enemy and ourselves as bullets continued to fly all around. 'Fall back, fall back!' shouted Hohmeyer as we all scrambled for our mounts.

Although we were mightily relieved to be getting away from that hotspot, the disaster that had befallen E Troop meant we were in grave need of swift re-organisation. The loss of Smith and Sturgis had robbed us of both our commanders. Hohmeyer's misgivings on the lack of officers had been proved so right. If he could've seen that then why couldn't our superiors? Though Yates now held overall command, his first duties lay with F Troop, leaving E Company in the hands of our First Sergeant. T'was akin to the first mate taking charge of a rudderless ship; and a foundering one at that.

Back on top of the bluffs, Hohmeyer and I breathlessly caught up with a white-faced Yates, now marshalling F's own fall back. Ne'er had I seen an officer look so shaken. 'We've bin dealt a grievous blow, sir,' gasped Fred. 'Lt Smith is wounded real bad and we lost Sturgis, Ogden and two others down there. Ogden ne'er stood a chance.'

I stared at Hohmeyer in disbelief. 'Ogden,' I repeated stupidly, 'you mean Johnny got it down there too?' 'Aye, him and Brogan and Rood,' came the sombre reply. 'Ogden's mount just took off when the shootin' started, must have took a bullet or somethin'. Carried the poor bastard straight into the hostile village and right inner the heart o' them savages,' Fred paused and turned to look back down at the river. 'Sure hope Johnny got the chance to use the Colt on hisself,' he added soberly, 'afore they cut him to pieces.'

My blood ran cold; in an instant, Ogden, my friend, bunkie, and companion on a thousand jaunts over the past four years was no more. He was gone in the blink of an eye and in my frantic efforts to tend Smith I'd been completely oblivious to his hideous fate.

How cruel that Sky Dancer, the horse Johnny loved with a passion, had unwittingly caused his ghastly end. Hohmeyer was probably right, the horse must have been hit by a bullet which caused him to take off straight into the village.

I felt bewildered at the disastrous manner in which events were going awry, yet also possessed of the terrible realisation that our position would only get worse. Shooting a glance back, I just couldn't believe my eyes at the sheer numbers of angry Indians now appearing. And they sure as Hell weren't running, they were coming right at us from across the river. As thick as grasshoppers, mad as Hell and right on our tails.

We spurred our skittish mounts away from that cauldron of noise back onto the bluffs and the rolling hills beyond. F Troop leading and us following. No-one spoke now. All the tall talk was over. I could tell that the boys was just as afeared about what was happening as I was. With both our officers gone there was a real danger of company discipline disintegrating in the face of what looked like overwhelming odds.

On our way up, we passed Kellogg, who was flogging his lumbering mule in a state of furious excitement. 'Ne'er thought I'd see the day when Custer's dogs of war turned tail in the face of the red man like a pack of whipped curs,' he spat. "Is this the dispatch you wish me to send? Stand fast, I beseech you! Stand fast I say!"

Custer and his force had made their way to a low hill to our right when Hohmeyer, following a quick parley with Yates, bellowed for us to dismount and form a skirmish line. Our defensive wall just had to buy the rest of our comrades some precious time. Mason yelled that it'd be utter folly to stand and fight and that we'd be better off retreating upstream and trying to hook up with Reno and Benteen whilst we still had time. The glowering Hohmeyer told him to hold his tongue and get on the line. I think he'd have shot him had Mason demurred.

We formed a skirmish line as we'd done so often in drill down the years. Each man down on one knee stationed five yards apart, every fourth soldier acting as a horse holder a few paces behind. 'Steady, boys, steady,' shouted Hohmeyer riding down behind the line. 'Hold your fire 'til I say; then make every shot count, d'ye hear?'

By now we were looking on open-mouthed as hundreds of angry warriors rose up from the valley afore us like a swarm of angry bees. As we watched the very ground seemed to grow Indians. We'd known we were about to tangle with the biggest number of hostiles ever previously encountered; no-one could have foreseen anything like this. 'Best start sayin' your prayers, boys!' I heard Mason cry. Whooping and shrieking, and sounding those infernal eagle bone whistles of theirs, the Indians had forded the river and was now stealthily creeping up the ravines and low hills that was all that separated us from them.

Seeing we were hopelessly outnumbered, an idea sprang into my mind. Might a number of carbine volleys in swift succession not only signal our predicament to Reno and Benteen but also guide them to our location? We sorely needed reinforcements; and needed them fast.

I immediately conveyed this notion to the anxious Hohmeyer who readily concurred. He ordered the boys to fire two rapid volleys of three; a searing explosion of gunfire that left ears deaf and ringing. I'd have ordered at least three volleys myself, but sensed Hohmeyer was already troubled by the need to conserve firepower.

Mason just wouldn't let it lie. He came up and yelled t'was down to me to take charge and try and save the troop by getting the boys to saddle up and ride out. Hohmeyer, he said, could go to blazes as we were all going to get shot to pieces if we stayed where we were. For an instant I was ready to be convinced as we were plainly being confronted by way more Injuns than we could ever hope to handle.

For a few agonising moments I was trapped by indecision. Yet we had no way of knowing precisely where Benteen and Reno were located or even if they and their troops still lived. Despite Mason's urgings I still hoped and prayed that reinforcements would ride to our salvation at any moment.

'Fire!' screamed Hohmeyer and around thirty Springfield carbines again roared into life, dropping at least two Indians some 250 yards distant. Yet there were way too many of them and far too few of us. My throat was now so dry that my first attempt at yelling an order ended in little more than a strangulated croak. Finding my voice with an effort, I roared: 'Come on! You're the finest shots of the Seventh Cavalry! You let those painted heathens know it!'

Again and again we worked those carbines, until fingers grew numb and barrels glowed hot, yet the Indians were elusive targets and still they kept coming, seemingly oblivious to our return fire, including the bullets I was desperately pumping out from my Winchester.

They'd pop up from behind the sagebrush, take a pot shot and duck back down again, only a lingering puff of black smoke betraying their position. 'How the Hell can we fight a foe we cannot see?' cried O'Connor in frustration.

Those Indians, I thought grimly, weren't only fighting to protect their village, but their whole way of life. What were we fighting for apart from saving our own hides? A handful of scalps and some tall tales to tell over a few beers down at the sutler's? Taking stock, I glanced down the line. We were holding steady and maintaining a murderous hail of lead, true, but our thin blue line was already at full stretch. What's more, I thought despairingly, the Indians were gradually cutting the distance 'twixt us and their fire power somehow seemed far greater.

How could they possess so many repeating rifles against our single-shot Springfields? And where the Hell was Benteen? I thought angrily, turning my head quickly to scan the prairie Eastwards. What a dreadful fix we were in; and to think we'd been so sure that these Indians would run in the face of a cavalry charge. They'd never stood their ground previous, much less poured forth in such numbers to take the fight to us.

Shooting a frantic glance back up on the ridge where Custer had positioned his headquarters, I could now see a number of figures fleeing from the East along it on foot, with what looked like a host of yelping mounted Injuns on their tail. Seemed like a seam of the battalion had given way which was pretty grim news all round. The elite regiment I'd been part of this past four years, the fighting body of men who'd ride through Hell and back without batting an eyelid, was falling apart afore my very eyes. Like Annie I'd had a bad feeling about this campaign all along. A fear in my gut I just couldn't shake. Why hadn't I obeyed my instincts and gotten out whilst I still had the chance? I'd given her all those assurances when in truth I hadn't believed them myself.

And how much longer could E Troop maintain our heavy and rapid fire? Our troopers were suffering jammed carbines as the soft copper shells became trapped in the breech. We'd all have been better off with repeaters. I lost my Winchester going to tend Davis when he was dropped. I'd managed to drag him a short way 'til his body shuddered from the impact of a second bullet. With what must have been his dying breath the young private told me he was done for and urged me to try and make good my own escape. I snatched up his Springfield and struggled to free his cartridge belt as bullets pinged all around. A few of the boys, already out of shells and too beleaguered to reach their mounts for more, were now having to use their revolvers which had a far lesser firing range.

After I'd got off a few shots my own Springfield, muzzle hot to the touch, seized up completely. Seeing my predicament, Walker, taking aim to my right, wordlessly tossed me the belt knife he'd been using on his own gun.

I swiftly prised out the jammed shell, but ramming home its replacement saw my hands shaking badly. Gritting my teeth while trying to compose myself, I could only hope Walker had been too busy to notice. Panicked cries behind us suddenly revealed a new and more serious threat; Indians were seemingly encircling our line and closing in fast.

Great clouds of black smoke billowed from the divide and towering spirals of dust made it impossible to see further than twenty paces. At one point I took a bead on some figure and was about to let fly when I realised it was clad in blue. Some fool trooper who'd become detached from the rest of us had damn near gotten his head blown off by a bullet from western Wales.

I could just about make out the ghostly silhouettes of our terrified greys as they bucked and reared and whinnied, ignoring the entreaties and oaths of their beleaguered holders, now coming under fire themselves from Indians who had crept up behind. 'Release the horses and git on the line!' I heard Hohmeyer cry. The horse holders did as ordered and, having dismounted and unleashed our squealing mounts, grabbed their own carbines and ran to our aid.

Within an instant our panicked greys, bearing extra ammo as well as precious food and drink, were charging

351

headlong through the gathering dust clouds back down in the direction of the river. And all I could think of was Annie's beautiful green agate I'd carefully packed in Scout's saddle pocket. Watching our mounts' wild flight, the thought occurred that this was where my life would end; a cavalryman without a horse is akin to a sailor overboard bereft of ship. Ev'ry spare man was needed on the line if we were to hold our ground, but I could now see that some of the boys were losing their nerve and, as company discipline started to fracture, tending to bunch up. I thought of Tom my brother and wondered if I'd die with my face to the foe.

'Spread out, for God's sake!' I yelled at the increasingly afeared troopers. 'Keep five yards apart!' I knew that the closer we moved together the easier it would be for the Indians to charge in among us.

Our return fire had to cover as wide an area as possible if we were to have any chance of repelling the hostiles, but what had been a tight, composed military unit moments earlier was now looking dreadfully frayed and ragged.

Our position was fast becoming hopeless and it seemed nothing would turn the tide. Soldiers were falling; Smallwood, Walker and then the valiant Torrey, flapping around on the ground like a winged pheasant, the nearest Indians now just over a hundred yards distant and getting ever nearer. Acutely aware of my shortening breaths and thundering heart I was momentarily relieved to hear Hohmeyer, now seemingly the sole mounted man among us, bellow at Moonie to sound Recall. Leastways, I told myself, there'd be greater safety in numbers up on Custer's knoll.

'Fall back towards the hill!' roared Hohmeyer. 'Maintain a steady fire an' keep your face to the foe!' Old Fred had truly earned his spurs this day, I thought; not that he'd ever live to get that medal pinned on his chest. How could I e'er have doubted him?

We backed up the ridge, making a fighting retreat

towards Custer and the remaining defenders in fair solid formation, although casualties continued to mount and we could scarce hear ourselves above the raging din.

All of us were fighting on sheer instinct now. Firing, reloading, backing up a few paces, pausing to free jammed carbines and then firing again, all the while knowing with a kind of sick dread that our ammunition was running dangerously low and that our extra bullets had been borne away by our escaped mounts, far beyond our reach.

As we fell back I caught sight of the fallen O'Connor struggle to his knees and beg for help. 'For God's sake!' he screeched, 'please don't leave me!' I'd once jumped into the sea to save a girl from drowning off Lower Town, though scared witless; how I now yearned to go back for that boy with every ounce of my very being.

O'Connor was little more than ten yards distant, but with bullets and arrows raining down like hailstones any rescue attempt would've spelt certain death. Unlike that girl off Lower Town I just couldn't save him.

Only an hour previous I'd jested about putting a slug plumb between the boy's eyes. Now, whipping my Colt from its holster, that's precisely what I did. What else in God's name could I have done?

E Troop spread out below the low hill where Custer had made his stand with perhaps seventy to eighty men around him. As if things couldn't get no worse, Indians were now close enough to unleash swarms of arrows at the desperate defenders above.

The deadly shower was in the main passing o'er our heads, but the shrieks and cries behind indicated those arrows were increasingly finding their targets. The gravely wounded Smith was somewhere up there being tended by Dr Lord; Custer nowhere to be seen, though I could hear the occasional reports of his Remington sports rifle ringing out. The remainder of those who still lived were lying prone and blasting away with their Springfields whilst praying for a miracle, as we were also.

The horror continued unabated. Horses' screams now rang out from the knoll. 'Holy Mother of God! They're shootin' the horses!' yelled someone to my left.

We all knew what this meant: a cavalryman shooting his horse to form breastworks was the last roll of the dice. Horseflesh would never stop a bullet, we all knew, but there was just no damn cover on those infernal slopes; not even a patch of sagebrush. We couldn't have picked a worse spot to fight a rearguard action. Outnumbered, outflanked, outgunned and abandoned ... 'It's all for nuthin', Will ... it's all for nuthin' ...'

In spite of all I felt sweet relief that I'd ne'er have to put a gun to Scout's noble head. I could ne'er, e'er, have pulled the trigger even in the face of my own impending destruction.

As if in a dream, I found myself scurrying down the line to try and keep the boys together.

Gaps were appearing where troopers had been hit by arrow or bullet and even as I approached I saw Meyer toss his Springfield aside, leap up and take off through the dust cloud towards the river.

Afore I'd reached the spot where he'd knelt, a second fellow also flung down his firearm and lit off in his wake. I momentarily thought of doing likewise, but those chevrons on my arm and that half-inch yellow line down the side of my light blue trousers anchored me to the spot.

'Hold the line!' I bellowed uselessly. Ghastly sights abounded. Hiley, spreadeagled on his back, glassy eyes wide and staring, legs twitching; arrow embedded deep in his throat from which a river of claret poured forth. John Heim cursing wildly while furiously pumping out shots from his carbine, seemingly oblivious to the arrow jutting from his side; Van Sant sprawled staring and lifeless beside him.

Swinging around, my eyes alighted on Brown, sitting

back on his haunches, jammed Springfield lying uselessly alongside a broken knife at his feet, blubbing like a whipped urchin as tears coursed down his cheeks.

Then I realised to my horror he was holding his Colt 45 in his right hand and slowly and deliberately raising the barrel to his temple ... 'George! No!' I screamed, just as the corporal's skull exploded in a shower of blood, brain and bone and his limp body, jerking in convulsions, flopped back into the dirt.

Next thing I knew, Hohmeyer had jumped down at my side, reins in hand, gesturing frantically at Eagan and Mason to run over.

The four of us got in a huddle, as low as we damn well could. Eagan's hand was dripping blood. 'T'is nothing,' he slurred, catching my gaze. 'For this we are soldiers.'

Hohmeyer must have felt as afeared as the rest of us, but, God knows, he wasn't about to show it. 'The Goddamn fight is lost, I fear,' he said, 'the enemy has scattered us this day. Should we remain here we'll all be slain like rats in a barrel ...' the first sergeant briefly hung his head. 'I shoulda gotten the boys out whilst there was still a chance,' he muttered. Mason, squatting to his left, twisted his head and spat viciously into the dirt. 'All them officers are lost ,' he told Hohmeyer. 'T'is down to us now. Us, and us alone.' 'What in Hell's name can we do?' Eagan asked Hohmeyer. 'We've no mounts and our situation is dire.

'Take your own horse, sarge. Won't you at least make a try for it? You've given your utmost, all our fellers have, but our ammunition is all but spent and as our fire power drops it'll give them red bastards free rein to charge.'

But a lone flight was the last thing Hohmeyer, eyes darting left and right, had in mind.

'We'll make for the river,' he said quickly. 'I'll lead an' you fellers must git as many able men as you can t' follow.'

Eagan and I exchanged looks. 'Ne'er was much good at

355

runnin',' he mumbled, 'guess now's a good time t'learn, huh?'

'Me and my bro was good at running,' I said. 'Running away from the constables, like.' Irish Tom grinned and damn-near crushed my knuckles with the fiercest handshake ever. 'What I'd give,' he croaked, peering towards the far river we both knew we'd never reach, 'for a pair o' fockin' wings.'

Anchoring the horse's reins under his boot, Hohmeyer took a deep breath and quickly pumped more bullets into his Colt.

'There are trees down yonder that'll give us some cover an' we may be able to round up some of our mounts,' he continued, snapping shut the revolver.

'I need you fellers to make damn sure the boys raise Holy Hell all the way down; git 'em to make as much noise as they can to try an' spook the Indians an', God willin', drive 'em back.

'If we stick together some of us may get through.'

T'was a last-ditch plan borne of desperation, but we were plain out of cards to play.

'Got any ideas?' asked Fred, looking straight at me.

'Nope, none I fear,' I replied, stooping as low as I could as another Indian bullet all but parted my hair.

I realised that I was hatless, pretty much all of us still left were, and though the sun continued to beat down ferociously I felt cold as ice. I was shivering so hard my teeth chattered.

'An' jus' you make darn sure, Sergeant James,' came Fred's voice, sounding a long way off as he re-mounted E Troop's only remaining horse, 'that you git them things back to my old lady jus' like we agreed; that is an order, soldier!'

I was struck by the anguished thought that those precious personal effects he'd entrusted in my care were in the saddle pocket the panicked Scout was bearing on his headlong flight down towards the Little Bighorn.

There was naught I could do about that now. Eagan, Mason and I ran up and down the remnants of our line, darting from man to man, making sure all knew what was about to happen. There were one or two terse nods of acknowledgement; a couple of hurried handshakes, but no-one spoke. There was damn-all left to say anyhow.

All knew we were caught 'twixt a rock and a hard place. Though still unscathed I was readied for the thump of arrow into flesh or the searing pain of a bullet burning its way through my soft body.

Never afore had I felt so small. I'd thought I was not afeared of death; now it was staring me in the face I didn't want the Grim Reaper to claim me.

Dear God, after all I'd gone through please not now. Not now I had Annie. And we still hadn't spent one single night together ...

'One day, Will James, youse gonna make someone real, real happy ...'

What we needed most, I thought desperately, was some covering fire, but as shots from the hill grew e'er more sporadic it was clear none would be forthcoming. Besides, might not our headlong flight spur some enraged defender to unleash a few bullets at our fleeing backs for what could be perceived as an act of mutiny?

Could we perhaps split into two platoons and cover one another as we made our way down? No, that ship had sailed. Most of us were out of bullets by now in any case.

None of us would ever leave this God-forsaken place, I thought bleakly. Our bones and those of our mounts would lie here for all eternity, pale and bleached by the unforgiving sun, to be scattered by wild animals; our unhappy grey spectres condemned to aimlessly wander these rolling hills until the Day of Judgement.

Dear God, if you really are there, please bring this nightmare to a sweet merciful end! Had Hohmeyer, Eagan and Mason not been so near I'd have wept at the thought I'd never see Annie again.

That vow I'd made her that day we'd rode out of Lincoln had been utterly sincere and straight from the heart; yet it had come to naught.

If only she could have known how hard I'd fought and that she was in my thoughts to the very last ...

Hell, no! I told myself fiercely. I will not die here this day! I'd been in some tight corners afore and somehow gotten through. I'd survived the Great Fire of Chicago, for God's sake, when hundreds had perished. I'd dodged a coffin on many an occasion during those wild old times in Opelika.

There were so many things I wanted still to do, so many places I hadn't yet seen. And above all else there was dear, sweet Annie awaiting me back at the fort.

'Right boys, now's your time; it's do or die!' I yelled, with a conviction I didn't possess. 'Stay bunched together, save what bullets you have, make damn sure those redskins know the Gray Horse Troop are coming and don't damn well stop 'til you hit that river!'

'Them Injuns won't follow us into them trees,' sang out a lone voice from somewhere down the line. I sensed we'd never be afforded the chance to find out.

Readying myself for the run of my days, I pulled off my high-heeled boots. I was the most fleet-footed in the company; I was going to give myself every blessed chance of making that river. If e'er there was a time our ill-starred family deserved a much-overdue change in fortune then this was surely it.

Hohmeyer still had his wits about him; he knew we had to regain our mounts. All too aware of the tortures of thirst our greys had endured I knew we wouldn't have to seek them out. They'd be watering themselves down at the river and Fred knew as well as I did that only a fellow on horseback would escape this stricken field.

I caught sight of Eagan gazing forlornly down at his now-silent Springfield, then despairingly back up at the oncoming savage hordes. 'Reckon we're done for, Tom?' I asked.

His answer surprised me. 'Nope,' he replied through clenched teeth, wiping sweat from his eyes with the back of his arm and pulling his Colt from its holster.

'There's always hope, Will, always hope. Dunno how I'm gonna do it, but I'm gonna fight my way outta here. Them red men won't be expectin' us to charge an' maybe ol' Benteen will quit his dallying and ride t' our rescue yet!' Had I sunk the amount of whisky Eagan had, I'd be talking the same, I thought darkly.

Mason, chest heaving, just stared hard at the ground with that wild look I knew of old, yet I could sense he too was still full of fight.

Then at his request I opened my Colt and handed him one of my last two bullets, keeping the last shell for myself. 'Ain't afeared o' dyin', but I wanna live,' he rasped, 'jus' so I git t'see a whole lotta fuckin' heads roll for this. If none of us make it out how'll anyone ever know what in God's name happened here?'

I swung around again to look East, but there was still no Heaven-sent sight of mounted bluecoats galloping over the divide, no fluttering guidons, no blaring bugles. We'd been greatly outnumbered, true, but another one hundred mounted men would have made all the difference. Just like those doomed explorers who'd crossed Australia all those years afore, salvation had been so close yet in the final reckoning heartbreakingly out of reach. Fate had now done for us all. Why, oh why, did it have to be us?

But then, those Cheyenne at the Washita had doubtless felt the same eight years back ...

I continued to gaze Eastwards but all I could see were those parched yellow hills that put me in mind of Pembrokeshire's Prescelis, 'cept they were carpeted by whooping mounted Indians and even more of the painted bastards running towards us on foot. They knew damn well they had The Seventh whipped even if we ourselves couldn't make head nor tail of how it'd happened.

We were supposed to have cut a swathe through that valley like angels of God. Now it'd be left to others to pick over the bones of this debacle; just like the crows and buzzards would feast on ours.

Those politicians in Washington had talked of driving Indians from the face of the earth; instead the fighting Seventh was being exterminated. There'd be no victory parade back at Lincoln, no triumphant headlines in the Bismarck Trib, no little ones running around that townhouse on Burnside ...

True to his word, First Sergeant Fred Hohmeyer was about to order a charge, e'en though all was lost. What mad folly was this? I asked myself, a cavalry charge bereft of officers, horses and sabres?

The Light Brigade had stormed into the Valley of Death all those years previous but, God in Heaven, at least those fellows still had their mounts. Maybe in the course of time, Hohmeyer's Charge would become the stuff of legend. The type of stirring tale some impressionable schoolboy sat at his desk back in west Wales might readily devour.

I quickly ran my eye over those who were left. To my right, Huber was panting, mouth agape, clutching his revolver and staring up at Hohmeyer with red, murderous eyes. He, for one, was evidently going to sell his life dearly; likewise Farrell, staunch and steadfast. 'If this is my time then I am ready,' I heard him say.

McElroy was next in the line, head bowed and weeping, hands clasped together in prayer. 'Forgive me Father for I have sinned ...'

Then came young Henderson, face ashen and shaking, nursing a wound to the arm which bled copiously.

He was ranting that if any of us got out of this alive we'd all be laughing stocks back East. As we got up to make that last desperate dash I swear I heard him chuckling to himself.

I felt a hand claw my shoulder. Turning aside I found myself staring into the most terrified pair of eyes I'd ever seen. It was Stella, one of our youngest recruits. His words, making little or no sense, poured forth in a torrent of sobs. He was babbling something about how when we made the river we could chop down some trees, build some rafts and sail them all the way downstream.

'Sure we can, son,' I answered, 'we can follow the Bighorn all the way down to The Far West. Just you stick with me and I promise that I'll be with you every step of the Goddamn way.' Stella nodded frantically. I was talking cock and bull, but could tell from the spark of hope and gratitude in those eyes that the wretched fellow truly believed me.

Wrenching myself free from Stella's grip I looked up again at Hohmeyer and we snatched a last sweaty handshake.

'It's been a privilege serving under you, Fred!' I shouted above the din. 'Don't forgit t' zig-zag!' he yelled back. 'You zig,' I answered, foolishly proud at how steady my voice sounded, 'and I'll zag.'

Then, in spite of my trembling right hand, I found myself standing to attention and saluting him as if he was an officer.

A loud report close by made me spin round. Stella lay there glassy-eyed, gaping hole in the side of his skull; smoking revolver in his right hand. Whilst my back was turned he'd stolen up from behind, pulled my Colt from its holster and spattered his brains with my last bullet. Gazing down at the twitching corpse I felt sickened to the depths of my soul.

The time had come; at that very instant Moonie's bugle sounded behind us. How'd he summoned up the spittle to blow?

And then, though those who remained were little more than a bunch of dead men, we fellows of E, all who were left of Custer's once-proud Gray Horse Troop, rose as one and set off down that slope in the wake of Hohmeyer and his rearing, plunging mount bellowing like a bunch of maddened grizzlies.

How many of us made that demented charge to oblivion I couldn't say. Two dozen, maybe more, along with a few mounted stragglers from F, all howling like wolves as we made for the river a full three-fourths of a mile distant; although to our anguished eyes it looked nigh on a hundred. No wonder the Indians in our path stood aside. We were making enough noise to rouse the recent-slain from their eternal sleep. To the Indians the last of Custer's bluecoats were no longer of right mind and shorn of rational thought.

Onwards we sped, that grey of Hohmeyer's our one guiding light. He was blasting away with his Colt right and left; how he hoped to hit anything God only knows. We'd no choice but to follow the course of his insane flight. Hohmeyer was striving to clear a path; his thoughts and concerns were for his men only.

Still we ran, leaping from one crop of sagebrush to another, whooping and screeching at the very top of our lungs and cutting a swathe through those Indians who, confronted by these crazed white men, backed off in silent and sullen incomprehension; their ranks opening up like the Red Sea.

In my right hand I stubbornly clutched poor dead Davis's empty Springfield; as cumbersome and useless as it now was, my years of training had compelled me to retain it like an appendage of my own being. Dispossessed of sabre, I'd have to rely on the carbine as a lone means of defence come the hand-to-hand fighting.

Through the brown grasses, parched scrub land and dust we stumbled, the doughty Hohmeyer continuing to blaze our doomed trail; he was out of bullets by now but would turn in the saddle every so often and urge us onward. 'Faster, men! Faster!'

We were all done in by now, and those trees and bushes down by the Little Bighorn just weren't getting any nearer. Shots rang out from either side and occasionally a soldier would go down; possibly from a bullet but more likely from sheer exhaustion.

T'was like some insane buffalo hunt; 'cept we were the ones being hunted down. Washington had invaded the land of the red man Hell-bent on trouble and it was us who were paying the price. At first, I'd indeed tried to dodge this way and that, knowing that a moving target was harder to hit. Anything to try and delay that agonising moment of pain and death.

By the time we neared the river, I was pretty much past caring. I was bounding through the lush green fields above Pencnwc, Spot prancing alongside, my brothers shouting at my heels and soon, very soon, I'd reach the sanctuary of the farmhouse kitchen and dear Mother's blessed arms …

Suddenly, a commotion up ahead; Hohmeyer and his mount had crashed sidelong to the ground raising a huge cloud of dust, the wretched beast whinnying in agony, legs kicking madly; its gallant rider pinned beneath.

Wild shrieks to the left of us and I was suddenly aware of a vast wave of hostiles rising forth, as if from a fissure in the ground, to swamp us. Out the corner of my eye I caught sight of a huge fearsome silhouette rearing from out of the dust, war club raised; a giant avenging angel poised to strike. The warrior moved like lightning and gave my exhausted self no time.

Instinctively I shot up my left arm using the Springfield to parry the blow. Stone clanged against steel, and the ferocity of the impact sent me toppling sideways, my right foot vainly seeking purchase yet finding mere air instead.

I felt myself tumbling helplessly over some steep precipice, striking hard earth and rock afore somersaulting over and over until, on hitting the bottom, all breath was expelled from my body …

I don't know how long I lay insensible … it probably amounted to mere instants. Feigning death would be futile, I knew, as the Indians would dispatch the wounded by slicing off hands, legs, noses and privates.

I'd hoped I was no more, that death had mercifully overtaken me, yet for now I breathed still. As I came round I sat up, spat soil from my mouth and sought to unscramble my senses.

I appeared to have fallen into a deep gully; my mouth was full of dirt and grit, my carbine had vanished and I stared in stark, mute incomprehension at the dreadful scenes above.

A few soldiers were scrambling down the ravine ahead; one, who might have been Eagan, turned and beckoned me, lips moving, yet I heard no sound. My hearing had gone completely and, having been knocked silly I was struggling to regain my wits.

Shaking my head to try and free myself of the roaring noise raging within my skull, my hearing abruptly returned and how I then wished it hadn't.

I could now hear the shrill whoops and eagle bone whistles of enraged Indians plus the dying screams of wounded men being chopped asunder.

Any fate was better than that, I decided, yet groping feverishly for my Colt 45 found its holster empty. The gypsy's curse had done for me. How cruel a fate to not even have the means to blow my own brains out, I thought, while awaiting the bullet or stone club that would finally dispatch me into eternity.

'Do you want to go to Heaven or would you rather not be saved? …' 'Ein Tad, yr hwn wyt yn y nefoedd …' (Our Father who art in heaven …)

Dragging myself to my feet with an effort, I tottered drunkenly after the soldiers fleeing down the draw, but could only manage four or five steps afore the dry creek bed rose up and hit me in the face.

Gasping, I turned on my side, realising I was down. I felt as weak as a new-born, drowsy as Hell, and just couldn't understand why. There was the same salty taste in my mouth I'd get after swimming at Pwllgwaelod.

Hauling myself to my knees I gazed down at my trunk and saw it drenched in blood. 'Oh, sweet Jesus ...'

I must have been wounded, yet I knew not where. Nor did I feel no pain.

'Sancteiddier dy enw ...
(hallowed be thy name)
'Deled dy deyrnas ...
(thy kingdom come)
'Gwneler dy ewyllys ...
(thy will be done)
Megis yn y nef ... 'Felly ar y ddaear fel hefyd ...
(on Earth as it is in Heaven)

Taking a series of deep gulps of breath, I rose again and managed to stagger a full ten yards to the far bank.

Steadying myself against a tree stump I gazed helplessly at the scene above as hordes of maddened Indians slashed and gouged and stabbed at all that was left of my troop.

The shrieks, wails and pleas of the dying were indescribable; soldiers little more than boys screamed for their mothers, others begged in vain for their lives. 'John! ... John! ... oh, John! ...'

My long plunge to the bottom of this gully was a descent into the very pit of Hell. And still I yearned in vain for my own end. I covered my ears with my hands and closed my eyes.

'Dyro I ni heddiw ein bara beunyddiol,
(Give us this day our daily bread)

'A maddau I ni ein dyledion,
(And forgive us our trespasses)
'Fel y maddeuwn ninnau i'n dyledwyr ...'
(as we forgive those who trespass against us)

Just as I felt consciousness slipping away I dropped my hands and prised open my eyelids at the sound of clattering stones and hooves approaching down the gulch.

A horse whinnied and my fevered eyes alighted upon a lone riderless grey, eyes rolling, nostrils flared, steam rising from his back, stumbling along the draw straight towards me.

My heart leapt in my breast and I gave a silent prayer of thanks as I understood what I was surveying. Pegasus, the white winged horse, had come to bear me from this butcher's yard at last ...

As the noble beast drew abreast, I lunged for the bridle like a drowning mariner clutching at the splintered remnants of his floundering vessel. Was this how Tom and Frank fought in their last moments?

Scrabbling frantically to gain a grip, my torn and bleeding bare foot missed the stirrup but my right hand seized the pommel of the saddle even though the force of Pegasus' movement almost ripped my arm off. Round and round we danced, partners in some mad waltz, as I feebly struggled again and again to hoist myself aboard. My once-prodigious strength had deserted me just when I needed it most ... 'Oh spare me that I may recover my strength before I go hence and be no more ...'

But then, despite my wounds and fading exertions, I found that inner fury I didn't know I still possessed; at the same time gaining some purchase on the bulging saddle pocket. 'Fate, don't fail me now!' I screamed silently, 'take me to the finish line!' And with one last heave I hauled myself across the saddle, lying there on my belly like some unwieldy sack of flour. I'd made that vow to Annie, I kept telling myself, and I always kept my vows.

Now that blessed little daughter of Kilkenny was beside me once more: begging and pleading and shrieking for me to hold fast ... 'Folks need someone like you to fight their corner, Will!'

God knows I was striving my utmost, but I was so dog-weary. All I craved was to lie down, snatch some blessed sleep on the cool riverbank and then press on; yet Annie implored me not to ... 'You gotta keep fightin' Will! ...'

Pegasus trotted on, me draped across his back, a dead and useless weight, legs kicking and flailing like an upturned crab on Newport Sands in my futile attempts to anchor myself in the saddle.

Still struggling to mount up I fumbled to my left, left hand again alighting on the pommel and, taking another deep breath, slowly and painfully dragged myself around while at the same time hauling my trailing right leg over my mount's heaving right flank ... ... 'I remember you sayin' there weren't no Injun alive that could kill ya ...'

The Herculean effort was so great I think I momentarily passed out ... 'Don't know how I'm gonna do it, but I'm gonna fight my way outta here ...'

Regaining my senses, I found myself hanging low over Pegasus' head, like a man riding through a hailstorm. Half-blinded with blood from an apparent wound to the head, I looked dispassionately down at Pegasus' white mane turning pink afore me ... 'Call me Ishmael ...'

'Ac nac arwain ni I brofedigaeth;
(And lead us not into temptation)
'Eithr gwared ni rhag drwg
(but deliver us from evil)
'Canys eiddot ti yw'r deyrnas ...'
(For thine is the kingdom)

On we trotted down the gully, passed on either side by screaming, shadowy figures seemingly fleeing in the opposite direction.

Pinned flat to Pegasus' back, face nestled in that sweaty white mane, I peered dully ahead at whooping, exultant Indians rushing directly towards us to our right. Instinctively I slid leftwards from the saddle, halfway down my mount's flank, low as I could go, right hand clinging to the pommel, desperately trying to conceal myself behind the horse's body while making Pegasus appear riderless. As I held my breath, the Indians continued past in the direction from whence we'd come, less than an arm's length away … 'The enemy has scattered us this day …'

Fighting an impulse to heave, I again hauled myself painfully back into the saddle. We were now so close to crossing the Cleddau; those damn constables hard on our tails.

On and on we pressed, until the gully's sides seemed to shrink, retreat and finally vanish. And all the while as I clung silently to Pegasus underpinning the beat of my racing heart I was aware of the drumming of that noble steed's hooves and the rhythmic motion of his flanks beneath me … 'You do love me, don't you Will? …'

Presently we broke into a canter, and as we did so I heard the powerful throb of massive wings above.

'Onward, dear Pegasus, onward …' I murmured, as the blessed ground fell away from beneath us, 'bear me to the Mountain of Angels …' '… I will not die here this day …'

Glancing down, I could now see the silver, glittering coil of the Little Bighorn River, sunlight dancing on its surface, as we rose high above, the sounds of death and destruction and wanton slaughter growing fainter and fainter by the instant until mercifully fading away into the distance.

Higher and higher the pair of us soared until the noise and din and heat of conflict was all but a memory. Off to the South I could now spy the peaks of the jagged Wolf Mountains shimmering in the heat haze on the horizon; beyond them the distant hills of Wyoming.

We continued to climb majestically; higher and faster and steeper as Pegasus soared like a white arrow discharged from its bow, upward and onward, onward and upward ... until the rays of the afternoon sun struck us full-on and flooded my eyes as well as my entire being with love, happiness and thankfulness ... and I thought that if we continued forth like this then afore too long I'd be reaching God ...

'A'r gallu, a'r gogoniant, yn oes oesodd ...
(The power and the glory)
(For ever and ever)
Amen.'

Ft A Lincone
Dakota Tr
June 26, 1876

Deerest Will

so pleesed to git yo letta a'v bin sleepin with it under ma pilow tho ah dont sleep so gud thees days hop ya keepin wel owt thar an' mebbe yous now on yors way home saw that nass Mrs Howmayer tother day sed she an the kids woz misin mr howmayer sumthin awful am misin yous jus as bad an ba the ways ah rote this leta missel tho Polly hada reed of it purty gud huh you lernt me gud Will padray told mee tother day yoo bois wil be jus faan as them injuns thay dont knows howta shewt strate ah shaw hop hes rite bout that hop yoos getin inuff ta eet tho when yous get back am gunna hav bakd yoo a hole lotta flapjax.

ya eva lovin
Annie

Mike Lewis

CHAPTER 20

Fishguard
May 12, 1905

It was a mild, misty and damp Friday evening as Arthur
Nicholas left his Bridge Street lodgings in Lower Town and,
turning left, headed down the street in the direction of the
Ship Inn. Normally he would spend Friday evening drinking
with his chums, John Kinsella and Henry Havard, either at
the Commercial Hotel on Fishguard Square or the Royal
Oak opposite or, if the weather was fine, perhaps go on a
stroll down to Llanpit or Lower Town Quay arm-in-arm with
Louisa.

Tonight, however, he did not feel like company but had
promised Louisa a meal out the following evening instead.
Now, nursing a splitting headache as well as a large glass of
Porter's, Arthur found himself sitting all alone in the corner
of the pub as he tried to make sense of the tragic tale he had
uncovered in the course of his investigation.

WBJ's trail had taken him on myriad of twists and turns
before finally leading 'Yr Unig Cymro' (The Lone Welshman)
to General Custer's blind alley at Little Bighorn out in the
desolate wilds of Montana. Arthur had established that James
was the sole Welshman lost that day. If nothing else, James'
personal odyssey had left Arthur with an abiding respect for
those hardy souls who had abandoned poverty-stricken lives
in north Pembrokeshire in search of a new life thousands of
miles away in the United States and Canada. Those doughty
emigrants had faced hardship and danger merely in crossing

the Atlantic. And once in America, they had been forced to contend with a vast and unknown wilderness inhabited by dangerous wildlife and hostile Indians. Sitting there in the Ship, Arthur was fairly sure he lacked the restless spirit and sense of adventure to have followed the path James had forged.

It was this country's great misfortune, he ruefully reflected, to have lost its true pioneering adventurers such as Will James, while stick-in-the-muds such as himself had been more than content to remain at home in their 'milltir sgwar' (own patch). Wales was undoubtedly all the poorer for it.

Yet what Arthur found most poignant about WBJ's letters from America was the yearning for the old country that 'strange wild boy from Dinas Mountain' evidently never lost. The reader could discern the man's loneliness and longing in almost every line. While Arthur accepted he would never know the real reasons behind James' departure, he liked to think that in the short time WBJ had left on Earth he had finally found some degree of happiness and contentment; perhaps even a love to rival the all-consuming, if ultimately destructive passion he and Elizabeth Morgans had held for one another.

And Arthur had not stopped thinking about the advice the now Elizabeth Evans had imparted. 'Seize the day, Mr Nicholas, as before you know it you'll be nearer the end than the beginning.'

Rising to his feet a little unsteadily, Arthur resolved at that moment that he would visit a Haverfordwest jeweller's the very next day and buy the finest gold engagement ring an apprentice solicitor could afford. It was the very least that the girl whose mother WBJ had saved from drowning off Lower Town over thirty years previously deserved.

How thankful he was to have found Louisa, a girl so sweet he could by now no longer contemplate life without her, yet how sad that the one man he would have most liked to see at the wedding, apart from his own dear father, lay buried in some God-forsaken part of Montana. Breaking off from his office work that evening, Arthur had spent much of the time sombrely thinking about all the blood that flowed away, across the ocean to the second chance; and how had it got on when it reached the promised land?

He had frequently found himself looking at the ocean and trying hard to imagine the way Will felt the day he set sail, from Liverpool, for eastern Canada. 'We should have held you,' Arthur muttered to himself as the drink took hold. 'We should have told you, but you know our sense of timing; we always wait too long.'

Over the previous twelve months Arthur felt he had formed a pretty good idea of the type of person James had been. Was that the reason he now experienced a sense of acute sorrow and loss? Was that why, try as he might, he just could not erase the memory of Elizabeth Evans' shattered features from his mind? She'd clearly borne an intense and enduring love for the man.

What was it his mam had said about someone whose memory he had been toasting all alone in one of the pubs the young Will James would doubtless have frequented? 'Despite getting into scrapes you could always count on Will to somehow find his way out of them.' All who'd known James as a young man agreed that his skills as a horseman were second to none. The feats he could perform on horseback were unparalleled. Something of a rascal, he was also undoubtedly courageous and resourceful.

Arthur knew that not one man under Custer's immediate command had survived the most famous battle of the American West on that red Sabbath. Every soldier in the five companies that had rode with Custer had been slain.

Yet if any of those desperate troopers could have beaten the odds at Little Bighorn on Sunday, June 25, 1876, it would have been the man from Dinas Cross known to all as Will Pencnwc.

Well, thought Arthur morosely, Custer's Last Stand had proved one predicament too far, one scrape too many; and one from which not even 'Will O' the Wisp' had been able to make good his escape ...

***

'He saw no man get away, but had heard four different eyewitnesses tell of one soldier who rode through the Indians on a very swift white horse which they could not catch.'

(Author Walter M Camp, interview with Foolish Elk, September 1908).

'One enlisted man on a white horse escaped ... this trooper somehow managed to ride through the encircling attackers and dash up the stream. He was pursued for a distance and the chase abandoned.'

(Unknown Indian battle participant, American Legion magazine, April 1927).

'Rain-in-the-Face, Red Cloud and Crazy Horse, Indian chiefs who fought in the battle; in statements at various times, all asserted that one trooper, severely wounded, got through their lines.'

(Oshkosh Northwestern, August 6, 1937; from 'Custer Survivor').

'One longsword escaped. His pony ran off with him and went passed our lodges. They told me about it in Chicago. I saw the man there, and I remembered hearing the squaws tell about it after the fight.'

(Chief Rain-in-the-Face, Hunkpapa Sioux, Coney Island, New York, 1894).

THE END

Mike Lewis

Acknowledgements

The author wishes to thank the following:

United Kingdom: Dr Hywel Bowen-Perkins; Ruth Bloom; the late Dr Reg Davies; Dinas Cross Historical Society; Rex Harries; Alis Hawkins; John Hughes; Hugh Jenkins; Lyn John; Tom Latter; Carol Lloyd; Claire Orr (Pembrokeshire County Archivist); staff at Pembrokeshire Archives, Prendergast, Haverfordwest; Edward Perkins; Peter Russell, Len Urwin.

United States: Darrell Dorgan; Mike Ferguson (Bismarck Tribune); Cindy Hagen (Cultural Resource Manager, Little Bighorn National Monument Museum, Montana); Diane Merkel (Little Bighorn History Alliance); Union County Museum (South Carolina); Frederic Wagner.

Canada: Library and Archives Canada; Bob Lloyd, Nicola MacIntyre.

Mike Lewis

ABOUT THE AUTHOR

Mike Lewis hails from the former fishing village of Aberporth, West Wales, where his family have farmed for generations.

Having joined a local newspaper straight from school, he proceeded to work as a writer and sub-editor on a number of national titles in London, including "The Guardian" and "The Daily and Sunday Telegraphs".

A lifelong rock and pop music fan, in the 1990s he co-authored biographies on Scott Walker and Syd Barrett, of Pink Floyd.

Mike later worked as "The Sunday Telegraph" boxing correspondent, covering the Beijing Olympic Games of 2008.

Having returned to his native West Wales to raise a family, and while working for the "Fishguard County Echo" he stumbled across the story of William James, the West Wales farmer's son who emigrated to the United States and joined the US Seventh Cavalry.

Mike subsequently found previously-undiscovered letters James had sent back to his younger brother from America which form the framework of If God Will Spare My Life...

A father-of-five, married to Sue, Mike combines his writing career with helping to run Cardigan Amateur Boxing Club.

BIBLIOGRAPHY

The following list encompasses books and articles read or consulted which provided both general background and specific knowledge.

Books

Brininstool, E. A., *Troopers With Custer*, Stackpole Books, 1994.

Chiaventone, F. J., *A Road We Do Not Know: A novel of Custer at the Little Bighorn*. Simon & Schuster, 1996.

Chorne, L. J., *Following The Custer Trail*, Trails West, 2001.

Connell, E. S., *Son Of The Morning Star*, Picador, 1984.

Donovan, J. A., *Terrible Glory: Custer and the Little Bighorn*, Little Brown, 2008.

Dube, S. *My Failings And Imperfections*, Carmarthenshire Antiquarian Society, 2011.

Harper, G., *The Fights on the Little Horn*, Casemate, 2014.

Hunt, Frazier and Robert. *I Fought With Custer: The story of Sergeant Windolph, Last Survivor of the Battle of the Little Big Horn*, Bison Books, 1987.

Koster, J., *Custer Survivor*, Chronology Books, 2010.

Michino, G., *The Mystery Of E Troop: Custer's Gray Horse Company at the Little Bighorn*, Mountain Press, 1994.

Philbrick, N., *The Last Stand: Custer, Sitting Bull and the Battle of the Little Big Horn*, Vintage, 2010.

Swanson, G. J., *G A Custer: His Life And Times,* Glen Swanson Productions, 2004.

Willey, P & Scott, D. D., *Health Of The Seventh Cavalry:*

A Medical History. Oklahoma, 2015.

Newspapers
Bismarck Tribune
County Echo (Fishguard)
Dewisland and Cemes Guardian (Solva)

Collections and Archives
Pembrokeshire Archives, Prendergast, Haverfordwest
Little Bighorn National Monument Museum

Websites
Men With Custer UK (www. menwithcuster. com)
Little Big Horn Associates Message Boards (thelbha. proboards. com)
Little Big Horn Associates Inc (Facebook Group)

Groups
The Dinas Cross Historical Society